MIDNIGHT

DEREK LANDY

MIDNIGHT

HarperCollins *Children's Books*

First published in Great Britain by
HarperCollins *Children's Books* in 2018
HarperCollins *Children's Books* is a division of HarperCollins*Publishers* Ltd,
HarperCollins Publishers
·1 London Bridge Street
London SE1 9GF

The HarperCollins website address is
www.harpercollins.co.uk
1

LIMITED EDITION ISBN 978–0–00–797291–3
HB ISBN 978–0–00–828456–5
TPB ISBN 978–0–00–828457–2
PB ISBN 978–0–00–828459–6

Typeset in Baskerville MT by Palimpsest Book Production Ltd, Falkirk, Stirlingshire
Printed and bound in England by CPI Group (UK) Ltd, Croydon CR0 4YY

MIX
Paper from
responsible sources
FSC® C007454

This book is dedicated to Reggie.

What is there left to be said about you, my friend?

You're smart, and yet wilfully stupid. You're good-looking, yet kind of ugly. You've got wonderful hair, yet you're always wearing hats.

You've saved my life three times now — in contrast to the measly once that I've saved yours — and you've taught me more about Icelandic cuisine that I ever wanted to know (seriously dude — hákarl? Seriously?), but there is something that I've been meaning to tell you for years, but I've never found the right opportunity.

Remember that girl, your pen pal, back when we were kids? Remember how you kind of loved her?

That was me. Sorry, dude.

*And from the nothing
came the everything.*

1

The old castle stood dark against the star-filled sky, its tall windows empty, its battlements jutting like teeth. Upon those battlements, and indifferent to the cold winds that scoured the mountaintops, stood Wretchlings, monstrous things of scabs and sores whose insides boiled with poisoned blood and decaying meat.

Lying on a blanket on a snow-covered perch 809 metres west and 193 metres up, Skulduggery Pleasant put his right eye socket to the scope of his rifle and adjusted the dial.

He wriggled slightly, settling deeper into the blanket, then went perfectly still. His gloved finger began to slowly squeeze the trigger, and Valkyrie raised her binoculars, training them on the closest Wretchling.

The gun went off with a loud crack that the wind snatched away, but they were so far from the target that it took a few seconds for the bullet to hit.

The Wretchling jerked slightly, and looked down at its chest. A moment later, it started to tremble. The stitches that held it together unravelled, and the Wretchling came undone, its body parts falling, its stolen entrails spilling out, and it collapsed on top of itself, a pile of meat steaming in the cold air.

Skulduggery moved on to the next target and adjusted the scope once more.

"You think they feel pain?" Valkyrie asked.

Skulduggery paused for a moment, and looked at her. "I'm sorry?"

"The Wretchlings," she said. "Do you think they feel pain?"

"Not really," he answered, and went back to aiming his rifle.

"But they have brains, right? Fair enough, they might not be thinking great thoughts, but they do still think. And if they think, they might be able to feel. And if their body can feel physically, can't their minds feel emotionally?"

Skulduggery fired again. Valkyrie didn't bother looking to see if the bullet hit its target. Of course it did.

"They do have brains," Skulduggery said. "They're stolen from the dead, along with the limbs and the internal organs, and they're twisted and warped and attached to the Wretchling like the parts of a machine – because that's what they are. They look alive, but it's all artificial. Are you feeling guilty about what we're doing?"

"No." She watched him acquire his next target. "Kind of."

"They're just like Hollow Men." He put his eye socket to the scope.

"But Hollow Men don't have brains."

"I don't have a brain."

"But Hollow Men can't think."

"Believe me, the only thing on a Wretchling's mind is the messiest way to kill someone."

Valkyrie looked through the binoculars. "So we kill them first? That's hardly enlightened, is it?"

"We're not killing them," Skulduggery said. "These clever little bullets are designed to dismantle, not destroy."

He fired, and she watched as the next Wretchling was dismantled. Black blood gushed.

Skulduggery stood. "That's the last of them," he said, taking Valkyrie's hand and pulling her to her feet. He left the sniper rifle on the blanket and she handed him his hat. It was black, like his three-piece suit, like his shirt and tie. Valkyrie was dressed all in black, too – in the armoured clothes made for her years ago by Ghastly Bespoke and the heavy coat with the fur-lined hood she wore over them.

Clouds were moving in from the east, scraping over the jagged peaks of the mountains, blocking out the stars. Below where they stood, the drop disappeared into gloom. The wind nudged Valkyrie, like it wanted to tip her over the edge, send her spinning downwards into the cold emptiness. She felt an almost irresistible urge to take a big step forward.

"Are you OK?" Skulduggery asked.

Her face, numb though it was, had gone quite slack. She fixed it into a smile. "Peachy," she said, taking off her coat. "Let's go."

He wrapped an arm round her waist. "Are you sure you don't want to try this alone?"

"If I knew I'd be able to fly, no problem," she said. "But I told my folks I'd be there for roast dinner, and if I plunge to my death before that they'll just think it's rude, so..."

They lifted up and drifted beyond the ledge, the world opening up beneath them. Skulduggery redirected the freezing winds so that not a single hair was disturbed on Valkyrie's head. It was strangely quiet as they flew, surrounded by the howls and shrieks of the mountains but tucked away from it all.

"The thought has occurred to me that maybe you'll only start flying when you absolutely need to," Skulduggery said.

"Do not drop me."

"Indulge me for a moment. The range of your powers is still largely unknown to us, yes? You can fire lightning from your fingertips, you certainly have destructive potential, and you have the burgeoning psychic abilities of at least a Level 4 Sensitive. Plus, you have flown before."

"Hovering is not flying."

"I bet if I were to drop you, you'd fly."

"I'm not sure if I can emphasise this enough, but *do not* drop me."

"The prospect of imminent death could release you from the mental barriers that are holding you back."

"It wouldn't be imminent death, though, would it? You'd catch me. There's no threat there. You'd save me because saving me is what you do, just like saving you is what I do. The only thing that dropping me would accomplish is to annoy the hell out of me."

Skulduggery was quiet for a moment.

"*Do not drop me,*" Valkyrie repeated.

He sighed, and they continued over to the castle, landing beside a pile of Wretchling remains. A sudden gust surrounded them with the stench of putrid meat and human waste. It filled Valkyrie's nose and mouth and she gagged. As Skulduggery sent the foul air away with a wave of his hand, Valkyrie lunged for the battlements, sure she was going to puke over the side – but she swallowed, managed to keep it down.

"Sometimes I miss having a sense of smell," Skulduggery said. "Tonight is not one of those times."

Valkyrie spat, wiped her mouth, and stayed where she was for a moment to recover. She felt sure that she'd once been told the proper names for the different sections of the battlements, but couldn't for the life of her remember what they were.

The wind whipped her hair in front of her face, so she tied it back into a ponytail, then took a wooden sphere, roughly the size of a golf ball, from her pocket. She gripped the sphere in both hands and twisted in opposite directions, and a transparent bubble rippled outwards, enveloped her and stabilised. The personal cloaking spheres didn't have nearly the range of their regular-sized versions, but they were just as effective, and a lot handier to carry around.

Skulduggery took out his own cloaking sphere, did the same, and vanished from her sight.

She slipped the sphere back in her pocket and stepped closer to him. Her cloaking bubble mingled with his and suddenly she could see him again.

Sticking by each other's side, they set off down a set of stone steps, a flurry of snow chasing them into the gloom. Skulduggery held up his hand just before they reached the bottom. A tripwire glinted on the final step.

"Sneaky," Valkyrie said.

They jumped the last few steps, and the moment before they landed Skulduggery caught her and kept them hovering off the ground.

"Pressure plates," he said.

"Even sneakier."

They drifted along the corridor, stopping at the end so that Valkyrie could push open the door. They touched down on the other side, took the next set of stone steps that spiralled downwards, Skulduggery leading the way.

Two guards with sickles on their backs stood at the open windows in the next corridor, their heads covered by black helmets. Rippers. It was freezing in here but they stood with their arms by their sides, as though the cold didn't bother them, keeping watch on the road leading to the castle.

"Which one do you want?" Skulduggery asked.

Nodding to the nearest Ripper, Valkyrie said, "This one," in a soft voice, even though she knew that her words wouldn't travel beyond the bubble that surrounded them.

"Count to ten," Skulduggery responded, and walked away, vanishing from sight.

Valkyrie moved up behind the Ripper, finished the count and stepped closer. Out of the corner of her eye, the second Ripper disappeared as Skulduggery did the same.

She wrapped her right arm round the Ripper's throat, grabbed the bicep of her left arm and hooked her hand behind the Ripper's helmet. His hands came up, trying to free himself. He put a foot to the wall and pushed out, shoving them both backwards. Valkyrie held on, her head down, her eyes closed. She kicked at his leg and dragged him backwards, laying him on the ground as his struggles weakened.

She looked up, watched as the second Ripper fell into view. He hit the floor and stayed there.

When her Ripper was unconscious, she released him and walked to the other end of the corridor. Her cloaking bubble intersected with Skulduggery's and he appeared before her so suddenly she jumped.

"Sorry," he said.

She waved his apology away. "I'm sure I scared you just as much as you scared me."

"Not really."

She took his hat and threw it out of the window, and was totally unsurprised when a moment later it floated in again and settled back on his head.

"Are you quite finished?" he asked, adjusting it slightly.

"It wouldn't kill you to admit to being a little startled every now and then," she said.

"I don't get startled," he responded, walking off again. She caught up to him before he left her bubble, and fell into step beside him. "I anticipate and adjust accordingly."

"You don't anticipate everything."

"Of course not. Where would be the fun in that?"

"I'm just saying you shouldn't feel like you have to keep up this unflappable demeanour around me."

"Has it occurred to you, after all these years together, that I just might not be flappable?"

"Everyone is flappable, Skulduggery."

"Not me."

They came to a door that took them to a tunnel that took them to a room, and in this room they chose an archway that took them to more stairs. Down they went, and down again, until the torches in brackets were replaced by bulbs and the steady thrum of power reverberated through the floor. They avoided large groups of Rippers, passed rooms where white-coated scientists murmured to one another, and kept going until they came to a perspex window overlooking a large laboratory packed with machines that blinked with volatile energy.

Doctor Nye sat on a stool, its back stooped, working on the intricate insides of a rusted device. Nye's thin limbs looked smaller than when Valkyrie had seen it last, when it had towered over her, its head nearly brushing the ceiling, but she wasn't altogether surprised. Crengarrions shrank as they got older, and their skin colour tended to lighten. Now it looked, at most, about ten feet tall, and its skin was a delicate ash.

"It looks old," she murmured. "Good."

They found the stairs, followed them down, arriving at the double doors that led into Nye's lab. Two Rippers stood guard.

"I've got this one," Valkyrie said, walking towards the Ripper on the right. She was halfway there when the cloaking sphere started to vibrate in her pocket.

Alarmed, she pulled it out. The two hemispheres were ticking towards each other quickly – much quicker than they should have – counting down to the bubble's collapse. She tried to twist them back, then struggled to merely keep them in place, but it was no good.

The bubble contracted.

2

Her boots were visible.

Valkyrie crouched before either of the Rippers caught sight of her. There were sigils on the wall – she could see them now. She recognised one of them: a security sigil that attacked Teleporters. She was pretty sure the other one was forcing her cloaking sphere to malfunction.

And it contracted again. Not all the way, just enough to reveal the top of her head. Time was running out.

Keeping low, she pocketed the sphere and hurried over to the Ripper. The bubble contracted again. He heard her footsteps and his hands went to his sickles.

Valkyrie pulled her own weapons – shock sticks, held in place on her back – and launched herself at him. The first stick cracked against his helmet, but he ducked the second, spinning away. Valkyrie's bubble collapsed completely now, as did Skulduggery's, and she glimpsed him throwing fire even as her Ripper attacked, sickles blurring.

Valkyrie knew the pattern and countered, slipped to the side and struck the Ripper's knee, then spun and caught him in the ribs. His clothes absorbed the electrical charge, and he didn't seem to register the pain.

He left her an opening and she fell for it, committing herself to a swing that she regretted instantly. A sickle blade raked across her belly, would have torn her open were it not for her armoured jacket. He kicked at her ankle, swept her leg, and she hit the ground and somersaulted backwards to her feet, defending all the while. His knee thudded into her cheek and the world tilted.

He leaped at her. She dropped the stick in her right hand and white lightning burst from her fingers, striking him in the chest and blasting him head over heels. He rolled and came up, his jacket smoking.

Valkyrie picked up the fallen stick, placed it end to end with the other one. They attached and she twisted, the staff lengthening, and when the Ripper ran at her she whacked it into his leg, then spun and cracked it against his head. He fell back and she followed, the staff striking him once, twice, and then a twirling third time. He dropped one of his sickles.

She went to finish him off and he dodged, dodged again, dodged faster than she could strike. He jumped over to the wall and rebounded, flipping over her head. She whirled but he was too close, and he grabbed the staff and pulled her into a headbutt that would have broken her nose had she not lowered her head. Even so, bright lights flashed, and she felt the staff being wrenched from her grip as she went staggering.

The Ripper let the staff drop, and swung his remaining sickle towards her neck. She raised an arm, her armoured clothes saving her once again, and snatched the weapon away. It fell, clattering against the stones.

Valkyrie ducked low and powered forward, grabbing him round the waist. Snarling, she lifted him off his feet and slammed him against the wall, then seized his helmet, searching for the twin releases, and tore it from his head. The Ripper fell back, blinking, and she swung the helmet into his jaw and he went down, and she hit him again and again until she figured that was probably enough.

She dropped the helmet and got her breath back.

"You got his helmet off," Skulduggery said, standing over the motionless form of the second Ripper. "How did you manage that?"

She shrugged. "I adapted accordingly. Come on. We have a doctor's appointment."

3

She pushed open the double doors and Doctor Nye waved a long-fingered hand.

"Do not disturb me," it said in that familiar high whisper. "I left strict orders not to be—"

It looked up then, and its small eyes widened and its wide mouth opened as it got to its feet, the stool crashing to the ground behind it.

Skulduggery held his gun low, by his hip. "The moment you set off an alarm, I will shoot you. I feel we ought to be clear on that from the very beginning."

Nye stopped moving backwards, and raised its arms. "I have no weapons."

Up close, Valkyrie could see that the threads that had once sewn Nye's mouth and eyes shut were still there, poking out of its skin. She walked forward. "You act like you're not pleased to see us, Doctor. That hurts my feelings. I thought we'd bonded that time you autopsied me."

"The years have been good to you," Skulduggery said, coming round the table. "I mean, you've obviously shrunk, but apart from that you look great. How have you been spending your time? The last I heard, you'd escaped from Ironpoint Gaol. Who was it that broke you out? Eliza Scorn?"

"How is Eliza?" Valkyrie asked. "Any word?"

11

"I haven't seen Eliza Scorn in years," Nye said. "I was not the only one she freed. There were others."

"But she set you up here," said Skulduggery. "You'd lost everything when we imprisoned you. We made sure of it. She helped you."

Nye licked its lips. Its tongue was small and pink. "She could see the importance of my work."

Valkyrie picked up a scalpel and walked over slowly. "Excavating the soul," she said. "How's that going for you? Found it yet?"

"I believe I have," said Nye.

"So what next? Now that you've found where it hides, what are you going to do with it?"

"Finding the soul was only the first step. Now I follow it to where it leads. I'm not hurting anyone. I'm not experimenting on anyone. You can search the castle. I have no patients here."

"No?" Valkyrie asked. "You don't have anyone strapped to a table somewhere, their ribcage open, their organs on a nearby tray while they look around, hallucinating friends and family come to rescue them? No? Well, I have to say that's an improvement. You're practically reformed. Skulduggery?"

"You're quite sure there is no one being tortured, Doctor?" Skulduggery asked. "Maybe having their skin peeled off? I heard about one experiment you ran during the war where you decapitated prisoners and then kept their heads alive in jars."

Nye backed up. "What do you want?"

"You're under arrest," Skulduggery said. "You're going back to Ironpoint."

"We'll be sure to request a smaller cell this time," Valkyrie said. "Something snug."

"Or you can make it easy on yourself," Skulduggery said. "You can tell us where Abyssinia is."

Incredibly, Nye paled even further.

"Wow," said Valkyrie, "your poker face sucks, dude. That means we get to bypass the bit where you tell us you don't know what we're talking about – and we threaten you and you eventually break – and go straight to the part where you answer our questions. So where is she?"

"I do not know."

"I'm just going to warn you that we've been looking for Abyssinia for almost seven months. Do you hear me? Seven months. And we haven't found her, or the flying prison she's commandeered, or any of her little anti-Sanctuary friends. We're both extremely annoyed about this. Our patience has worn thin, Doctor. When we found out that she paid a visit to this charming castle no less than two days ago... Well, I'm not going to lie: I cried a little. Tears of happiness. And when we learned that you were working here? It was like all my birthdays had come at once. Not only do I get to see my old friend Doctor Nye, but Doctor Nye gets to help us in our search, and tell us where Abyssinia has gone."

"I promise you, I do not know."

"Then why was she here?" Skulduggery asked.

"If... if I tell you, you must let me go."

"OK."

"I think you are lying."

"Of course I'm lying. You're going back to prison, Doctor. The only choice you've got is the size of your cell."

Nye hesitated, then sagged. "It was not a thing she was looking for. It was a person. His name is Caisson."

"And who is Caisson?"

"Abyssinia said he is her son."

"I see," Skulduggery said, taking a moment. "Does he work here? Is he a scientist or manual labour?"

Nye hesitated.

Valkyrie folded her arms. "He was a patient, wasn't he? You may not be experimenting on anyone right now, but up until two days ago you were."

"When I came here, this facility had already been running for decades," Nye said. "I was brought in to replace a scientist who had gone missing. My instructions were clear: I was to continue the work of my predecessor. On my initial tour, I was shown the room in which Caisson was being kept – but I was not the one who worked on him."

"How long had the experiments been going on for?"

"As far as I am aware, for as long as this facility has been operational."

"Which is?"

"Sixty years."

Valkyrie frowned. "He's been experimented on for sixty years?"

"No," said Nye. "He was experimented on *here* for sixty years. I do not know where he was before this."

"What else do you know about him?" Skulduggery asked.

"Nothing. Experimenting on Caisson was not my job."

"So who did the work?"

"An associate. Doctor Quidnunc."

"Is he in today?" Valkyrie asked.

"I have not seen him in a week, since Caisson was removed from this facility."

"Caisson was removed a *week* ago?" Valkyrie said. "So when Abyssinia came for him, he was already gone? Why was he moved?"

"I do not know for certain," said Nye, "but I imagine somebody learned that Abyssinia was drawing close and we were told to evacuate as a result. Caisson was the first to be moved."

"Then why are you still here?"

"I, and a handful of other scientists, refused to leave. I can only speak for myself, but my work had reached a critical stage and I could not possibly depart."

"Abyssinia wouldn't have been happy that her son wasn't here," Skulduggery said.

"She was not," said Nye. "She killed many Rippers."

"Did you tell her where he was moved to?"

14

"I did not, and do not, possess that information."

"Who took him?"

"I do not know. A small team of people. The owner of this facility sent them."

"Which brings us back to Eliza Scorn."

Nye shook its head. "Eliza Scorn does not own this facility. As far as I know, she was merely obeying orders when she delivered me here."

"Then who's your employer?"

"I am afraid I do not know."

"You're working for someone and you don't even know who it is?"

"What does it matter?" Nye asked. "My work is important and needs resources. I do not care who provides them."

Valkyrie sighed. "What about Abyssinia? Did she say anything that could lead us to her? Remember, you really want to make us happy."

"She provided no such information."

"Did you tell her about Quidnunc and his experiments?" Skulduggery asked.

"Yes."

"Did you tell her where she could find the good doctor?"

"I do not know where he is."

"Then how are you still alive?" Skulduggery asked. "You don't know anything helpful, you worked in the same facility where her son was being experimented on... Why didn't she kill you, Doctor?"

"Because I did to her the same thing as I am doing to you," Nye responded.

"And what is that?"

"Delaying you."

The shadows converged and twisted and from the darkness stepped a woman in a black cloak, her face covered by a cloth mask so that only her eyes were visible.

15

Skulduggery raised his gun and the woman's cloak lashed out, and Skulduggery ducked and fired. The cloak absorbed the bullets and whipped again, slicing through the table to get to him. Skulduggery jerked to the side, his hand filling with flame, but the cloak twisted back, covering him – and when it whipped away, Skulduggery was gone.

The woman turned to Valkyrie, but Valkyrie had already moved behind Nye and was buckling its legs. It dropped to its knees and she gripped its throat, keeping her eyes on the newcomer.

"Have to admit," Valkyrie said, "that was pretty cool, even for a Necromancer. But, if you try anything like that on me, I will fry the stick insect here."

The woman in black didn't respond. Her cloak coiled around her.

"You would not kill me," said Nye, its voice a little garbled. Its skin felt oily in her grip.

"I wouldn't *want* to kill you," Valkyrie corrected him. "I wouldn't want to kill anyone. But, if your awesome bodyguard tries to kill me, I'll kill you faster than your beady little eyes can blink."

Nye made a small sound, like a laugh. "Then it seems that we have reached an impasse."

"Not at all," said Valkyrie. "An impasse implies that we're evenly matched. But we all know that's not true." She glanced at the woman in black. "I dabbled with Necromancy. Did you know that? Solomon Wreath taught me a few things. So I know that you can shadow-walk. That's what you did with Skulduggery, right? But I also know that the range for shadow-walking is limited – so he's already on his way back here and he's coming mighty fast. We only have a few seconds before he bursts through these doors, and when that happens... it's not going to be pretty. All I have to do is wait, because time is on my side. But for you the clock is ticking. Can you hear that? The tick-tock in your head?"

"I am not going back to Ironpoint," said Nye. "I only have a few years left in my life. I will not spend them in a cell. Whisper – kill her."

"Whisper – wait," Valkyrie said, tightening her grip. "Why is it always killing, huh? Why is it always fighting? Why is violence always the default position?"

Nye held up a hand to Whisper, even though the woman had not moved. "You offer an alternative?" it asked.

"Give me Quidnunc, and I'll let you go before Skulduggery gets back."

"I do not know where Quidnunc is," Nye said. "But I do know one thing that could possibly lead you to him."

"Did you tell this one thing to Abyssinia?"

"I did."

"So we'd be playing catch-up."

"Yes."

Valkyrie considered her options, of which there were none. "OK," she said. "Deal."

"First, you must release me."

"I don't trust you enough to release you, Doctor."

"Then you had better make a decision before the Skeleton Detective gets here, Miss Cain. Time is ticking away."

Valkyrie almost smiled. She took her hand from Nye's throat and stepped back as it stood. It turned, looking down at her, as Whisper came up behind it. Her cloak swirled around them both.

"Quidnunc suffers from liquefactive necrosis," Nye said, and the shadows convulsed and Valkyrie was left alone.

"Huh," she said.

The doors burst open and Skulduggery stormed in, gun in one hand and fire in the other. "Where are they?" he demanded.

"Gone," said Valkyrie. "You just missed them."

Skulduggery stood there for a moment, then shook the flames from his hand and slipped the gun back under his jacket. "That's annoying," he said. "Are you OK?"

She shrugged. "Grand. Quidnunc has, um, liquid active necrosis."

17

"Do you mean liquefactive necrosis?"

"Let's say that I do. What is it?"

"A form of organic rot that Mevolent had weaponised during the war."

"That the same thing Tesseract had? So Quidnunc wears a mask, like him?"

"Perhaps," Skulduggery said. "In any case, he will need the same serums that kept Tesseract alive, and those serums are hard to come by. If we find who makes them, we'll find Quidnunc."

"Cool. Although Nye told Abyssinia, y'know, about the liquid factor thing."

"Liquefactive necrosis."

"He told her about that, too."

"Then we have no time to waste," Skulduggery said, stalking to the door. He spun round. "Unless you're hungry. Are you hungry? You haven't eaten since noon."

"I'm pretty hungry, yeah."

"Then we'll stop for pizza," Skulduggery said, and marched out.

4

Education, Omen Darkly mused as he examined the test he'd just got back, may not have been the area in which he was destined to excel.

While Corrival Academy was indeed a school for sorcerers, that didn't mean all the lessons were about throwing fireballs or shooting streams of energy out of your hands/eyes/mouth – although there was a fair bit of that stuff.

Mostly it was sitting at desks, reading textbooks and scribbling answers – pretty much the same experience Omen had had when he'd gone to a mortal school, back in Galway. A lot of the time, in fact, things at Corrival were worse. Because there were more subjects to cover – Omen not only had to study history and science, but also mortal history and mortal science – the school day was longer. PE wasn't just about combat training and self-defence, as tough as those things could be – it was also about picking a sport and playing it, magic not allowed. Students were taught to be the best sorcerer they could be, but they were also taught how to live, behave and thrive in the mortal world. Which meant more work, more tests, and more opportunities to fall short.

Omen folded the test paper, hiding the big red E from view. It wasn't that big a deal. It had been a difficult test – everyone said so, even the smarter kids. What chance did he have, really, when even the smarter kids were finding it tricky? Sure, they still technically passed, as did just about everyone else in his class, but he wasn't a big believer in grades anyway. He preferred to get his education out there, on the streets. Where it mattered.

Omen chewed his lip. That said, his parents were probably going to kill him if they found out.

He stuffed the test paper down into his bag. That was one of the good things about Corrival being a boarding school, he supposed – less exposure to disapproving parental figures. Of course, there was a pretty fair chance that they wouldn't actually care about a failed test. Omen had, quite by accident, cultivated a relationship with his folks that depended entirely on their low expectations. He sidled along in the background of their lives while their focus was on his twin brother, Auger – the subject of an actual prophecy, destined to face the King of the Darklands in a battle to save the world. In order to aid him in this battle, Auger had been born strong, fast and smart – not to mention naturally talented, extremely hard-working, courageous, decent, resourceful, charming, funny, tall and good-looking. Because being good-looking was obviously a vital quality in any self-respecting Chosen One.

Omen had missed out on being the Chosen One by virtue of being born second, so he didn't possess any of Auger's attributes. What he did have, however, was a plucky demeanour and a never-say-die attitude – but he didn't really have them, either.

Life was one bitter disappointment after another. Sure, there had been glimmers of hope along the way. His best friend was pretty cool, for a start, and seven months ago he'd helped Skulduggery Pleasant and Valkyrie Cain stop an ancient evil from being reborn. Well, sort of.

No, he *had* helped. He had been right there, sharing in the adventure. He'd come away with the bruises to prove it. The problem was that the ancient evil hadn't *actually* been stopped. Abyssinia, after all, had succeeded in coming back to life. Taking this into account, he supposed that meant he had helped Skulduggery and Valkyrie *fail* in their mission. Which may have explained why they hadn't called on him since.

What made things worse was that word of his involvement hadn't spread through the school like he'd expected. A few people knew a little of what happened, but it was as if his fellow students couldn't be bothered to spread cool rumours about him. There were no whispers in the corridor as he passed, no wide-eyed stares, no clusters of girls giggling whenever he smiled. After a brief spell as an adventurer, he was returning to being that insignificant little speck of a boy he'd always been.

Unless he did something about it.

His stomach in knots, Omen went over what he was going to say once more in his head. He'd practised this conversation again and again, planning for all possible contingencies. A part of him wondered about the grade he would have got in the test if he'd devoted as much time to it as he had to rehearsing how he'd ask out Axelia Lukt, but he easily swatted such thoughts from his mind. He had more important things to worry about.

Axelia sat in the common room, chatting and laughing with her friends. She was so nice, so smart, so pretty, and she had the loveliest accent and the happiest laugh Omen had ever heard. He could have listened to her laugh all day, as weird as that would have been.

Omen stood up, took a deep breath, and walked over.

He bumped into October Klein and mumbled an apology, turned round and went back to his corner.

He took another deep breath, and another. And another. He went light-headed, and collapsed back into his chair.

When he felt certain he wasn't going to faint or fall over, he got back to his feet. Focusing on breathing normally, he made his way across the common room without bumping into anyone, and was about to open his mouth when a firm hand gripped his elbow and steered him away.

"Hey," said Auger, all smiles today. "How'd you get on in the test?"

"Um," said Omen.

Auger nodded and then, in that casual tone he always used when he was hiding something, said, "That's cool, that's cool. Hey, have you seen Mahala around?"

"I saw her right before breakfast," said Omen. "Everything all right?"

Auger's voice dipped. "Yeah, yeah, just, when you saw her, did you notice anything different about her? Anything unusual?"

"Like what?"

Auger shrugged. "Like was she acting any different? Was she talking any different? Did she have glowing green eyes? Did she appear confused...?"

"It's funny," said Omen, "out of everything you just said, it was the glowing green eyes thing that stood out."

"She's, kind of, slightly possessed right now," Auger said. "If you see her again, let me know. Stay away from her, but let me know."

"You need any help? I could help."

"No, really, it's fine. I've got Kase. We'll sort it out. If it gets too much for us, though, I promise I'll give you the nod."

"Sure," said Omen. "That sounds good."

"Anyway, sorry for interrupting. You looked like you were talking with Axelia." He steered Omen back, depositing him in front of the most beautiful girl in the school and her friends.

"Hey, girls," he said.

"Hi, Auger," they chorused.

Auger nodded to Omen, and walked quickly away, and Omen froze.

Axelia looked at him and smiled. "Hi, Omen."

"Hi," he said. His mouth was suddenly so ridiculously dry. "Could I talk to you for a moment?" he managed to say. "Maybe go for a short walk?"

Axelia's friends widened their eyes, like Omen had just dumped a dead bird at their feet, but Axelia had the grace to keep her smile.

"Sure," she said.

Omen smiled back and they walked out of the room side by side. This was good. She hadn't yet said the word no, and neither had she laughed at him. If he could keep that going, he was in with a chance.

"What do you think of all those refugees?" she asked as they walked.

"Yeah," Omen said. "Aw, it's really... It really makes you think, doesn't it? Like, who... who are they?"

"Um, we know who they are."

"Well, yes, but what I'm asking is... uh..."

"You haven't heard about them, have you?"

"I'm not really sure what you're talking about, no."

Her beautiful blue eyes widened a little in surprise. "You didn't hear about the portal that opened up yesterday, right outside the city walls? It's literally just over the west wall, Omen. It's been on the Network all day. It's all anyone is talking about."

"A portal to where?"

"To the dimension where Mevolent still rules."

"Seriously?"

"How have you missed this?"

"I really don't know."

"We spent all of last class talking about it. You were there."

"I was daydreaming. And there are people coming through?"

"Thousands of them, all mortals."

"Do we know why?"

"They're slaves over there. Wouldn't you want to get away from that if you could? I mean, it's Mevolent."

Omen nodded. "He's pretty bad, all right. Do you think he'll come after them?"

Axelia hugged herself. "I don't want to think about that. We got rid of our Mevolent – we shouldn't have to deal with someone else's. Anyway, that's all I know. You really should start paying attention in class, Omen. Especially after the result you got in the test."

"You, um, you know about that?"

"I sit behind you. I saw your mark. Sorry."

"But I'm not the only one who failed, right? Like, there were a few of us. That was a hard test."

"Was it?"

"Not for you, maybe, because you're really smart and stuff. But for us ordinary people it was hard."

"I'm not that smart."

"Yes, you are," Omen said. "You're dead brainy."

She laughed. "What did you want to talk about, Omen?"

They stopped walking. There was no one around. It was all suddenly very still and very quiet. Omen nodded again. He was aware of how much he was nodding. It was a lot.

"Well," he said, trying his best to keep his head still, "in the last few months, um, I'm really glad about how we've become friends. You know, with our little jokes and things."

Axelia's brow furrowed a smidge. "We have little jokes?"

"Yes. Don't we? The little jokes? The little..." his mouth was dry again, "jokes? That we have. You don't notice them?"

"I'm afraid not, Omen."

His laugh sounded panicked. "That's OK. It's not important. Basically, what I wanted to say was: we're friends. Aren't we?"

"Of course."

"And that's so good," he said, both hands covering his heart. "It's so good to have friends. Real friends, you know? And I, I think you're great. I think you're funny, and smart, and, like, so cool."

"Aww, thank you."

"You're way cooler than me."

"No, I'm not."

"You so are."

"You're cool, too."

"Well, I'm not, but thank you for saying so." He laughed, and so did she. This was going well. Omen felt the time was right for the part he'd rehearsed in the mirror. "I'm really glad you're my friend – that means so much to me, you have no idea. And I don't want to ruin that, I really don't, and what I'm about to say... well, it's risky. But I couldn't live with myself if I didn't at least try."

Axelia nodded. "OK."

"You're probably going to say no," he said, veering away from his script. "And that's fine. Saying no is absolutely fine. It's expected, actually. I'd be, to be honest, I'd be stunned if you said, you know... yes. So I realise that that's not going to happen. So please, please don't feel bad. The last thing I want is to make you feel bad."

"Thank you, Omen."

He laughed, even as the pit in his stomach opened wider. "No problem," he said. "But, again, I have to, you know, at least try."

"Of course."

"So... um... The thing I was wondering was maybe, and, not expecting a yes to this at all, in the slightest, but the thing I was wondering was maybe you would, um, like to, you know..."

"Yes."

His heart burst into fireworks in his chest. "Yes?" he repeated, laughing. "Really?"

Axelia reached out, touched his arm, a look of grave concern on her face. "What? No, I was just... I said 'yes?'"

His laughter died instantly. "Right."

"I didn't say 'yes'," she said, "I said 'yes?', you know? Although it may have come out as 'yes', without the question mark after it. I'm sorry, Omen, English is not my first language."

"You're really good at it."

"Thank you."

"You know so many words."

"I interrupted you," she said. "I'm sorry. Please say what you need to say."

Omen chewed his lip and nodded. "Uh-huh," he said. "Right. Uh... I think we both know how it's going to go, though, don't we? I think we... I think we do."

"Probably," Axelia said. "We could stop, if you like?"

Omen nodded, doing his best to consider it even though his brain appeared to be broken. Then he shook his head. "Actually, I feel I have to try. If I don't at least say the words, then... then it'll be hanging over me. Are you OK with that?"

"Of course. Go ahead."

He forced a laugh. "Hey, Axelia, will you go out with me?"

"No," she said sadly.

His world crashed down and he said, "Yeah."

"I do like you," she said, "and I don't want to say 'as a friend', but..."

"As a friend," Omen said, and nodded again. "That's fine. I expected it, I really did. I hope this doesn't make things weird between us. Does it?"

"Of course not."

"Because it means a lot to me that we're friends."

"I know. It means a lot to me, too."

"Well, um... I suppose I'll see you around."

"I suppose so." Axelia smiled, gave his arm a squeeze, and walked away. Omen went round the corner, sat on a bench and was sad.

5

They came through, three abreast, the adults laden down with bulging bags and the children clutching raggedy dolls and carved wooden animals. Their footsteps were heavy, their shoulders stooped, their spines curved with exhaustion.

They weren't too tired to look scared, however. Their eyes flickered over everything, trying to spot the differences between this reality and theirs, but avoided the gaze of Valkyrie or anyone who stood watching. This was a battered people. All they wanted was to stop walking, to lay down their packs, to get some sense of a journey completed, but that wasn't about to happen just yet. As they came through the portal, the doorway sliced from their universe to this one, they were directed to follow a trail of flags to the makeshift town of tents that had sprung up along the outside of Roarhaven's west wall. Shrinking away from the grey-suited Cleavers on either side, the mortals trudged onwards in a broad, unbroken line.

"Thirteen thousand in thirty-six hours," Skulduggery said.

"What are we going to do with them?" Valkyrie asked. "China wouldn't send them back to their own reality, would she? We send them back and Mevolent's army will either execute them or use them as slaves. Maybe they could stay in Roarhaven. There are plenty of uninhabited districts. Loads of empty houses."

"Roarhaven is a city for sorcerers," Skulduggery said. "I don't know how welcoming its citizens would be to mortal families moving in beside them."

"What's wrong with them moving in? We're supposed to live in peace, aren't we? That's why Sanctuaries exist."

"Roarhaven *has* a Sanctuary," Skulduggery pointed out. "It isn't *itself* a Sanctuary."

"I don't think we have a choice," she said. "It's not like we can send them to live in Dublin or London or anything. They're mortals, but they're not like *our* mortals. They've lived their entire lives in a reality ruled by sorcerers."

Skulduggery nodded. "It would definitely require a period of adjustment."

"I think China's going to do the right thing. She knows she has to set an example as the Supreme Mage, so I reckon she'll hand over all those empty houses to these nice people from Dimension X."

"That's not what it's called."

"We can't call it the Leibniz Universe. It's boring, and nobody knows who Leibniz is."

"He was a German philosopher and physicist back in the late seventeenth—"

"Exactly," said Valkyrie. "No one's ever heard of him. And I think I should be the one to name it because I'm the one who discovered it."

"You didn't discover it."

"Well, OK, maybe not discovered it, but I found it."

"It wasn't lost, Valkyrie. It had billions of people living in it."

"And I found them, too."

He shook his head. "Silas Nadir shunted you over there. By your rationale, he should be the one naming it."

"He's a serial killer. He'd pick a stupid name."

Temper Fray walked through the portal, saw Skulduggery and Valkyrie and immediately started over. One of the Cleavers moved to block his way, but he flashed his City Guard badge and the Cleaver backed down.

"What did you find out?" Skulduggery asked.

Temper frowned. "No hug?"

"Oh, I'm sorry," said Skulduggery. "Valkyrie, hug him."

"I'm hugging him with my mind."

"You two are weird," Temper said. "It's telling that I get back from a twelve-hour trip to an alternate dimension and you two are the strangest things I've seen all morning. How was your little jaunt to the mountains, by the way? Meet anyone interesting? And by interesting I mean anyone tall, green and ugly?"

"Not quite so tall or so green any more," Valkyrie said, "but Nye is still as ugly as I remember. We chatted, yes. We have a lead, a man named Quidnunc."

"Never heard of him."

"Neither have we," Skulduggery said. "We're hoping once we get to him, he'll lead us to Abyssinia and then we'll be able to stop her from doing whatever it is she's planning on doing."

"You still haven't found out what that is, huh?"

"Not even close," Skulduggery said, "but I've known her a long time, and, whatever her master plan is, it will not be good news for the rest of us."

Temper frowned, and looked at Valkyrie. "Is he downplaying it?"

"I think he's downplaying it."

Temper nodded. "There's definitely some downplaying going on. Come on, Skulduggery – you had a thing with her. There's no need to be embarrassed."

"I'm not embarrassed."

"She's a very good-looking lady – you know, once she grew her body back and all. I've always found that ex-girlfriends with bodies are better than ex-girlfriends who are just internal organs locked away in a box somewhere. But I'm old-fashioned like that."

Skulduggery sighed. "Can we stop talking about this?"

"We can," Temper said, "once you accept that there is no shame in dating a murderous psychic who sucks the life out of people. No shame at all."

"Thank you, Temper."

"There's a *bit* of shame in losing her to someone like Lord Vile, though. I mean, that dude was evil."

"Are you finished?"

Temper grinned. "Not even close. But for right now? Yeah, I'm finished."

"Thank you," said Skulduggery. "We just got back into the country a few hours ago and we were going to follow up on this Quidnunc person, but decided to take a little detour here instead. Correct me if I'm wrong, Temper, but this portal wasn't here when we left, was it?"

"It was not," Temper said, and clapped his hands. "OK then, first things first: that is one messed-up reality they have back there. Seriously. Why anyone would venture into it, I have no idea."

"You ventured," Valkyrie said.

"I'm a City Guard now – I have my orders."

"I heard you volunteered."

"It's a portal to another dimension," Temper said. "What, am I *not* gonna go through? Anyway, there are thousands of people lining up on the other side of that thing. More coming every hour. With anyone else, I'd be expecting a stampede, but these folks are just so beaten down I doubt they could muster the energy to panic."

"Did you see any of Mevolent's men?" Skulduggery asked.

Temper shook his head. "Not a one."

"We were told there's a device that's sustaining the portal. Is that true?"

Temper scratched his jaw. "Never seen anything like it. It's a metal box, roughly the size of a car battery, with all these sigils carved into it. I don't know if the device did it all, or if a Shunter opened the rift and this device is just keeping it open. I don't know how it works, and no one knows how to shut it down, but then I guess the sorcerers in the Leibniz Universe have gadgets we don't understand yet."

"We're calling it Dimension X now," Valkyrie told him.

"No, we're not," Skulduggery said quickly. "Have you spoken to the people? Have they said anything about the Resistance?"

"They won't talk to me," Temper answered. "You've got to understand, these folks are almost as afraid of the Resistance as they are of Mevolent's army. To them, all sorcerers are super-powered psychopaths who topple buildings on to innocent mortals."

"Then hopefully we can show them a new, warmer kind of sorcerer," Skulduggery said, as a child dropped her doll. He stepped forward, using the air to lift the doll into his hand, and presented it to the little girl. She looked up at him and screamed, and her parents pulled her away.

"Sometimes I forget that being a skeleton is unusual," Skulduggery murmured. He tossed the doll to the girl's father and returned to Valkyrie's side. "Do you have any idea what the best course of action might be?" he asked Temper.

"For me, the best course of action is a shower and bed," Temper answered. "For the situation, I'd send a squadron of Cleavers through to make sure the mortals are protected while they wait. I heard stories of bandits closing in."

"As far as we know, China's not sending any Cleavers," said Valkyrie.

Temper sighed. "Then maybe you could talk to her? She's got a soft spot for you, Val, everyone knows that."

"If we could actually get in to speak to her, maybe," Valkyrie replied. "But we've been trying to arrange a meeting with China for weeks, to discuss our progress – or lack of progress – in this Abyssinia situation, and all we hear is how busy she is."

Temper chewed his bottom lip for a moment. "Those refugees are easy targets. They need someone to keep them safe." He sighed. "I guess the shower can wait."

Valkyrie raised an eyebrow. "You're going back through?"

"Looks like it."

"Can't you send some of your City Guard friends through instead?"

Temper smiled. "I've been a Roarhaven cop for five months, and in that time I have discovered that the City Guards are not friendly people. Commander Hoc has changed things since you were in charge, Skulduggery. We report only to him, and he reports only to the Supreme Mage. My colleagues don't trust me – probably because they see me talking to the two of you so regularly."

"They think you're our spy," Skulduggery said.

"Yes, they do."

"Good thing you're our spy, then."

"It certainly keeps things simple." Temper looked back towards the portal. "Either of you want to join me?"

Valkyrie held up her hands. "I have things to do today, and bad memories of that place. Thanks, but I think I'll stay in this dimension."

"You mentioned bandits..." Skulduggery said.

Temper nodded. "Bands of them."

"Bands of bandits. That doesn't sound good."

"It really doesn't."

Skulduggery looked at Valkyrie.

"Good God," she said, "you don't have to ask me for permission to go play with your friends."

"It's just there are bandits," Skulduggery said. "I like bandits. There's no guilt involved when you hit them."

"When have you ever felt guilty about hitting anyone? Go. Battle bandits. Have fun. I'll make a few calls, see if anyone can help us track down the guy who makes Quidnunc's serum." She held out her hand. "Keys."

Skulduggery tilted his head. "Sorry?"

"Car keys. You drove us here, remember?"

"But… can't you get a taxi?"

"Back home? That'd cost a fortune."

"Have Fletcher take you."

"It's a school day, and Fletcher's busy being a teacher. Come on. Keys."

He hesitated, then handed them over. "The Bentley is a special car."

"I'm not going to crash it. I'm going to make a copy of the key, by the way. Just so you know."

"Drive very slowly. Especially round corners. And along straight roads."

"Can you please trust me?"

"I trust you with my life," Skulduggery said. "Just not necessarily my car."

6

Decorum. That's what it was all about.

Cadaverous Gant insisted on doing things the way they were supposed to be done. It may have been an old-fashioned philosophy to live by, but it was clear-cut, and he appreciated that kind of simplicity in this world — a world he increasingly disapproved of.

When he'd been a young man, he hadn't approved of progressives. When he'd been a professor, he hadn't approved of the lackadaisical approach his students took to their studies. When he'd been a serial killer, he hadn't approved of people interrupting the murders of said students.

It was why he built his house, after all.

A wonderful house in St Louis, built to his own design by a succession of contractors who didn't know what the others had worked on. Piece by piece, the house had come together, a labyrinth of corridors and traps and doors that opened on to brick walls.

The perfect lair for a serial killer.

His father had taught him all about the proper way to do things. Here's how to chop down a tree. Here's how to catch and skin your dinner. Here's how to take a beating. And, when his father was gone, it was institutions that had taken over, reinforcing this work ethic, carving him into the man he had become – a man who understood decorum and the proper way to do things.

Which brought him to Abyssinia, the Princess of the Darklands.

Over the past few months, ever since she had been reborn, she had been wearing a variety of flowing robes and elegant dresses, garments that worked well with her delicate features and her long silver hair. Cadaverous had watched, approvingly, as she experimented with styles and fashions, searching for herself in mirrors and in the admiring eyes of her devoted followers.

But the dresses and robes, it seemed, had only reminded her of the centuries she had spent as nothing more than a dried-out heart in a little box, so she had abandoned them and gone for something new — a red bodysuit, tighter than necessary and more than a little garish.

Cadaverous didn't know where the Darklands were, but he doubted this was appropriate attire for their princess. And that was another thing that annoyed him, this lack of a straight answer. She'd been calling herself that for years, back when she'd been a voice in his head as he lay on that operating table, guiding him back from death, giving him a purpose. A focus. His mortal life had ended with that heart attack, and it had come crumbling down around him with that illegal search warrant, but he had seized the focus her voice had given him right when he'd needed it most.

His old life was nothing. His career in academia had been a waste. Those young people he'd killed mere practice. The sharpening of a blade. The loading of a gun. Preparation for what was to come.

The magic that had exploded within him had altered his perceptions in ways no mortal could possibly comprehend. Suddenly his life was so much bigger. He no longer needed his old house of traps and dead ends — now he could transform the interior of whatever building he owned into whatever environment he could imagine.

His newly found magic allowed him to distort reality itself.

If only he'd experienced it as a younger man. If only he'd grown up with magic, cultivated it, the possibilities could have been infinite. Who would he have been? he wondered. What would he have become?

He would have stayed young. That he knew for certain. The magic would have rejuvenated him. Instead of looking like a seventy-eight-year-old man, he would have looked twenty-two. He would have stayed strong and healthy. His back wouldn't have twisted; his shoulders wouldn't have stooped. He'd still be tall and handsome and his body wouldn't ache and fail him.

The others around him were far older, but looked a third of his age. Razzia, the tuxedo-wearing Australian, as beautiful as she was insane. Nero, the arrogant whelp with the bleached hair. Destrier, the little man, fidgeting in his ill-fitting suit. They were all damaged, in their way, but the faces they showed to the world hid the worst of it behind unlined skin.

For all his irritations, he did appreciate Abyssinia for opening his eyes to a world beyond his old one. The question that weighed heaviest on his mind, though, was why she had taken so long.

She stood at the floor-to-ceiling window of Coldheart Prison's control room, looking down at the tiers of open cells as the convicts – the ones who had elected to stay – huddled in small groups. Discontent had been spreading through this floating island like a slow-moving yet incurable virus. It was not an easy thing to keep hundreds of people fed on a daily basis, and it had fallen to Cadaverous to somehow deal with the problem.

"Do you think my little army is plotting against me?" Abyssinia asked.

"Probably," Razzia answered.

"They wouldn't dare," said Nero.

"That's what I would do," said Abyssinia. "I would lead a charge and overthrow the people standing right where we're standing. Then I'd take this flying prison and use it like a pirate ship, plundering whole cities around the world." She sounded almost wistful.

"We freed them," said Nero. "They owe us. And they could have left with the others, but they chose to stay. That shows loyalty." He looked around. "Right?"

Destrier was too busy muttering to himself to reply, and Razzia just shrugged.

"Cadaverous," said Abyssinia, "you've been unusually quiet of late. What do you think?"

He chose his words carefully. "I think they are unhappy."

"Because we have failed to feed them?"

She didn't mean we, of course. She meant Cadaverous.

"That is undoubtedly part of it, yes."

She turned to him. "And what is the other part?"

He could have said anything. He could have demurred. He could have made it easy on himself in a hundred different ways. Instead, he said, "When we freed them, we made promises. We promised them purpose. We promised them revenge. We promised them power. We have yet to deliver on any of these things."

He didn't mean we, of course. He meant Abyssinia.

"You think I have been distracted by the search for my son," she said.

Before he could respond, the door opened and Skeiri and Avatar strode in. Skeiri was a slip of a girl, dark-skinned and serious, while Avatar was muscle-bound, handsome and eager to serve. They had emerged from their cells all those months ago, and Cadaverous could see a time in the not-too-distant future when Avatar, in particular, was the one issuing the orders, much like Lethe and Smoke had done, and Cadaverous would have to obey. Again.

They held someone between them, a man with blood dripping on to his shirt, his wrists shackled, his magic muted. Avatar and Skeiri stepped back as Abyssinia approached.

The prisoner narrowed his eyes. They were remarkably piercing eyes. "I'll never—"

"Shush," said Abyssinia. "Listen to me. I want you to resist. I'm going to enter your mind and find out where you're keeping Caisson. And I want you to try to stop me. You're one of Serafina's top people – you'll know how to keep a psychic out of your head. Use all your training. Use all the tricks. Give me a challenge."

The prisoner's jaw clenched. It was a remarkably square jaw. "You won't get anything from—"

"That's the spirit," Abyssinia said, and the prisoner's face contorted. He clutched his head and let out a whine, his knees buckling. He dropped to the ground, face still stricken, and then, as soon as it began, it was over, and he sagged.

"My son is in a private ambulance," Abyssinia said. "They're keeping him sedated and moving. Right now they are somewhere in Spain. He's accompanied by five of Serafina's sorcerers." She looked down at the prisoner. "You disappoint me. That was far too easy."

He shook his head, the colour returning to his face. He murmured something and Abyssinia hunkered down.

"Pardon?" she said. "What was that?"

He met her eyes. "I wasn't ready."

"Oh!" she said. "I do apologise. Are you ready now?"

He cried out, face twisting, hands clutching at his head.

"You're three hundred and fourteen years old," Abyssinia said. "You watched your childhood friend die in a freak accident. The smell of tequila makes you physically sick. You've had a song you hate running through your head for the last three days, a song called 'Uptown Girl'."

The prisoner gasped and fell forward, and Abyssinia placed her hand on him. "Were you ready for me then?"

She drew the life out of his body, his skin cracking, his bones creaking, and his strength flooded her and she stood, kicking the empty husk of him to one side. She took a moment, shivered with her eyes closed, and calmed herself. She looked at Avatar. "Find this ambulance. Do not act until I say so."

"Yes, Abyssinia," Avatar said, bowing.

She walked back to the window. "Cadaverous."

She had a task for him. He was surprised. He straightened. "Yes?"

She waved a hand. "The body."

He frowned. "Yes?"

"Get rid of it."

7

"Chicken or fish?" the man in the hairnet asked, tongs hovering.

Omen pursed his lips, looking closer at the options available. The dining hall was filling up. There was a queue of students waiting behind him. He knew they were getting annoyed, but he couldn't help it. Lunch was one of the most important meals of the day – he had to get it right.

"What kind of fish is it?" Omen asked.

"The dead kind," said the man in the hairnet.

"Is it fresh?"

"Does it look fresh?"

"I don't know," said Omen. "You've covered it in breadcrumbs."

The man in the hairnet shook his head. "We didn't do that. It swims around in the ocean like this, covered in breadcrumbs and missing its head. We just catch 'em and cook 'em."

"I, uh, I don't think that's right."

"I wouldn't lie to you, boy. I'm a Food Service Assistant. We take an oath."

"Hurry up," said someone in the queue.

"Yeah," said the man in the hairnet, "hurry up. Make a decision, short stuff. Fish, chicken, vegetarian or vegan."

"What's the vegan option?"

"Spiralised Asian quinoa salad."

"And what's the vegetarian option?"

"Vegetables."

Omen's stomach rumbled. "I don't really like vegetables."

"Then it's a good thing you're not a vegetarian."

"I'll... um... OK, I'll have the chicken."

"The chicken? After all those questions about the fish?"

"Well, you see, I don't really like fish."

"Then why did you ask about it?"

"I thought I might try it. Then I changed my mind."

"You're the reason I hate my job," said the man in the hairnet, and he dumped Omen's lunch on to a tray and handed it over. "Next!"

Omen sat at one of the long tables. Across the hall, Axelia was chatting with her friends. They laughed. He wondered if they were laughing about him.

Never joined him at the table, sitting opposite. She had her hair down, and she was wearing a hint of make-up that really brought out her eyes.

"Lunch guy does not like you," she said, digging into her salad.

"You were in the queue?" Omen asked.

"I'm the one who told you to hurry up."

"Oh, cheers for that."

"I made a promise to myself to interact with you in public at least three times a day. I figure it'll make you more popular with people."

"So I can expect a third interaction this evening?"

Never took a swig from her bottle of water. "This *is* our third interaction. Me telling you to hurry up was our second. The first one was when I threw that ball of paper at your head this morning."

"That was you?"

"You should have opened it up. It had a picture inside, a caricature of Mr Chicane that was quite satirically brilliant, if I do say so."

"What do you think of him anyway?" Omen asked.

"Chicane? His eyes are a bit too close together, a feature I captured splendidly in my artwork, but he's OK."

"You don't think he's a bit... off?"

"In what way?"

"Like... he only teaches for a few weeks every year."

"Because he has a speciality," Never said. "He only gives a few modules every couple of terms."

"I think he's up to something."

Never put down her fork. "Omen, as your only friend, I have no choice but to be the one to tell you – stop."

"Stop what?"

"Stop *this*," said Never. "Stop looking for bad guys and conspiracies. Yes, Lilt was working for Abyssinia, but that doesn't mean any other member of the faculty is involved. Yet you think there's something about Chicane, just like you thought there was something suspicious about Peccant, and before him it was, what, the ground staff, wasn't it? For the last seven months, you've been searching for an adventure."

Omen blushed. "No, I haven't."

"I get it. You were part of something huge. We both were. But it's over."

Omen gave a little laugh. "No, it's not. Skulduggery said he'll call me when he needs me."

"Why would he need you? You're fourteen, and you're not exactly at the top of your class, are you? They don't need us, Omen."

"That could change at any moment."

"Yes," said Never, "it could. And, if it does, awesome. But the problem is that you're waiting for it like it's a sure thing. It's not. Adventure happens to some people. Skulduggery and Valkyrie. Your brother. It intrudes upon their lives whether they want it or not. But the rest of us don't live like that. I wish we did. I'd love to be off adventuring with Auger or Skulduggery. Maybe not

Valkyrie, because she's responsible for murdering thousands of people, including my brother."

"Never, you know that was Darquesse."

"I didn't say Valkyrie did the murdering, did I? I just meant she bears some responsibility for her evil dark side going nuts and obliterating a quarter of the city, that's all. Anyway, I admit it, like you, I'm waiting for the call to adventure. But, unlike you, I'm not putting everything else on hold while I wait."

"I'm not putting anything on hold."

"How did you do on that test yesterday? You got the results back, didn't you?"

"I did fine."

"Did you?"

"Yes."

"Did you pass?"

"Almost."

"And how many assignments have you started?"

Omen folded his arms. "That's a trick question. We haven't been given any assignments."

"We've been given four," said Never.

"Oh."

Never sighed, and leaned forward. "I know you, Omen. I look across the room and you're sitting there, daydreaming, and I know exactly what you're thinking about."

"No, you don't."

"It's always the same two things. The first is Axelia Lukt."

"Well, obviously."

"I heard about that, by the way. Tough luck."

"Yeah."

"And the second thing you're daydreaming about is Valkyrie kicking the door open and saying she needs your help to save the world. Am I close?"

Omen said nothing.

"See? Knew it. That's not going to happen, but you want to

believe, so much, that they're going to swoop in and take you away from all the normal stuff that you're not actually doing any of the normal stuff."

Omen picked up his knife and fork again, and started cutting into his chicken. "Can we stop talking about this? I know you mean well, but you're starting to annoy me."

"I don't want to annoy you, Omen," Never said gently. "I don't want to be the serious one in any friendship I have, I really don't. I hate being the serious one. I'm the funny one. I'm the quirky, gender-fluid friend with a heart of gold and abs of steel."

"You don't have abs."

"That's only because I don't like to sweat. My point is, I don't want to be the one to give you bad news. But no one else cares enough."

They ate in silence.

Once they'd finished, Never reapplied a little lipgloss. "How do I look?"

Omen sighed. "Low-key glamorous."

This got a smile. "That's what I'm going for. Are you mad at me?"

"No," said Omen. "You can, you know, tell me whatever you think you need to tell me, just like I can choose to listen to you, or choose to ignore you. Because we're friends."

"We are friends," Never said, smiling. "But you can't ignore me. Nobody ignores me. I'm way too cool."

"Yeah, you are."

"So what do you think about all this Leibniz Universe stuff, eh? Isn't it crazy?"

"It *is* crazy."

"Omen, do you know what the Leibniz Universe is?"

"Not really."

"It's Mevolent's universe."

"Well, why don't they call it that? I'd remember it if it was called that. Who's this Leibniz person anyway?"

"Nobody knows."

"Do you think he'll come through? Mevolent, I mean?"

Never brushed a strand of hair away from her eyes. "Naw, I don't think so. He can stomp around his own dimension as much as he wants because there's no one there to oppose him. But here, we have a whole *world* that'd fight back."

"Yeah," said Omen. "Maybe. But you know the way all the wildlife – all the deer and rabbits and squirrels and stuff – run out of the forest when there's a wildfire? What if it's like that? What if the mortals are just trying to get away from what's following along behind?"

"You're worrying over nothing," said Never. "We don't know what things are like over there now. All we have are the reports Skulduggery Pleasant and Valkyrie Cain made after they got back, and that was, what, eight years ago? Besides, we already killed our own Mevolent. If the other one shows up, we'll just do the same to him."

"How, exactly? No one knows who or what killed our Mevolent."

"Skulduggery killed him," Never said, shrugging. "Everyone knows that. Just because it's not in our textbooks..."

"If Skulduggery killed him, he'd talk about it," said Omen. "He talks about everything else."

Never sighed. "Because you know him so well?"

"I don't claim to know him well. I'm just saying that he wasn't the one to kill Mevolent."

"It doesn't make any difference. If we get invaded, we'll still send them packing. They have magic, but we have magic and technology."

"So do they."

"But we have nukes."

"Seriously? You'd nuke them?"

"Of course. Wouldn't you?"

"I don't know. It's a bit... drastic, isn't it?"

"War is a drastic thing," said Never. "Ooh, that should be on a bumper sticker."

"I think I'd keep the nuclear bombs as a last resort," said Omen. "We have the Sceptre of the Ancients, don't we? Skulduggery and Valkyrie stole it from Mevolent's dimension, too, so using it to push back his army would be... uh..."

"The word you're looking for is *ironic*."

"Is it? OK. It'd be ironic."

"That's a good plan, Omen. Ignoring the fact that no one's been able to even *find* the Sceptre since Devastation Day, that's a wonderful plan."

"Well, like, we have other God-Killer weapons. One little nick from the sword and even Mevolent drops dead."

"The sword's broken."

"Then the spear," Omen said irritably, "or the bow or the dagger, whatever, it's the... What?"

"Nothing. I'm just quite impressed that you could name all four God-Killers."

"Really? Three-year-olds can name the God-Killers."

"Yeah, but they're *three*, Omen."

Omen nodded. "Because infants are smarter than me. Yep, I get it. That's funny."

Never grinned. "Feeling overly sensitive today, are we? I wouldn't blame you. Tell you what, I won't tease you again until you really, truly deserve it, I promise. Come on, tell me more about how you'd beat Mevolent."

"No."

Never laughed. "Oh, please? I was really enjoying that conversation."

"Tough."

"So you'd use the God-Killers on him, and...?"

Omen shrugged, looked away, happened to glance at the door just as Miss Wicked walked in. Tall, blonde and terrifying, he watched her look around, and immediately glanced away when her eyes fell upon him.

"Oh, God," he said.

"What's wrong?" Never asked.

"Miss Wicked caught me looking at her."

"She's coming over."

"Is she?"

"Coming straight for you."

"Are you joking? Please tell me you're joking."

"Omen," Miss Wicked said, and Omen yelped and swivelled in his seat.

"Hello, miss," he said. "I mean, hi. I mean... yes?"

She looked down at him. "Omen, you have been summoned."

He blinked. "I have?"

"Tomorrow morning," she said, "ten o'clock, in the headmaster's office."

He paled. "But... tomorrow is Saturday."

"It is."

"But there's no school on a Saturday."

"The school is still open at weekends, Omen."

"But there aren't any classes..."

"Correct. Which means I shouldn't be coming in. And yet I am."

"Is... is this because of the test?"

"Why would I be coming in if this was because of a test? No, Omen, this is not about a test. Grand Mage Ispolin, of the Bulgarian Sanctuary, is visiting Corrival Academy and he has requested that both of us be present when he arrives."

"Jenan's dad? Why would he want me to be there?"

"Jenan has yet to return home. I'm sure the Grand Mage wants to discuss the events that led to his son running away."

"Am... am I in trouble?"

"I really don't know, Omen."

"Are you in trouble?"

"Grand Mage Ispolin is probably going to try to have me fired."

"But why? You didn't do anything wrong!"

47

"Your vote of confidence will go a long way, I'm sure. Ten o'clock, Omen. Don't be late. I have no truck with tardiness."

She walked away.

This, Omen thought, was not at all the call to adventure he had been hoping for.

8

Valkyrie didn't get the headaches any more. That was one good thing about working on her Sensitive side, as Skulduggery liked to call it – the more Valkyrie practised, the easier it got. And she *had* been practising – but not even Skulduggery knew just how much.

She'd been eighteen when her true name had walked away from her, when Darquesse had become a separate entity, a person all of her own. When Darquesse left, she'd taken Valkyrie's power, leaving her dulled and weak and, once again, mortal.

Nature abhors a vacuum, however, and a new kind of magic had rushed in to fill the void. Valkyrie had just turned twenty-five, and they still couldn't explain how she could control that strange energy, or how she could see people's auras, or how she could do all those things and be a Sensitive as well. They didn't even know what to call her.

She was a one-off, she'd been told. An oddity. In a world of weirdos, she was a freak.

She tried not to take it personally.

The truth was, her power scared her. She felt it in her blood, twisting in her veins, eager to become whatever she needed it to be. But, for all its destructive potential, it also allowed her glimpses into the future, a future of darkness and pain that had lodged itself in her thoughts. Sometimes it was all she could think about. Sometimes it was all there *was* to think about.

Death was coming for the people she loved, unless she could learn enough about the future to avoid it.

And so here she was again.

She pulled up and got out of the Bentley. Standing beside the door to Cassandra's cottage was a piece of Darquesse that Darquesse had left behind when she'd departed this universe. Tall and strong and dark-haired, physically identical to Valkyrie in every way, she had taken to calling herself Kes.

"Hey," said Valkyrie. "Sorry I'm late. I was in the Alps yesterday, doing a thing, and then we got back this morning to find out that there's this portal that opened up at Roarhaven and... anyway. Sorry. Have you been waiting long?"

"Only a few hours," Kes said. "Well, a day."

"Seriously? I am so sorry."

"It's OK."

"How did you pass the time?"

"Oh, that was easy," Kes said. "I was standing over there for a few hours, then I stood over here. The time flew by."

"We really need to get you a phone."

"If you can find one I can hold, I'm all for it. Ah, it's fine. It's not like I have anything better to do with my time. You are literally the only person I have to talk to on this entire planet. I can't interact with anyone else in any meaningful way. I can only do tiny amounts of magic before I fade away and recharge. I'm... I'm bored."

Valkyrie smiled. "I thought you told me last week that gods didn't get bored."

"Well, as you took delight in reminding me, I'm not a whole god, am I? I'm a splinter of a god. A fragment of a god."

"I believe the term I used was 'crumb of a god'."

"Whatever I am, I get bored, OK? But you're here now, so let's get to it, what do you say? Ready to see the future?"

Valkyrie sighed. "I suppose I am."

She took the key from beneath the old pot and led the way into the house. The first time she'd come here after Cassandra died, when Skulduggery had wanted to test her burgeoning psychic abilities, she had taken a few minutes to process her feelings about being back in such a warm and welcoming environment. Today, she just walked straight through and took the stairs down to the cellar. This was her seventh time here without Skulduggery, and she had settled into a new, simpler routine.

She stood in the middle of the cellar. The floor beneath her feet was little more than an iron lattice, treated with magic to prevent it from heating up when the flames burned through the bed of coals beneath. The walls were brick, and reverberated with psychic energy, making Valkyrie's mind vibrate like a tuning fork. The ceiling was criss-crossed with pipes, designed to spray water.

Months ago, Valkyrie had had to project her visions on to the clouds of steam that billowed upwards. But she didn't need to do that any more.

She closed her eyes, let her thoughts scatter, and worked to find the peace within that chaos. When she found it – the quiet place – she let it grow and expand and fill her up until it pushed the noise away and, for a moment, for a single blissful moment, there was nothing in the world but her breathing.

She opened her eyes.

The vision filled the cellar, dissolving its walls, and she was suddenly outside, in the refugee camp, surrounded by the displaced and the scared. She felt their relief at escaping Mevolent's army, but also the rising fear of once again being at the mercy of a society of sorcerers they had no reason to trust. Valkyrie drifted through the camp, alert for any new deviation, but there were no extra details for her to absorb today. Satisfied, she allowed her mind to move on, and the camp vanished and she was in darkness.

"Here he comes," Kes said, from somewhere to her right.

They'd taken to calling him "the Whistler". He signalled his arrival with a tune. Most of the time it was 'Dream a Little Dream of Me'. Twice, it was 'Blue Moon'.

Today, he was whistling as usual, and, for only the second time, Valkyrie could see his outline. He was maybe her height, maybe six foot, and slender, but that was all she could discern. His outline was solid, but everything within that swirled and flipped too quickly to identify.

"Bring him closer," said Kes.

"I can't," Valkyrie answered. She took a few steps towards him, but the Whistler stayed at the same distance. Out of all the elements in her visions, all the bloodshed and death that was to come, his presence was the thing that unnerved her the most.

The vision moved on.

"You actually think you're going to win?" someone said behind her, and she turned, and a burning town built itself up around her. Dead bodies littered the streets. Car alarms wailed.

Auger Darkly fell to his knees in front of her, clutching his shoulder. Blood soaked his shirt. Omen ran out, picked him up, his brother gritting his teeth against the pain. Together they hurried on. They were being chased. There were people chasing them. People with guns.

Valkyrie moved in. This time she'd see their faces. This time she'd find out who they were so she could stop them before this happened.

They came round the corner, guns up, and passed right through her. Dressed in black, wearing body armour. Helmets. No insignias. Moving like soldiers, or SWAT teams, relentlessly tracking their prey.

She watched them spot the Darkly brothers. They opened fire. Bullets punched Omen in the back and he flopped on to the pavement as Auger went stumbling. Valkyrie did her best to ignore it. It was a scene she knew well, and it tore at her insides each time. But today she didn't curse or cry out – she just listened. Waited. Waited for one of them to say something. Anything.

"Target down."

The vision swept away and Valkyrie was confronted with the Plague Doctor, who held a child in his arms. Valkyrie stepped closer and the child vanished and the Plague Doctor's hands went to his mask and he pulled it off, but before Valkyrie could see his face he was gone, and Saracen Rue was lying dead on the ground.

"There's Tanith," Kes said softly, and Valkyrie turned to watch her friend back away from an unseen enemy, her sword in her hand.

Then Tanith was gone and China was lying in that field of broken glass Valkyrie had seen again and again. Just a flash of that, and then they were standing in the Circle, in Roarhaven. Smoke and flames billowed from the High Sanctuary and the Dark Cathedral was in ruins, and marching towards them was an army with Mevolent leading the way.

Valkyrie had glimpsed this before, but the vision stayed with Mevolent longer this time. She didn't know what that meant. Was this future more likely now? Was it closer?

The army was almost upon her, and her heart hammered in her chest.

She looked away and Cadaverous Gant walked by, holding a rag doll in a blue dress. A house appeared, tall and pointed and radiating darkness, and Cadaverous went into the house and the door stayed open, like it was inviting Valkyrie to follow.

Valkyrie started to walk, but Kes pointed. "There," she said.

A figure was slowly coming into focus on the other side of the room. A woman with silver hair, standing with her head down.

"Leave," Kes said.

"Not yet."

"You have to."

"There's something about that house."

"Valkyrie," Kes said, "leave now or she'll see you."

Valkyrie hesitated, but she knew she had no choice.

She let it go, let it all go, and the house vanished and the vision washed away and the cellar came back.

Kes looked at her. "You OK?"

"No," said Valkyrie, walking for the stairs. "I hate seeing the future."

9

For a solemn occasion such as an execution, the mood in Coldheart Prison was something approaching a festival.

The convicts lined the tiers, eager for the show and struggling to contain themselves. Every so often an excited whisper would drift down to the broad dais that hovered above the energy field. On that dais the teenage members of First Wave stood in the costumes that Abyssinia had ordered to be made for them – black, with shiny belts and polished boots – to give them the false sense that they were an elite military unit. To Cadaverous, they were scared little children, no matter what they happened to be wearing.

He stood with Razzia and Destrier and Nero. Beside them, and yet apart, were Avatar and Skeiri. Abyssinia's new favourites. The up-and-comers. Cadaverous despised them even more than he despised First Wave.

The only member of First Wave not dressed in her finery was the annoying girl with the habit of constantly flicking her hair out of her eyes. Dressed in civilian clothes, she stood on the very edge of the dais, a mere step away from a lethal plunge to the force field below. The bracelet she wore was cheap but solid and needed a key to remove it. It also bound her magic.

"Please," she said through the tears that were streaming down her face, "I just want to go home."

Abyssinia stood beside Parthenios Lilt, their heads down,

seemingly consumed by disappointment. They didn't answer the girl. That wasn't down to them. That was down to First Wave's leader, the arrogant whelp Jenan Ispolin.

He strode forward awkwardly, as if his knees had locked. The bravado that he usually carried with him – even here in Coldheart, surrounded as he was by genuine threats – seemed to be missing at this moment. He was pale, and afraid, and he looked as young as he was.

"Isidora Splendour," he said, his voice trembling slightly, "you have been found guilty of betraying your true family."

Isidora shook her head. "I didn't betray you, I swear."

Jenan continued. "We are destined for greatness. We have been chosen to change the world. This is the highest honour."

"Jenan, please."

"And yet, you jeopardised this sacred mission with your cowardice."

She turned. "I don't want to kill anyone," she sobbed. "None of us do. Mr Lilt, please. You're my *teacher*. Please help me."

Lilt shook his head sadly.

"Abyssinia," Isidora tried, "I'm begging you, we don't want to do this, but we're too scared to tell you. Please don't make us. We're only children. We don't want to hurt anyone."

Abyssinia looked to the rest of First Wave as they huddled together. "Is this true?" she asked gently. "Have you reconsidered? Have you had second thoughts? We are training you, making you stronger, better, more powerful. Your old classmates would barely recognise you, you have advanced so much. You have evolved. You are my dream made flesh." Her smile faltered. "But if this traitor's words are true, if you do indeed see yourselves as only children, you must tell me. Please, I beg you – be honest. Open your hearts. If you doubt me, if you doubt my plan and you have lost faith in our future together, a future that is on the horizon, now is the time to make this clear. Speak, my loves."

It was as if the entire prison held its breath and was silent.

Isidora fell to her knees, crying.

Abyssinia nodded slowly to Jenan. "Continue, my loyal warrior."

The boy's chest puffed out ridiculously, and he looked down at his weeping friend. "Today, you tried to leave," he said. "You knew the punishment for that."

Isidora shook her head again. "I didn't know," she said. "We were never told that! Please, give me another chance! This isn't fair!"

The boy hesitated, then reached down, took Isidora's hands, and pulled her gently to her feet. For a moment, Cadaverous thought he might give her a reprieve, but then he saw Abyssinia close her eyes, and knew she was in Jenan's head.

Jenan put his hands to Isidora's shoulders and pushed, and Isidora shrieked and toppled from the dais. The other members of First Wave looked away, covered their mouths, gave little cries of shock, and Jenan stepped backwards, a look of horror on his face.

"My loves," said Abyssinia. "Come to me."

She spread her arms and they walked to her, hesitantly at first, but Cadaverous could feel the waves of empathy Abyssinia was giving out, even from where he stood. When they huddled around her, they were safe and warm and they belonged.

Just like he used to.

Cadaverous followed Abyssinia back to her quarters. When she saw him, she sighed.

"Do you mind coming back later?" she asked. "We just had to execute one of the children."

"I was there," Cadaverous said. "You handled it well."

She sat. "Thank you."

"Do you think they'll be ready?"

"Of course," she responded.

"You're putting an awful lot of faith in a group of scared teenagers," Cadaverous said. "You have hundreds of followers now – most of whom would be all too eager to engage in some mindless slaughter for you."

"But it's not mindless," Abyssinia said. "There is a point to it all, even if you can't see it."

"You could help me see it. You could explain it to me."

"When you're ready, I'll tell you. Is there another reason you're here, Cadaverous?"

"There is. But, now that I have you alone, I almost don't know where to begin." He took a breath. "We believed in you. We brought you back."

"And I love you for it."

"We love you, too. I can say that with absolute certainty because, before you, I didn't know what love was. I knew it as an abstract thing, something other people said. Something other people felt. But your voice in my head, lying on that operating table... that was the voice of love. And I was hearing it for the first time."

"That's sweet of you to say."

"You're here because of us, and we're here because of you. Because of the mission."

"The mission," Abyssinia said. "Yes."

Cadaverous hesitated. "Only... only I think the search for your son has distracted you in recent months."

The good humour drifted from Abyssinia's face. "Do you indeed?"

"I have to be honest with you, Abyssinia. That's what love means, isn't it? Honesty? I feel, since you returned, that your focus hasn't been on the mission."

"I see."

"The rest of us, the ones who brought you back, we're starting to feel..."

"Yes? Starting to feel what, Cadaverous?"

"Neglected."

A ghost of a smile. "Huh. Like children, I suppose? Everyone's vying for the mother's love, jealous of anyone she dotes on. Is that what you are, Cadaverous? Are you a child? Should you be in First Wave, too?"

He didn't answer.

"What would you prefer? Would you like it if I spent more time with you, is that it? Would that be enough for you, I wonder? Would that coddle you?"

Cadaverous bristled. "I'm not asking to be coddled."

"You're not? Because it seems like you are."

"You made promises."

She rose. "You dare make demands of me, Cadaverous Gant? After everything I have given you? After I called you back from death itself? After I gave you purpose? Now you want more? You think you deserve more?"

"I think I deserve the truth!"

Abyssinia was upon him in an instant, pressing him back against the wall, her open hand hovering in front of his face.

"You insubordinate little nothing," she whispered. "You deserve only what I tell you you deserve. You have grown disillusioned with me, have you? Well, I have grown disillusioned with *you*, Cadaverous. You are not the man I hoped for. I have watched you shrivel in these last years, ever since your precious Jeremiah fell from that walkway. Your hatred of Valkyrie Cain has turned you from the path I had set you on. All those murderous urges you gave in to when you were mortal? I allowed you to make peace with them, to channel your rage. I calmed the demons in your head so that they no longer control you — and how do you repay me?" She stepped away. "By doubting me. By questioning me. By betraying me."

"I have not betrayed you!" he snapped.

"You betray me every day!" she shot back. "With every disappointment, you betray me! You were my loyal soldier! My favourite!"

Cadaverous snarled. "I was never your favourite. Smoke was your favourite, and then Lethe, when he came along. I'm always there, but always pushed to the back by the bright and the new. I should be your second. I should be your lieutenant. Instead, I arrange the food for the convicts and the criminals while people like Avatar and Skeiri waltz in and catch your eye."

Abyssinia shook her head. "Jealousy does not become you, Cadaverous."

"You've kept us in the dark long enough, Abyssinia. We're starting to feel as if we're not on this mission you told us about. We're starting to feel that you've lied to us."

"Get out," she said quietly.

10

Tea and biscuits were already laid out when Sebastian Tao crept into the house through the back door.

It was all back doors these days – back doors and skylights and narrow windows and a lot of sneaking around. Dressed as he was – all in black, with the curved beak mask and the wide-brimmed leather hat and the flowing coat – it was difficult to walk down the street, even at this time of night, and not attract curious stares or invitations to fight. Sebastian didn't like to fight. He hated violence. He'd had enough of that growing up.

He stepped into the living room. "Hello," he said.

The small group turned, smiling and nodding.

"Welcome, Plague Doctor," said Lily. "Cup of tea?"

They laughed. Sebastian chuckled politely. They knew very well that he couldn't take his mask off. Not that he needed to. His suit provided him with all the sustenance he required – although he eyed the biscuits on display longingly. What he wouldn't give for a taste.

But no. He had a mission.

"Let's hurry this along," Tantalus said, standing up from the floral couch. "Some of us have lives to get back to."

The others went quiet. Tantalus was the unofficial leader of their little group of Darquesse-worshippers, primarily because he lacked any identifiable sense of humour. He just seemed like the kind of man people would take orders from, although Sebastian had yet to witness any actual leadership abilities.

Tantalus cleared his throat. "I hereby call this meeting of the Darquesse Society to order. Blessed be her name."

"Blessed be her name," the others echoed.

"We have gazed into the face of God and we found love."

Sebastian repeated it along with everyone else.

"All right then," Tantalus said, scowling at Sebastian, "why are we here?"

Tantalus didn't like Sebastian, and he wasn't shy about letting it show.

Sebastian nodded to Forby. "Tell them what you told me," he said.

Forby, a small man with fantastic hair, cleared his throat. "Um, OK, so, the portal – the portal that all these Leibniz people are coming through. The mortal portal, I call it." He laughed. "Anyway, I'm on the team. The investigating team."

"Congratulations," said Bennet. "That's pretty high-profile. It's good to see you getting recognition in your job."

"Thank you," said Forby. "It's a real boost to my confidence, I have to admit. I've been working at the High Sanctuary since it opened; before that I was at the old Sanctuary for eighteen years... I mean, I've put in the time, you know? I've put in the work. It's just really nice to have—"

"Tell me we're not here just to congratulate Forby for doing his job," Tantalus said.

"We're not," Sebastian assured him. "Forby, get to the bit about the box."

Tantalus frowned. "What box?"

"A device," said Forby. "I was part of the team that went through the portal to examine it. I'm fairly certain that the device opened the portal."

Tantalus folded his arms. "So?"

"If I'm right, and I think I am, once we reverse-engineer it, once we figure out how it works, I can use the device to open a portal to wherever Darquesse happens to be, and we won't even need a Shunter to do it."

"This is good news," said Lily, her eyes widening. "This is great news!"

Tantalus held up a hand for silence, and kept his eyes on Forby. "That is good news. I agree. Or it would be, if we knew where Darquesse is. But we don't, do we?"

"Not yet," said Forby. He glanced at Sebastian, and Sebastian stepped forward.

"We've been talking about this," he said.

Tantalus scowled again. "Who's we?"

"Forby and me," Sebastian said.

"And what exactly have you been discussing?"

Sebastian chose his words carefully. "I don't know a whole lot about this stuff, but I do know that while it is possible to track energy signatures through dimensions, to go looking for one, even one as powerful as Darquesse's, would be a waste of time."

Forby nodded. "That's true."

"But then I asked Forby," Sebastian continued, "if it would be easier to track the Faceless Ones instead, seeing as how there's a whole race of them."

Tantalus's eyes narrowed. "Why would we want to do that?"

"We all know that Darquesse left this reality to find a new challenge. Fighting the Faceless Ones was that challenge."

"The Plague Doctor posited the idea that Darquesse might very well still be fighting them," Forby said, "so to find them would be to find her."

"And apparently, that's entirely possible." Sebastian paused. "We just need some Faceless Ones' blood."

Tantalus laughed. "Oh, is that all? Well, I'll nip down to the shops, shall I? Anyone want anything else while I'm picking up a jar of Faceless Ones' blood? How are we for milk?"

"I know where there's some blood," Lily said.

63

They all looked at her.

"There's a scythe in the Dark Cathedral," she said. "I saw it on a tour I took there. They have it sealed off with a bunch of other stuff. The little sign said that it was splattered with the blood of one of the Faceless Ones that came through at Aranmore. Would that do?"

Sebastian looked back at Forby, who shrugged.

"I don't see why not," he said.

"So what are you suggesting?" Tantalus asked. "That we break into the Dark Cathedral and steal this scythe right from under their noses? Do you have any idea of the amount of security they have? Do you have any idea what they'll do to us if they catch us?"

"Probably kill us," said Lily. "I don't think I should go."

"No one's going!" Tantalus snapped. "The only way this wouldn't be a suicide mission is if someone knew a secret way in. Do you? Do any of you?"

Beneath his mask, Sebastian smiled, and raised his hand.

11

Valkyrie woke and lay there, scrabbling for the last threads of a departing dream. It was almost within her grasp – a normal dream, this time – when her thoughts tumbled in, filled her head, sent the dream scattering. She reached for the bottle of water by the bed, found it empty. Her throat was parched.

She got up. It was cold. She pulled on her bathrobe, tied it and hugged herself as she unlocked her bedroom door. The landing was dark. Her fingers trailed across the wall, finding the three light switches. She pressed the middle one. The light came on downstairs. Hugging herself again, she went down, narrowing her eyes against the glare until she was used to it.

She left the light, walked through the gloom to the kitchen. She could see well enough. Xena raised her head when she stepped in, just to check, and then went back to sleep. Valkyrie smiled at her, opened the fridge as quietly as possible, took a bottle of water and turned to go. Abyssinia stood watching her.

Valkyrie yelled in shock and dropped the water, white lightning crackling around her fingertips. Xena leaped up, barking, came running over, ignoring Abyssinia entirely to sniff at Valkyrie's legs, tail wagging with sudden excitement. Abyssinia looked away, her mouth moving, holding a conversation Valkyrie couldn't hear with somebody she couldn't see.

Valkyrie let the energy die. Abyssinia was looking down, not at Valkyrie at all. Valkyrie was seeing her, but she wasn't seeing Valkyrie. She started to fade. In seconds, she was gone.

Valkyrie slid down to the floor, her back against the fridge. Xena came and sat beside her, then laid her head across Valkyrie's lap. Her fur was warm and soft and reassuring.

"Good girl," Valkyrie whispered. "Everything's going to be all right. Good girl."

She reached for the bottle of water, and took a swig.

She stayed like that until the sun came up.

12

Omen was a morning person. He didn't like getting out of bed, but when he did he was invariably bright and optimistic. Mornings, he often thought, were bursting with potential. Every morning was the start of what could become the best day ever.

True, the brightness tended to dull a little once the day began to beat him down, and his optimism never lasted that long when faced with the disappointment that came with being who he was, but that didn't change how much he liked mornings. Especially a Saturday morning, when half of the students went home for the weekend and the other half chatted and hung out and bonded as people. He imagined.

This Saturday, however, was determined to squish him before he'd even had his breakfast.

His room-mates had snored. This was not unusual. What was unusual was the sheer determination they displayed, as if they were working together to deny him sleep. From then on, it was one minor catastrophe after another. He'd dropped his toothbrush in the toilet. His phone hadn't charged. Grendel Caste sneezed on his breakfast. And now here he was, sitting outside the Principal's Office.

Filament Sclavi walked by, then stopped and turned round. He sat down next to Omen.

"I heard," he said.

"Heard what?" Omen asked, even though he knew.

"You asked out Axelia Lukt, and Axelia Lukt said no."

"Ah," said Omen. "That's what you heard. I'm surprised people care enough to gossip."

"People gossip even when they don't care," said Filament. "It's what people do. So how are you? How is your heart? Is it broken?"

"Naw," said Omen. "It's ever-so-slightly dinged. It's fine. I'm fine."

Filament looked at him. "You don't have to be brave in front of me, Omen."

"I'm... not. I swear."

Filament patted his arm. "I can see that you are fighting back the tears."

"I'm really not, though."

Filament smiled sadly. "Then why is your lower lip quivering?"

"I think that's just what it does."

"You know what? You should ask her again."

"You think she's changed her mind?"

"Not yet, but she might if you pursue her. Have you never seen a romantic comedy? Have you never seen the nerd get the hot girl? How does he do it? He proves himself worthy of her affection. He devotes himself to wooing her."

"Am I the nerd?"

"Well, you're certainly not the hot girl."

Omen laughed a little. "Yeah, I suppose."

"My sisters – I grew up with sisters – they love the romantic comedies. Have you seen *10 Things I Hate About You*? Heath Ledger pursues Julia Stiles. You should sing to Axelia during morning assembly."

"That's a terrifically bad idea."

"A Partridge Family song, maybe."

"I'm not sure who they are."

"They were a musical group. One of my older sisters, she loved David Cassidy when she was a teenager. David Cassidy was in the Partridge Family. According to my sister, he was the main Partridge."

"Did they have costumes, or...?"

"I don't know if they dressed up as partridges, I just know the David Cassidy song. But you can't do that song – that was used in the movie. You want another one, a song that may once have been cheesy, but now is sort of cool."

"I don't think I'm going to sing to her, though."

"That's a pity," said Filament. "It would work. I'm sure of it. But there are other ways to woo a lady. Send flowers every day. Write her poems. Or appear at her door one evening with cue cards professing your love."

"Is that wooing, though? Or is it, you know... stalking?"

Filament frowned. "How can it be stalking? It's for love."

"I get that, I do, but everything you've just mentioned sounds a little like harassment. I'd really prefer to be the guy who, you know, is rejected and then is kind of cool about it. I don't want her to regret knowing me – that's basically what I'm trying to say. I don't want to be the bad guy, or the guy who can't take the hint. You know?"

Filament didn't respond.

"Filament?"

"Your words have made me sad," Filament said.

"Oh."

"All those romantic comedies I watched."

"It's fine for movies."

"No," said Filament. "No. I shall never watch another. From here on out, it will be horror movies and only horror movies. Not even musicals."

"Musicals are OK."

"Maybe one or two musicals, like *Grease*."

"*Grease* is funny."

"It was nice talking to you, Omen, even if you did make me sad."

"I'm really sorry about that."

"I will try to be as brave as you."

"I'm not being brave, though."

Miss Wicked approached. "Filament," she said, "it's a Saturday morning. Do something better with it than sitting outside the Principal's Office."

"Yes, miss," Filament said, and hurried away.

Miss Wicked frowned at Omen. "It's ten o'clock. Why are you out here?"

"I, um, I haven't been told to go in."

"Our appointment is for ten," she responded, striding to the door. "We go in at ten."

She walked in and Omen hopped up and hurried after her.

He'd never been in Principal Rubic's office before. He was immediately struck by the number of books on the shelves and the huge window behind the desk. Rubic himself sat at his desk, an elderly man with a face that longed for a beard it didn't have. Standing before him was a tall man with dark hair swept back off a high forehead, a man who looked just like his son.

"Ah, Miss Wicked, Omen," said Rubic, waving them in, "I was just about to call for you. Of course, you will both recognise Grand Mage Ispolin, here from the Bulgarian Sanctuary. The Grand Mage is, very naturally, concerned about Jenan's well-being."

"It's been seven months," Ispolin said, "and nothing has been done." His accent, like that of so many sorcerers, was both distinct and soft, the result of hundreds of years of living. "My son remains missing, and this woman is still teaching at this school. I'm here to demand answers."

"Of course," Rubic said, "of course. Your concern is understandable."

"For seven months, I have been met with nothing but excuses from the High Sanctuary."

Rubic nodded sadly. "Investigations of this nature do, unfortunately, tend to take a lot of time, Grand Mage."

"I am aware of the amount of time investigations take," Ispolin said slowly. "What I am interested in learning is why this woman is still employed here."

"I believe you know my name," Miss Wicked said.

Ispolin looked up. "What?"

"My name," she said. "I believe you know it. Please use it. Every time you say 'this woman' I look around, wondering who you're talking about. I am here, I gather, because of the altercation outside the boys' dormitories. Is that right?"

"That's right," Ispolin said. "When you attacked Jenan. Is this the type of teacher you have here, Mr Rubic? One who goes around assaulting your students?"

Omen cleared his throat to speak, but could only croak. Ispolin glared at him.

"Yes? You have something to contribute?"

"I'm sure Omen was about to remind you that the altercation began when your son attacked him," said Miss Wicked.

Ispolin sneered. "So he claims."

"Now, now," said Rubic, "we have no reason to doubt Mr Darkly's version of events."

"Jenan attacked me," Omen whispered.

Ispolin folded his arms. "And I say that you are a liar."

Omen flushed red.

"Look at his face," Ispolin said. "Only the guilty blush."

"Nonsense," said Miss Wicked. "Omen blushes at the mention of his own name. Please don't make my student feel any more uncomfortable than he already does, Grand Mage Ispolin. Blushing means nothing, and Omen is not a liar."

"How can you be so sure?" Ispolin fired back. "His brother is the Chosen One, isn't he? Jenan told me all about him, and, from where I stand, this is a boy who has been starved of attention his entire life. His brother is the one people know. His brother is the one people remember. But this boy here is so desperate for a moment in the spotlight that he has fabricated this entire story."

"I didn't," Omen said, shaking his head.

"You're a liar!"

"Grand Mage!" Rubic said, rising slightly in his chair, "I must ask you to calm yourself!"

"I want him expelled."

Rubic frowned, and sat back again. "I... Grand Mage, I cannot do that."

"I want him expelled and I want her fired."

"Grand Mage, please..."

Miss Wicked adjusted the sleeve of her blouse. "Are we done with this nonsense?"

Rubic held up a hand. "Just a moment—"

Miss Wicked ignored him, and focused on Ispolin. "I walked by and found Jenan choking the life out of Omen. I intervened. Jenan proceeded to physically attack me. I restrained him."

"You nearly broke his arm!"

"It could have been far, far worse. Headmaster, you realise this, do you not? I could have hurt Jenan far, far worse than I did?"

"Of course," Rubic sighed.

"In which case, I restrained him with an admirable amount of, dare I say it, restraint. For which I should be thanked. Of course, I don't do this for the thanks. I do this for the love of teaching, of moulding young minds."

"If this happened the way you say it happened," said Ispolin, "then you won't mind a Sensitive verifying it to be the truth."

Miss Wicked smiled. "No Sensitive is going to poke around inside my head, Grand Mage. You are just going to have to take my word for it, as an educator."

"I'm afraid I can't do that."

"I'm afraid you don't actually have a choice," said Rubic. "Miss Wicked has been before a Review Board, and we have cleared her of any wrongdoing. Grand Mage, we have taken this meeting with you as a courtesy, but please don't be under any illusion that you have any sort of jurisdiction here."

Ispolin glowered, and Rubic turned to Omen and Miss Wicked. "Thank you both for coming."

Miss Wicked gave a curt nod, and led the way to the door.

"Not the boy," said Ispolin. Omen turned. "She can leave, but I haven't finished with the boy."

Omen looked to Miss Wicked for help, but her face was impassive.

"Very well," said Rubic, sighing. "Omen, stay behind a moment, would you?"

"I will take my leave of you," said Miss Wicked, opening the door. "But, as I had foreseen something like this occurring, I have arranged for someone to come in and speak on the boy's behalf."

She left, and Omen frowned. Then he heard footsteps. Familiar footsteps.

They entered the room with a flourish – Emmeline Darkly and Caddock Sirroco, grand and good-looking and imperious. The room seemed to shrink around them, like a lens being refocused. Rubic stood up quickly and even Ispolin diminished slightly in their presence.

"Hi, Mum," said Omen. "Hi, Dad."

His mother threw him a sharp glance, but his father was too busy looking furious to acknowledge him.

"We were listening," Caddock said, turning his gaze on the Grand Mage. "So you haven't finished with the boy, have you? *The boy?*"

Ispolin bristled. "I have a legitimate grievance to—"

"*The boy* is our son," Emmeline cut in. "*The boy* is a Darkly, and his brother is destined to save the world. You should be thanking him. You should be thanking us for our very existence."

"Instead," Caddock said, "we find ourselves being dragged from our commitments – at the weekend – to defend our son for, what, exactly? For surviving *your* son's attempt to murder him?"

"How dare you—"

"How dare we?" Emmeline shot back. "How dare we what? How dare we side with the truth?"

"Jenan did not attack anyone."

"Jenan is part of the First Wave," Emmeline said. "That's what they're calling themselves now, is it not, this little group of terrorists formed here, at the Academy, by Parthenios Lilt? The headmaster has enough questions to answer about how he allowed this man to teach here, how he allowed this rot to fester in his own school, and they are questions that he will answer, but today, Mr Ispolin, we are focusing on you and your son."

Ispolin smoothed down his tie, though it looked perfectly smooth from where Omen was standing. "Jenan is easily led. His friends pressured him into joining. It's this teacher, this Lilt, who is responsible for what happened."

"I don't think you're giving Jenan enough credit," Caddock said. "Everything we've heard indicates that he's a natural leader – and now he's with this Abyssinia person, in a flying prison populated by convicts and criminals. He's the enemy, Mr Ispolin. We didn't do that to him. Our son didn't do that to him. He did that to himself."

Ispolin glared. "It's Grand Mage," he said. "Grand Mage Ispolin. You will refer to me as such."

Emmeline observed him with a sneer on her lips, and turned to Rubic. "I presume we are done here, Mr Rubic." It was not a question.

"Of course," Rubic said, nodding quickly. "Thank you for coming in. Omen, would you see your parents to the gate? There's a good lad."

13

"I'm sorry about that," Omen said to his parents as they walked away from Rubic's office. "I know how busy you are."

"We are very busy," said Emmeline, examining everything that they passed. "Please tell that teacher not to call on us again."

"I will," said Omen, though he knew he wouldn't.

"Where's Auger?" Caddock asked. "We were hoping to see him before we left."

"I'm not sure," Omen said. "I can pass on a message, if you like."

"We don't have a message," said Emmeline. "We just wanted to see him. Never mind."

"I could show you around," Omen suggested brightly. "If you have time, like. If you're not rushing back."

"We are rushing back," Caddock said.

"Oh, OK. I'll walk you out, then."

They walked on, Caddock a few steps in front. Silence descended.

"How are your classes going?" his mother asked eventually.

"Good," Omen responded. He wondered for a moment if they'd heard about his failed test. But no. His parents were formidable people, but they weren't omnipotent. "Really good. They're all going well. Even maths, and I'm terrible at maths."

"Are you?"

"Um, yes. I've always been terrible at maths. Remember?"

"Of course," Emmeline said in a tone that let Omen know she didn't, not at all. "And that's going well for you, is it?"

"Yep. I mean, I still don't understand most of it, but I don't think that's too important."

Caddock looked back. "You don't think understanding maths is important?"

Omen shrugged. "Not really. As long as the numbers fit, that's the only thing that matters, isn't it?"

Caddock sighed irritably, a sound Omen knew only too well. "Understanding a subject enables you to master the subject. What you're doing is skating along the surface of your education, Omen. It's time you committed. It's time you took it seriously."

"OK," Omen said quietly.

"Auger takes his studies seriously," Caddock continued. "Wouldn't you like to be like that?"

"I suppose."

"There you go again. Humming and hawing. You've got to be more decisive. You can't go through your life like this. Be definite. Do something. Commit to something."

"I'll try."

Caddock turned and Omen had to stop quickly to avoid bumping into him. "You're not listening to me at all, are you?"

"I am."

"You're hearing me, you're just not listening to me."

"I'm going to be late," Emmeline said, glancing at her watch. "Omen, do something with your life, will you? Auger volunteers for things; he gets involved in extra-curricular activities. He puts the work in at school, but he also has so many outside interests. Be more like that. Now we have to go."

"OK," said Omen, watching them walk on without him. Then they turned a corner and they were gone and, as usual, he was left feeling curiously empty.

He didn't know what to do so he went walking. He should

have been used to it by now, his parents' ability to rob him of himself. In the same way that Ispolin had seemed diminished around them, Omen became lesser in their presence. Smaller. Even more insignificant. He wished it had gone on longer, their defence of him. Even though he knew their outrage was actually about Ispolin's assault on the family name, he had enjoyed listening to their words. It had almost been like they cared. It had almost been like they approved of him.

But of course they didn't. Their approval was reserved solely for Auger who, Omen admitted, more than deserved it.

Not for the first time, though, he wondered what he'd be like as a person if he'd had his parents' approval. Would he be more confident? Would he be more popular? Would he be more daring?

Miss Gnosis was setting up a table outside the dining hall, a table with a blank clipboard resting on it. He liked Miss Gnosis. She'd made him rethink his attitude towards Necromancers. Sure, her discipline was death magic and she wore black like all Necromancers, but she was bright and fun and a really good teacher. Plus, she had red hair and she was in her twenties, and she still had her strong Scottish accent.

"Good morning, Omen," she said. She pursed her lips and turned her head slightly, looking at him from a new angle. "Everything OK? You look a little down in the dumps."

"I'm fine. I was just... No, I'm fine."

"I heard about Axelia."

"Seriously?" said Omen. "Even the teachers have heard?"

"Staffrooms are sad places unless we have something to gossip about. Guys like you, Omen, they get the girls later in life. You just wait till you hit your twenties."

He blushed, and tried to hide his smile by nodding to the clipboard. "What's this about?"

Miss Gnosis held it out. "We're collecting food and blankets for the Leibniz refugees. Would you like to sign up? We're going down to the camp on Monday to distribute whatever we've got, and we need all the help we can get. You interested?"

"Would... would this count as, like, an extra-curricular activity?"

"It's practically the definition of the word."

"And signing up for it, that would be a commitment, wouldn't it?"

"It certainly would."

"Yes," said Omen, and paused. Then he said, "Yes," again, more forcefully.

"Good man," said Miss Gnosis.

"I'll do it."

"All right then."

"I'll help."

"I have to tell you, Omen, this sounds like it's a bigger deal to you than it is to me. Put your name down there like a good lad, and I'll explain what you'll have to do."

14

Valkyrie was curled up on the couch with Xena, watching Saturday evening TV, when she saw Skulduggery drop slowly from the sky and land outside the window.

She moved the dog to one side and got up, padded on bare feet to the hall and opened the door.

Skulduggery's jacket had bullet holes in it.

"You look like you've had fun," she said, leaning against the doorjamb.

"I punched many bandits," Skulduggery responded. "Temper did, too, but I punched more. Not that it was a competition. But, if it had been, I'd have won."

"Well, I'm proud of you for winning what wasn't a competition. Have all the refugees passed through the portal?"

"Not even close. By the time we were returning, there were perhaps two thousand waiting to go through, with plenty more arriving every few minutes. China finally sent in a battalion of Cleavers to offer protection."

"Well, that was nice of her," said Valkyrie. "Any sign of Mevolent's army?"

"Not so far."

"Well, you know, be grateful for small mercies, or whatever it is that people say. Also, have you seen your jacket?"

"Ah," he said, "yes. Most unfortunate."

"Do you even have anyone to fix it any more?"

"Of course. Ghastly wasn't the only tailor in town – just the best. I see, by the way, that the Bentley is in one piece."

"Naturally," said Valkyrie, taking the car keys from the side table and handing them over. "When I borrow something, I return it in pristine condition, and I am shocked that you would ever doubt me."

"I never doubt you," he replied, and handed her a key in return.

She raised an eyebrow. "What's this?"

"A spare," he said, "for the Bentley. In case I ever lose my own."

"You're giving me a key to your car?"

"Just to mind."

"Does this mean we're now sharing the Bentley?"

Skulduggery stiffened. "Dear me, no. Not in the slightest."

She clutched the key to her chest. "You mean I now own the Bentley? You're *giving* her to me?"

"OK, I'm changing my mind about this whole thing," he said, and reached for the key.

"No take backsies," said Valkyrie, and shut the door.

15

The President of the United States was in a bad, bad mood.

Martin Maynard Flanery had been elected fair and square and, try as they might, the leftist losers and the liberal media couldn't take that away from him.

His presidency was beyond legitimate. He had won the electoral college on a scale no one had ever seen before or even dreamed *possible*. Yet he had done it, because he was smarter than everyone else, shrewder than everyone else, and smarter than everyone else. He was a winner.

"I'm a winner," he said to the Oval Office, but the Oval Office didn't respond.

There was a knock on one of the doors.

"Not now!" he called out. Beyond that door was a line of people, all with demands on his time, with reports and briefings and files and folders that would clutter up his perfectly bare desk. He didn't want to let them in. He could feel them hovering out there, full of nervous energy that would get under his skin. Even thinking about it made him uncomfortable.

Flanery stood, went to the window, stared out through the bulletproof glass. From here, he could see Secret Service agents, sworn to protect him, trained to give their lives for his.

But would they? Would they die to protect him? He narrowed his eyes. He couldn't trust them to do what they'd sworn to do.

If his time as president had taught him anything, it was that he couldn't trust anyone.

He had enemies everywhere.

There was a knock on the other door, and, before he could order them to go away, the door opened and Wilkes slipped in.

"I'm not to be disturbed," Flanery snapped.

"Oh," said Wilkes, freezing in midstep. He looked around, eyes flicking to the empty desk. "What... what are you doing?"

Rage boiled. "You don't ask me questions!" Flanery snarled.

"No, sir," said Wilkes, immediately wilting. "Sorry, sir."

Flanery gripped the back of his chair. "I'm thinking," he said. "I'm planning. I'm deciding. I'm doing many things."

"Yes, sir," said Wilkes. "Um, I've received requests from a few members of staff. They really need to speak to you on some pretty urgent matters..."

It was pitiful, the way he stood there, riddled with weakness. Flanery hated weakness. He hated Wilkes.

"Have you handled the witch?" Flanery asked.

Wilkes winced. He didn't like talking about the witch in the Oval Office. He'd even proposed they use code words. Flanery enjoyed seeing him squirm.

"She is under control, yes, sir."

"How can we be sure she won't refuse my orders again?"

"I, um, I made it very clear what the repercussions would be."

"What did you say?"

"I, ah, relayed, uh, what we had discussed in—"

"*Uh!*" Flanery blurted. "*I relayed what we had, uh, duh, duhhh...* Why can't you just answer the question, eh? Why can't you do that? What did you tell her?"

Wilkes swallowed. "I told Magenta that if she ever disobeyed your orders again, she'd never see her family."

"And what did she say?"

"She... she started crying, Mr President. She apologised, and said she would do as she was told in future."

Flanery pursed his lips. "She cried, did she?"

"Yes, sir."

He smiled. "I'd have liked to have seen that. I bet that was something to see, this high-and-mighty witch reduced to tears. Was she on her knees when she was crying?"

"Um... no, sir."

"Next time, make sure she's on her knees."

"Yes, sir."

Flanery sat behind his desk again. "I want you to call Abyssinia," he said. "Tell her I've decided to move up the operation."

Wilkes went pale. "Sir?"

Flanery pretended not to notice his shock. "The mainstream media are producing more fake polls saying I'm the most unpopular president in history. They're turning the people against me, Wilkes."

"The people love you, sir."

"I know that!" Flanery snapped, his anger rising again. "But they're being lied to. They're being misled. We need to do something to unite the country behind me. So move up the operation." Wilkes hesitated, and Flanery glared. "Well?"

"Mr President," Wilkes said, "that might not be possible. The plan is... is delicate, sir. We have to get *our* people in place and Abyssinia has to get *her* people in place, and the timing has to be just right."

"They're calling me the most unpopular president in history, and you want me to wait on *timing*?"

"Sir, Abyssinia's plan requires—"

Flanery leaped up and Wilkes flinched.

"Abyssinia's plan?" Flanery roared. "Abyssinia's? This is my plan! I'm the one who thought it up! I'm the genius here! She's nothing but another witch! What do we do with witches, Wilkes? What do we do with them? We make them get on their knees and weep. Isn't that right?"

"Yes... yes, sir."

"And then what do we do with them?"

"I'm... I don't know..."

"We burn 'em, Wilkes. We burn the witches."

"Yes, sir."

"The same goes for the freaks and weirdos and sorcerers and whatever else they're called. They're all gonna burn, Wilkes, and when they do the entire country will stand behind me and they'll shout my name and they will love me."

"Yes, sir."

Wilkes wouldn't meet Flanery's eyes.

16

The fifteen-minute drive to Haggard took over twenty minutes. Valkyrie decided on the scenic route, right along the coast, the road clinging to the shoreline like the hem of a dress. There was a boat on the water, somebody parasailing. It looked fun.

She could have driven for hours, but Haggard reached for her, pulled her in, and no matter how slow she went, her childhood home drew closer, until she was suddenly parked outside. She turned off the engine and took a breath. She was excited to see her family. She wanted to see them. But there was a part of her that crouched in the shadows of her mind, and that part whispered to her, telling her to turn round, to leave them in peace. They'd be happier without her, it said. They'd be happier if she left them alone. Safer.

She'd killed her own sister, after all, just so that she could use a weapon. It didn't really matter that she'd resuscitated her immediately afterwards. What kind of person, the voice whispered, could bring themselves to do that to someone they loved?

Valkyrie got out of the car, slammed the door shut. She wasn't going to let the voice win today. She wasn't going to let all those bad feelings come crashing down on her, like they had so many times in the past.

She was getting better.

She walked up to the front door and paused, immersed in a

feeling she still hadn't become familiar with. This was her home and yet it wasn't. Her childhood lived here. The young girl called Stephanie Edgley lived here. This was where she'd watched TV and read her books and done her homework. This is where she'd listened to her mum and dad crack jokes and riff off each other. This was where her little sister hurtled around the place. This was the house where normal lived.

She walked in. The house was warm, and smelled of good food cooking. She went immediately to the kitchen. Her mum was chopping carrots, her back to her.

Valkyrie opened her mouth to say something, and realised she didn't know what that something should be. She waited for the chopping to stop, then she just said, "Heya."

Her mum looked round, and a smile broke out and she hurried over. "Sweetheart," she said, wrapping Valkyrie in her arms. Valkyrie spent so long trying to figure out how much pressure to apply to her own hug that it was over before she'd really committed to it.

"Do you want a cup of tea?" her mother asked. "Sit down, I'll put the kettle on."

Valkyrie nodded and smiled as her mum busied herself with the mechanics of tea-making. The kitchen looked exactly the same, apart from the refrigerator. The refrigerator was different.

"You got a new fridge," Valkyrie said.

"Hmm? Oh, yes. Well, three or four years ago. Didn't you see it when you were here for your birthday?"

"I don't think I came into the kitchen."

"Oh, well, there it is: the sort-of-new fridge. Now, dinner won't be ready for about a half-hour or so. Are you hungry? I think we have some biscuits, unless your father ate them."

"I'm OK."

"You're sure? They're chocolate chip."

"I'm fine."

The front door opened and closed.

"There's a strange car parked outside," came her father's voice. "We should be on the lookout for odd people acting oddly in the neighbourhood."

He walked in, grinning.

"Hi, Dad," said Valkyrie.

"Hello, oddball," her father replied, coming over to give her a hug. "Good God! It's like hugging a statue. Melissa, you've got to try this."

"We've already hugged."

"It's like hugging a statue!"

"Yes, dear."

"Obviously, a statue that I love very much, and a wonderful statue full of life and warmth and all those other things, but holy God, those are some hard muscles." He poked Valkyrie's arm.

"Ow, Dad."

"Sorry," he said, then poked again.

"Ow."

"Sorry."

"Des, stop poking her."

"Right, yes," he said, and stepped away. He poked his own arm and his face fell. "Why don't I have muscles like that?"

Valkyrie's mum passed her a mug of tea. "Because you don't work out like your daughter does."

"But why can't they be hereditary?"

"That's not how hereditary works. Things are passed *down*, not up."

"Stupid DNA," he grumbled. "Do I at least get a cup of tea?"

"You do if you make it yourself," said her mum. "I made one for Stephanie because she's a guest."

"No, she's not. This is her home and I, for one, refuse to treat her any differently. Stephanie, fetch me my pipe and slippers."

"No."

"Ah, go on."

"You don't even have a pipe," Valkyrie said.

"My slippers, then."

"I don't fetch, Dad. I'm not a dog."

"Where is your dog, by the way? Did you bring her?"

"She's at home, guarding the house."

"And how is life up where you live? Up there in foreign climes, with your strange customs and language and everything?"

"It's fifteen minutes away."

"Which begs the question: why haven't you been down to see us more?"

"I've just been busy, that's all."

"Too busy to call in on your way past?"

"Des," her mum said, "she keeps unconventional hours, remember."

Her dad shrugged. "Ah, yeah, but we've barely seen her in six months. How's work?"

"It's OK. I mean... yeah, it's OK. I've been easing back into it."

"Saved the world lately?"

"Not quite. But working on it."

Her mum leaned forward slightly. "You are keeping safe, aren't you? You wouldn't do anything silly now."

"No, Mum. I'm keeping safe."

"Because I still have nightmares about—"

"Hey now," her dad said. "We had an agreement, didn't we? We don't talk about that day at the dinner table. It puts everyone off their food and puts some of us in a bad mood. Besides, we have to watch what we say around the munchkin."

And, right on cue, Alice came running into the room. "Stephanie!" she cried, delighted.

"Hey there," said Valkyrie, getting off her chair just in time to catch Alice in a hug. She laughed as her little sister squeezed her with all her tiny might. "I love your top."

"Thank you," said Alice, stepping back, full attention now on her clothes. "Do you like the sequins? They catch the light."

"They do catch the light," Valkyrie said. "That's a very grown-up thing to say. They're lovely."

"Thank you. Do you want to see my shoes? Look at the heels."

"Oh! They have lights!"

"Red lights and orange lights," said Alice. "Do you wish you had lights in your shoes?"

"I do. I really do."

"They don't make them for grown-ups, though, I don't think. Mom, do they make them for grown-ups?"

"I don't think so," said Valkyrie's mother.

Alice nodded. "They don't. They're only for small feet like mine."

Valkyrie raised an eyebrow at her mother. "*Mom?*"

Melissa sighed. "All the kids call their mums mom these days. I think the young moms kind of encourage it."

"Do you want to see my dolls?" Alice asked. "I have princess dolls and soldier dolls. Today, the princess dolls rescued the soldier dolls from the evil dragon."

"Sounds exciting," said Valkyrie.

"It's very exciting. Would you love it very much to play with me?"

"I would love it very much."

"Hold on, hold on," Desmond said. "Don't rush off yet. You can play dolls with Stephanie after dinner, OK?"

"But can I show Stephanie my room?"

Desmond sighed. "Of course you can."

Alice took Valkyrie's hand and led her upstairs, to Valkyrie's old bedroom. The walls were light blue with interlocking rainbows traced along the borders. It was the same bed with brighter sheets, the same bedside table and dresser. The same wardrobe.

Valkyrie opened the wardrobe. There was a new mirror on the inside door, to replace the smashed one, the one her reflection used to step out of. That was one of the main secrets Valkyrie still kept from her parents, the fact that they had had a duplicate daughter living with them for years and they never suspected she wasn't the real thing.

"Do you like my clothes?" Alice asked.

"I do," said Valkyrie, and closed the wardrobe. "This used to be my room. There were books everywhere and weird posters on the walls... You keep it a lot tidier than I ever did."

Alice nodded. "That's what Mom says." She picked up a small doll, dressed in green with wings and pointed ears. "This is Sparkles. She's my fairy."

"I like her wings."

"She uses them to fly. When there are no humans around, Sparkles comes alive, but when humans come back, she has to pretend to be a toy again."

"That's pretty cool," Valkyrie said, sitting on the bed. "Is she your friend?"

Alice nodded. "My best friend, along with Molly and Alex in school."

"Wow, you've got a lot of friends."

"It's important to have friends. They like me because I'm always happy."

Valkyrie smiled. "Always? You never get sad?"

Alice frowned. "I don't think so. Molly and Alex are sad sometimes. Sometimes they're not friends, and they get sad because of that. But I never get sad, even when people aren't friends with me."

"You're a smart girl."

"Do you get sad?"

"Sometimes."

"You should be happy like me."

"I should, shouldn't I?"

"What do you get sad about?"

"Different things. But it all goes away, isn't that right? Even when you're really sad about something, you always feel better after a while."

"I don't know," said Alice, looking puzzled. "I'm always happy, I said."

Valkyrie laughed. "Of course. Sorry. I forgot."

"Do you want to see my other toys?"

"Sure."

They stayed up there until they were called downstairs. In the kitchen, the table was already set and Melissa was carving the roast chicken.

Valkyrie's stomach rumbled. "Oh, wow, that smells amazing."

"How amazing?" Desmond said, his eyes narrowing.

"Very amazing."

"Then would you be interested in a trade? This dinner for a teeny, tiny favour?"

"Des," Melissa said. "She's getting the dinner anyway. She doesn't have to do anything for it. She's our daughter."

"What favour would that be?" Valkyrie asked, tensing despite herself.

Her parents exchanged a glance.

"We were wondering if you'd be free to babysit on Thursday," Melissa said. "It's our anniversary, and we thought we'd spend the day getting pampered in the Lakeview Hotel."

Valkyrie hesitated. "Babysit?"

"If you're not too busy."

She looked at Alice. "Babysit this squirt?"

"I'm not a squirt," Alice said, frowning.

"You'd have to pick her up from school at quarter to three," Melissa said, "and we'd be gone until the next morning."

"So I pick up this squirt from school, and then I get to spend the rest of the day with her? And she gets to spend the night at my house?"

Alice's eyes widened. "Your house? Would I have my own bed?"

"You'd probably have to, wouldn't you?"

Alice nodded quickly.

Valkyrie grinned, and shrugged to her folks. "I think I could manage that."

"Yay!" Alice cried, thrusting both hands in the air and dancing.

Melissa laughed. "Everyone sit. Hope you're all hungry."

"I'm starving," said Valkyrie.

"I'm starving, too," said Alice.

Valkyrie sat at the table in her usual spot. It felt strange, especially with Alice settling into the chair beside her. But as soon as Alice was seated she hopped up again.

"I forgot Sparkles!" she said, and ran upstairs.

"Have you met Sparkles?" her dad asked, helping Melissa serve dinner.

"I have."

"All her schoolfriends have them. They're like that elf, you know, at Christmas, that comes alive when all the humans leave the room? Creepy little things. Expensive, too. You never had anything like that when you were a kid, did you?"

"Nope," said Valkyrie. "No elves. No fairies. I didn't even have an imaginary friend."

"I did," said Desmond. "His name was Barry. He was always getting me into trouble."

"I didn't have time to have an imaginary friend," Melissa said. "I had a very full social calendar, even back then. I've always had lots of friends, actually. Then I got married and they all kind of drifted away."

Desmond grinned. "That's the effect I have on people."

"I know you're joking," Melissa said, "but you can be quite rude."

"It's not me," Desmond protested. "It's Barry."

Melissa sighed. "Gordon was the same. A wonderful man, such a big heart, but completely oblivious."

"Yeah," said Desmond, "we Edgley men are great."

There was a knock on the door and Desmond went to answer it. Melissa put a plate of food in front of Valkyrie. Roast chicken, roast vegetables, peas, and the most perfectly roasted potatoes.

"Thank you," said Valkyrie.

"Um," said Melissa.

"Yes?"

Her mum winced. "We should have told you. I thought it'd be a nice surprise, but I regret now not telling you."

"Not telling me what?"

"That was a lie. I didn't tell you because I wanted it to be a surprise – I didn't tell you because I thought you might say no."

"Say no to what?"

Desmond came back into the kitchen and Skulduggery stepped in after him, his hat in his hand.

"Sorry I'm late," he said.

17

Valkyrie frowned. "I don't get it."

"We invited Skulduggery," Melissa said.

"You did?"

Skulduggery tilted his head. "You didn't know?"

Valkyrie held up a hand to him. "Hold on, you." Then, to her parents, "How did you invite him?"

"We called him last night," said her mum.

"How do you have his number?"

"You gave it to us, remember? In case you... weren't in contact with us for any length of time."

Valkyrie narrowed her eyes. "You were only supposed to use it in case of emergencies."

"This is an emergency," Desmond said. "A social emergency. We thought it was important that we all sit down and... chat. About things."

"Do you mind?" Melissa asked. "Skulduggery is such a big part of your life. We want to get to know him – and we want to get to know you. Does that make sense? Is that weird?"

"It's not weird, no, but it's..." Valkyrie shrugged. "It doesn't matter. Skulduggery, take a seat."

"Thank you," Skulduggery said. "I thought you knew."

"It's cool."

"I haven't been invited to dinner in about three hundred years, so I said yes without even bothering to check."

"People don't invite you to dinner?" Desmond asked, putting a plate of food in front of him.

"I don't eat," Skulduggery said, and Desmond nodded, and took the food away. Alice came down the stairs and Skulduggery activated his façade, turning to her when she ran in. "Hello."

"Hello," she said.

Skulduggery tilted his head. "Why are you so short?"

"I'm only seven," Alice said.

"That's no excuse. When I was your age, I was twice as tall as you. You should grow taller."

"I will, when I'm older."

"You're not just being lazy, are you?"

"No."

"Do you promise?"

"I promise."

"Come over here."

Without hesitation, Alice crossed the room.

"My name is Skulduggery," Skulduggery said. "It's a big word. Can you say it?"

"Skuduggery."

"Skulduggery."

"Skulduggery."

"Very good. And you are Alice. We've met before, when you were even smaller than you are now. You were a baby the last time I saw you."

"Now I'm seven."

"That's right. You're a little girl now. It's very good to meet you again, Alice."

"It's very good to meet you."

"Are you joining us for dinner?"

"Yes." She turned to Valkyrie. "I can't find Sparkles."

Valkyrie looked thoughtful. "Well, she does come to life when we're not there, so she's probably playing hide-and-seek with you. If you were a fairy, where would you hide?"

"In the clouds."

"OK, but I don't think the window's open, so she's probably still in your bedroom. Maybe in your bed? Under the blankets or—"

"Or under the pillow!"

Valkyrie clicked her fingers. "I bet that's where she is!"

Alice ran upstairs again.

"I have questions," Desmond said, as he and Melissa sat down.

"Go ahead," Skulduggery said.

"Is this your actual face, from when you were alive?"

"No," Skulduggery answered. "It's a random selection. Sometimes they repeat; sometimes they're brand new."

"Do you have magic toilets?"

Valkyrie sighed. "Dad..."

"What? I just want to know if there are magical versions of everyday items. A magic toilet would be a good idea, wouldn't it? Maybe the pee disappears before it hits the bowl."

"Des," said Melissa, shaking her head.

"What? I'm curious. If the pee disappears, where does it go? Does it evaporate or is it, I don't know, transported to another dimension? When we spoke last night, you said you'd just got back from a parallel dimension. Is there an entire dimension that is just filled with our pee? Or is there a parallel dimension that is just like ours, but our pee is their rain? Every time we pee, are we peeing on millions of people?"

"No, Desmond," Skulduggery said. "That doesn't happen."

Desmond nodded. "That's probably a good thing."

"There aren't magical versions of every household item. Sorcerers use the same things mortals do. We live side by side, after all."

"Not any more you don't. You live in Roarhaven now."

"Not all of us," Skulduggery said.

Desmond leaned forward. "What about wands?"

"We don't use wands, Dad," said Valkyrie.

"Then how come they're a thing? Why did they become associated with magicians?"

"A few hundred years ago," Skulduggery said, "some sorcerers did indeed use wands."

Valkyrie raised an eyebrow. "I didn't know that."

"It was a passing fad," he explained. "Embarrassing to all who witnessed it and, as it turned out, quite damaging. In much the same way that Necromancers use an object to channel their power, sorcerers of different disciplines used wands to focus their abilities. Necromancers, however, need to use objects as their power is too unstable."

"How was using wands damaging?"

"Magic is instinctual. As such, it's affected by our moods. If a sorcerer panics, their control is diminished. Channelling their magic through wands meant they were unconsciously limiting their own potential. It's called the Wand Principle."

"That makes sense," Desmond said, nodding. "The Wand Principle. I like that."

Alice hurried in, Sparkles in one hand. She sat at her place. Nobody was eating.

"Well, I'm hungry," said Valkyrie, and picked up her knife and fork.

"Please, all of you, begin," Skulduggery said. "Don't mind me."

The others started to eat. The food was everything Valkyrie had remembered.

"So," Melissa said, "what have you been up to for the last five years, Skulduggery? Stephanie told us that an ex-girlfriend of yours has been brought back to life. That's an unusual situation."

"I suppose it is," Skulduggery said. "Yes, Abyssinia and I have a history, but that was hundreds of years ago. A lot has happened for both of us since then."

"Wasn't she just a heart in a box for most of that, though?" asked Desmond, his mouth full.

"Well, yes, you're right, which brings to mind some intriguing questions about how internal organs perceive the passage of time – but Abyssinia managed to communicate with people and entities telepathically while she was in there, so I think it's fair to assume that she experienced at least some growth as a person."

"Still, anything involving an ex is bound to be awkward, especially one that you... um..."

"K-I-L-L-E-D," Skulduggery finished, glancing at Alice. "Yes, that brings with it its own unique complications. We still haven't spoken, though, since she was resurrected, so I'm afraid I can't give you a definitive answer."

"I don't want peas," said Alice.

"Just eat a few of them," Melissa said, before turning back to Skulduggery. "What are you working on now? Anything exciting?"

"Just the usual," Valkyrie said before Skulduggery could answer. "People with strange names doing strange things for strange reasons."

"Anything dangerous?"

"No, not really. Not what I'd call... Skulduggery, what do you think? I wouldn't call it dangerous. Would you?"

"No," said Skulduggery. "Not dangerous. Not at all."

Valkyrie nodded, and went back to eating.

"It's not exactly safe, either," Skulduggery continued, "but dangerous is... I've always felt that it's a word loaded with unhelpful connotations."

Valkyrie chewed faster, but Melissa was already asking a follow-up. "Just to clarify – how not-safe is it? Stephanie? Could you get hurt doing whatever it is you're doing?"

Valkyrie swallowed. "I could get hurt crossing the road, Mum."

"Which is why you were taught to look both ways."

"She still does that," Skulduggery interjected. "She's very good at crossing the road."

"Thanks," Valkyrie said, giving him a glare before smiling reassuringly at her parents. "I'm safe. I'm taking care of myself. I'm not in any danger."

"What about this ex-girlfriend? Anyone that can come back from the dead sounds like she might be trouble."

"The High Sanctuary has people working on that," Valkyrie said. "That isn't what we do any more. We're Arbiters now. We're not sent out; we're not assigned anything. We get to pick and choose the cases we work on. And I'm still easing back into things, remember? I'm taking it nice and slow."

Melissa put down her knife and fork. "Skulduggery, do you promise to keep our daughter safe?"

Valkyrie closed her eyes. She knew what was coming.

"I'm afraid I can't do that," Skulduggery said. "We have no way of knowing where a line of investigation will take us or how dangerous it will get. But you can rest assured that I will do my very best to keep your daughter alive. My very, very best."

Valkyrie's parents looked at him.

"So how's Fergus and Beryl?" Valkyrie asked them quickly.

Melissa hesitated, reluctant to move to a different subject. "They're doing... fine, we think. We don't really see them much. They've been having some trouble with the girls."

"What's happened?"

"Ah, it's nothing. People change. They grow up and they grow apart. Even sisters. Even twins. Carol got a job in a solicitor's office and she's moved into her own apartment. She's doing fine. I think she even has a boyfriend. Crystal is still living at home."

Desmond frowned. "She had a bit of a nervous breakdown," he said. "She's been to see a psychiatrist, the poor mite. She started thinking that Carol was an imposter. There's a name for it, some kind of delusion..."

"Capgras delusion," Skulduggery said. "It's a misidentification syndrome, commonly found in paranoid schizophrenics."

Or people whose sisters had been murdered and then replaced by reflections. Valkyrie looked down at her plate. "Is she OK?"

"She's got pills she takes," Melissa said. "And she talks to her psychiatrist once or twice a week. She's perfectly fine apart from... apart from when Carol's around."

Valkyrie's throat burned. "Maybe I'll call in," she said quietly.

"I'm sure she'd like that," Melissa said.

Skulduggery's phone rang. "I do apologise," he said, taking it from his pocket. "Ah, it's Temper. I'm afraid I'll have to take this."

"I'll talk to him," Valkyrie said, whipping the phone out of his hand as she stood up. She walked into the hall and then out of the front door as she answered the call.

"I have news," Temper said.

"Tell me."

"Valkyrie? Is everything all right? Is Skulduggery in trouble again?"

"No," she said, "he's fine. He's having dinner with my parents. I just... I needed to get out of there. What do you have?"

"The chemist who makes Quidnunc's serum – I found out his name. Gravid Caw. He's got a house in Black Cat Drive. Don't have a whole lot more on him, I'm afraid – if he's a bad guy, he's stayed clear of the City Watch."

"Gravid Caw, Black Cat Drive. Got it. Thank you."

"You want me to have someone haul him in for you to question?"

"Naw, it's OK. We only have a limited number of times we can do that before your City Guard buddies get annoyed at being used to pick up our suspects. Besides, we prefer to catch bad guys in their natural environment. It's more fun."

Valkyrie went back into the house. "We have to go," she said, handing the phone to Skulduggery.

"Already?" her mum asked, standing. "You can't stay a little longer? Even just for dessert?"

"We really can't," Valkyrie said. "Mum, thank you so much

for dinner. I haven't had food that good in ages. Dad, thanks for asking about magic toilets." She gave them both a kiss.

"And thank you for inviting me," said Skulduggery. "It was very nice of you."

Valkyrie hugged Alice. "I'll see you on Thursday, OK? We'll have the best day."

"I can't wait," Alice said, grinning.

Valkyrie and Skulduggery left. The Bentley was parked at the corner. Valkyrie unlocked her own car. "Gravid Caw is the chemist. He lives on Black Cat Drive. Meet you there?"

"Of course," Skulduggery said. "Valkyrie, are you all right? Your parents called me after I'd arrived home yesterday evening. I wouldn't have come if I had known I'd be interrupting."

"You weren't interrupting."

"I know how much you were looking forward to spending some time with your family. Believe me, I understand."

She smiled. "Thanks. But you're never an interruption, you got that? Now quit being considerate. It's weird, and it makes me want to laugh nervously and run away."

"You are an odd woman."

"Yep," she said.

18

Even in Coldheart, a scream so full of terror was a curiosity worthy of further investigation, so Cadaverous hunted it down like he'd hunted all those idiotic co-eds through his house of horrors, finally turning a corner to see Razzia leaning over the barrier.

"Are you throwing people off again?" he asked, walking up to her.

She didn't look round. "He's the last one," she said.

"Did you get him to apologise?"

"He got down on his knees and begged me to forgive him. He said he got confused in all the excitement."

"You didn't forgive him, obviously."

"We let them out of their cells to attack Valkyrie and the skeleton. They should have known better than to attack me, too." Her voice was low, her face expressionless. Then she brightened, her unhinged smile returning. "You should've seen the way he evaporated, Caddie. The moment he hit that energy field he just went *zzaap*," and she clicked her fingers.

"I'm sure it was lovely."

"It was, actually. Very pretty. I might write a poem about it later. What rhymes with evaporated?"

"Not much."

"Maporated. Is that a word?"

"Not a real one."

"It's not easy being a poet."

"Stick to what you're good at, Razzia. Extreme violence and making people uneasy in your presence."

She sighed unhappily, and took a crumpled ball of foil from her pocket. "I want to try new things, though. I want to stretch myself."

"You're bored, aren't you?"

"Dunno," she said, opening the ball. "I've never been bored before, so I don't know what it feels like. I've always had someone to kill or hunt or torture. I don't even view it as work, you know? Is it even work, when you're doing what you love?"

"It's a vocation, is what it is. But even someone like you needs direction, and I don't think you've been getting that lately."

The foil contained a few small pieces of raw meat. Razzia brought her other hand close. "Things are different," she said. "Before we got Abyssinia back, it was non-stop, you know? We were always busy. Always focused."

"But now that's all changed," Cadaverous said.

"We still have our plans, though. Abyssinia has her people in place, and First Wave are getting ready to strike." Razzia's palm opened slowly, and the parasite poked out. A black tentacle with a head slightly thicker than its body, it had no eyes but plenty of sharp, tiny teeth. It hovered over the foil, then dipped down, snatching the meat into its jaws.

Cadaverous couldn't take his eyes off it as it fed. "But is that enough to keep life interesting, Razzia?"

"No, it ain't. She won't even send me on the simple jobs because she thinks I'll do something crazy and kill a bunch of people for no reason."

"I know."

"I always have a reason, Caddie."

"I know that, too."

"But she sends Skeiri instead, because apparently she has more 'self-control'. What's so good about self-control?"

"Nothing that I can see."

"I hate Skeiri."

"I know."

"She's basically just a sane version of me. We even have the same pets!"

"What are the odds?"

"Her pets aren't as well-trained as mine, though. And see this guy? He's longer than Skeiri's, and he's not even fully grown yet. And her pets are green. Can you imagine it? How ugly."

"Very ugly."

"Can I tell you something? And promise you won't tell anyone else?"

Cadaverous dragged his eyes away from the parasite. "Of course."

"I'm not sure that I have any friends here. Like real, actual mates. Nero makes me want to stab him every time I talk to him and Destrier's always working on his little projects, and he's a weirdo anyway... For so long, Abyssinia was my friend, a voice in my head that only I could hear. But she barely does that any more, and when she does it just feels... weird."

"I'd like to think that I'm your friend, Razzia."

She smiled. "Yeah. I reckon you are." She looked down at the parasite as it ate. "But you're a psychopath, so I don't think you count."

"Do you want to know a secret?" Cadaverous asked. "I've been having the exact same thoughts as you. I'm bored. It's as if all Abyssinia wanted was for us to bring her back to life, so she filled our heads with all these wonderful ideas of an anti-Sanctuary and getting revenge on the people who've wronged us... and, now that she's back, all she cares about is herself and her son."

"You really think she was fooling us?"

"I don't know," Cadaverous said, shrugging. "I hope not. But that's how it seems. That's how it feels."

The parasite finished its lunch and retracted into Razzia's palm.

She crumpled up the foil and tossed it over the side. "I think I'm having a midlife crisis."

"We just need to remind Abyssinia that we're here, and we're valuable. We just need some way to impress her again." Cadaverous gave a little shrug. "Oh, well. If anything occurs to you..."

He let his words hang, and started walking away.

"What about..." Razzia said, and her voice trailed off.

Cadaverous turned. "Yes?"

"Nothing."

"No, go on. What were you going to say?"

She hesitated. "Well, if all Abyssinia cares about is getting Caisson back, then she'd be, like, super happy with us if we found him."

Cadaverous frowned. "But she's assigned Avatar to that job, and, from what I gather, he is mere hours away from finding the ambulance route. He's going to get all the praise. He's going to get all the fun jobs."

"Yeah, but we could, you know... kill him."

"Kill him?"

"Just a little," Razzia said quickly. "Just slightly."

"So what you're suggesting is that we wait for Avatar to find the ambulance's route... and then we kill him, sneak off ourselves, and rescue Caisson."

"Well, I mean, yeah," said Razzia. "Why not? We bring her son back, Abyssinia's gonna love us."

Cadaverous smiled. "You're not as insane as you seem, are you?"

Razzia laughed, then turned deadly serious. "Oh, no, I am, but. I really am."

19

It was late evening by the time they found Gravid Caw standing with a small group of people at the steps of the High Sanctuary. They were chanting and waving placards, calling for the refugees to be sent home while impassive Cleavers stood so still they might have been carved from granite.

Valkyrie walked up and stood beside him. He didn't notice for the first few seconds – he was far too busy chanting and waving his placard.

"I like your sign," said Valkyrie, and Gravid turned his head to her. His eyes widened when he realised who she was. "There are no typos, for one thing. I've always thought, what's the point of hating someone if you can't be grammatically correct about it?"

"I, uh, I don't hate anyone," Gravid mumbled, and went to move away. Then Skulduggery was on his other side.

"Well," he said, "you hate mortals a *little*."

"No," Gravid responded, growing noticeably paler. "We're just... we're here to ensure they're treated fairly."

Valkyrie raised an eyebrow. "*This* will be interesting."

The chanting died down once the protesters saw who had joined them. Valkyrie smiled. Skulduggery waved. The protesters glanced at each other, glanced at Gravid, and then moved away, abandoning him to restart their protest a little further on. Gravid's shoulders slumped.

"You were saying," Valkyrie prompted, "about your struggle to ensure the mortals are treated fairly."

Gravid cleared his throat, then cleared it again. "We just don't think it's, you know, fair that they're being kept in tents and things. They're not animals, after all. They have their dignity."

"First of all," Valkyrie said, "yes, they do have their dignity, thanks for reminding us. That's very important. Second, how many animals do you know of that are kept in tents? Is that a thing, keeping animals in tents? I mean, cattle can be kept in sheds, and horses in stables, but I've never heard of an animal that is kept in a tent."

"It's, uh, metaphorical."

Valkyrie frowned. "Which part, the animals or the tent?"

"I have a question," Skulduggery said, taking the placard from Gravid's hand and examining it. "It says here: Keep Mortals Out of Roarhaven. So obviously you're not inviting them in. You don't want them outside in tents, you don't want them inside in houses... so where do you want them?"

Gravid didn't answer.

"Do you think we should send them to Dublin, or Cork, or Belfast?" Skulduggery continued. "Do you think they could assimilate into mortal culture here? That would be troublesome, though, wouldn't it? They're from an alternate dimension. It would be quite the security risk."

Gravid mumbled something.

"Sorry?" Valkyrie said. "What was that?"

Gravid cleared his throat once more. "We could send them back."

"Send them back where?"

"Back where they came from."

Skulduggery didn't say anything. He was leaving this to Valkyrie. She joined him in silence for a moment, enjoying the effect it was having on poor little Gravid. He was practically squirming in his shoes.

"Do you know why they came here?" she asked.

Gravid girded himself. "The unfortunate circumstance they find themselves in should not be our concern."

"But do you know?"

"Why should we be held responsible for—"

"Yes or no answer, Gravid," Valkyrie interrupted. "Do you know what they're running from?"

"Yes, but that's got nothing to do with us."

"So you know that they're fleeing from, basically, genocide, yes?"

"I have sympathy for them," Gravid said, "of course I do, but we have to help our own before we can even think of helping others."

"Well, you're definitely not thinking of helping others, so you're halfway there already."

"Look—"

"Look?" Valkyrie repeated, stepping closer. "Are you losing your patience with me, Gravid? Are you getting angry? Are you upset that I'm not just accepting your nasty little excuses like the rest of your sign-waving friends? What do you intend to do about that, eh? You want to bully me? Intimidate me? Tell me to go back where I came from?"

Gravid swallowed. "We're having a peaceful protest. I'm not losing my patience with anyone."

"I'm losing my patience with *you*, Gravid. *Gravid*. What does that name even mean, anyhow?"

"It means meaningful," Gravid said quietly.

"It also means pregnant," Skulduggery said.

"I didn't know that when I chose it," Gravid muttered. "But I'm doing nothing wrong, OK? You can't arrest me for standing on the street and voicing an opinion. I'm entitled to it."

Valkyrie frowned again. "Who told you that?"

"Who told me what?"

"That you're entitled to an opinion," Valkyrie said. "Who told you?"

"But... but I am."

"So no one told you. You just heard it somewhere and decided it was true. You're not entitled to an opinion, Gravid. You're faced with right and wrong. You're choosing wrong, and, because you can't defend that choice without admitting that you're wrong, you claim that you're entitled to believe in a lie if you so wish." She leaned in. "I hate people like you, Gravid. I despise them. You're not even strong enough to be honest about how rotten you are."

"Besides," Skulduggery said, clamping a hand on Gravid's shoulder, "who said we were here to arrest you? I never said anything about arresting you. Valkyrie, did you say anything about arresting Gravid?"

"I thought it," Valkyrie said.

"She'd do it, too," said Skulduggery. "That's the problem you face when you deal with Arbiters. We don't answer to anyone. We could arrest you, throw you in a cell, and you'd languish there until we remembered to ask you those questions we'd been meaning to."

"What, uh, what questions?"

"It's about your day job, actually. Nothing to do with standing on pavements and waving signs about sending people back to get murdered. No, this is about your job, not your hobby."

"I'm unemployed."

"In this economy? How can that be? Roarhaven is thriving. There's work for everyone."

"Maybe you're not looking hard enough," Valkyrie said. "Or maybe you're too busy making illegal drugs."

Gravid shook his head in an unconvincing attempt at appearing unconcerned. "I don't know what you're talking about."

"The drugs, Gravid," Skulduggery said. "She's talking about the drugs you make in your basement, illegally, that you then sell to people. For money."

"I don't... I don't do that."

"You are possibly less convincing than you think you are, but I'm afraid we've just come from your basement."

Gravid's eyes widened. "You're not allowed to do that! You need a warrant to search someone's house!"

"For someone who doesn't view mortals too highly, you seem to think that a lot of their laws apply to you. We don't need warrants, Gravid. We're Arbiters. We knocked, you weren't home, and very gently we let ourselves in."

"You're going to need a new door," Valkyrie said.

Skulduggery nodded. "It's possible you might need a new door, but that's only if you like doors. Personally, I think the gaping hole lets a lot of light in. While we were there, in your house, we happened to find the hidden entrance to the basement. Well, I don't mind telling you, we were surprised. We certainly didn't expect to find the entrance in the wall, did we, Valkyrie?"

"We did not."

"I mean, we thought it might be there, but we weren't sure."

"You're going to need a new wall, too," said Valkyrie.

"Just a slight wall," Skulduggery nodded. "The west one. It's got some holes in it. Four small ones and a big one. Anyway, once we found the hidden basement, we found all the paraphernalia that you use to make the illegal drugs. There was a lot of it."

"So much," said Valkyrie.

"A huge amount. We told the City Guard about that, by the way. A friend of ours, a nice American man, you'll like him, is on his way to see you. I don't want to spoil anything, but you're looking at a lot of gaol time."

"So much," said Valkyrie.

"A huge amount."

Gravid tried to bolt, but Skulduggery grabbed his arm and squeezed his shoulder and he rose to his tiptoes and cried out.

"But before all that," Skulduggery said, "we were wondering if you could answer a few questions. It's got nothing to do with the protest, don't worry, and nothing to do with the illegal drugs, either. Another drug you make – a perfectly legal one, so good for you on that – is to combat necrosis. You make that one for a man named Quidnunc. We need to find this man. Where is he? Do you know?"

"All... all this just to find Quidnunc?"

"Yes."

"Breaking into my house, finding the drugs, calling the City Guard... and you just wanted to know where Quidnunc is? I would have told you! If you'd asked, I would have told you, no problem!"

Skulduggery nodded to Valkyrie. "See? I told you he'd be nice. Where is Quidnunc, Gravid?"

"He's staying at the Sadists' Club."

"I've never heard of it."

"It's really secret."

"Is it a club for sadists?"

"Yes."

"Clever."

"I don't know where it is – Quidnunc never said. Did you really call the cops?"

"Yes."

"Aw, man. I would have told you. You just had to ask. Like the woman did."

Valkyrie narrowed her eyes. "What woman?"

"A woman in red came to see me, asking about Quidnunc, but she didn't pull any of the stuff that you just pulled. She simply asked, and left."

"Did she have silver hair?"

"Yes."

"Did she say anything about her plans? Anything that could help us figure out where she is? If you have something useful, we could talk to our American friend and he could take it into account when your charges are being filed."

"OK," said Gravid, "OK, yeah, she did, she said, uh..."

"True things only," Skulduggery said. "Lies will result in even more gaol time."

Gravid sagged. "Then no. Nothing."

They took Gravid Caw to the nearest Cleaver and handed him over.

"That was fun," said Valkyrie

"You really got into it that time."

"He annoyed me. So – the Sadists' Club. Any idea where it is?"

"Not yet, but I'm sure I know just the people to ask. Would you like to accompany me?"

"Will there be punching?"

"Probably."

"Then, if it's all the same to you, I'll give it a miss. If I can go a full day without having to hit anyone or inflict physical pain, I'm going to do it. That's my New Year's resolution."

"You're about nine months too late."

"I meant my Chinese New Year's resolution."

"Then you're about eight months too late."

"Then it's just something I've decided."

"That's fair enough. I'll meet you here in the morning?"

"Cool. I'll be here around nine."

Skulduggery doffed his hat to her and walked towards the Bentley. Valkyrie turned and headed off in the opposite direction.

Once in her car, she left Roarhaven behind her, and the roads got bumpier before widening again and smoothing out. She joined the motorway. This time of night, there wasn't very much traffic. She turned on the radio, sang along with the music, allowing her mind to drift. She changed lanes and adjusted speed without giving any of it much thought. After a bit, she stopped singing and turned off the radio and just drove in silence. Her mind settled into the rhythm of the road. The drone of the tyres filled the car slowly until she was all alone in the world.

Abyssinia walked across the motorway and Valkyrie cursed and braked and swerved and went right through her.

The car rocked to a stop.

Valkyrie jumped out, energy crackling between her fingers, crackling from her eyes, her teeth bared, ready to fight, but the road was quiet and empty, and Abyssinia was neither lying there nor standing there. She wasn't there at all.

A hallucination, that's all it was. A hallucination or a vision, brought on by the meditative state she'd been sinking into. So Valkyrie was either having flashbacks to psychic episodes or having psychic episodes without meaning to – she didn't know which was worse. She got back in the car, restarted the engine and did a slow U-turn.

Back on track, the car drove straight and steady like nothing had happened, but Valkyrie's hands shook as they gripped the wheel.

20

Down below, the energy field hummed with power, its light flickering off the lower tier of cells.

Cadaverous took the folded paper from Avatar's hand and opened it. Printed upon the three sheets was a detailed route through Europe, complete with timings, rest stops, and distance in both miles and kilometres. Everything a group of sorcerers would need to keep a private ambulance moving smoothly, and everything a certain other group of sorcerers would need to ambush said ambulance.

"You've done good work," Cadaverous said. "Very good work, actually. I didn't think you had either the contacts or the intelligence to pull this off, if I'm being honest. I thought you were all muscle and no brains – but it seems Abyssinia was right about you."

Avatar didn't answer.

Cadaverous chuckled. "Don't look so surprised. I can admit when I'm wrong. Do you mind if I take this? You don't? That's so nice of you. This... this is what I love. I'm one of the originals, you started following Abyssinia after she released you from your cell, but here we both are, working together. As a team."

Cadaverous folded the sheets and tucked them into his pocket, then lifted Avatar off the ground, grunting slightly with the effort.

He dragged him the short distance to the balcony, and heaved him over.

Zzaap, as Razzia would say.

21

It was a Monday morning, which meant that Omen had already missed a double maths class and, as he handed blankets to a never-ending line of wary, hungry mortals, he was now missing civics. He was glad to miss maths – when was he ever going to have to add numbers in his adult life? – but he regretted missing civics. His classmates were being given their first lesson on how to forge an ID. Those kinds of things would be useful to know in the next few hundred years.

Instead, here he was in a sort of market, right in the very centre of the City of Tents, a proud member of Miss Gnosis's volunteer team of nine. He'd never volunteered for anything before, and he was starting to remember why. It was boring, for a start, and the mortals were hardly any fun, what with them hating and fearing anyone who could do magic. He wondered how they felt about people who could *barely* do magic, like Omen himself, but decided against asking. He probably didn't know them well enough to make jokes.

Someone tapped him on the shoulder.

"Miss Gnosis says I'm to relieve you," Axelia said.

"Oh," said Omen, and blushed, and stepped aside, and Axelia started handing out the blankets. She'd been weird with him all morning, everyone had, probably because they all figured he'd only volunteered because she'd be here.

He wandered over to Miss Gnosis, who was supervising the food distribution. "Um, miss? What'll I do now?"

"You're on your break," Miss Gnosis said, flicking through the pages of her clipboard. "Go mingle."

Omen didn't really know how to mingle. He'd watched Never do it, but hadn't ever come close to mastering that particular skill himself. Two of Axelia's friends were giving him the side-eye and whispering to each other, however, so he plunged into the crowd of mortals to escape, and found himself jostled and jumbled and then spat out the other side, nearly colliding with a stall lined with pots. The girl behind the stall narrowed her eyes at him.

Omen looked at her, then decided to smile. He may have overdone it, because the girl recoiled slightly.

"Hi," said Omen. "Um. Hello."

"Hello," said the girl.

Omen stuck out his hand. "My name's Omen," he said. "Omen Darkly."

She observed his hand for a moment before shaking it. "Aurnia."

"Hi, Aurnia. Very good to meet you. You're the first person from another dimension that I've ever actually spoken to."

She didn't say anything to that, so he continued.

"I mean, obviously, I spoke to the people when I was giving them blankets, but it wasn't anything that you'd call a conversation. It was mostly just, *Hello, here's a blanket*, and then they'd walk away. So..." He cleared his throat. "It's a school thing, the food and blankets. I volunteered. Do you have schools where you're from?"

"Yes."

"Yes. Of course. Who doesn't have schools?" Omen laughed. "They're all the same, no matter which universe you're from. It's all a drag. I hate school, y'know? Well, it's OK. Some of the teachers are nice, but I think I'm just not very smart." He was saying the wrong things. He didn't know what the right things to

117

say were, but he was not saying them. "So what do you think of our universe?" he continued. "Pretty cool, right?"

"It's warm enough."

"Sorry?"

"It's warm. It's fine."

"Oh," Omen said. "Oh, I get it. Um, when I say cool, I don't mean cold. It's an expression we have here. It means something good. Y'know, hey, that's cool. I'm cool. You're cool. It's an expression. Do you have expressions where you're from?"

"Yes."

"Cool. Well... it was very good to meet you." He waved, and backed off, and battled his way through the crowd.

"Making friends?" Miss Gnosis asked.

"I don't think so," said Omen. "She didn't look very happy to talk to me."

"She's been through a lot. They all have. Remember that their culture is vastly different from ours, and also she probably sees you as evil."

"Right."

"Which probably explains her reluctance to chat."

"I suppose."

"I don't think it's anything personal."

"Maybe it's my face."

"Your face is fine."

"I don't think girls like it, though."

She passed him a badge. "Here. Invite your new friend to be one of the ambassadors. Let her see that you're not a bad guy."

The crowd had thinned by this stage, so Omen returned to Aurnia's stall without making a fool out of himself.

"Aurnia?" he said. "Um, I was wondering if you'd like to be an ambassador, maybe? We're giving out these badges to people that we'd like to talk to, going forward, to come up with ways to help out. We're interested in hearing what you need, what your concerns are, that kind of thing."

118

She eyed the badge suspiciously. "What we need?" she repeated.

"Yes. If that's more food, or more blankets, or medicine, or... whatever. We want to open a dialogue with your people."

"I don't speak for them."

"But you can," said Omen. "That's what this little badge does. It lets you speak. I mean, it doesn't *let* you speak, you don't *need* it to speak, but it kind of puts you in a position where you can get heard. If you like. If that interests you."

"That little button does all that?"

"Yes." He held it out to her. "If you want it."

Aurnia considered it, then took the badge. "My people are scared," she said. "We didn't know what was on the other side of the portal – all we knew was that if we stayed in our homes we'd be killed. Now people are saying if we stay here we'll be killed."

"No," said Omen, his eyes wide. "No, no. We don't kill people. God, no. You're innocent, and you're unarmed, and you're mortal. We don't kill mortals. Sorcerers protect mortals."

"From what?"

"Uh, mostly from other sorcerers."

"Like Mevolent."

"Yes," Omen said. "We had our own version of him, in this dimension. We stopped him. He's dead here. If the Mevolent from your home tries to follow you through the portal, we'll kill him, too."

Aurnia didn't appear to be reassured. "What are you going to do to us?"

"We're, um, we're not... I'm sorry, what do you mean?"

"If you're not going to kill us, where will you put us?"

"To be honest," Omen said, shrugging helplessly, "they're still trying to figure that out. Supreme Mage Sorrows – she's in charge – is a very smart lady, though, so she'll think of something. You're safe now. You can relax."

"We're not safe," Aurnia replied. "We're in a strange world and we're surrounded by sorcerers."

"We're not all bad," said Omen. "I know your experience with people like me has been pretty terrible. I've heard about what it's like over there, in your reality. But things are different here. The mortals are free and happy. Well, not all of them, but in general. Kind of. What I'm trying to say is that this is their world."

"They rule over you?"

"Well, no, because they don't even know we exist."

"They have their own cities?"

"They have all the cities," Omen said, "all except this one, and Roarhaven is kind of invisible. This isn't a perfect universe, and not everything is fair or good and not everyone is happy, but I'm telling you, you don't have to be scared of us."

She looked doubtful. "And you," she said, "you promise you're a good sorcerer?"

"I, uh... I promise I try to be a good *person*. I don't think anyone would really say I'm a good sorcerer."

She gave a reluctant smile. It was a pretty one. "I don't mind that at all," she said.

Omen smiled back, suddenly seeing the upside of volunteering for stuff.

22

After almost crashing her car the previous night, Valkyrie decided to let Skulduggery pick her up. She left Xena outside so that she could run around, and got in the Bentley. Skulduggery's façade was a tanned gentleman with a blond moustache.

"Nice," said Valkyrie. "Have you found out where the Sadists' Club is?"

"Not yet," he said, swooping the car round and heading for the gate. "But I'm expecting a call from one of my contacts who will – hopefully – relay that information."

"Is Temper the contact?"

"No."

"He's usually the contact."

"I have more than one contact, you know."

She shrugged, and sank into a silence that lasted until they'd reached the motorway.

"Is everything OK?" Skulduggery asked.

"Sorry?"

"You seem quiet."

"Do I?"

"I think I know why."

Valkyrie looked at him, and didn't say anything. There was no way he knew about the visions. No way.

"It's about the dinner, isn't it? I ruined your family dinner and you're mad at me."

"I'm not mad at you," she said, relaxing. "You know what happens when I'm mad at you."

"You tend to throw mugs at me."

"And have I thrown any mugs? Do you even see any mugs? No. So I'm not mad at you. I'm not mad at my parents, either, even though they invited you without asking me. I understand why they did it. They're worried about me; they think getting more involved in my life will ease their minds."

"It won't, though," Skulduggery said. "At all. In the slightest. If they knew more about what you did—"

"They'd never sleep again," Valkyrie said. "Exactly. But, y'know... they're parents. It's their job to worry about me, just like it's my job to protect them from what's coming." She winced even as the words escaped her lips, hoping fervently that he'd let it go. But of course he didn't.

He looked at her. "Do you think about that a lot?"

"Think about what?"

"About what's coming. The things you saw in your vision."

Valkyrie tried to give a nonchalant shrug. "A bit. But, if I feel it getting me down, I just remind myself that we've seen the future before and we've seen the future change, so..."

"So you're hoping to change the future."

"Y'know... yeah."

"That's quite a burden to carry."

"Is it?"

"It's almost as if you're taking all responsibility for the bad things that are going to happen."

"Well," Valkyrie said, giving a little laugh, "they won't happen if we change them, will they?"

"We were able to alter aspects of the future that Cassandra Pharos saw," Skulduggery said. "But it was only aspects. Are you hoping to avoid this new future altogether?"

"I don't know," she said. "I mean, it's not out of the question, is it? The future I saw only exists because certain things happen along the way. We change those things, and that future vanishes. It's not like we're battling against fate or something, right? I don't believe in destiny. Auger Darkly isn't *destined* to face the King of the Darklands – it's just been foreseen. By psychics. There's a difference. So if there's no fate, and no destiny, what are we left with? God? I've seen no evidence of a higher power controlling everything, and I've been Darquesse. If anyone could have sensed the presence of an upper-case God, it's her."

"All that may be true," Skulduggery said, "but we know from experience that changing the future is not easy. In order to ensure it doesn't happen, we'd need to know a lot more about what's coming. You'd need to delve deeper into your vision."

"Well, OK," Valkyrie responded. "Then let's do it."

"Unfortunately, that brings its own complications, as you well know. In order to safely navigate the psychic highways, you'll need training. Safeguards will have to be put in place."

"That'll take years."

"You don't know that," Skulduggery said. "There's never been a Sensitive like you before. The ability essentially exploded inside you. Maybe it won't take that long."

"You told me it'd take three years minimum before I could start exploring the vision seriously. Have you changed your mind?"

Skulduggery hesitated. "No," he said at last.

"And, while I'm spending the next three years – minimum – studying to be a Sensitive, the world is going to hell around me? No, thanks. What I should be doing is just diving into the vision, head first."

"Far too dangerous."

"You don't know that. It might be fine."

"Or it might have huge, untold side effects," he said. "You could lose control. You could lose your mind."

"I'm strong enough to take it."

"If anyone could, then yes, I agree, it would be you. And I freely acknowledge the fact that this caution goes against every instinct I have. I much prefer to plunge into danger. It's more fun. But something like this... is different."

"If you were me," she said, "would you do it?"

Skulduggery didn't answer. The eyes of his façade remained fixed on the road.

"Yeah," she said. "See?"

His phone rang. She answered, then hung up and told him where the Sadists' Club was.

They got to Roarhaven, drove through and parked, then walked a little, coming to a metal door with a shelf riveted on to it, level with Valkyrie's chest. Skulduggery knocked, and a small voice piped up. "Who goes there?"

"Visitors," Skulduggery said, "just passing through. We heard this would be a good place to meet like-minded people."

There was a moment of hesitation, and then, "Skulduggery? Is that you?"

Skulduggery frowned. "It might be. Who is this?"

A slot opened, and a man no taller than Valkyrie's outstretched hand stepped out on to the shelf. He was wearing a green suit and orange tie, and he had wings and pointed ears.

"It's me," said the small man. "Cormac."

"Whoa," said Valkyrie.

Skulduggery deactivated his façade, and peered closer. "Cormac?"

The little man grinned. "I thought that was you! How've you been?"

"Fine," Skulduggery said. "You look... different."

"Ah, yeah, I shaved the beard."

"That must be it. Also, you've shrunk."

Cormac's face soured. "The faerie genes kicked in three years ago. My ears went pointy and I grew the wings and I got all that faerie magic that'd been promised me since I was a kid, but...

124

well. As you can see, my parents left out some pretty pertinent information."

"Hi," said Valkyrie. "My name's Valkyrie. How are you? Could I ask a question?"

"Go ahead," said Cormac.

"Are your parents faeries, too?"

"Yes, they are. Proud members of the fae community."

"And are they... small?"

He folded his arms and sighed, like this was the hundredth time today he'd had to explain this. "They're people-sized. All faeries start off people-sized. Some faeries develop the ability to switch back and forth between sizes. Some – and this is the part I didn't know until three years ago – shrink down to this size and are then stuck like this. It hasn't been easy. I have to wear modified dolls' clothes, I can't form meaningful relationships with anyone taller than twenty centimetres, and cats keep trying to eat me. Also, I lost my job."

"What were you?"

"I was a hand model. I modelled wristwatches in photo shoots, things like that. I have good wrists. Lightly haired."

"Right."

"And now I'm here, stuck doing security for the Sadists' Club." He winced. "Damn. That's supposed to be a secret."

"That's why we're here," Skulduggery said. "Could you let us in? We're looking for someone."

"Can't do it," Cormac replied. "Wish I could. You and me go way back, and I always look out for my friends – but this is my job, Skulduggery. Do you know how hard it is for a faerie of my size to find gainful employment? First, I have to overcome the stigma of being a faerie in the first place. You think that's easy? That was hard even when I was people-sized. You know the problem? There are so few faeries left in the world that nobody knows a thing about us or our culture. All they have to go on are tired old tropes and stereotypes, with the clapping and the fairy dust and the constant Tinkerbell references. I struck it lucky with this job. Yeah, the clientele are not exactly my kind of people, but you gotta do what you gotta do."

"So how do we get in?"

"You really want to do this? There's a whole thing. You want to do this?"

"If you wouldn't mind," said Skulduggery.

"No, we can do it. I can pretend I don't know you, we'll go through the process, and, if you pass, you get in. Fair's fair."

"What do we do?"

Cormac put his tiny hands on his tiny hips. "One of you has to fight me."

23

Skulduggery tilted his head. "Really?"

"If you don't have a member to vouch for you," Cormac said, "it's trial by combat, yeah."

Skulduggery looked at Valkyrie. "Do you want to do it?"

"No, thanks," she said.

"Are you sure?"

"Not a chance."

"Right then," Skulduggery said, "it looks like it's you and me, Cormac."

Cormac flew straight at Skulduggery's jaw and swung a tiny fist that launched Skulduggery backwards.

"I'm awesomely strong now, by the way," Cormac called out.

Skulduggery threw himself forward and Cormac met him in mid-air. Valkyrie noticed the door creak a little, and with a gentle push it opened. She sneaked in, closing it behind her. She found herself in a small courtyard with white stones gathered round three green bushes. She passed through an archway into an enclosed patio area with wrought-iron tables and chairs. Upon the tables were upturned wine glasses and a menu.

A waiter came out of the doorway to her left, smiling as he approached.

"Good morning," he said, "and welcome to the Club. You

must be a new member – I would have remembered you otherwise."

"It is my first time here. Is it always this quiet?"

"It is on a Monday morning, yes. Can I get you a drink?"

"Actually, I'm just here to meet someone. Doctor Quidnunc. Have you seen him recently? I had his number, but then dummy here went and lost her phone, so..."

The waiter smiled. "I've been there. I'm on my third phone in two years because I keep losing them."

"Wow," said Valkyrie, giving a laugh. "Well, at least I'm not that bad. Quidnunc wouldn't happen to be in today, would he?"

The waiter rolled his eyes. "Quidnunc's in every day. Apparently, he's on the run."

"No way."

"Yep. He's availing himself of the facilities here, and the rooms upstairs, to do a little hiding out until the heat wears off. As a matter of fact, he asked that none of the waiting staff answer any questions about him, especially questions posed by people we've never seen before..."

The waiter's voice grew increasingly quiet, and his face grew increasingly worried.

Valkyrie flashed him her best smile. "That's probably wise. So no one else has come looking for him, then? No woman with silver hair?"

The waiter didn't answer.

"I'll take that as a no. He's upstairs, is he? How do I get to him?"

"Now that I think about it," the waiter said, "you do look awfully familiar."

"Then at least I'm not someone you've never seen before."

"I think I've seen you kill thousands of people."

"Ah," Valkyrie said. "That wasn't me. That was Darquesse. I didn't kill anyone. The stairs are through here, are they?"

"That means you're Valkyrie Cain," said the waiter. "You work for the High Sanctuary."

"Actually, no, I'm an Arbiter now."

"What's that?"

"We don't work for the Sanctuaries. We're our own bosses, with our own jurisdiction."

"But you're still a detective, aren't you?"

"Oh, yes. Very much so."

"Am I in a lot of trouble?"

"Not from me," said Valkyrie, "as long as you tell me where Quidnunc is."

The waiter sagged. "Through there and up the stairs. He's in the East Room. Please don't tell him I told you."

"You have my word."

He took out his notepad, flipped to a blank page and held it out. "Could I have your autograph?"

Valkyrie frowned. "I'm sorry?"

"I've never met a famous person before."

"I'm not famous."

"I've heard of you."

"But that doesn't mean I'm... Listen, I don't give autographs. That's weird. It's weird that you would ask me and it's weird that you think I'd do it."

"There you are," Skulduggery said, walking in behind her and brushing at his suit.

"Who won?" Valkyrie asked.

"We fought to a standstill," Skulduggery said. "Do we know where Quidnunc is?"

"Upstairs."

"Then let's go talk to him."

"Excuse me," said the waiter, and held out his notepad and pencil. "Can I have your autograph?"

"Of course," Skulduggery said, signing with a flourish before handing the notepad back. "Valkyrie, lead the way."

They left the waiter and went upstairs, followed the signs to the East Room and came to the closed door. They heard the splash of water from within, and Skulduggery waved his hand and the door burst open.

It was a good-sized room, with a large bed and a little table with flowers on it, and a bathtub with clawed feet in the middle of the floor. A naked middle-aged man stood with one foot in the tub, his eyes wide and his mouth open.

"Ew," said Valkyrie.

The man screeched and scrambled, knocked against the table, the vase of flowers smashing to the ground. He dropped to his knees on the other side of the bed, his modesty covered.

"Thank you for that," said Valkyrie. "Doctor Quidnunc, is it? We've been looking for you."

"And we're not the only ones," Skulduggery said, taking a bathrobe from behind the door and tossing it to him. "Do cover up, Doctor. There are ladies present."

"He's talking about me," said Valkyrie. "Where's your mask? I was expecting a mask."

"Wh-why would I be wearing a mask?" Quidnunc asked, pulling on the robe.

"Because of your thing," Valkyrie said. "The liquor-fat-sieve thing that rots your skin."

"Liquefactive necrosis," Quidnunc said. "I don't need a mask or bandages or anything. I caught it early. My serum keeps it under control."

"Oh," said Valkyrie. "That's disappointing."

"You've got to help me. My life is in danger."

"Then you should have turned yourself in before now. You'd be safe in a cell."

"I didn't want to be in a cell," Quidnunc said, tying the robe as he got to his feet. "I didn't want to get arrested. But now that you're here, and I don't have a choice – arrest me. Please."

Skulduggery folded his arms. "First, you tell us where Caisson is."

"No," Quidnunc said. "First, you take me somewhere safe, somewhere with Cleavers, and then I'll answer whatever questions you have."

"We can stand here arguing," Skulduggery said, "or you can do it our way and we'll bring you straight to the High Sanctuary and lock you in their very safest cell. Once again – where is Caisson?"

"I... OK, I don't actually know the answer to that particular question. I'm sorry. They took him away; they didn't give me any warning whatsoever. They just arrived, told me I'd better scram if I wanted to live, told me Abyssinia was probably on her way and that she wouldn't be too happy to learn about all the experiments I'd been doing over the last few decades, so I said OK, I will get myself gone, and I didn't ask any questions or—"

"Stop," said Skulduggery. "You talk an awful lot and you say very, very little of any actual relevance. Who are the people who took him?"

"I don't know their names," said Quidnunc. "There were five of them. Very professional, but rude, you know? They didn't have time to chat. Not that I did, either. I mean, my life was in danger."

"It still is," Valkyrie said. "Who do they work for? Who do you work for? We asked Nye but it didn't know."

Quidnunc hesitated. "Uh... I'm not supposed to say."

"Say it anyway."

"I really don't think I should."

"You don't have a choice," Skulduggery said. "Abyssinia is following the same trail we followed to get here – which means you don't have an awful lot of time. Tell us who you're working for."

Quidnunc sighed unhappily. "She is going to be so mad with me. She has a thing about loyalty, you know?"

"Who does? Eliza Scorn?"

"No, no. Miss Scorn worked for her for a time, but... no. I work – we all work – for Serafina."

Valkyrie didn't need to ask Skulduggery who that was. She'd heard the name a few times over the years, always in passing, always related to the Faceless Ones, or the war.

Serafina of the Unveiled. Mevolent's wife.

Skulduggery grunted. "Well, that's... lovely. OK, tell us about Caisson."

"Um, sure," said Quidnunc. "He told me all sorts of things. When you, um, experiment on someone for that long, you build up this strange kind of rapport, you know? It's almost like a friendship."

"Except not really," said Valkyrie.

"It's a sort-of friendship."

"Where one friend is physically torturing the other."

"I never tortured," Quidnunc said quickly. "I experimented on."

"What kinds of experiments?"

Quidnunc exhaled loudly. "All different kinds. Like his mother, Caisson feeds on the life force of others, which meant I could keep healing him whenever he was in danger of dying. He really was the ideal specimen, you know." He smiled wistfully. "The perfect subject."

"This is getting disturbing," said Valkyrie, "so let's get back to the questioning. What did he tell you?"

"I'm sorry, can I put on my slippers? There's a broken vase on the floor and I'm afraid I might step on it."

"You're going to have to focus here, OK? What exactly did Caisson tell you?"

"Everything."

"Let's get a little more specific. What did he tell you about Abyssinia?"

"He told me about the last time he saw her, how she was attacked. He mentioned you," Quidnunc said, looking at Skulduggery. "He told me you were there."

"He wasn't lying."

"He said you and the rest of the Dead Men, plus the Diablerie, attacked her. The battle went on for days. Abyssinia was winning. On the last day she told Caisson to sneak away, but one of you caught him. China Sorrows. She caught him and she was going to kill him if his mother didn't stop fighting."

"Did he tell you what happened next?"

"His mother surrendered. You killed her."

Skulduggery towered over him. "Then what? What did he do after that? Where was he raised? What's he like? Who is he?"

"I... I don't really know how to answer..."

"Try."

"He's... savage. Intelligent. Resourceful. I guess he's everything you'd expect from someone with parents like his."

"Who was his father?"

Quidnunc swallowed. "Take me to Roarhaven and I'll tell you."

"How about you tell us now?" Valkyrie said. "I don't particularly like to hurt people any more unless I absolutely have to, but Skulduggery still finds the humour in it."

Skulduggery shrugged, and pulled his glove tighter round his right hand. "I'm old-fashioned that way."

"Don't hit me," Quidnunc said immediately. "Please don't hit me."

Skulduggery tilted his head. "For a proud member of the Sadists' Club, you seem very squeamish when it comes to violence."

"Just violence perpetrated upon myself," Quidnunc said. "It's ironic, I know. Maybe even hypocritical. But if that's the worst thing people say about me—"

"It's not," Valkyrie said, cutting him off. "Tell us what we want to know. Caisson's father. His name."

Quidnunc chewed his lip. "And then you'll take me to Roarhaven?"

"Pinky promise."

"Vile," said Quidnunc. "His father was Lord Vile."

Valkyrie blinked. A distant part of her mind counted the blinks. She blinked four times before turning to look at Skulduggery.

"Well," Skulduggery said, "that's interesting."

24

Valkyrie took hold of the collar of Quidnunc's bathrobe and hauled him along after her. She opened the wardrobe, shoved him in and closed the door, then came back to Skulduggery.

She hesitated a moment, then smiled calmly and, keeping her voice low, said, "Can I ask a personal question?"

"Go ahead," Skulduggery said.

"Remember when you were Lord Vile? Remember those days? Now, I know you were dressed in armour and everything, and you were all big and scary and whispery and sinister, but you were... you were still a skeleton, right?"

"Yes."

"So, and I mean this in the nicest possible way, there is absolutely no way that you could have had a kid... right?"

"Right."

"At all?"

"In the slightest."

"OK."

"Probably."

"What?" Valkyrie said. "There is *probably* no way you could have had a kid? Where did this 'probably' come from?"

"We're talking about magic," Skulduggery said. "People do tricky things with magic."

"I paid attention in biology, all right? Well, I didn't, but my reflection did, and what I remember about the whole baby-making process is that eggs don't fertilise themselves."

"If Quidnunc is telling the truth, then Caisson was either lying to him, or Abyssinia lied to Caisson about his father."

"Yes," Valkyrie said. "That makes sense. That seems obvious. Because you're totally not the dad, right?"

"Totally."

"OK."

"Probably totally."

Quidnunc knocked on the inside of the wardrobe. "Hello? Can I come out now?"

Valkyrie opened the door, pulled him out. "Get dressed," she said. "We're going to want to talk about this a lot more when you're in your cell."

"Yes," Quidnunc said, grabbing his clothes off the floor. "Thank you, yes. Could I make one request?"

"No requests," said Skulduggery.

"It's just, as a co-operating witness, I thought maybe I'd be granted one small request."

"You're not a co-operating witness. You're under arrest."

Quidnunc looked surprised. "Am I?"

Skulduggery tilted his head. "Aren't you? Didn't we place you under arrest? We may have forgotten. Doctor Quidnunc, you're under arrest. Put your trousers on."

"You haven't even read me my rights."

"Why does everyone think we operate according to mortal rules? We don't have mortal trials, do we? We have Sensitives who can read your mind and proclaim your guilt or innocence."

"So I don't have any rights?"

"Not any we have to read to you. Haven't you ever been arrested before?"

"No."

"Well, now you'll know for next time."

Quidnunc zipped up his fly and pulled on a shirt. He picked

a shoe up off the floor and looked around. "Can either of you see my other shoe? It looks just like this one."

"We know what a shoe looks like," Valkyrie responded. "It's under the chair."

"Ah," Quidnunc said, moving to the other end of the room. He put both shoes on and started tying the laces.

Skulduggery held the car keys out to Valkyrie. "You'd better bring the car round."

She raised an eyebrow. "You're trusting me with the Bentley twice in the space of a few days?"

"I should stay with the doctor in case Abyssinia arrives. Pull up on the street outside and we'll be waiting. Do not crash."

Valkyrie took the keys, went to say something bitingly funny to Quidnunc – but Abyssinia was suddenly standing behind him.

25

Nero and another woman had teleported in with her and Skulduggery moved at once, using the air to throw Nero off his feet, but Abyssinia had grabbed Quidnunc before they could stop her. "Hello, my darling," she said to Skulduggery.

Skulduggery froze. "Hello, dear."

"And Valkyrie," said Abyssinia. She was wearing red. It was tight. "It's so good to meet you. Formally, I mean. When I'm not sucking your life force out of you. I think perhaps that was rude. As was instructing Cadaverous Gant and Jeremiah Wallow to remove you as a potential obstacle on my path back to life. As it turns out, you were vital to my rebirth. You have both my thanks, and my apologies."

Valkyrie did her best to appear nonchalant. "It happens."

Abyssinia smiled. It was a beautiful smile, though it did seem unsettlingly wide. "Forgiveness is truly a sign of a good soul."

Nero stood up, scowling.

"My soul is not good, I'm afraid," Abyssinia continued. "I've always had a problem with forgiveness. This man here, for example... I suppose I could forgive him for what he did to my son."

"Yes," Quidnunc whimpered, his head held between her hands. "Please."

"But then I think about all those experiments he carried out,"

138

Abyssinia continued, "and all that pain he inflicted, and I am unable to think clearly."

"I can tell you things," Quidnunc said quickly. "I can describe the people who took him."

"I know who took him," Abyssinia responded. "Serafina's people. Five of them. I know they have my son in a private ambulance, and they're driving through Europe in a futile attempt to stay ahead of me."

"I know other things," Quidnunc said. "I know lots."

"Do you?" Abyssinia asked.

Quidnunc winced suddenly, and Valkyrie felt a pressure in the room, like she was on a plane coming in to land, and then the pressure was pierced and Quidnunc cried out.

Abyssinia shook her head. "You lie, Doctor. There's nothing else that interests me in your memories, apart from all those decades of torture you put Caisson through."

"It wasn't my fault," Quidnunc said, crying now. "I was ordered to do it. Serafina told me—"

"I know what she told you to do," Abyssinia said. "And, unlike you, I know why she told you to do it. I suppose you're not the real villain here. You're the instrument she used."

"Yes," Quidnunc said. "I'm just the instrument."

She put her lips to his ear. "But even the instrument must be broken, Doctor."

Quidnunc gasped and went pale, then purple, then yellow, his cheeks hollowing, his eyes drying up in their sockets, his body shrivelling beneath his half-buttoned shirt.

Glowing with stolen health, Abyssinia allowed the husk of his remains to fall at her feet and looked up. "It's so good to be around you again, Skulduggery. I missed you when I was a heart in a box. I missed our talks."

"I would imagine good conversation is hard to come by when you're an internal organ."

"You see? You understand me. You always have." She switched

her gaze to Valkyrie. "This is not the first time *we've* spoken, either, is it?"

"I saw you in my vision," Valkyrie said. "You touched me. How did you do that?"

"I am the Princess of the Darklands. I can do many things." She turned slightly. "Nero, Skeiri, leave us, please."

"Uh, is that wise?" Nero asked.

"You are such a sweet boy," Abyssinia said. "Thank you, but I'm perfectly safe here. I'll contact you when I need you. Go on now."

Nero glanced at the woman called Skeiri, but she remained impassive. A moment later, they vanished.

"There," Abyssinia said. "Some privacy. I have to admit, Valkyrie, there are... gaps in my memory when it comes to you. I think it happened when I drew from your strength. You're something of a mystery to me – which I find delightful, by the way. You're a book I have yet to read."

"No one's called me a book before."

"I've sensed you since that day, haven't I?"

"Not me," Valkyrie said. "Must be somebody else." She pressed on before Abyssinia revealed too much in front of Skulduggery. "So this Darklands – is that a place, or more like a state-of-mind-type thing?"

"It's here, Valkyrie. All around us. To the Faceless Ones, this entire planet is the Darklands. It's why they sought it out. It's why they fought so hard to stay. This is their holy land. It's why they want to come back."

"Huh. I hadn't heard that before."

Abyssinia smiled. "Of course not. You haven't read the Book of Tears, have you? You haven't listened to its sermons. I would recommend it, if you have the time. It could change your life."

"I don't think so," said Valkyrie. "To be honest with you, I never liked going to regular church, let alone crazy church."

Abyssinia laughed. "You think the mortal religions sound any less fantastical? At least our gods are real. You faced them, didn't you? You were there when they visited, ten years ago."

"I was there, all right. They came back, my head felt like it was going to explode, and they killed a bunch of people. Mostly their own worshippers, so... that's one good thing about them. Pity you missed it."

"Yes, it is. I do so love a family reunion."

Skulduggery tilted his head. "Family?"

Abyssinia bit her lip. "Here it comes – everything I kept from you when we were... dating. Could you call it dating? Let's call it dating. I'm royalty, darling. My bloodline can be traced back to the Faceless Ones themselves."

Valkyrie frowned. "I don't get it."

"My family comes *directly* from the first Faceless One to take human form. Not to possess a human body, mind you, but to actually *become* a human body. It was to be the start of a whole new species, before the Ancients rebelled."

"And I thought we shared everything," Skulduggery murmured.

"Oh, don't be mad with me, my love. My father swore us all to secrecy. If our enemies, of which there were many, learned of our heritage, they would seek to destroy us."

"Wait," Valkyrie said. "Skulduggery, are you actually believing her?"

He shrugged. "You're descended from the Last of the Ancients – why can't she be descended from the Faceless Ones?"

"Because at least my ancestors were human, not an insane god who put on a human face and went out and got lucky. Abyssinia, are you sure your family wasn't just full of it?"

Abyssinia's smile dimmed. "Do not speak ill of my family."

"Sore subject?"

"My mother was a beacon of love, and my father had the blood of gods in his veins. You have no idea how better off the people of this world would have been if my parents ruled over them."

"We've been to a world overrun by the Faceless Ones," Skulduggery said. "It was not a fun place."

"My father had no intention of bringing them *back*," Abyssinia said. "Why would he? They had their time, and that time ended. Now it was our turn. A thousand years ago, my father was about to reveal the truth to the world and rally the righteous to our banner. We would have overthrown the mortal civilisations. We would have cured disease, ended famine, made countless lives better..."

"So long as the mortals knelt before you."

"A little kneeling never hurt anyone," said Abyssinia.

"Your dad," Valkyrie said, "would he be the King of the Darklands, by any chance?"

"That was his title, yes."

"It's not any more?"

"When I was still a child," said Abyssinia, "my father was betrayed by his most gifted – and trusted – student. Murdered on the cusp of greatness."

"Ooh, I hate that," Valkyrie said. "I hate being murdered on the cusp of things."

"You're quite an insolent young lady, aren't you?"

"I have my moments," said Valkyrie.

"This gifted student," Skulduggery said, "who was he?"

Abyssinia smiled thinly. "You haven't figured it out yet?"

"I have," said Skulduggery, "but I want confirmation. He killed your father. Both your parents? I imagine your whole family. Maybe you were the only one who escaped. He was probably unaware of this, as he wouldn't have stopped hunting you if he'd known you were alive. So that means you, or more likely someone still loyal to you, killed a child of roughly the same age and appearance and presented the body to him as your own."

"Who are we talking about?" Valkyrie asked.

"The gifted student," Skulduggery said, "who went on to unite the disciples of the Faceless Ones and start a war that would last for centuries."

"Mevolent," Valkyrie said slowly. She looked back at Abyssinia. "But then that means... your father was the Unnamed."

"That's what they called him."

Valkyrie nodded. "I don't know what to do with that information."

"So why does Mevolent's wife have your son?" Skulduggery asked.

"Does it matter?" Abyssinia responded. "It's Serafina. Serafina does what Serafina does, and she always has. Have you met her, Valkyrie?"

"I haven't."

"You wouldn't like her. Would she, Skulduggery? She wouldn't like her. Serafina is... unlikeable, wouldn't you say?"

"I've always thought so," Skulduggery said.

"Yes, she's beautiful," said Abyssinia. "Yes, she's alluring. Yes, every step she takes is a sensuous moment to be savoured by all who bear witness... but there are more beautiful. China Sorrows, for example. A more beautiful person I have never seen than China Sorrows. There are those more alluring, also, whose footsteps are even more sensuous than Serafina's." She sighed. "Even so, as unlikeable as she is, she does possess a certain... something. Does she not, Skulduggery?"

"I suppose she does."

"Would you say Serafina is more beautiful than me?"

"I would not."

Abyssinia laughed. "Come now, you can be honest. With our history, with what we've shared, honesty is surely the least we can expect from each other."

"I am being honest," Skulduggery said. "My criteria for judging beauty have broadened considerably since the last time we spoke. Serafina may be physically attractive, but she's a monster."

"This is true."

"Of course," Skulduggery continued, "you're a monster, too."

Abyssinia smiled. "We're all monsters here. Such darkness I see before me. Lord Vile and Darquesse. How many innocent lives have you two snuffed out? How much blood is on your hands?"

"Plenty," said Valkyrie.

"Plenty," Abyssinia echoed. "This is indeed true. Everyone knows about you, Valkyrie. They fear you, don't they? They resent you. They positively hate you. But Skulduggery's dark side remains a secret. It's why I sent Razzia and Nero away. A secret is only fun when it's kept. How would the Sanctuaries around the world react, I wonder, to the truth? Maybe I should tell them... Oh, Skulduggery, how I wish you had a face! I would love to see if you were scared, or nervous, or resigned at the very notion! Instead, all I get is this... blank skull. Does it bother you, Valkyrie? Does it bother you that you can't tell what he's feeling?"

"I can tell," Valkyrie said.

Abyssinia looked at her, and didn't say anything.

"Quidnunc let slip something interesting," Skulduggery said. "Something Caisson told him when he was being tortured."

Abyssinia took a moment to take her eyes off Valkyrie. "Oh?"

"He seems to think Lord Vile is his father. Why would you lie to him about that?"

"You think it's a lie?"

"I may not remember every single thing I did when I wore that armour, but I'd recall fathering an impossible child."

"Not impossible, my love. There have always been ways to conceive a child with magic, even back then."

"I'm not his father."

"Oh, Skulduggery. You don't know what you are."

"What about your anti-Sanctuary friends? Do they know about any of this? Do the First Wave kids? They all know you're looking for Caisson, obviously – but do they know he's the future King of the Darklands? Do they know of his heritage?"

"We are united, if that's what you're wondering."

"You're united because you're lying to them," Skulduggery said. "You sold them on a sorcerers-rule-the-world idea – but what you're talking about now is something different. You're talking about you ruling the world. Your son taking his rightful place on the throne, and you standing behind him. That's why you sent Nero and Skeiri out, isn't it? You're afraid if they find out what you're really up to, they'll leave."

Abyssinia smiled. "I suppose we all have our secrets. But that's not the only reason I sent them away. I seek a truce, Skulduggery."

"After everything you've done?"

"Not for me. For Caisson. You murdered me before he'd even taken a name to protect himself. He's never known a mother's love, let alone a father's. He's had the cruellest of lives, and once I get him back he will assume the title of the King of the Darklands – the same King that Auger Darkly is prophesied to battle and possibly kill. I implore you, I beseech you, to talk to the Darkly boy, convince him not to hunt down our son. In return, I will take Caisson and leave, and you will never hear from either of us again."

"You want to negotiate? That's unlike you."

"Not when it comes to our son."

"Don't call him that."

"He's like you, you know. He grew up tall."

Valkyrie interrupted. "Why don't you go after Auger?"

"I've thought about it," said Abyssinia. "It would, admittedly, solve my problems to just kill the boy. But prophecies are complicated things. Who's to say that an attempt on the Darkly boy's life wouldn't lead him to this fateful confrontation with Caisson three years from now? No, a peaceful solution is the most desirable, I think."

"You'll walk away?" Skulduggery asked. "You'll abandon the people who follow you?"

"They'll follow someone else. I've given them what they needed.

I've started them on the road. Some of them are already beginning to turn away from me. It was inevitable, but they refused to see it."

"Tell us where Coldheart Prison is and we'll talk."

"Oh, no, no, Skulduggery. This truce I offer is for me and Caisson only. You'll have to deal with my friends on your own. Will you let us walk away?"

"I'm sorry, Abyssinia – you're too dangerous. You've always felt that the world owes you something. Now that I know you think it owes you fealty, I can't trust you. You're a threat. You'll always be a threat."

Abyssinia sighed. "So you are turning down my offer of a truce?"

"Unfortunately, yes."

"Then you know what has to happen now."

"I do."

Valkyrie tensed.

Nero and Skeiri teleported in. Skulduggery pulled his revolver and Nero dived on him and they both disappeared. Valkyrie raised her arm, energy crackling, but Skeiri's palm opened, just like she had seen Razzia's do, and a tentacle – just like Razzia's, except green – shot out, and that tentacle plunged right between the open zip of Valkyrie's jacket.

Straight into her chest.

26

Valkyrie gasped. Stepped back. Both hands closed round the tentacle. It was warm. Slick. It pulsed with life.

She dropped to her knees.

Inside her chest, the head of the parasite squirmed.

Skeiri held up her other hand. Her palm opened. The second parasite readied itself. Aimed right at Valkyrie's face.

It launched but Valkyrie caught it one-handed. It snapped at her.

With her free hand, Valkyrie grabbed a shard of broken vase and slashed, severing the parasite's head from its body. Skeiri screamed and both tendrils retracted into her palms and she staggered back, clutching her right wrist, sobbing.

Blood drenching her T-shirt, Valkyrie got up. Abyssinia took hold of her, threw her against the wall. A framed picture was dislodged. Fell.

Valkyrie's weak knees. Hot blood against cold skin. Abyssinia's hand on Valkyrie's head, her mind peering into Valkyrie's thoughts. Confident. Arrogant.

Vulnerable.

Valkyrie's hands clutched Abyssinia's head.

27

Valkyrie drowned in memories.

They overwhelmed her. She was lost to them, her own identity nothing but a drop in the vast ocean of Abyssinia. Pain and love and conflict, hatred and strength, peace and vengeance. Faces and voices Valkyrie had never known, suddenly as sharp as those of her own parents.

Valkyrie went under. This was a mistake. Doing this was a mistake, but there was no way out now. She was being crushed by a life she'd never lived, where everything was new, where everything was alien.

And yet, in all that newness, something familiar.

She swam towards it.

She was on a hilltop, hunkering in front of a dying man. Blood seeped from a wound in his belly. She prodded him in the chest with her finger. He winced, and opened his eyes.

"Oh, no," he said when he saw her.

Valkyrie smiled. "Hello," she said.

No. It was Abyssinia. Not Valkyrie. This was Abyssinia's memory, and yet it was Valkyrie who spoke.

"They left you behind, did they?" she said. "A terrible thing to leave a comrade behind. You go to the trouble of attacking a village and killing all of these fine, fine people... and, at the first whiff of a stab wound to the gut, they leave you in their wake. You have my sympathies, brave warrior."

"Please," said the dying man, "I know who you are. Help me."

Valkyrie laid a hand on his shoulder, and looked him in the eye. "I will help you. I would be honoured to help you. But first, I am in need of some information about these friends of yours."

"Ask me anything," said the dying man, but Valkyrie shook her head.

"You don't have to speak," she said. "Conserve your strength. Let me do the work."

She ignored his look of confusion and sent her thoughts into his, like the tip of a spear sliding into soft flesh. She felt his alarm and she pushed it to one side, focusing instead on his memories. They opened before her, every intimate detail of this dying man's life. But she cared little for the intimate details. She absorbed the recent memories. The moment the dying man and his eleven companions came across this village of mortals. The death they brought, with steel and magic and cudgel. She watched, through his eyes, as one of the mortals, a desperate woman defending her children, ran him through before she, too, was cut down.

"They abandoned you," Valkyrie said, leaving his mind. "After all you've done for each of them, they left you to die here alone."

"Please," the dying man said. "Help me."

"Of course," said Valkyrie, and rested her hand across his forehead, drawing out what remained of his life and taking his energy for herself. The empty shell of his body toppled sideways and she straightened.

"Eleven of them," she said, "going north. Six hours ahead of us."

Skulduggery stood over another corpse, his hood up, casting his skull in darkness. The wind plucked at the tail of his coat. His sword lay heavy across his back.

Valkyrie walked over. "Did you hear what I said?" she asked.

"Eleven of them," he repeated to her. "Six-hour head start."

Valkyrie touched Skulduggery's arm. "They're just mortals," she said gently. "There's so many of them in the world that I doubt anyone will notice their loss."

He turned his head to her, ever so slightly. "You think I grieve for them?"

"You don't?"

"Maybe once I would have. Maybe once such mindless slaughter would have stirred grief within me, or righteous fury..."

Valkyrie bit her lip. "But no longer?"

"Now I feel nothing but contempt," Skulduggery said. "For their weakness. For their short, vulnerable lives. For the sheer pedantry of their existence."

A smile broke across Valkyrie's face. "My love," she said. "You have finally joined me."

She pulled away from the memory, heaving herself back into the ocean. She was herself again. Valkyrie Cain. And Valkyrie Cain had parents and a sister and a dog, and she wasn't Abyssinia and she hadn't been the one to encourage Skulduggery's descent.

Because, of course, Skulduggery didn't *need* any encouragement.

Valkyrie was in darkness, watching, as Skulduggery donned the black armour. Cold flame flickered off the walls. He worked slowly, methodically, with buckles and straps and belts. Piece by piece the armour went on, each segment sliding into place, covering him, burying him, sealing him away, until at last the helmet went on and Skulduggery Pleasant was gone.

And there was only Lord Vile.

No.

She didn't want to see this. She didn't want to see Skulduggery like this. She didn't want this memory. It wasn't even hers. It belonged to Abyssinia, and Valkyrie wasn't Abyssinia: she hadn't watched her father die and she hadn't joined Mevolent's army in order to get close to the man who'd killed him.

She was in the hall, in the great hall in Mevolent's castle, and she was talking, making a speech while they all looked on.

She was at the top table. Mevolent's wife may have been seated at his right side, but Valkyrie was seated to his left. She could see the resentment in the eyes of the gathered sorcerers – Serpine in particular. Baron Vengeous was without expression, and beside him China Sorrows smiled, as if she was delighted that Valkyrie had been chosen as Mevolent's favourite.

All her plans had led her to this point.

As she spoke, Valkyrie glanced behind her, to where Lord Vile stood. Upon hearing certain words, he would strike, plunging his sword through Mevolent's back. And then, while he killed Serafina before she could even stand, it would be she herself who took Mevolent's head.

And yet.

Fate had a cruel sense of humour, it seemed. Her plans, as careful as they were, as precise in their execution as their planning, had scattered before her mere hours earlier, when she had learned of the child growing within her.

Suddenly her thoughts of vengeance were nothing but smoke on the wind. Mevolent had robbed her of her family – though he did not know it – and yet she had the potential for a new family. She didn't need to kill him. She didn't need to take what was his. She could slip away in the night and seek happiness elsewhere.

Behind her, Vile waited for words that would never come.

Valkyrie paused in her speech, took a drink of wine, and found herself with her hand on her belly. She looked down, and smiled. This would be her final night in the castle.

And it was.

The tip of the sword slid through her chest and Valkyrie frowned. There were cries from the crowd.

She was lifted off her feet as the pain blossomed. Vile. He had betrayed her. She almost laughed.

Her feet kicked feebly as he carried her to the window on the end of his sword. Mevolent and Serafina, she noted, never even looked up from their meal.

Lord Vile threw her into the glass and it shattered around her and she fell into darkness, the wind snatching at her clothes and her hair and she fell and fell and the rocks met her at the bottom and broke her body.

She blinked up at the stars. It was all she could do.

Her strength had saved her from an immediate death, but that strength was leaking from her with every moment. She tried to touch her belly, but could not move her hands. Tears mixed with the blood on her face.

I'm sorry, she thought, for her lips could not form words. *I'm sorry, my child.*

Sadness overtook the pain and Valkyrie wept, and tore herself from the memory, and gasped, and looked down at herself, and saw the hole in her chest.

She was back in the East Room, back in the Sadists' Club, back in Roarhaven, and Abyssinia was stumbling away and Valkyrie sank down, her back against the wall, while Skeiri wailed in the corner.

Skulduggery and Nero came back, Nero crying out, Skulduggery kneeling on him, pressing the revolver into his head. He looked up, saw Valkyrie, immediately left Nero where he lay and hurried over.

Nero pushed himself up, recognised a no-win battle when he saw it, and vanished, along with Abyssinia and Skeiri.

"Valkyrie," Skulduggery said, pressing his hand against the wound. "Valkyrie, can you hear me? You're going to be OK. You're going to be fine."

She tried to speak but couldn't, and as he lifted her into his arms the world drew in and darkness swallowed her.

28

The first classes of the day were business studies and double combat arts. Omen didn't mind combat arts. He'd been through it all before when the best trainers in the world had taught Auger how to hit and Omen how to get hit. Now it was different. Now Omen was no longer the punchbag, and it was quite startling – to his classmates, to his teacher, to Omen himself – how much of that training he had absorbed over the years.

The only thing that prevented Omen from being one of the best in the class was the fact that he appeared to possess absolutely no aggression. At all. In the slightest. Which was a problem when it came to fighting.

These two classes turned out to be more theory than practical, and nobody broke much of a sweat, which meant Omen could skip the weekly torture of showering with the rest of the boys. Instead, he got dressed quicker than usual and found Never in the corridor.

"Hey," he said.

Never looked up, hesitated, and smiled. His hair was tied back today. "Hey."

"I was thinking," Omen said, "about what we were talking about on Friday."

Never frowned. "Remind me."

"Y'know... we were talking about the fact that I'm sitting

around, waiting for Skulduggery and Valkyrie to call me off on an adventure."

"That was you?"

"I was thinking, maybe... I mean, obviously you had a point."

"I *am* me."

"And, if I reacted badly to it, then I'm sorry. I just... I don't want to be boring. I don't want to be like everyone else and I had a taste of what it's like to have a life like that, like Auger's, and I..." He sighed.

"Don't worry about it," said Never.

"Well, I am worrying about it," Omen said. "And you know me better than probably anyone, and you were only trying to make me see sense."

"Seeing sense is good," Never said.

"Are we friends again?"

"When did we stop?"

"I mean, we haven't really chatted in the last few days and I thought you were mad at me or something."

"I'm not mad at you, monkey. I've just been busy. I'm a very busy person, you know. Like, right now? Right now I'm busy."

Omen laughed. "Right now you're talking to me."

"And I'm busy, so, like, wrap it up."

"Oh," said Omen. "Oh, right, sorry. Um... well, that's it, I suppose."

Never put a hand on Omen's shoulder. "Good talk. I'm glad we did this. It's important, I think, to be able to talk about stuff."

"So who are you waiting for?"

Never took his hand back. "I'm not waiting for anyone."

"Is it a new boyfriend?"

"How do you know I'm not still with Wilder?"

Omen grinned. "He's not your type at all. He's too loud."

Never shrugged. "Also, he'd never been out with someone as amazing as me, so I think he got intimidated. Ah, well, his loss."

"So who's the new guy?"

"There actually isn't one. I'm off the market at the moment. I feel I need some space to reconnect with myself, to rediscover my own vitality."

"What kind of books have you been reading?"

"Books with words and no pictures, so they'd be of no interest to you." He checked his watch. "OK, I've got to get going. Omen, you have a good one."

Omen laughed. "I'll try my very best, but I will find out what you're—"

And Never teleported away.

"Omen."

Omen turned as Aurnia ran up. He blinked, not expecting to see her in the school corridor like this. "Aurnia! Hi! What are you doing here?"

"I'm lost," she said. Her eyes were watery, like she was about to start crying. "All of the ambassadors are being brought in to discuss our concerns, and I was with the group and then I got distracted. This school is... huge. This is the biggest building I've ever been in. Back home our school is a single room in my uncle's house."

"So you got lost," said Omen. "OK, that's cool. I can help you. Come on."

They started walking, Aurnia hugging herself and sticking close to his side. He noticed her shrink away from the people they passed, like a mistreated cat.

"Do you remember what room you were supposed to be heading to?" he asked.

"No," she said. "I wasn't really listening. I've barely heard anything that's been said since we arrived here. How does anyone get anything done here?"

"I still haven't figured that out myself, to be honest."

"You said that mortals have schools here, too – proper schools. Are they as big as this?"

Omen shrugged. "It depends. I mean, I suppose some of them are, the really exclusive ones, but most of them aren't."

"What was it like growing up here?" she asked.

"Oh, I didn't. I grew up near Galway. Do you have Galway in your dimension?"

"Yes."

"I grew up near there, in a small town, all very normal. My family's magic, but Roarhaven wasn't a city back then so we lived among mortals and basically pretended to be like everyone else. We even had mortal names and stuff. I liked it, actually, being just like everyone else. I suppose I fit in better as a mortal than I do as a sorcerer."

"Why don't you fit in as a sorcerer?"

"I'm just not very good at it. My brother, Auger, he's good at it. He's really good at it. But then he's so good at everything. I was never much good at anything."

"But you can do magic?"

"Yes," he said. "Not much, but I can. Do you want to see?"

Aurnia looked alarmed and shook her head.

"OK," said Omen quickly. "That's cool."

She actually smiled. "You used that word again. Cool. Why is cool a good thing?"

"I don't really know. I suppose it came from, maybe, America, from back in the 1960s when everything was cool and groovy and stuff."

"Ah," said Aurnia, "so that's why we don't use the word like you do. We don't have an America where I'm from."

"How can you not have a country?" Omen asked, frowning.

"Well, we have it, it's there, it exists, but no one lives there any more. Mevolent killed everyone in America hundreds of years ago and poisoned it all – the land, the water, the air..."

"Wow."

"Yes."

"So you guys don't have Elvis or Jennifer Lawrence or Spider-Man... or anyone."

"I don't know who they are."

"Elvis was a singer, and Jennifer Lawrence is in movies, and Spider-Man swings from buildings and stops crime."

"Is he a sorcerer, too?"

"No, he was just bitten by a radioactive spider. It's so weird that you don't have those things."

"Not really," Aurnia said, shrugging. "From where I stand, it's normal, and actually having an America with people in it, *that's*, like you said, the thing that's weird."

He led her up the west staircase. She was no longer hugging herself. With every step she took, she was growing in confidence. He wished he was like that.

She laughed suddenly. "I'm sorry," she said. "I never thought this would happen."

He grinned along with her. "What would happen?"

"This," she said, gesturing to their surroundings. "Sorcerers everywhere and I'm just walking through them all."

"It's a different world."

"Yes, it is."

Axelia passed, eyes on her phone, and Omen waved to get her attention and said, "Axelia, hey."

She looked up, smiled automatically. "Hey," she said.

"Axelia," said Omen, "this is Aurnia. Aurnia's part of the volunteer group, from the camp? Do you know where the rest of them are?"

"I was just helping out with them," Axelia said. "They're in Meritorious Hall. The meeting hasn't started yet, so you'll be fine. It's very good to meet you, Aurnia."

"And you," said Aurnia.

Axelia smiled again and walked on, and Omen took Aurnia right and down a corridor.

"She's very pretty," said Aurnia.

"Is she?" said Omen.

"Everyone here has such wonderful hair. Is it because of the shampoo?"

"You don't have shampoo where you're from?"

"Maybe the sorcerers do, but mortals use soap. My family received a bottle of shampoo in one of our care packages, though, and last night I washed my hair and... and it's wonderful."

"Your hair does look extra shiny today."

She laughed again. "Thank you."

The door to Meritorious Hall was open. Inside, sorcerers and mortals were finding their seats.

"Here we are," Omen said.

Aurnia clasped her hands. "Thank you, Omen. Thank you so much."

"No probs. Problem. No problem."

She looked at him for a little bit, and then looked away. "Well, I'd better go."

"Wait!" he blurted.

"Yes?"

"Um... would you like to do something?"

"I am doing something. I'm walking."

"No, like, do something."

"I don't think I understand."

"With me," said Omen. "Would you like to do something with me? Tomorrow, maybe? It's just that I enjoy talking to you, and spending time with you, and I was wondering if maybe you'd like to, um, do it again?"

Aurnia frowned. "Are you trying to court me?"

"I don't know. I think so?"

"Huh."

"So... what do you think?"

"We have strict rules for courting where I'm from," said Aurnia. "First, you must ask my parents."

"Yeah, right, that makes sense."

"And then my brother. He's very protective of me, though, so that might be difficult."

"I can do it."

"And then you have to seek permission from the twelve village leaders."

"All twelve?"

"And, before they make their ruling, you must do the Love Dance in the streets."

"Wow. I don't have much rhythm but, well, I suppose I could get my dancing shoes on."

"No shoes," she said. "The Love Dance is performed without clothes. When the dance is over, you must sing the traditional ballads, also naked. Then and only then will we receive the blessing of my people, and we shall be wed. My family will be expecting a child within the first year, so naturally you will have to commit to a lifetime of..." She grinned suddenly, a grin so pretty it made Omen's heart lurch. "I'm joking. We don't have strict rules for courting, and we don't have to get married or have babies. The look on your face, however..."

Omen barked out a laugh and felt the tension rush from his body. "That was mean. That was very mean."

"I would like to talk to you tomorrow, Omen. So the answer is yes."

He gave a grin of his own. "Cool," he said.

29

Here in this small town in Tuscany, where the streets were impossibly narrow, was where the flaw in the otherwise flawless route that Serafina's people had planned out would be exploited.

This was where Cadaverous would ambush the ambulance.

Sitting in the shade, Cadaverous glanced at his watch. It was just gone midday, the ambulance was almost here, and there were no mortals about. This was beyond perfect.

"She cut it off," Razzia said. "Just... swish. Cut it right off."

Cadaverous didn't respond.

Razzia looked up. "She deserved it, of course. Skeiri, I mean. *Ooh, I'm so great, I'm taking Razzia's place...* and now she has one less tentacle. That's the moral of the story, right there."

Nero teleported in. "They're coming," he said.

"Did it look like it hurt?" Razzia asked. "What Valkyrie did to Skeiri?"

Nero sighed. "Are you still talking about this? It was ages ago, OK? It was yesterday. How am I supposed to remember what happened or what hurt or what didn't? All I know is, she wouldn't stop moaning about it."

Cadaverous stood. "In positions, everyone," he said.

Nero scowled. "And why are you the one giving orders? I'm the one who should be in charge."

"Is that so?"

Nero shrugged. "You're all getting sidelined, now that Abyssinia has her pick of people from Coldheart. I'm the only invaluable one. I should get to call the shots."

If you're so invaluable," Razzia said, "how come you're here with the rest of us?"

"I really don't know," Nero answered. "Pity, maybe?"

"Or perhaps," said Cadaverous, "for all your stupidity, you have still managed to recognise how easy it is to fall from Abyssinia's favour. Let's be honest, you didn't exactly acquit yourself well during that encounter with Pleasant and Cain, did you?"

A glowering stare. "I did OK."

"You're here to prove yourself," Cadaverous told him. "And, until you do, you take orders from your betters."

"Whatever," Nero muttered.

"Destrier," Cadaverous said, "if you would...?"

Destrier nodded, and walked to the middle of the road.

For a few seconds, there was silence. The warm breeze kicked up a little dust on the road.

"It's not like I don't have sympathy for her," Razzia said from behind cover. "I wouldn't like to lose my guys. They're my guys. But Skeiri shouldn't have tried to take my place."

"Razzia," Cadaverous said, "maybe we should focus now, if that's OK?"

She nodded. "Fair point, mate. Absolutely."

She settled, and Cadaverous readied himself.

The ambulance, to all outward appearances a beaten-up old truck, came round the corner. Upon seeing Destrier, the driver immediately picked up speed. The passenger window whirred down and a gun poked out. But by then Destrier already had his hand raised.

The ambulance slowed so much it looked like it had stopped, but Cadaverous could still see the wheels turning, could still see the little pine car freshener – in the shape of a strawberry – caught

161

in time-compressed limbo as it tried to swing from the rear-view mirror. The faces of the men inside, frozen into grimaces, didn't register Razzia strolling up and opening the driver's door.

She reached in, unbuckled the driver and hauled him out. His fall was a fall through treacle, but Razzia was already kicking the passenger out of the other side. Then she settled in behind the wheel, and gave Destrier a thumbs up.

Destrier dropped his hand, and time around the ambulance returned to normal. The driver and passenger hit the road – hard – and flipped and rolled, and Razzia brought the ambulance to a gentle stop.

Cadaverous approached the back of the ambulance. The driver and passenger were groaning, moaning, trying to get up. Razzia hopped out of the van, broke the driver's neck and opened her hand towards the passenger, now stumbling to his feet. Her palm opened, and the parasite shot out, spearing the passenger through the neck before retracting.

The ambulance doors burst open. A woman lunged at Cadaverous, fire in her hands. Nero teleported her away before she could actually do anything, and Cadaverous climbed in.

Caisson lay strapped to a gurney. He was tall, thin and malnourished. His skin was waxy, his silver hair cut short, clumps of it missing, showing his scalp. His eyes were closed. He looked dead.

Cadaverous pulled away all the tubes and electrodes and undid the straps. Grunting slightly with the effort, he pulled Caisson on to his shoulder and crab-walked to the door. He dropped down.

"I could help," said Razzia.

"No, it's OK," Cadaverous said, nodding behind her. "You're going to need your hands free."

Three sorcerers stood there, legs apart and fists clenched. They looked impressively intimidating.

"We're going to need that back," said the biggest one.

"You mean Caisson?" Cadaverous responded, as Destrier and

Razzia moved to stand beside him. "No, no, no, we're not taking him. We wouldn't take him without asking. How rude! We're just borrowing him. We'll bring him back, honest."

"He is the property of Serafina."

"Then where is she? If he's so important to her, let her come and present her case. We will absolutely return him to you if she does that. If Serafina gets on her knees and begs."

The big one's eyes narrowed. "You shouldn't say the things you're saying."

"Why does she want him, anyway? Why is she doing this? Torturing someone for sixty years – that's a commitment few people would be willing to make. What's he done that's so terrible?"

"You can ask Serafina yourself, providing we let you live long enough."

"I hate the talking bit," Razzia mumbled.

"Sorry?" the big one said, his irritation rising. "What was that?"

"The talking bit," she repeated. "I hate it. It's boring. Can we get to the killing bit? That's where the fun is."

"Take it from me, beautiful, you don't want us to get to the killing bit."

Razzia swivelled her head. "Did you just call me beautiful?"

The big one smiled. "What can I say, sweetheart? I have a thing for lunatic blondes."

"Sweetheart. Beautiful. Lunatic blonde." Razzia shook her head slowly. "I have a name. I know I have a name because I picked it myself. Now, while I may be a sweetheart, and I sure am beautiful, and I am undoubtedly both a lunatic and a blonde, my name is Razzia, and that is what you'll be gurgling as I kill you."

Razzia ran at them. Destrier moaned reluctantly but joined her, and Nero appeared right behind Serafina's people.

Cadaverous just turned, and carried Caisson away from the ambulance.

The breeze was picking up as he lay Abyssinia's son on the ground and once again sat in the shade. He faced away from the fighting. He didn't need to see it. No matter how good Serafina's crew were, he had faith in his own. They'd been through a lot together. For years, they'd worked behind the scenes, carrying out Abyssinia's commands when she was nothing but a heart in a box. Yes, back then they'd had Smoke and Lethe to bolster their strength, and yes, their loss had weakened the team considerably. But they were more than a match for their opponents.

Cadaverous took a gun from his jacket and flicked off the safety. It was a pity, what was about to happen.

When the last moan of pain was abruptly cut off, he stood and turned. Destrier, Nero and Razzia: triumphant, as expected, walking away from the dead bodies of their enemies.

"My friends," said Cadaverous as they came forward, "I would just like to take this opportunity to tell you how much I appreciate your talents. We may have had our disagreements over the years, we may have exchanged angry words, we may have said things we each regret..."

"I haven't," Nero muttered.

"But there is no one else I would have even attempted this with," Cadaverous continued. "You are some of the best, the most loyal, and the stupidest people I have ever had the pleasure to know."

Nero frowned. "What?"

Cadaverous struck Destrier on the temple with the butt of his gun and grabbed Nero before he could react, jamming the muzzle under his chin.

"My dear Razzia," he said, "if I see you raise an arm, I pull this trigger and Abyssinia loses her only Teleporter."

Nero tried to pull away, "What the hell are you doing, old man?"

"Shut up, boy," Cadaverous said, spinning him round and pressing the gun into his back.

"I don't get it," said Razzia, looking genuinely confused.

"Sincerest apologies," Cadaverous said, "but Caisson isn't being returned to his mother. If she wants him, she'll have to come to me."

"I still don't get it."

"She doesn't care about us, Razzia. We're disposable. She doesn't care if we get hurt. She doesn't care that Skeiri lost a pet. Not really. You can't see it because you don't want to see it, but she lied to us, she misled us, she tricked us into finding her heart and bringing her back to life. Those plans of hers, where we topple the Sanctuaries and do as we please? That was never going to happen. She was always going to rule over us all – her and her son. She betrayed us, Razzia."

"Kinda like how you're betraying me right now."

"I am sorry about that. You're not my enemy – unless you try to stop me. Are you going to try to stop me, Razzia?"

"Not when you've got a gun, no."

"People always think you're crazier than you actually are."

"Oh, I'm pretty crazy all right," Razzia said, "but I'm not crazy enough to steal Abyssinia's kid. She's gonna blow a gasket, mate. She's gonna rip you apart."

"She'll try."

Razzia made a face. "Nero's crying."

"Is he?" Cadaverous said. "Nero? Are you?"

"You're gonna kill me," Nero sobbed. "You are, aren't you? You're gonna make me teleport you somewhere and then you're gonna shoot me to stop me from bringing Abyssinia to you before you can escape. I don't want to die, Mr Gant. Please don't kill me."

"Oh, I won't kill you, Nero. Why would I do that? After all we've shared? Remember that gentleman we killed in France, the man with the three eyes?"

Nero managed a happy gurgle. "The Three-Eyed Weirdo, yeah."

"Those are special moments for me, Nero. I'm not going to kill you. You're going to teleport Caisson and me to that three-eyed gentleman's airfield, remember it? I have a small plane waiting for me there."

"What are you going to do with me then?"

"I'm going to have to render you unconscious."

"You're gonna hit me?"

"A mere tap. You'll wake with a headache, nothing more."

"You don't know that," Nero argued. "You might give me brain damage."

"I guess that's true – but it's either that or I shoot you."

Nero sagged. "You can hit me."

"Thank you." Cadaverous looked back to Razzia. "Don't come after me."

"I won't have to."

"You take care now."

"Enjoy being alive," she said. "While it lasts."

30

Valkyrie opened her eyes.

"Welcome back," Reverie Synecdoche said, barely raising her gaze from the chart at the foot of the bed.

"Hey," Valkyrie muttered, her tongue heavy. They were in Reverie's clinic, a building Valkyrie was getting to know well. She had a bandage taped to her chest. She was hooked up to a drip. The bed was comfortable, the pillow cool. It occurred to Valkyrie that the pillows in the clinic were always cool.

"Skulduggery told me to tell you that he's over at the High Sanctuary, waiting to talk to the Supreme Mage," Reverie said. "He doesn't fancy his chances."

"Do you have magic pillows?" Valkyrie asked.

"Why would we have magic pillows?"

"Because they're always cool."

"We flip them a lot. How are you feeling?"

"Disappointed about the pillows, but otherwise OK." She frowned. "I feel drunk."

"That will fade. You had quite a nasty injury."

"Oh, no."

"You were lucky. It missed your heart."

"I'm very lucky."

"Yes, you are."

"I went into her mind."

"Did you?"

Valkyrie nodded. "Abyssinia's mind. I went in. Saw her memories."

"That's nice."

"It wasn't really. I'm not used to feeling drunk, you know. I don't drink. Well, I mean, I have drunk, you know. I have imbibed the alcohol. I'm just not used to it. I don't like being drunk."

"Of course you don't," Reverie said, coming closer and checking the drip. "You're a control freak."

Valkyrie's eyes widened. "I am offended. I am not a control freak. How very dare you. I just like being in control of the situation at all times. Is that bad? Is that wrong?"

"Not at all," Reverie murmured, making a note on the clipboard.

"Things have a habit," Valkyrie continued, "of spiralling out of control. You think everything is one way, and then it goes poof, and it's all everywhere. I like to keep a handle on it. Try to keep it all together. You know what happens when things go all everywhere? Bad things happen. I've seen it. So I try to scoop it all back into the basket. Did I mention the basket? There was a basket somewhere in this anatomy. Anatomy?"

"Analogy."

"Analogy, yes, thank you. There was a basket that I forgot to mention. The basket was holding everything and then..." She sighed. "Anyway. I'm not a control freak." Her eyes widened. "I cut off one of Skeiri's thingies."

"That doesn't sound nice."

"Her thingy. Her... thing. With the snapping and the biting. The same as Razzia. Razzia has the same snappy and bitey thing."

"This is an interesting conversation."

Valkyrie waved her arm like a snake, her hand snatching at the air.

"Ah," said Reverie. "The parasite."

"*Yesssss*," said Valkyrie. "I cut it off. I feel so bad. Do you think it's like I killed her pet? I don't want to kill her pet. I love animals."

Reverie replaced the chart at the end of the bed, checked her watch, and looked at Valkyrie. "Was the parasite trying to attack you?"

"Oh, yes, Reverie, it really was. It was all..." She made a scary face.

"Well now," Reverie said, "it sounds to me like you had no choice."

"But I love animals." Valkyrie started to cry.

Reverie patted her head. "It's OK. You did the right thing."

"Do you think it'll grow back?"

"The parasite?"

"Do you think it'll grow back, like a foot?"

"Feet don't grow back, Valkyrie. You're thinking of lizard tails. The parasite won't grow back, I'm afraid."

"Oh, *noooo*."

"You were defending yourself. If this Skeiri person really cared about her parasites, she wouldn't have sent them to attack you, would she?"

"I suppose not." Valkyrie sniffled, and wiped her nose. "When can I leave?"

"I'll have a nurse come by in about twenty minutes, take the tube out of your arm, and you'll be free to walk out of here."

"Cool. Can I take the pillows with me?"

"No. They're ours."

"Just one of them, then. This one."

"No."

"What about that one?"

"No."

"Both?"

"Neither."

"Half?"

"A nurse will be in soon."

"You're mean."

"They're not your pillows, Valkyrie."

"You're still mean."

Half an hour later, Valkyrie was feeling a lot less drunk. She got dressed and the nurse gave her fresh gauze to change her dressing.

Militsa Gnosis was waiting in the lobby when Valkyrie walked out.

"I heard you'd been injured," she said. "Thought I'd call round. I was going to bring flowers and grapes, but it occurred to me that you don't really seem like a flowers person."

"I'm really not," said Valkyrie. "But I do like grapes."

"I should have brought grapes, then. You want to go for a coffee?"

"To be honest," Valkyrie said, "I would love to."

They stopped at the first coffee shop they came to and took a table at the back.

"So what was it that injured you?" Militsa asked. "Bullet? Knife? Arrow?"

"Tentacle."

"Seriously?"

"A tentacle with teeth that shot out of a lady's hand."

"Wow."

"Yeah. It's a parasite. It's called a... well, it's called whatever it's called, but most people just call it a parasite."

"She hot?"

"The parasite?"

"The lady."

"Um... I suppose. Although Razzia's hotter."

"That's the Australian?"

"Yep. They both have the parasites, but Razzia has the most beautiful mouth. I think you'd like her."

"I *have* always been partial to a bad girl," Militsa said, and sipped her coffee. "You want to talk about it?"

"About what? Getting injured? I'm always getting injured."

"Well," said Militsa, "you *were* always getting injured, but then you went away and you didn't get injured for years."

"Ah, I still got injured," Valkyrie said. "I still trained. My instructor didn't exactly take it easy on me."

"Or you didn't take it easy on yourself."

"Meaning?"

Militsa took another sip. "I've known you, what, six months? Seven? Around that? I might be way off here, but when you left Ireland you were so wrapped up in guilt over what Darquesse had done, over what you yourself had done, that you were looking for exciting new systems of punishment. So you hid for five years from the people who loved you, and... what? How did you spend your time?"

"I fixed up an old house."

"OK."

"I got a dog."

"Good."

"I read a lot."

"Excellent."

"And I trained."

"You fought?"

"I trained. I worked out. I sparred."

"And you got hurt?"

"You can't train to fight without the risk of getting hurt."

Militsa shrugged. "OK. I get that. Who was your instructor?"

"Someone I found."

"You found someone good enough to train you, after you'd spent years training with Skulduggery? That's a high bar to match."

Now it was Valkyrie's turn to shrug.

"I get the feeling you don't want to talk about this," Militsa said.

"My mind's just not on it, that's all. There's a lot going on – and not just with me. Like, wherever you look there's drama.

What do you think of this whole refugees-from-another-reality thing? Isn't that nuts?"

"Have you seen it? The portal?"

"Yeah. I usually view dimensional portals as a bad thing, but the people coming through just look so scared..."

"We're helping them out at the Academy," said Militsa. "It started with food and blankets, but the High Sanctuary seems to have handed us full responsibility for their well-being – which, you know, because they're still coming through is a lot more than we can handle."

"Are you in charge?"

"Well, I'm spearheading it, yes, but there's a load of volunteers."

"Then it'll be fine," Valkyrie said. "So long as you're involved, they'll be all right."

"Thanks for the vote of confidence," Militsa said, smiling. "But it is not what I signed up for. I'm a researcher and a teacher. I can barely organise my desk, let alone relief aid for thousands of terrified mortals. I keep imagining that one of these days I'll grow up and become someone who knows what they're doing, but so far that hasn't happened. Do you ever think about that? Growing older, I mean?"

Valkyrie shrugged. "That's the good thing about magic, isn't it? Growing older isn't something we'll have to think about for another few hundred years."

"That's growing old. We won't have to worry about growing old. Growing older is different. We still do that."

"I suppose," Valkyrie said, her mind drifting to Alice – wondering what it would be like to watch her little sister grow up and age naturally, reaching her thirties, her forties, while Valkyrie still looked nineteen.

"Sometimes I look at people like the Supreme Mage," Militsa was saying, "or the headmaster, or even Skulduggery... All of these people are hundreds of years old and, I don't know, I start to wonder what effect that has on them."

Valkyrie drank her coffee. "I'm not sure I get what you're talking about."

"I study magic," Militsa said. "It's what I do. It's what I love. But, when I look at sorcerers who've been alive for centuries, I start to ask questions. About whether or not it's worth it."

"I am so not getting this."

Militsa laughed. "Never mind. I'm talking nonsense!"

"No, no," said Valkyrie, "come on. What do you mean?"

Militsa hesitated. "They lose something, I think. The more lifetimes go by, the less... human they become. I don't mean that in a bad way – at least, not in general. But I think there's a sacrifice you make when you embrace magic."

"Maybe there is," Valkyrie said, "but I don't agree with you about the less human thing. Yeah, OK, China's a bit of a mystery, but Skulduggery's a good person."

"To you."

"To the world, which he has saved a few times."

"I didn't mean to offend you."

"I'm not offended. Really."

"I just think... there's a price to pay. We're not immortal, and yet compared to the mortal people we grew up with, our old friends and neighbours, compared with those poor people from the Leibniz Universe, immortal is exactly what we are. And I think there's a sacrifice we have to make in order to live like that. A piece of yourself you cut away. How else are you going to be able to watch the mortals in your life grow old and die while you stay young?"

Valkyrie smiled, and leaned forward. "I do not wish to think about this right now."

Militsa leaned forward, too. "I do not blame you. Let us never speak of it again."

"That works for me, gorgeous."

Militsa blushed. A blush on a redhead was extremely noticeable.

"You're scarlet," Valkyrie said, and laughed.

"Shut up," Militsa replied, looking away, to the front of the café. "Oh, thank God. A change of subject."

Valkyrie looked round. Skulduggery nodded to her from the door.

She smiled at Militsa. "Be right back," she said, and joined Skulduggery outside.

"How are you feeling?" he asked.

"Sore. Did you manage to speak with China?"

"I did not. I should have stayed at the clinic. I should have been there when you woke."

"What for? You've seen me in one hospital bed, you've seen me in them all. I looked into her head, you know."

"Abyssinia?"

"I took her by surprise, I think. She... It's like she opened the door into my thoughts, but instead of her walking through into my mind, I barged straight into hers."

"What did you see?"

Valkyrie hesitated.

Skulduggery nodded. "You saw me."

"Yeah. Sorry. I kind of used you as an anchor to get through her memories. I saw you put on Vile's armour, I saw the night you stabbed her and threw her out the window... It's weird because it was me. I was experiencing her memories as her, so it was me you stabbed."

"Oh. That's most unfortunate. I sincerely apologise."

"I'm over it."

"That's good to know. Did you happen to see if the child..."

"Is really yours? I didn't. Do you think he could be? You told Abyssinia you don't remember everything you did as Lord Vile. I didn't know that."

"There are periods that are hidden to me," Skulduggery said. "Blank spots in my recollections."

"But you remember everything."

"Apparently not."

"Skulduggery... is Caisson your son?"

"I don't know."

"Would you want him to be?"

Skulduggery watched a tram pass, and didn't answer.

"Militsa's waiting for me," Valkyrie said. "Call me in the morning, OK?"

"I will. I'm glad you're alive, Valkyrie."

"Me too."

She went back inside.

31

Omen waved frantically, but neither Skulduggery nor Valkyrie saw him, so he sat back in his seat, oddly dejected. A fellow tram passenger glared at him disapprovingly.

The tram stopped at Shudder's Gate and he went the rest of the way to the City of Tents on foot. Sorcerers passed without even glancing at him, and the Cleavers stood silently on either side of the path. He could see his own reflection in their visors. He looked nervous, and his shirt had come untucked.

He tucked it into his jeans again, tried to smooth down his hair, and fixed his eyes straight ahead as he walked. He didn't particularly like his reflection. It reminded him of what other people were seeing when he'd much rather forget about things like that.

There was a fence now surrounding the camp, but he found the entrance and made his way to the market. He went up to Aurnia at her stall.

"Hi," he said, unable to stop a smile from spreading across his face. "How are you? You look really nice."

"Hi, Omen," Aurnia said. She sounded deflated at the prospect of their date, and, as much as he couldn't blame her, he did kind of feel hurt. Still, he pressed on.

"I was thinking that I could take you on a tour of Roarhaven," he said. "There are some really cool parts, especially around the Arts District, that are just awesome."

"I can't go."

"Oh," he said. "Oh, OK, that's fine."

"No, I mean I can't physically go. They won't let me."

"Who?" Omen asked. "The village leaders?"

"We don't have village leaders," Aurnia said. "That was a joke. But no, it's not any of my people. The Greycoats won't let us through."

"The Cleavers? Why not?"

"We're not allowed to leave the camp without official supervision. I think they're worried that we won't go back, or maybe that we'll steal something or cause trouble."

"But you'll be with me."

"I mentioned your name to the man in the uniform. He asked if you were the Chosen One, then another man in uniform said no, the Chosen One's name was Auger, and he didn't know who you were."

Omen sagged. "I get that a lot. Well, maybe you can show me around the camp, instead? Maybe I could meet some of your friends?"

Aurnia hesitated, and not in a good way.

"Or not," said Omen.

"My friends don't understand," Aurnia said. "My family doesn't, either."

"Understand what?"

"You. To them, all sorcerers are the same. They're all dangerous. I tried explaining that you're not like that. I told them about you. I told them what you were like."

"Oh, really?" Omen said, trying not to smile. "What did you say?"

"I told them you were harmless."

He frowned. "Well, I mean... I'm not harmless. Harmless is, like, a puppy, or a... baby cow."

"It's called a calf."

"I'm not a calf. I mean, I'm no threat to you, or them, but I'm..."

"I didn't mean it as an insult."

"No, no, of course not. But I've done stuff. Brave stuff. A few months ago, my life was in danger and I was fighting. I even broke a guy out of prison."

"Why did you do that?"

"No, no, he was a good guy, and it was a bad prison. My point is, I'm not... I don't want you to think that I'm boring. I mean, yes, most of the time, I'm nothing, but I am capable of more."

"I've hurt your feelings."

"You haven't."

"I have. I'm really sorry."

Omen shrugged. "Don't worry about it. Really. I actually know some pretty important people – I could talk to them. I'm sure I can arrange something. And, even if I can't, the Cleavers aren't going to keep you confined forever, right? Once everything is cool, you'll be able to, like..."

"Go free," Aurnia said.

"Well... yeah."

"Maybe we will. If we're allowed."

"It's really not like that, though. They're keeping you all in one place because it's safer."

"For who? We can't hurt you. You're sorcerers."

"Safer for you, then."

"I thought you said we were safe here."

"You are, but some people, they don't know if they can trust you. Just give them time, I swear, and they'll realise that you're not a threat and everything will be cool."

Aurnia nodded slowly, and stepped back.

"It was... very nice seeing you again," said Omen.

"Yes."

He didn't know what else to say, so he gave her a little wave, and walked back to Shudder's Gate. He took a tram back to school, but at the stop at the Circle he saw his brother sprint past. Omen jumped up, squeezing through the doors right before they closed. Already Auger was disappearing round the corner.

Omen ran after him, followed him into a side street and lost him down an alley. Omen chose a turn at random, then another, and was about to give up and head back when he heard the unmistakable sounds of fighting.

Unable to think of any use he might actually be in a fight, Omen nonetheless followed the sounds down a narrow canyon of brick and cement, stepping through stagnant pools of water, his fists clenched, his heart beating madly.

Suddenly there was a rush of footsteps and then Mahala was there, her eyes glowing green, and she barged into him, and Omen hit the wall and she sprinted on. She'd barely even noticed he'd been there.

"Omen," said Auger, limping up. "What are you doing here?"

Omen scrambled up. "I saw you," he said. "I thought I'd come and see if you needed any help. Are you OK?"

"I'm fine," Auger said. His shirt was ripped. "Did you see Mahala?"

Omen nodded. "Her eyes were doing that glowing thing you talked about."

Auger sighed. "Yeah. That's proving to be a problem."

Kase shuffled by, his face a mess of cuts and bruises. "Hey, Omen."

"Hi, Kase," Omen said, and Kase shuffled on.

"Since you offered," said Auger, "you mind helping me walk for a bit? I'm already healing, but I could use the assist."

"Sure," said Omen, and took his brother's weight as they made for the street. "And hey, you know what you're doing and everything, and I don't want to intrude where I don't belong... but shouldn't you call someone? Like, not even Skulduggery or Valkyrie, but the City Guard, maybe?"

"We were going to," Auger said. "I don't know if you've noticed, but the City Guard are not the most thoughtful of people. This is Mahala we're talking about. It's going to take some pretty weird magic, a few more punches to the face, and some good old-fashioned friendship, but we're going to help her and we're going to banish whatever's possessing her back to whatever hell it came from."

"Right," said Omen. "Yeah, I can understand that. Do you need any help?"

Auger laughed. "Dude, from what I've heard, you've got enough on your plate already."

"What do you mean?"

"I heard about Axelia."

Omen sighed. "Of course you did."

Auger smiled. "She's a cool girl. A smart girl."

"Smart enough to turn me down."

"Hey now, come on, don't be hard on yourself."

"Ah, I'm OK about it. I knew she was going to say no."

"So you knew it was going to end badly, but you still had to try, huh? I will never understand people who say we're not alike."

They emerged from the alley. Kase was waving a green amulet about. It started to vibrate in his hand.

"She went this way," he said.

Auger stood on his own. "We gotta go."

"Are you sure you don't need my help?" asked Omen.

"We've got this," said Auger. "Kase, you agree?"

"We've got this," said Kase.

"And what'll I say if the teachers start asking where you are?"

Auger grinned. "Just tell them we're back where we belong," he said, and Kase laughed and they started jogging away.

Omen watched them go, and didn't bother wondering what the hell Auger was on about.

32

Skulduggery called at a little after nine the next morning, shaking Valkyrie from a dream.

"Did I wake you?" he asked.

"No," she croaked.

"It sounds like I woke you."

"Hold on." She grabbed the bottle of water from her bedside table, downed what was left. "OK," she said. "I can talk now."

"Abyssinia has Caisson."

Valkyrie sat up. "Dammit," she muttered.

"Five dead sorcerers," Skulduggery said, "all connected in some way to Serafina, were recovered in Italy yesterday evening. The private ambulance was empty."

"So she has him. Well, that's wonderful." Valkyrie sighed. "What do we do now?"

"We talk with China."

"Any idea why she's been avoiding us?"

"A few," he said. "If I can't arrange something by the end of the day, I'm kicking down doors until I get to her."

"Well," Valkyrie said, getting slowly out of bed, "you have fun kicking those doors, OK? I'm still recovering from getting stabbed in the heart."

"You didn't get stabbed in the heart."

"Close enough."

"It was five centimetres away."

She went to the mirror, examined the bandage. "Five centimetres isn't very much when you're getting stabbed," she said. "Anyway, today I'm recuperating, and spending time with my sister."

"What if I require your assistance?"

"Temper will help you."

"Temper has his duties. What if I require *your* assistance?"

"If it's really important, give me a call."

"What if I'm bored and just want someone to talk to?"

"Then you need more friends."

"Most of my friends are dead."

"And that's exactly the cheery start to the day I've been looking for."

She hung up.

Xena was waiting for Valkyrie when she went downstairs. She poured fresh food into the dog bowl and had her breakfast, then went walking through the woods that surrounded the house. Xena disappeared into the undergrowth, darting across her path every now and then on the trail of some mysterious scent.

Valkyrie had a late lunch, got in the car and drove to Haggard, where she parked across the road from her old primary school and walked up to the gate, barely resisting the urge to go in and take a look around. There'd been an extension built since she was a pupil here, which essentially tripled the size of the place. She wondered if her old classroom was the same, or if her old teachers were still there.

More cars pulled up and parents walked over. The end of school was approaching.

"Stephanie?"

Valkyrie turned as Hannah Foley came forward, clad in yoga pants and a hoody, her blonde hair tied back into a ponytail. Valkyrie realised they were hugging a few seconds after it started.

"Ohhhhh," Valkyrie said. "Hi..."

Hannah stepped back, hands on her stomach and a smile on her face. "How are you? Janey Mac, I haven't seen you in ages!"

"Janey Mac indeed," said Valkyrie. The way Hannah was patting her belly, it was like she was inviting Valkyrie to comment on the rather obvious pregnancy. Instead, Valkyrie said, "So what have you been up to?"

"Well, I'm pregnant!" Hannah said, laughing. "I know what you're thinking: *again?* I just can't get enough of it! I didn't know you had a child here."

"I don't," said Valkyrie. "I've got a sister."

"A sister?" Hannah said, clearly astonished. "What age is she?"

"Seven."

"That's quite a gap!"

"I suppose so."

"So tell me about you, Steph! What are you doing with yourself?"

Valkyrie kept her smile. "Keeping busy."

"At what? Sure, you don't even need a job, do you? Don't you have your uncle's money? I remember everyone talking about that back in school – we were all so jealous that you were a millionaire. We couldn't understand why you kept coming in, though!"

Valkyrie nodded along while Hannah laughed, and said, "Money can't buy friendship."

"Ah, now this is true," Hannah said. "And it can't buy happiness, either, isn't that what they say?"

"I've definitely heard it said."

"I mean, don't get me wrong, I imagine it was wonderful to suddenly be rich – but wait till you start having children, Stephanie – then you'll find out what real happiness is."

"Yeah."

"I'm due to pop with this one in six weeks – though, knowing me, it'll probably arrive a few days early!"

She laughed again, like that was funny, and Valkyrie sneaked a glance at her watch.

"No engagement ring, I see," Hannah said, calming down. "Is there no one special in your life, or has he just not bothered to get a claim in?"

"I'm not looking to get married," said Valkyrie.

"Oh, you should, Stephanie, you should! Marriage was the best thing that ever happened to me – after becoming a mom, of course."

"Of course."

"Finding someone special, sharing your life with them, bringing life into the world... That's true happiness. You can have all the money you ever wanted, you can have millions and billions, but if you don't have a family of your own, what's the point, isn't that right?"

Valkyrie gave a tight-lipped smile and shrugged with her eyebrows.

Hannah took in Valkyrie's car. "Is this yours? A bit too flashy for me. You wouldn't fit a baby seat in the back! That's mine over there, the people carrier. We're determined to fill it, as you can probably tell!"

"You certainly have a lot of children."

"It's hard work, believe me. On one level, I envy you. Your time is your own, you have no responsibility, you can head off on holiday whenever you want – but there is no way I would trade places. I just wouldn't. You look like you don't believe me!"

Valkyrie was pretty sure her expression was completely neutral.

Hannah continued. "I didn't inherit millions, but I'm rich in kisses and hugs and smiles and laughter and love."

Valkyrie blinked at her. "Right then."

The bell rang, signalling the end of the school day, and suddenly there were kids swarming out of the door. It was alarming.

"Stephanie!" Alice squealed, launching herself into Valkyrie's arms.

Valkyrie laughed, picked her up as easily as she'd pick up a doll. She turned to Hannah. "Well, gotta go. Good luck with the pregnancy thing."

"Oh, thank you! Janey, I'm an old pro by now!"

Valkyrie hurried to the car before Hannah could invite her to meet her child.

"Who is that?" Alice asked from the back seat as she buckled her belt.

"An old friend of mine," said Valkyrie.

"Is she a mommy?"

"She is."

"Why aren't you a mommy?"

"Because I don't want to be."

"Why did she call you Janey?"

Valkyrie smiled. "She didn't. She meant Janey Mac. It's just something people say."

"What people?"

"Irish people," Valkyrie said, pulling out on to the road.

"Why do they say it?"

"I'm not sure. It's just something they say."

"Why don't you want to be a mommy?"

"Because children are gross and yucky."

Alice laughed. "I'm a child!"

"No, you're not," said Valkyrie. "You're, like, eighty."

Alice giggled. "I'm not eighty! I'm seven!"

"Are you sure?"

"Yes!"

"I could have sworn you were eighty."

"I'm only seven!"

"Then why do you look so old?"

"I don't look old!"

Valkyrie pointed at an old woman they were driving past. "See her? The old woman with the wrinkly face and all that loose and saggy skin? You look exactly like her."

Alice gasped theatrically. "Is that what I'm going to look like when I'm your age?"

"Oi!" Valkyrie said, and Alice giggled, and Valkyrie found

herself struggling to keep her smile. In eighty years' time, Alice might very well end up looking like that – while Valkyrie wouldn't have changed one little bit.

She shook the thought from her mind. "Want to grab a milkshake on the way home?"

Alice cheered.

33

In the small room filled with cleaning equipment on the east side of the Lacuna Underground Car Park, the wall rumbled and slid open, revealing the tunnel beyond.

Tantalus peered into the darkness, and frowned. "This leads into the Dark Cathedral?"

"Yes, it does," said Sebastian. "The Cathedral is full of secret passageways like this."

"And how did you know about it?"

Sebastian shrugged. "I told you, I've had an interesting past."

Tantalus turned to him. "Or you're one of them. You're a disciple of the Faceless Ones – you're one of Creed's agents sent to take us down from within."

"Tantalus, come on," Bennet said. "Why would Arch-Canon Creed even care about what we're doing?"

Tantalus glared. "For one thing, we're about to break into his Cathedral and steal one of his artefacts. For another, if Darquesse returns, then everyone will turn away from *his* gods and start worshipping her, just like we do."

"I'm not working for Creed," Sebastian told him. "And does it really matter how I know that this tunnel is here? We have a way in, don't we? So why are we standing around talking about it when we could be finding the scythe?"

Tantalus raised his finger, pointed it right into Sebastian's face, so close it almost tipped against his mask. "I don't trust you. You've got secrets."

"We all have secrets."

"Not like yours. You won't tell us where you're from or what you're after."

"I want to bring Darquesse back, just like you."

"Guys," said Bennet, "we don't have an awful lot of time here."

"Shut up, Bennet," said Tantalus. "The beaked weirdo here may have won over you and your equally gullible friends, but I'm not so stupid. I've been watching you, Plague Doctor. I've been listening to you. You think you have all the answers, don't you?"

"Not even remotely."

"And, after all this time, you still won't let us see your face. Why is that?"

"Tantalus," said Bennet, "we've been through this. The Plague Doctor's uniform is a pressurised suit that keeps him alive. If he takes it off, he dies. OK? Now, if we're going to go through the tunnel like we planned, can we please do it before we're discovered and someone calls the City Guard? What do you say?"

Tantalus glared again, then grunted, and clicked his fingers, summoning flame into his hand. Bennet did the same, and Sebastian took out a torch and flicked it on.

They walked along the tunnel, pushing the darkness ahead of them, watching it squeeze by and fill up the space behind.

"What are we going to do when we get into the Cathedral?" Bennet asked. "I mean, we probably shouldn't split up, right?"

"We're splitting up," said Tantalus.

"Aw."

"We'll find the scythe faster that way, plus we'll have less chance of being caught."

"But if we *are* caught," Bennet argued, "staying together would make it easier to fight our way out."

Tantalus scowled. "We won't have to fight our way out if we're not caught in the first place. Bennet, I told you not to come. I knew you'd do this."

"Do what? I'm not doing anything."

"You don't want to split up because if you're caught, you know you can't fight."

"I can fight."

"Closing your eyes and flailing your fists is not fighting."

"I don't fight like that."

"Yes, you do. It's ridiculous, and so are you."

"Hey," Sebastian interjected, "hey, let's calm down."

"I'm not ridiculous," Bennet muttered.

"What was that?" Tantalus said, stepping closer. "What was that you said?"

"I said I'm... I'm not ridiculous."

"Really?" Tantalus said, and laughed. "So out of everyone here, Bennet, whose wife left him for a Hollow Man? Eh? Granted, we don't know if the Plague Doctor's wife left *him* for a Hollow Man because we don't know anything about the Plague Doctor –"

"I'm not married," Sebastian said.

"– but we know for certain that *my* wife didn't leave *me* for a walking bag of green gas because I left her years ago. So that only leaves *you*, Bennet, as the most ridiculous man here."

Bennet blinked quickly and said nothing.

They carried on walking. Sebastian glanced at Bennet. His head was down and his lip was quivering. There was an unspoken rule in the group that nobody should mention what happened between Bennet's wife and the Hollow Man – a rule that Tantalus had just hurled to the floor and kicked to death.

Ten minutes later, they came to a wall.

"All right," Tantalus said, "how do we get through?"

"Look for a switch," said Sebastian, moving his hands over the surface.

Tantalus sounded surprised. "You mean the all-knowing Plague Doctor doesn't know where it is?"

"It'll be here somewhere."

"I am shocked," Tantalus said. "My faith in humanity has been destroyed. Who will I believe in now that the omnipotent Plague Doctor has revealed himself to be just another—"

"Will you stop?" Bennet shouted. "Will you just stop?"

Tantalus turned to him. "What?"

"I am sick of the sarcasm and the constant petty remarks," Bennet said. "What are you, a child? No, forget that, my son was never as bad as you. OK, we get it, you feel threatened by the Plague Doctor's presence."

Tantalus bristled. "I'm not threatened."

"But you know what the rest of us are doing, while you're acting out? We're getting on with things. Yes, we don't know what he looks like. Yes, we don't know much about him. But he has brought more purpose to our little group in the last seven months than we have had in the last seven years. So get over it, all right?"

"Don't... don't you speak to me like that."

"You can't order me around, Tantalus. You know why? Because we're about to go sneaking through a very scary place run by some genuinely dangerous people. If we're caught, do you know what's going to happen to us? I don't. No one does. Because people who go sneaking through these kinds of places are generally never heard from again. Faced with this situation, do you really think I'm going to be intimidated by a bully like you?"

"Bennet, you'd better—"

"I'd better what?" Bennet said, stepping right up to Tantalus. "I'd better watch my mouth or you'll insult me again? You'll mock me? You'll bring up the fact that my wife left me for a Hollow Man? Go ahead. You know something? I'm glad Odetta is with Conrad, because I was a lousy husband. He can at least give her the love and comfort that I never could. That's my fault. That's on me. But you don't get to use that against me, you understand? You ever mention them again and I will close my eyes and flail my fists. Yeah, it may not be the coolest way to fight, but I can guarantee you, some of that flailing will actually hit you. So go ahead, Tantalus. Make my day."

The tunnel was cold and quiet as Tantalus decided on his next move.

He turned away. "You're ridiculous," he said.

"Yeah," Bennet said, "I'm ridiculous."

"You are."

"That's right."

"So ridiculous."

"Yeah."

Sebastian waited until they'd finished, then said, "I've found the switch."

They didn't say anything to that, so he pulled the lever and the wall parted like curtains. They stepped through into an empty corridor, the overhead lights flickering on as the tunnel sealed behind them.

There was no more arguing. They were deep in enemy territory.

Tantalus turned to them. "You know what we're looking for. Lily said the scythe's on display with a bunch of other Faceless Ones junk. Once we have it, we send out a message, and we all meet back here. If someone sees you, pretend that you're meant to be here. Act casual. Only run as a last resort. Bennet, you go left. Plague Doctor, you go right. I'm going this way. Questions? OK." He took a deep breath. "Good luck."

They split up. Sebastian found some stairs and followed them to a higher floor. The Cathedral was quiet. He ducked back when people passed – clergy, mostly. They wore red with black piping, stylish robes designed to attract potential worshippers, a stark contrast to the drab garments worn by the Arch-Canon, Damocles Creed.

"Stop."

Sebastian froze.

"Turn round. Slowly."

Sebastian did as he was instructed. Two Cathedral Guards

approached, their black armour moulded to their pecs and their eyes glaring from beneath their helmets.

"Who are you meant to be?" one of them asked.

"Um, I'm the Plague Doctor," Sebastian said. "How do you do?"

"Take off the mask."

"I'm afraid I can't do that for health reasons."

"Are you meant to be here?"

"Yes. Definitely."

"Do you have a pass?"

"They said they'd get me one, but they haven't yet. They told me to wait here."

"Who told you?"

"Uh... Jimmy. And Clive."

The guards glanced at each other, then the talkative one pressed a button on the wall and a security door slid down behind Sebastian, leaving him with nowhere to run.

They came closer. "Put your hands over your head."

"But that's where my hat is."

"Put your hands up!"

"Hey," another Cathedral Guard said, coming up behind them. "What's going on? Who is this?"

The other two stood to attention. "We caught an intruder, ma'am. We're bringing him in for interrogation now."

"I'm not an intruder," Sebastian said. "I'm waiting for Jimmy and Clive."

"I don't know a Jimmy or a Clive," the female guard answered.

"You don't?" Sebastian said. "Jimmy's short? Clive's tall? Clive has a moustache and he walks with a limp? You're sure you don't know them?"

"Pretty sure," she said, and gestured to the security door. "Why is this shut?"

"Um... this is what we're meant to do if we find an intruder," said the talkative one. "It's standard operating procedure."

"Oh, yeah," said the female guard. "So it is."

She kicked the guard behind her, just spun and threw her leg up and whacked it into his head. She continued the spin, dropped low, swept the first guard's legs from under him. He fell and she swung her staff into his face so hard his helmet flew off, and now both guards were unconscious.

She straightened up, took off her helmet and turned to Sebastian.

"Now," said Tanith Low, "just who the hell are you?"

34

Sebastian did his very best not to wave. "You can call me the Plague Doctor," he said.

Tanith nodded. "The Plague Doctor. Right. What's your real name?"

"That's the only name you need to know," Sebastian said, and squawked a little when Tanith grabbed the beak of his mask and yanked it down low, bending him over. She started pulling him in a circle.

"I'm afraid that's not going to cut it," she said. "I'll have to insist."

Sebastian tried to pull her hands away, but she was twisting his mask and it was hurting his neck. "Ow. Stop. Please. I'm the Plague Doctor. You don't need to know my name."

With her other hand, she batted the hat from his head and rapped her knuckles on his mask. It echoed loudly in his ears. "Don't try to tell me what I need, all right? Who are you, and why were you sneaking around?"

"Why are you sneaking around?" Sebastian countered, because it seemed like a good idea at the time. She twisted his beak again and he cried out. Again.

"I'm sneaking around because I'm here to do bad things," Tanith said. "Why are you here?"

"I have to steal something!"

"What?"

"I can't tell you!"

"Why do you have to steal it?"

"I can't tell you that, either!"

He finally broke free, stood up to his full height and readjusted the mask, glaring at her through the glass eyeholes. "I am here," he said, "on a secret mission. It looks like you are here on a secret mission, too. I can't tell you what my mission is, just like I'm sure you can't tell me what your mission is."

"I'm here to kill someone."

Sebastian blinked. "Oh. It... it's not me, is it?"

"Well, I don't know," said Tanith. "Maybe it is. What's your name? If it's not the name of my target, I'll let you live."

"Really? You think I'm that stupid? I'm not telling you my name, and that is final." He didn't know why he did it, but as he was speaking he watched his hand come up, one finger extended, and as he said the word final he prodded Tanith once, in the chest. He immediately regretted it. He regretted it even more when she grabbed that finger and twisted, forcing him to his knees.

"Please!" he cried. "Don't break my finger! I need it to point at stuff!"

"Your name."

"I can't tell you!"

"Your name."

"Sebastian!" he howled. "Sebastian Tao!"

She released him and he cradled his hand.

"Hello, Sebastian," she said.

"Hello, Tanith," he moaned.

"You know who I am, then."

He got up. "Yes. Of course. Everyone knows who you are."

"And you're not going to ask why I'm here to kill someone?"

"I don't have to," Sebastian said. "I know you're a Knife in the Darkness. I know you went back to them after Desolation

Day. If you're here to assassinate someone, I'm sure they have it coming."

"You seem to know a lot about me."

"Well," said Sebastian, shaking out his sore hand, "I know a lot about a lot of people. It's one of my gifts. I promise you, we're on the same side."

"I'll make up my mind about that. Seeing as how you know so much, Sebastian, do you know how to get this security door open? I can crack just about any lock, but this door doesn't seem to have one."

"Is that where your target is?"

"It will be."

"I think that's where I have to go, too. Maybe we could team up."

"Yeah? You want to help me kill someone?"

"Uh, well, not quite, but... Actually, I was thinking more along the lines of you protecting me until I find what I have to find, then we kind of... go our separate ways."

"Tempting," said Tanith. "So tempting. Or I kill you."

Sebastian frowned. "What? Why would you kill me?"

"Because you know who I am. You might tell someone."

"I won't. I swear."

"I want to believe you, Sebastian. I do. You have an honest mask. But look at this from my point of view: life would just be a lot easier if I kill you before you have a chance to mess anything up for me."

"Unless I know how to open this door, right? Like, if I open the door, you don't kill me?"

"I don't kill you."

"At all?"

"Right now."

Sebastian hesitated, then nodded. "I'll open the door. Because I trust you."

"It's nice to be trusted."

He went to the spot on the wall he'd seen the Cathedral Guard press, and found the button. The security door slid open.

Tanith put her helmet back on, and marched in. Sebastian followed.

"What are you doing?" Tanith asked.

"Coming with you," said Sebastian.

"I thought you wanted me not to kill you."

"Tanith, listen. I can't tell you what I'm after... actually, I can. It's a scythe they have in their collection here. But I can't tell you why I'm after it. You just have to trust that I'm doing the right thing."

"The right thing for whom, exactly?"

"I probably shouldn't tell you that."

"You're a man of mystery, Sebastian, in a completely non-alluring way. But, seeing as how any alarm you raise would alert my target, you can stick with me until you find your scythe."

"Thank you."

"Then you get out of my way," she said. "Or I *will* kill you."

35

Valkyrie roamed around downstairs while Alice went to her room to pack a small overnight bag. She stopped at the mirror in the hall, pulled down her T-shirt to check the gauze, then chewed on a leaf to keep the pain away.

She went into the living room, smiling at the framed family photographs on the mantelpiece. She came to one of her nana and suddenly missed her terribly.

Alice ran in behind her, bag in one hand, Sparkles in the other. "Will you teach me how to do magic?" she asked.

Valkyrie turned slowly. "What?"

"I want to learn," said Alice. "I'm good at learning. Miss Donohoe says I'm her prize pupil."

"What, uh, what kind of magic do you think I know?"

Alice shrugged. "Magic magic."

"Oh, right. And why do you think I can do magic?"

Alice laughed. "Because you can! Mom and Dad are always talking about it when they think I'm not listening, but I'm always listening."

"What else have you heard?"

"Skulduggery is magic, and he's a real skeleton. But I'm not supposed to say that to anyone except you and Mom and Dad. You get hurt a lot."

"Do I?"

"That's what Mom says, and Dad tells her that you're big and strong and able to handle yourself. Sometimes Mom cries about it."

"I see."

"So will you teach me?"

Valkyrie hesitated, then sat. "I don't know if I should. Some magic is dangerous. It can hurt you."

"I'll be very careful."

"I know you will, but some magic can hurt you even if you're the most careful person in the world."

"Then don't teach me that magic," Alice said. "Teach me the safe magic."

"Sweetie, I don't know if I can. Maybe when you're older."

"When I'm eight?"

"Maybe a little bit older than that. I was twelve when I first learned magic."

"But that's ages away! That's..." She counted. "Five years away!"

"You're very smart."

"I know," Alice said, and grinned, and then looked serious. "But that's too long. I want to learn now."

"I can't teach you until you're twelve. Sorry. It's the rules."

"Then can you show me magic?"

"Um... well, I suppose so."

Valkyrie held up her hand, and sent energy crackling between her forefinger and thumb.

"*Wowwwwww,*" said Alice. "Can I touch it?"

"No," Valkyrie said, "it'd hurt a lot. You ready to go?"

Alice held up her bag. "Yes!"

"Is Sparkles ready to go?"

Alice held up Sparkles. "Yes, she is!"

Valkyrie's phone rang. It was Skulduggery.

"Hold on just a second," she said, and answered. "What's up?"

"China's free for a chat in an hour," Skulduggery said.

"She can finally see you?"

"She doesn't know it yet, but yes."

Valkyrie stood up. "You don't have an appointment, do you?"

"No, but I took a look at her schedule, and she doesn't have an appointment, either. So what do you say we drop by unannounced?"

"I can't," said Valkyrie. "I'm with Alice."

"Bring her with you," Skulduggery responded. "China hasn't met her yet, has she? It'll be a good ice-breaker. We'll probably need one."

"There's no way I'm doing that."

"I need you there, Valkyrie. China actually likes you. I'm not going to get any answers if you're not there."

Valkyrie smiled down at her sister. "I don't have a babysitter."

"Alice will be fine on her own."

"She's seven."

"That's not old enough to be left alone?"

"No, it isn't."

"Then can you drop her back to your parents?"

"I'm in Haggard right now – I said I'd take her for the night, remember? It's their anniversary."

"Oh. Well, how about asking Fergus and Beryl to mind her?"

"What? No. I would *never* do that to her."

"Isn't there anyone else?" he asked. "I need my partner with me."

Valkyrie sighed. "Unless you know of anyone offering a babysitting service, I can't think of..."

"Valkyrie?"

She shrugged. "I thought of someone."

"Oh," Skulduggery said. "Me, too."

36

Omen raised his hand to volunteer, and Mr Peccant chose someone else. Omen put his hand down. He'd known the answer. It wasn't often that a teacher asked a question in class that Omen knew the answer to, so he liked to seize the chance whenever it cropped up. But teachers, like life, had a habit of passing him by.

October Klein gave the wrong answer, which turned out to be the right answer, and Omen was glad now that he hadn't been picked, but still felt aggrieved nonetheless.

He sank lower in his chair, and deeper into despondency. Never had been right. Omen had been waiting for Skulduggery and Valkyrie to call him to adventure, and of course they were never going to do that. The last time was a fluke. They'd needed someone inconspicuous to spy on a group of students. That was a very specific set of circumstances, unlikely to ever be repeated.

Omen had to face it – he'd had his adventure. It had been terrifying and exhilarating and brilliant and terrifying, and then it had ended. Skulduggery and Valkyrie and Auger were bottomless cups into which adventure could be poured and they would never fill up. Omen's cup had already spilled over, and as usual he was left with a soggy mess and a widening puddle.

He turned to Never, a few seats away, and mouthed the words: *You were right.*

Never frowned back at him, and mouthed: *What?*

You were right.

I was white?

You were right.

About what?

What you said.

What did I say?

About me wasting my time, waiting to be called on another adventure.

Never stared. *What?*

The stuff we were talking about last week.

Use shorter sentences, muppet.

You were right.

I got that much.

About me.

Yes.

Wasting my time.

Please hurry up.

Waiting for adventure.

You're waiting for a denture?

Adventure.

A denture?

Adventure.

I was right about you waiting for adventure?

Yes.

Never frowned. *I know.*

Oh.

That's why I said it.

I just wanted you to know that I agree with you.

What?

I agree with you.

So?

I wanted you to know that.

Is that all?

Yes.

Can we stop doing this now?

OK.

Never nodded, and went back to paying attention to whatever Peccant was saying while Omen thought a little more about what he'd been thinking about. When he'd finished, he tried to catch up with the rest of the class, but they were all scribbling furiously.

"Mr Darkly," Peccant said.

Omen looked up. "Yes, sir?"

"You look confused."

"No, sir."

"You're not confused?"

"No, sir."

"So that's just your face, then, is it?"

"Yes, sir."

"That's good to know," Peccant said, and went back to whatever it was he was doing.

Omen managed to not get in trouble until the bell rang for the end of school. He went to talk to Never, but she turned a corner and vanished, leaving him alone in the crowd.

He saw Mahala approaching and he shrank back, barged into some First Years, finally stumbled to the bench along the wall. He sat, watching her pass, digging for his phone to call Auger – but then his brother appeared. Mahala didn't attack him. Come to that, her eyes weren't glowing green. Omen watched them talk, very intently, and then Auger nodded, smiled grimly, and watched Mahala hurry away.

If that had been Omen standing there, the crowd would have thrown him about like a leaf in a stream. But the stream parted for Auger.

Auger saw him and raised a hand in greeting, then came over, sat beside him on the bench.

"I see you've got Mahala back," Omen said.

"Yes," said Auger, and a moment passed and he nodded. "Yes."

"Um... how's she doing?"

"She's good. She's doing OK. Back to normal, at least. She's blaming herself for everything she did when she was possessed, but I think that's only natural."

"And the thing that was possessing her? Did you banish it back to the hell it came from, like you'd planned?"

Auger hesitated. "Not quite."

"Oh?"

"We got the spirit out of Mahala, which was great, but then it went into Kase. So now Kase is possessed and he's, like, extra-angry. So if you see him, and his eyes start glowing... just run. OK? Just get the hell out of there."

"I'll do that."

"I'll take care of it, you know? I just need a little time to come up with a new plan."

"Any help I can give..."

"I know, dude. Thanks." He shook himself out of his sombre mood. "So, hey, who's this mortal girl you've been showing around the school?"

Omen sighed. "Of course you heard about that. Her name's Aurnia."

"Do you like her?"

"She's very nice."

"You gonna see her again?"

"I don't know. Hopefully. I mean, it can't go anywhere, I know that."

"Why not?"

"Are you kidding?" Omen asked, and laughed. "Can you imagine what'd happen if Mum and Dad heard about it?"

"So what if they freak out? Don't listen to them, dude. She's still a person, right? You're allowed to like her."

"I don't think I am, though. When you fall in love with a Necromancer girl or you start to date a mermaid, they pretend not to notice, but if I tried to go out with a mortal girl from another dimension they'd be terrified that it'd tarnish the Darkly name."

"Hey," Auger said, holding up a finger. "I never dated the mermaid. We just... hung out."

"I always meant to ask you about that, actually."

"Ah," Auger said with a shrug, "don't."

Omen laughed. "You know something? I can't wait for you to face the King of the Darklands, because can you imagine what they'll be like once you beat him and the prophecy is complete? All those centuries of waiting and expectation will be over, and they'll no longer be the parents of the Chosen One. They'll just be normal sorcerers again. I can't wait to see their faces when they realise that."

Auger nodded, but Omen noticed that the smile was gone. He softened his tone.

"Um, what are you going to do afterwards?" he asked.

"After I face the King?" Auger said. "Assuming I survive?"

"You will survive," said Omen, frowning. "You have to. They don't make prophecies about people who fail – they make them about heroes. Heroes who win."

"I've been thinking about this more and more," said Auger, looking around. "You know, I'm kind of invincible right now. I'm invincible for the next three years, until I'm seventeen and I go up against the King. Until then, nothing much can stop me. It doesn't mean that I'm not careful. I can still be hurt. I can still be injured. And hell, I can still be killed, because, as everyone knows, no prophecy is guaranteed. But in general, as long as I'm smart, I'm invincible."

"That must be pretty cool."

"It is. Mostly. But I've been wondering... what happens after? If I defeat the King of the Darklands, I'll emerge alive, yes – but I'll have lost that invincibility. Suddenly I can trip and fall off a cliff, or get hit by a bus, or get sick or something. Suddenly anything can kill me."

"You'll still have the talents you were born with," said Omen. "You'll still be faster and stronger and smarter than most people."

"But none of that has kept me going," Auger replied. "The one thing that has propelled me through all of these crazy adventures I've had is the confidence that I'll survive them. That's my secret. It's not power or ability, it's just... I dunno. Pure belief in myself. That's who I am. It kinda defines me."

"I would love that."

"I know you would, dude. Sometimes I wonder what you'd be like if you had even a tenth of my confidence. That's what holds you back, you know."

Omen waved his hand. "We're not talking about me right now. So you think that once the prophecy has been fulfilled and the King is defeated, you'll, what... lose yourself?"

"Maybe, yeah."

"I've never thought about it like that."

"See, I know who I am right now. I've always known who I am, why I'm here, what I'm meant for... But I don't know who I'll be once it's over."

"Who do you want to be?"

Auger looked up suddenly. "What?"

Omen blinked. "Did I... did I say something wrong?"

"No," Auger said, staring at him. "It's just... I don't think anyone's ever asked me that before." His phone beeped, and he looked at it and sighed. "The call to action," he said, and stood. "Good talking to you, bro."

"Be careful."

He grinned. "Invincible, remember?"

Auger hurried away, and the moment he was out of sight Omen's phone rang. The screen lit up with Valkyrie's name, and he jumped to his feet.

"Hello?" he said, his mouth dry.

"Omen," Valkyrie said, "hey."

"Hi," said Omen. "Hi, how are you? What's up? Is anything wrong?"

He heard her hesitate. "Would you happen to be doing anything right now?"

"Nope," Omen said immediately. "Nothing."

"Are you busy for the next, maybe, two hours? Three at the most?"

A teacher walked by and Omen turned away, keeping his head down and talking quietly. "I'm free. I'm ready. What do you need?"

"I need your help, to be honest. I'm a bit stuck."

He froze. "Oh, God. You're trapped?"

"No, no, nothing like that. How are you with kids?"

Omen frowned. "Like... fighting them?"

"What? No, Omen. Minding them. I need a babysitter. You in?"

He sagged.

"Omen?"

The call to action. "I'm in," he said.

37

Valkyrie got changed into her black clothes, and zipped her jacket all the way up. On her way downstairs she glanced through the window, saw Never and Omen standing beside her car. Never was looking irritated, and teleported away while Omen was still talking.

Valkyrie waited until Omen knocked before opening the door. She waved him in.

"Hey," she said. "Thank you for doing this. Seriously."

"Of course," he said.

"Is everything OK between you and Never? He seemed annoyed. Is it me? I know he doesn't like me a whole lot."

"No," Omen said. "No, it's definitely not you. OK, it might be, just a little, but mostly... I don't know. He's been acting a little odd lately, that's all. Keeping secrets, maybe."

"We all have secrets."

"I suppose."

Alice poked her head out of the kitchen.

"Alice, come over here," said Valkyrie. "She's not usually this shy. Alice, this is my friend. His name is Omen."

Alice hesitated, then hurried over, and Omen waved.

"Hi, Alice."

Alice waved from behind Valkyrie's leg.

"There's food and drink in the fridge," Valkyrie said, grabbing her car keys, "and probably some snacks somewhere in the kitchen. If you want a pizza or something, I think there's a menu floating around, but I'll only be gone for two hours or so."

"I'll be fine," said Omen. "We'll be fine."

"Just put the TV on," Valkyrie said. "Or, I don't know, she might want to do homework. Could you help her with that?"

"I think I can manage," Omen said, trying to sound confident.

"Right," said Valkyrie, "OK. I wouldn't be doing this if it wasn't important, so thank you."

"No problem."

Valkyrie bent down to Alice. "I won't be gone long. Omen will take care of you – he's really nice, you'll really like him."

"Is he magic, too?" she asked.

"We don't talk about magic, remember?"

"Yeah, but is he magic, too?"

Valkyrie sighed. "A little. Omen, don't show her any magic."

He nodded. "Probably wise."

"You're going to be nice to Omen, aren't you? You're going to behave and do what he tells you?"

"Yes."

"When I get back, we'll go to my house and I'll show you your room, OK? That sound cool?"

"Yes."

"And when you speak to Mum and Dad about this tomorrow...?"

"I'm not to tell them you left," Alice said.

"Good girl. That's very important." Valkyrie straightened up. "Right. I'm off. Be good."

She left the house, got in her car, and drove to Roarhaven. She met Skulduggery in the High Sanctuary's lobby and together they slipped away from the sorcerers who were not doing a good job of keeping a surreptitious eye on them. Using their personal cloaking spheres, they passed between the Cleavers standing guard, and waited at the double doors to China's Room of Prisms.

Skulduggery checked his pocket watch. "Any moment now," he said.

Valkyrie heard footsteps on the other side, and the handle turned and the left door opened. She dodged back, avoiding the man who came through. He went to close the door after him, but Skulduggery put a hand to it and Valkyrie slipped under his arm. The sorcerer frowned, but Skulduggery was already following Valkyrie in. The door closed behind them.

They deactivated their cloaking spheres as they walked between the hundreds of thin columns of mirrored glass. China, reading through a file as she sat upon her throne, gave no indication that she saw their shifting reflections, until she closed the file and leaned back, a single eyebrow arched. "Arbiter Pleasant. Arbiter Cain. To what do I owe the etcetera...?"

"It's been a while, China," Skulduggery said. "We were almost thinking you were avoiding us."

China smiled, and stood. Her dress was an extravagant affair, a low-cut thing of purple and indigo, tight everywhere but the sleeves and studded with beading that slowly changed its colours. Her dark hair was longer than Valkyrie remembered, and arranged in deceptively simple braids.

"Nothing quite so dramatic, I'm afraid," China said, coming down the steps. "I've just been busy. It's not easy running a city and overseeing practically every Sanctuary around the world. Every hour brings fresh challenges. Disputes, power struggles... even violence. And then we get challenges no one could have prepared for, like those poor people from the Leibniz Universe."

"Are they all through?" Valkyrie asked.

"Thankfully," said China, kissing her cheek. "Our technicians shut down the portal device this morning. Astonishing thing, apparently. Discovering how it works will be quite revelatory."

"What's going to happen to the mortals?" Skulduggery asked.

"That has yet to be decided. I wish there were an easy option, I wish we could allow them to assimilate with the mortals of our world, but I'm afraid they pose a substantial risk to our continued safety. Come," she said. "You look like you have things on your minds. I have to rush off to my next meeting, but we can talk as I get ready." She led them away from the throne.

"I've heard the First Bank of Roarhaven is about to open its doors," Skulduggery said. "Congratulations. I know you've been working at this for years."

Valkyrie caught China's thin smile reflected in the mirrors.

"Thank you," China said. "All my hard work is finally coming to fruition."

"I have to admit," Skulduggery continued, "I didn't think Grand Mage Vespers was going to pull it off. The last I heard, the entire enterprise was floundering. Where did he find new investors at this late stage?"

"There will always be people willing to take a chance on something they believe in."

"I heard some of the names of these investors," Skulduggery said. "Familiar names, actually. People with, shall we say, a history."

The wall opened before them, and they stepped on to a raised platform. It slowly began to rise into the darkness.

"You went to Arch-Canon Creed for help, didn't you?" said Skulduggery. "The members of his Church are some of the richest sorcerers in the world. The bank was about to fail before it had even got started, and he convinced his flock to invest and swooped in to the rescue. What did he get in return, I wonder?"

"The Religious Freedom Act," China said, turning to face them. "We'll be announcing it next month, but it's already in effect."

"I see. Can I assume that the Act allows people to practise whatever their faith demands, no matter how murderous it might be?"

"It gives churches autonomy, yes." Something new flickered behind China's eyes. Doubt, maybe. "It makes the grounds of every church sacred, and according to our laws—"

"Sacred ground remains outside everyone's jurisdiction," Skulduggery finished, "Arbiters included. You've given him free rein to do whatever he wants."

"Actually, we're keeping a very close eye on him," China said. "We have insisted that Grand Mage Vespers be allowed to oversee all Church practices. Nothing happens without Vespers' consent."

"And you've got your precious bank."

"Roarhaven needs it if we ever want to reach our true potential."

The platform came to a gentle stop and the doors opened. They walked out into China's chambers, a luxurious apartment on the very top floor of the High Sanctuary.

"Is that why you want to talk to me?" China asked as she walked towards the bedroom. "Finance and investments?"

"Actually, we want to talk to you about Abyssinia."

She opened the clasps of her dress and let it fall just as she walked out of sight. "Go on," she said.

Skulduggery and Valkyrie stayed at the doorway.

"Abyssinia has spent the last seven months searching for her son," Skulduggery said. "A man named Caisson. He, in turn, has spent the last few hundred years being experimented on at Serafina's pleasure. Last night, we believe mother and son were reunited."

There was no answer from the bedroom.

Irritated, Valkyrie walked in. China stood with her back to her, looking at clothes in her vast wardrobe.

"Caisson is the King of the Darklands," Valkyrie said, "the one in the Darkly Prophecy. Abyssinia's father was the Unnamed. China, this is serious, and Skulduggery and I are the only people investigating. We need Cleavers. We need you."

China turned. Her face wore a slack expression Valkyrie had never seen before. Unguarded. "He's still alive," she said softly.

Valkyrie frowned. "Who is? What?"

China stood taller, became more alert. She pulled an outfit from the wardrobe, threw it on the bed, began to dress. "When the Diablerie teamed up with the Dead Men," she said, "were you told about this?"

"Yes," said Valkyrie. "About ten years after Vile betrayed Abyssinia, she turned up alive. Started killing people on both sides of the war. The Diablerie and the Dead Men decided to co-operate, tracked her down and killed her."

"We killed her *eventually*," said China, pulling on trousers, "after battling her for days. She had somehow become extraordinarily powerful in the intervening years. During the course of this battle, I became separated from the others. I didn't stand a chance against her alone. But she didn't kill me. I suppose, in our way, we had been friends. So we talked."

"About what?"

China buttoned her top. "Her son. I knew her well enough to recognise genuine love when I saw it. She may have been able to withstand our attacks, and maybe even defeat us, but the boy was vulnerable. I offered her a chance to spare his life."

"How?"

"By sacrificing hers," said China. "She would allow herself to die, and her son would live. A fair trade, I thought. Abyssinia, being Abyssinia, had a condition."

"Which was? China? What was the condition?"

China looked at her. "That I raise the boy in secret," she said.

Valkyrie stared. Skulduggery walked into the room behind her.

China continued. "Naturally, if I'd had any choice in the matter, I would have laughed and walked away, but my life was being threatened, so I assured her that it would be an honour to care for her child. I miraculously escaped her clutches, she told the boy what was about to happen, and he allowed himself to be captured."

"After which," Valkyrie said, "Abyssinia surrendered and Skulduggery cut out her heart."

"And I took Caisson in," China said. "I passed him off as my servant's child, but I was the one who raised him."

"I've never pictured you as a mother," Valkyrie said as China put on her shoes.

"I can be nurturing. I nurtured you when we first met, didn't I?"

"You forced me to do nothing when Serpine was torturing Skulduggery."

"I meant after that. I'm sure there were moments of nurturing."

"You might be thinking of someone else."

"Perhaps," said China.

"Did Abyssinia tell you who his father was?" Skulduggery asked.

China looked at him. "She said it was Lord Vile. But I never believed it."

The pain from Valkyrie's injury was starting to nag at her, so she took a leaf from her pocket and started chewing. "What kind of a mother were you to Caisson?"

"A wonderful one, I should imagine," China said, crossing to the dresser to change her earrings. "I was educational, informative and succinct."

"All the hallmarks of a great mum."

"Thank you."

"What was he like?" Skulduggery asked.

China paused. "Troubled. I was part of the group that killed Abyssinia, after all, so there was a sustained period of adjustment. Nevertheless, he proved himself a capable young man, so I kept my promise, as dangerous as it was. If Mevolent had known that the son of Abyssinia was in his own castle, he'd have had him killed without even thinking about it. But it was getting harder and harder to stop Caisson from drawing attention to himself – and his hatred of Mevolent was growing. So I took him away. We sneaked out under cover of night. I sent word to my brother, who arranged a meeting with Eachan Meritorious. It was agreed that I would provide the Sanctuaries with vital information in the war against Mevolent, and I would be allowed to return to Ireland – under strict conditions, of course."

"Caisson is why you defected?" Valkyrie asked.

"Essentially."

"Huh. I never would have thought it'd be because of someone... else. Someone that isn't you, you know."

China nodded. "Because I'm so legendarily selfish."

"Well... yeah."

"So it surprises you, to know that I'm capable of sacrificing so much for someone else?"

"It does. I'm actually impressed."

China's smile dropped away. "Don't be," she said. "In this story, I may have come to love the boy, but I revert to my selfish ways eventually."

"What happened after you defected?"

China pulled on a jacket. "Despite my very best efforts, Caisson grew into an angry young man. He hated Mevolent, because he thought Mevolent had forced his father, Lord Vile, to attack his mother, and he hated Skulduggery for subsequently killing her. Sorry about that, Skulduggery."

"Understandable," he responded.

"Mevolent was beyond Caisson's reach for the moment, but Skulduggery proved an easier target. Or so he thought."

Skulduggery tilted his head. "He came after me?"

"And you beat him, easily and emphatically. You almost killed him, in fact."

"When was this?"

"I doubt you'd remember. So many people have tried to kill you over the years. Caisson would undoubtedly have died of his injuries if a woman named Solace hadn't discovered him on my doorstep and nursed him back to health. They fell in love."

"How sweet," said Valkyrie.

China walked out of the bedroom. They followed. "For a long time, I thought the love they shared was enough to heal them both. Not of physical wounds, but the invisible wounds we all carry around with us. Solace was, in her own way, as

215

troubled as Caisson. She had been one of Serafina's handmaidens before fleeing that wretched place. I actually thought they had found their peace within each other. Almost a hundred and sixty years went by. I didn't see much of either of them. And then another one of Serafina's handmaidens happened to glimpse Solace on a quiet street. A chance encounter that changed everything."

"They grabbed her?" Valkyrie asked.

China nodded. "And took her back to Mevolent's castle, where Serafina planned to torture her for her disobedience. Serafina has a long memory, and does so love to torture."

"And Caisson went after them."

"Of course. He'd spent his teenage years in that castle – he knew every secret it possessed. He sneaked in, intent on his mission to rescue his lady love... but I don't think he could resist the opportunity when it presented itself."

"What opportunity?" Valkyrie asked, frowning.

"Caisson killed Mevolent," Skulduggery said.

"He did," said China. "Stabbed him repeatedly to weaken him, and then drained his life force. Then he rescued Solace and they returned home. A happy ending... until Serafina came knocking on my door, full of questions and accusations. She thought it was Solace who had somehow killed Mevolent, you see, and demanded to know where to find her. I told her the truth, however, that it had been Caisson who'd done the dreadful deed, and I told her where to find him."

"You... you betrayed him?" Valkyrie said.

"I warned you that I would revert to my selfish ways."

"But you raised him like he was your own child."

"But he wasn't my child," China said. "Remember that." She looked at her watch. "I have to go."

She walked by them. Skulduggery had his head down, as still as a statue.

He looked up suddenly. "You're the Supreme Mage," he said.

"You don't have to worry about being late for an appointment. Who are you meeting that's so important?"

China smiled coldly. "It was so nice to see you both again," she said. "Do keep me updated, won't you? And, if you need any help, just ask." The doors slid open silently and China stepped on to the platform and turned. "You can let yourselves out," she said. The doors closed.

Valkyrie and Skulduggery looked at each other.

"Say it," she said.

"You say it."

"She's changed."

"Yes, she has."

They walked out on to the balcony, and Skulduggery took Valkyrie in his arms and they dropped slowly down the side of the building to the street far below.

"I'm just thinking," Valkyrie said, her head resting on his shoulder.

"I did recommend more of that."

"There is a possibility, as weird and unlikely as it may be, that you and China are kind of..."

"Parents," he finished.

"Yes. She may not be Caisson's mother, but you could definitely say she's his stepmother. A wicked stepmother, which I think would surprise no one. Does this change anything in how we go forward?"

"It might," Skulduggery replied. "China's emotional reserves may never have been overflowing, but they do exist. Her connection to Caisson may affect her decisions in this matter."

"So we can't rely on her."

"If we ever could."

"And what about you? What about your connection?"

"So we're believing Abyssinia now, are we?"

"No, not believing her. But not *not* believing her, either."

"I don't know, Valkyrie. I don't know what to think."

They touched down on the street. Passers-by gave them guarded looks as they veered round them. "Go home," he said. "Spend time with your sister. Tell her I said hello."

"What are you going to do?"

"Temper has promised me an update on the preliminary examination of the portal device."

"Ooh," Valkyrie said, "that sounds like fun."

"I know you're being sarcastic, but I'm quite looking forward to it."

"Such a nerd."

"That's why you love me."

She shrugged as she walked off. "One of the reasons."

38

It wasn't easy entertaining a seven-year-old. For one thing, Alice flitted from activity to activity like a bright-eyed butterfly. At first, she seemed content to watch TV, but quickly grew bored. Then she wanted to play a game on her tablet. After that, she wanted Omen to play a game on her tablet, and laughed as he tried to figure out what the rules were, what the controls were, and what the point was.

Eventually, she asked him if he wanted her to put on a show. She sang two Disney songs, one of them twice, then bits and pieces of Ed Sheeran and a song Omen didn't know. It was cute, but got boring very fast.

When Alice swung her arms wide and bowed dramatically, Omen clapped.

"Well done!" he said. "That was brilliant!"

"Thank you," said Alice, nodding at his wisdom. "What was your favourite part?"

"The bit at the start, and then the middle, and that bit at the end. It was all great, it really—"

"Do you want to play hide-and-seek?"

"Um, sure."

"Do you know how to play?"

"I do."

"Did you used to play hide-and-seek when you were small?"

"I did, yes, with my brother."

"Is your brother older or younger than you?"

"He's older, but only by a few minutes."

"My sister is eighteen years older than me."

"I know."

"Is my sister your girlfriend?"

Omen laughed. "No. She's much older than me, too."

"Do you have a girlfriend?"

He thought about it. "I think so."

"What's her name?"

"Aurnia. She's very nice."

"Do you love her?"

"Ha. Not yet."

"How can she be your girlfriend if you don't love her?"

"Because I like her a lot."

Alice nodded. This answer satisfied her.

"So do you want to play hide-and-seek?" Omen asked.

"No," she said.

"Do you want me to, uh, read you a story or something?"

"Yes."

"Do you have any books?"

"We keep half of my books in my bedroom – they're for bedtime stories – and half in that bookshelf. They're for daytime reading."

"Well, OK," Omen said, wandering over to the bookcase and hunkering down. "What one do you want? *Jack's Amazing Shadow*? *Little Legends*? Alice? Which book would you...?"

Alice didn't answer. She was staring out of the back window.

"Alice? What are you doing?"

She pointed. "There was a man there."

Omen straightened up. "Where?"

"Outside the window," she said. "He was looking in."

Fear's cold fingers immediately started to tap their way down Omen's spine. He went to the window. "What did he look like?"

"He was old," said Alice.

"Have you seen him before?"

She nodded, and he relaxed.

"Oh, good," he said. "Where have you seen him before?"

She pointed behind her. "At that window over there."

The fear came back.

It was probably nothing. It was probably a neighbour, or maybe someone had broken down and needed to call a tow truck, and they hadn't heard that everyone had mobile phones these days so there was no reason to leave their car.

He stepped into the hall and froze.

The front door was open.

Omen backed away. "Alice," he said softly. "Alice, come here."

She wandered over and he took her hand and knelt down. "I want you to be very quiet," he whispered. "Can you be very quiet for me?"

She nodded earnestly.

He took out his phone.

"This is a surprise."

Omen cried out and whirled round.

Cadaverous Gant stood by the stairs.

"I was expecting parents," Cadaverous said, "feeble mortal minds that I could command to deliver my message. Instead, I have the lesser of the Darkly brothers. I can't command *you*, can I? But what do you do when life hands you lemons? You make lemonade."

"What do you want with me?"

"I don't want you, little boy. I want her." He smiled at Alice. "Hello there."

Omen pulled Alice behind him. "You're making a mistake," he said. "A huge mistake."

Cadaverous smiled. "You see, it's that kind of thinking that meant this has never happened before. Until now, no one bothered to follow Valkyrie home. No one bothered to find out where she lived, who her parents were, if she had any cute and adorable siblings. At first, I fully expect it was because to strike at Valkyrie Cain would be to incur the wrath of Skulduggery Pleasant. But that changed, I think, and suddenly it was the wrath of Valkyrie herself that frightened people off.

"But I'm not scared of Miss Cain, and I'm not scared of the skeleton. I'm not scared of anyone, now that I come to think about it. Not even Abyssinia – not any more."

"Why do you want her? She's only a kid."

"There's no need for you to worry about the whys and wherefores. I was going to use her parents to deliver the message, but I can just as easily use you. Your corpse will make it even more dramatic, I daresay."

Omen darted to the fireplace, grabbed the poker, held it before him in both hands. "Stay away."

"I'm not one for fisticuffs, little Darkly, but we both know that I'm strong enough and fast enough to whip that poker out of your hands before you can swing it. So, please, have a little dignity in your final moments."

"Alice," said Omen, "when I tell you to, you run to the neighbours, OK?"

Out of the corner of his eye, Omen saw Alice nodding.

"Run!" Omen yelled, and launched himself at Cadaverous.

The old man batted the poker away and then slapped Omen so hard he spun and collapsed, his thoughts falling silent for a moment.

Dimly aware of Cadaverous speaking, when he blinked and looked up again, Alice was walking calmly back into the room.

"Good girl," said Cadaverous. "Don't be scared, Alice Edgley. Don't panic. Don't try to run."

Omen looked around for the poker, but couldn't find it. He clicked his fingers, doing his best to summon a flame into his hand, but all he did was attract Cadaverous's attention.

"Did you ever think, little Darkly, that perhaps magic just isn't for you?"

Omen got to his feet. Cadaverous walked towards him, backing Omen into the corner.

"You don't have to kill me," Omen said.

"I'll make it quick."

"You can tie me up or lock me away somewhere."

"Hush now," Cadaverous told him, "and come here."

"Please don't kill me."

Omen's back hit the wall. Tears ran down his face. Cadaverous reached for him – and stopped.

They stood there, frozen, while Cadaverous considered his options.

"I'm not going to kill you," he said suddenly. "I was going to kill you. I still might. But I probably won't. It might be more fun for Cain to come back and listen to your pathetic excuses." He held out his hand. "Phone."

Omen wiped his eyes. "Sorry?"

"Your phone, boy," Cadaverous said. "Give it to me."

Omen passed it over. Cadaverous dropped it and slammed his heel into it three times. Then he took another phone out of his pocket and tossed it to Omen.

"There is one number in that phone," he said. "When Cain gets back, tell her to call it. When is she due home?"

"Uh, half an hour, maybe."

"Perfect. You are to wait here. You are not to call anyone or alert anyone. You are not to step outside that door. Do you understand me?"

"Yes."

"If the skeleton comes in with her, make an excuse. Do not let Skulduggery Pleasant know what is going on. Alice's life will depend on it."

"OK. I promise."

"Sit on the couch there, like a good little boy. Sit and wait."

Then he was gone, and Alice was gone with him.

39

Like shadows, they drifted through the Dark Cathedral.

Or at least, Tanith did. She was magnificent to watch. She became the darkness, melted into it. She walked along walls and ceilings. She vanished when she had to.

Sebastian was less like a shadow, more like someone wearing a leather suit that creaked when he moved, with an awkward mask that curtailed a good deal of his peripheral vision. He also didn't quite melt into the darkness so much as lunge desperately. But he managed not to be seen, which was the main thing.

Tanith had another advantage over him – she knew where she was going, and led him straight to the display area. Set out in a large room like a museum, there were all manner of exhibits and books and stuff he didn't care about – and in the middle of it all was the scythe, turning slowly within a glass case and held aloft by the small sigils carved into the base. Sebastian reached for it, and Tanith smacked her staff against his hand.

"What is wrong with you?" she asked. "Are you actually trying to get us caught?"

He narrowed his eyes. "You think it's rigged to an alarm?"

"Yes, Sebastian, I do."

"Um... would you know how to dismantle it?"

She looked at him like he was an idiot. "Why did you come

here, why are you doing this, if you're not prepared for exactly this sort of thing? Are you always this ill-equipped?"

"Not always," Sebastian said.

Tanith sighed, and passed her hand over the lock. It clicked open.

"Cool," Sebastian said, and once again Tanith hit him with the staff.

"Ow," he said.

"I've unlocked it," she told him, "but the alarm is still active."

"Oh."

"You know, I'm not entirely convinced that you're cut out for this line of work," she said. "You are, and I have refrained from using these words until right this second, incredibly incompetent."

"Bit harsh."

"Not really. I know you think you have a mission, but I sincerely believe that you'd be better leaving it to someone else."

Beneath his mask, Sebastian smiled. "I wish I could, Tanith. I really do. But no one else can see what's going on, and no one else understands what has to be done."

"Then you should really just think about quitting, because you're going to get yourself killed."

"Maybe. But I have to try."

"What are you after, Sebastian? Why are you doing this?"

"The world needs help."

"Surely there are more qualified people to provide that help."

"You'd think so, wouldn't you?" He examined the glass case. "Do you think we could cut the wires or something?"

"The alarm isn't electronic," Tanith said. "See that sigil, in the corner? The little one? The moment the scythe is touched, that little sigil will start screaming like nothing you've ever heard."

"Can you disable it?"

"I don't know a whole lot about sigils."

"Pity China Sorrows isn't here."

"That would be incredibly handy," Tanith murmured. "Your

only chance, as far as I can see, is to grab it and run as fast as you can."

Sebastian peered at her. "That's it? Your advice is to grab it and run?"

"As fast as you can, because the Cathedral Guards will be right on your heels. You have a way out?"

Sebastian nodded.

"Then I'd do some warm-up exercises and get ready to sprint."

"Huh," he said. "This heist plan is not as intricate as I'd been hoping."

"Oh, don't worry, I'm going to provide a distraction," Tanith said. "I probably won't be able to get to my target without witnesses, so, when I strike, the alarm will be raised. That's your cue."

"And do *you* have a way out?"

"Of course."

"So, what, I wait here until the assassination?"

"Unless you want to help me kill someone."

"Not really."

"No offence, but I wouldn't have accepted your help even if you'd offered it. Find somewhere to hide, Sebastian. You'll know when my target is dead." She started to walk away.

"Hey, Tanith? Thank you."

She turned, looked back. "I don't know what your mission is, but I hope it works out for you."

"Same here. I mean, y'know, good luck killing the person. I'm sure they deserve it."

"If anyone deserves it," said Tanith, "it's China Sorrows."

40

Valkyrie pulled up outside her parents' home, struggling to wrench her mind away from thoughts of Abyssinia and Caisson and all this history that was suddenly starting to infect the present. So many secrets. So many hidden lives. She was no stranger to that, of course, but she had to keep it separate, had to keep it away from Alice.

Valkyrie tried smiling. Tried again. On the third attempt, it took.

She got out, entered the house.

"Hey," she called. The house was quiet. Omen sat alone in the living room. "Thanks for this," she said, walking in. "Seriously. Was she any trouble?"

Omen stood. It was pretty clear he'd been crying.

"What's wrong?" she asked. Then she looked around. "Where's Alice?"

"He took her," Omen said.

Valkyrie took a step forward. "What?"

He hesitated before answering. "Cadaverous Gant."

She was on him before he'd finished speaking, her hands curling into his shirt, forcing him back, pinning him to the wall. "*What?*"

"I'm so sorry," Omen said, crying again. "He was going to kill me. He said I've to give you this."

He had a phone in his hand. She released him, grabbed the

phone. The screen lit up. There was one number, ready to be dialled. She hit the button and waited.

"Hello, Valkyrie," said Cadaverous.

"Bring her back," Valkyrie said, walking away from Omen. "I'll do whatever you want, just don't hurt her, and bring her back."

"You'll be wanting to shut up now," Cadaverous said. "I hear one word from you that isn't an answer to a question, and I'll end this right now by killing her. Is that understood, you arrogant brat?"

She stiffened. "Yes."

"For the duration of this phone call you will refer to me as sir. Is that understood?"

"Yes, sir."

"That's much better. As you have probably guessed, I took your sister in order to lead you into a trap."

"You don't have to lead me anywhere. I will willingly go wherever—"

"I didn't ask a question."

Valkyrie froze. "Sorry," she said.

"Sorry what?"

"Sorry, sir."

"OK," Cadaverous said. "That's your first and only warning. You do that again and I'll kill her and throw her body in a ditch. We're going to play a little game, Valkyrie. Do you like games? I hope you do. This is a fun game. I call it Let's Save Alice. The objective is simple. You've got to find her before midnight. That's it. The rules are: you have to do this alone. Omen didn't factor into my plans, but let's face it – even if you take him with you, you're still basically alone. So, when this call ends, you leave your own phone where it is, you leave those little shock sticks of yours behind, you don't tell anyone – especially not the skeleton – and you and the Darkly boy get in your car and you drive. Are you with me so far?"

"Yes, sir."

"Good. I'm not going to tell you where your sister is – that's for you to figure out. Your first stop will be to see a man called Palter. He's waiting at The Iron Bar, in Roarhaven. He'll let you know what you have to do once you get there. Is that clear?"

"Yes, sir."

"If I find out that you are cheating, or if you fail to retrieve her by midnight, your sister dies. What time is it, brat?"

Valkyrie checked her watch. "It's almost six, sir."

"Then you have just over six hours. We'll be waiting."

He hung up. She stared at the phone.

"I'm so sorry," Omen said.

Valkyrie turned. She'd forgotten he was there. "Did he say anything? Anything about where he was taking her or what he was going to do? Anything at all?"

"No," Omen said. "He just told me not to call anyone. He said Alice's life depends on it."

"Yeah, I got that part."

"I'm so sorry. I let him take her. I didn't even fight him."

"He would have killed you." Valkyrie pulled her keys from her pocket. "OK, come on."

She stalked out of the house. He followed.

"I'm coming with you?"

"You're part of this now," she said. "Close the front door, then get in."

She got in. Started the engine. Her hands gripped the wheel. Her heart was cold and pounding. She wasn't sure if she was thinking clearly.

Omen got in beside her. She pulled out on to the road as he was buckling his belt.

"Was she scared?" Valkyrie asked.

"I don't think she knew what was going on," Omen said. "He was controlling her, telling her not to be afraid and to keep calm."

She nodded. That was good. The idea of her sister being out there, alone and terrified, would have been too much for her to take right now.

41

He followed Tanith at a distance, trying to figure out the best way to go about what he had to do. His mind, never the best place to go for ideas, remained stubbornly blank.

He watched Tanith crouch by a balcony. Making sure he wasn't seen, Sebastian scurried to the nearest curve of the same balcony and looked over. Walking below and deep in conversation was the Arch-Canon, Damocles Creed. Beside him was China Sorrows.

Sebastian started to creep round the curve.

When he came to the broadest part, he could see Tanith again, her back to him. She was focused on Creed and China, preparing to vault over the balcony.

He didn't want to do this. He really didn't want to do this.

He charged.

Tanith heard him and turned, saw him coming, made a face, gestured for him to go away.

He stopped charging because it was stupid, and instead walked up to her. She straightened, and moved away from the balcony.

"What the hell are you doing?" she whispered.

"I... I'm sorry, Tanith," he answered, speaking softly. "I can't let you kill her."

Tanith observed him coolly.

"I understand that you have your reasons," he continued. "I

get that, I do. But I need China to stay alive. I can't... I can't have the disruption that her death would bring. Do you see? For my plan to work out how I need it to, she has to stay alive. I'm so sorry."

"You think you're going to stop me?" Tanith asked.

"I'm hoping you'll just... walk away."

"And if I don't?"

He swallowed. "Then I'll have to do my best to stop you."

Tanith stepped closer. "Do you have any idea what she's done? Any idea, at all, about the people she's had killed? She was bad enough before she crowned herself Supreme Mage, but now that she has actual power? She's a monster, Sebastian – and you want to save her?"

"I can't let you kill her."

Tanith sighed, and shook her head. "Fine," she said, laying her staff on the ground. "Stop me."

Sebastian winced. "I am really, really sorry about this."

"Whatever."

He feinted low and went high and she hit him, square in the solar plexus. His suit did a decent job of absorbing the punch, but it still forced some of the wind from his lungs.

He lunged and she caught his wrist, twisted his arm, led him one way and then flipped him on to his back.

He got to his knees and grabbed for her leg, but she moved sideways and kicked him and he went tumbling.

Sebastian got up and ran at her. At first, it looked like she was going to dodge, but then she rammed her elbow into his chest, hit him a few times about the head and caught him with another kick that sent him flying.

He came to a rolling stop, and below them he heard a door close.

Tanith's eyes widened, and she hurried to the balcony and looked over. Sebastian watched her stiffen with fury, and she stalked over, standing above him.

"You made me miss my target," she said.

"I'm sorry, but I couldn't let you—"

"Who are you to stop me from doing anything? You'd have been hauled off in shackles if it wasn't for me. You'd have been interrogated and tortured. That stupid mask of yours would have been cut from your face, and, when they were done with you, they'd have dumped your body in a shallow grave somewhere. I saved your life, you little toad."

"I need China to stay alive."

"She's a tyrant."

"I'm sorry. I am."

"I should kill you for what you've done."

"Are you going to?"

She looked so mad that he was actually surprised when she shook her head. "This was my chance," she said. "China never leaves the High Sanctuary."

"You know there was no guarantee you'd have actually been able to kill her, right? She's pretty powerful. Plus, you'd have had to deal with Creed as well, and he's... formidable."

"You know him?"

"We've crossed paths."

Tanith took a moment, and shook her head. "You owe me, Sebastian Tao."

"I know."

"Go on," she said, pulling him up. "Go back and grab the scythe and get out of here."

"Thank you for your help. Seriously."

"I wish I hadn't met you."

"Yeah."

She walked over to the balcony and jumped it as easily as Sebastian would take a breath, and she was gone.

He hurried back the way he'd come. As he moved, he sent Bennet and Tantalus a message, telling them to meet him at the tunnel. He put his phone away when he reached the glass case.

He prepared himself, going over the escape route in his head. And then he grabbed the scythe.

The alarm split the air and he was off, sprinting through corridors, barging past clerics, staying ahead of the Cathedral Guards who gave chase. He lost them, took the stairs down, his legs burning. He found Tantalus in the tunnel, waving him on.

He ran in and Tantalus pulled the lever and the wall closed, sealing them in darkness.

Sebastian doubled over and fought to get his breath back.

"Is that it?" Tantalus asked, summoning a flame into his hand. "Let me see."

Sebastian let him take the scythe, and straightened. He took out his torch, swung it around. "Where's... Bennet?"

"I sent him on ahead," Tantalus said, examining the blade. "There was no point in both of us risking our lives to wait for you."

Sebastian didn't say it, but that little bit of nobility surprised him. Tantalus guessed what he was thinking. "I don't like it that we don't know your name or your face," he said. "But you're one of us, and we look out for each other."

"Thank you."

"But I still don't like you."

"Understood."

"At all."

"Gotcha."

"OK," Tantalus said. "This seems to be the genuine article." He hesitated, then handed it back.

"I've got a very good reason for hiding my identity, you know," Sebastian said, his breathing under control. "I can only imagine how hard it must be to trust me, but it will all make sense eventually. I promise."

"Trust isn't easy," said Tantalus. "Especially for us. Once most people find out that we worship Darquesse, they... they're quick to judge."

"I get that."

"But you've come through for us," Tantalus continued. "Tracking Darquesse through dimensions is your idea. And when you arrive back with the scythe, when Bennet and I both failed to find it... Any remaining doubts will be swept away."

"I hope so."

"You'll establish yourself as a guiding light. They'll probably want you to lead us."

"I'm no leader."

"What's that line, about how some people are born great, while others have greatness thrust upon them?"

"I think that's it, yeah."

"That's you. The reluctant leader."

Sebastian shone the torch at Tantalus, about to reassure him that he had no intention of replacing him, and the light glinted off the knife. He tried dodging but Tantalus grabbed him, jabbed the blade at his belly. Sebastian felt the sharpness through his clothes, but they were tough and the blade didn't get through. He dropped the scythe and the torch, the light spinning crazily across the ground, and seized Tantalus's wrist with both hands and they tripped over each other. Sebastian fell with Tantalus on top.

They rolled into darkness, rolled back into light. All those years Sebastian had trained for this and all he could do was hold Tantalus's knife hand away from him. If that blade cut through his suit, his mission would be over, followed quickly by his life.

Sebastian jerked his head up, the point of his beak stabbing Tantalus in the eye. Tantalus cried out and Sebastian heaved, turned them over, one hand pinning Tantalus's knife hand to the ground while he punched with the other. His fist twisted with the first impact, but he hissed against the pain and kept going.

Finally, Tantalus dropped the knife, and Sebastian swiped it away, then fell back as Tantalus scrambled up.

Sebastian grabbed the torch and straightened up. "What the hell, man?"

Tantalus, one eye squeezed shut, had both hands pressed to his nose as blood ran between his fingers. "I'll tell the others of this! They'll know what you've done!"

"You attacked me with a knife, you nutball!"

Tantalus shook his head. "You've got no witnesses. And I didn't even do that."

"Just stop, all right?" said Sebastian. "You can't pretend you didn't attack me when the attack fails. That's not how this works. I know what you did and you know what you did."

"You attacked me for no reason."

"There's only the two of us here! Why are you lying about this?"

"You're the one who's lying."

"You actually tried to kill me! Why? Because I'd be the one bringing back the scythe?"

Tantalus shook his head again.

"Are you so insecure? Are you so lonely?"

Tantalus pointed a trembling finger. "You arrive with your stupid mask and your stupid 'Call me the Plague Doctor', and all your plans and direction, and what am I supposed to do? This is my group! I started it! I'm not going to let you take that away from me! When the others hear what you've done, that you attacked me for no reason, they're going to kick you out."

"You're insane, you know that? You're deluded."

"I... I cast you out."

"What?"

"From the group. As leader, I cast you out. You're gone. You're not allowed to come to our meetings any more."

"Tantalus, stop embarrassing yourself."

"No."

Sebastian sighed, and rubbed his wrist. He was afraid he might have sprained it. "Fine. Do what you like. You're an idiot." He bent to retrieve the scythe.

"Leave that," Tantalus said.

Sebastian paused, then slowly picked it up. "I found it. I'm taking it."

"Give it to me."

"Not a chance. What, are you going to attack me again? That didn't work out too well for you last time, did it?"

Tantalus clicked his fingers, summoning another flame.

"My suit's fire-resistant," Sebastian said. "Do yourself a favour – walk away. We'll each give our version of events to the others, and see who they believe. That sound good to you?"

Tantalus looked around, his eyes settling on the knife.

"Don't do it," Sebastian said. "Dude, seriously, don't. I've got a scythe."

"It's been in a glass case for years."

"It's a Cleaver blade. They stay sharp forever. Everyone knows that."

"I don't."

"Then you're the only person who doesn't. It's woven razor."

Tantalus took a step towards the knife.

Sebastian sighed. "You know what? This is the second fight I've been in today, and I've had enough. I'm taking the scythe, and I'm going home." He turned away from Tantalus, and started running.

42

It was dark by the time they got to Roarhaven, and they wasted twenty minutes driving around before they found The Iron Bar. Omen sat very quietly while Valkyrie cursed. She was scary when she was angry, and right now she was raging. And, of course, it was all his fault.

He hadn't done anything. He'd just let Cadaverous take Alice. He'd allowed it to happen without even putting up anything remotely resembling a fight.

No one else would have done that. Auger would have already saved the day by now.

"Finally!" Valkyrie said, yanking the wheel to the left. The car mounted the pavement and she jumped out, ignoring the angry beeps of the cars behind. Omen reached over, turned off the engine and took the keys, then ran after her into the pub.

"Palter," she was saying loudly. "I'm looking for Palter."

It was a small place, with a stage in the corner that was obviously never used and a handful of surly patrons. Omen counted eight, plus the bartender.

"Palter!" Valkyrie said again.

"Don't know anyone of that name," the bartender told her, talking slowly. "Maybe you should run along home before someone recognises you."

Valkyrie walked up to him. "I don't have time for this. Palter. Where is he?"

The bartender chuckled without humour. "I swear I don't know who you might be talking about." He raised his voice. "Anyone here know anyone by the name of... Palder? Walter? What was it again?"

Valkyrie put one hand on the bar and sprang over it.

"Hey," the bartender said, "you can't come back here!"

She hit him. It whipped his head round and he stumbled back, broke a few glasses. She kicked him in the shin and he howled, and she grabbed him, smashed his head into the fridge. The bottles inside were still rattling as he collapsed.

"Palter!" she called.

Out of the corner of his eye Omen saw a hand light up. He was about to shout a warning, but Valkyrie was already ducking the stream of energy that smashed the mirror behind her. She threw a bolt of white lightning in return, caught the guy in the chest, sent him flying backwards.

It all went to hell after that.

Valkyrie sprang back over the bar. Omen watched as fists flew and Valkyrie caught them, dodged them, blocked them or got hit by them. She threw her own in return, along with some elbows, along with some headbutts. There was a tussle, and they were on the ground, and she snarled and snapped and bit and they yelped and cried out and gave way, one by one, falling while she kept going, a whirlwind of rage. She smashed and cracked and bashed them. She sent them to the floor, to the wall, sent them over the bar.

The last one ran to his coat, tried pulling a gun from one of the pockets. Omen charged at him, got shoved away, hit a broken bar stool and fell even as Valkyrie blasted the guy and he went down, the gun spinning across the floor.

"Palter!" Valkyrie screamed. "Palter!"

"I'm Palter," said a man with long hair, stepping in through the door, frowning at the carnage. "I'm Palter Grey. Sorry I'm late. The traffic was... What happened here?"

Valkyrie grabbed him, pinned him against the wall. He dropped the bag he was holding and looked terrified.

"Where's my sister?" she snarled.

"I don't know anything about a sister!" he said. "I was just... Listen, I think there's been a misunderstanding, OK? I'm just here because this old guy paid me! I don't even know his name!"

Omen scrambled up and hurried over. Keeping his voice soft, he said to Valkyrie, "He's who we came here to see. Maybe you should let him speak."

Valkyrie took a moment, and stepped back. "Gant," she said. "The guy who paid you is Cadaverous Gant."

Palter gave a cautious shrug. "Cool. You're Valkyrie Cain, aren't you? I recognise you. You look just like Darquesse."

"What did Cadaverous pay you to do?"

Palter frowned. "He... he didn't tell you? Aw, man... he said he told you. He said you were OK with it."

"OK with what?"

"Um, well..."

Valkyrie stepped closer and he flinched. "I don't have time for a big long thing. When I ask a question, you give me an immediate answer. Got it? What did he pay you to do?"

"I have to carve two sigils into you," Palter said immediately.

"A tattoo?" Valkyrie said, frowning. "You're here to give me a tattoo? What does it do?"

"It... I don't really know how to say this..."

"Better say it quickly."

"I'm really sorry, this isn't how it should go, but... he wants me to carve sigils into your eyes."

Valkyrie stared. "What?"

"I thought you were cool with it."

Omen stepped forward. "He wants you to tattoo her eyelids?"

240

"Not her eyelids. Her eyes."

"Jesus," said Valkyrie.

"I mean, I can do it," Palter said. "You don't have to worry. I'm not going to blind you. They won't interfere with your vision at all, and they won't be visible when they're done."

"What'll they do? The sigils?"

"Um... they'll let him see what you see."

Omen looked at her. "He wants to spy on you."

"It's not, as you can imagine, it's not a very common sigil to carve," Palter said. "A few hundred years ago, they'd be carved into the eyes of convicts released from gaol, so that Sanctuaries could make sure they were staying out of trouble. But these days that's looked on as being a little barbaric, so..."

"Right," Valkyrie said. "Fine. How long will it take?"

Palter frowned. "Not long. Not long at all. About... I don't know, maybe fifteen, twenty minutes. But wait – if you didn't know about this until just now, why would you go through with it?"

"He wants to make sure I don't break the rules. Come on, where do we do this?"

"We just need a chair."

Valkyrie picked one up and sat down. "Let's get it over with."

Palter hesitated, then opened his bag and took out his tools.

"Omen," Valkyrie said, "stand at the door. Make sure nobody comes in."

Omen nodded dumbly and did as he was told. He was glad she'd sent him away. He didn't think he'd have been able to watch something like that.

He wished Auger was here. Auger would know what to do. Or even Never. Never could teleport straight to Skulduggery and Skulduggery would sort this out.

Valkyrie was too close to it. She was panicking too much to think straight. Her love for her sister put her in danger of making a mistake that might cost her or even Alice their lives.

Nobody tried coming into the pub, and by 7.30 it was done. Omen walked back as Palter packed his instruments away. "How are you feeling?"

Valkyrie blinked. "Eyesight's blurry."

"That'll pass," said Palter. "I think."

Omen frowned at him. "You think?"

"I've never done this before."

"But you did it right, didn't you? You haven't damaged her eyes or anything?"

"I didn't damage anything, I promise. I did everything the way I was supposed to. Her eyesight should clear in a few minutes."

Valkyrie stood, and went to the broken mirror behind the bar. "So he can see what I'm seeing now, is that it?"

"Yes," said Palter. "I've already carved a corresponding sigil on to him which will basically receive what you're transmitting. I doubt he'll be watching every single second, though – he has to focus on you in order to see through your eyes."

"But he can't hear us, can he?"

"No," said Palter. "It's visual only."

Valkyrie glared at her reflection, glared right into her own eyes, and Omen knew she was hoping Cadaverous could see the anger boiling behind them.

"This isn't cool," said Palter. "I get the feeling that you're being coerced into all this. Do you want me to call someone? You hang around with the Skeleton Detective, don't you? Want me to call him?"

"Don't call anyone," Valkyrie said.

Something in Palter's bag started beeping.

"Is that a bomb?" Omen said, backing away.

Palter took out a metal box. "It's my money. He's unlocked it remotely. Now I just have to..." He tapped in a code on the keypad and the lid clicked, and he opened it. A thick bundle of cash lay inside. "I don't feel right about taking this."

"Take the money and go back to your life," Valkyrie said. "He didn't say anything, did he? About where I have to go next? About where my sister might be?"

"He didn't mention anything about that, sorry." Palter took out the cash, shoved it in his pocket – then frowned, rubbing his thumb and forefinger together like he was wiping off residue. "Aw, man," he mumbled, and collapsed.

Omen stared.

Valkyrie hurried over, checked Palter's pulse. "He's dead," she said. "Money must have been poisoned."

"Oh my God."

The phone rang. Valkyrie took it out of her pocket. "I'm here," she said. "Give me my sister."

She paced away from Omen, and stopped.

"Sir," she said, struggling to be polite. "Yes, sir. Yes." Another pause. A longer one. "What? You can't... I can't do that."

She looked round, locked eyes with Omen. He didn't say anything.

"Yes, sir," she said, then hung up.

"Valkyrie?" Omen said.

"Stay here," she responded, and walked quickly into the gents' toilet.

43

It reeked in there.

Valkyrie went straight to the sink, gripped the sides, stared at her reflection in the water-flecked mirror. Cadaverous was watching, she knew he was. She snarled at him, then looked down, and focused.

She closed her eyes, controlled her breathing, reached out with her mind. The world was a mass of grey, but there was a single light shining in the gloom and that's where she sent her thoughts. Then she felt it – an acknowledgement.

She opened her eyes again. Kept staring down at the sink. At the filthy plughole.

"Ow," Kes said from behind her. "What did you do?"

"I called you," said Valkyrie. "I wasn't sure if I could do it."

"Well, don't do it again – my head is splitting. What the hell do you want? Jesus, are we in the men's toilets? This place is disgusting."

"Cadaverous Gant took Alice."

A moment. "Our Alice?"

"My Alice," Valkyrie said. Then, "Our Alice, yes."

"Let's go get her back," Kes said, urgency biting into her words. "Where is she?"

"I don't know. Not yet. Omen's with me."

"Why? The kid's useless."

"Cadaverous told me to bring him. Now he... Now he wants me to kill him."

"What?"

Valkyrie struggled to keep her voice down. "In order to get to Alice, Cadaverous wants me to kill Omen."

"Are you going to?"

"Of course not. That's why I called you."

"Why aren't you looking at me?"

"He can see what I see."

"What?"

"He had a guy tattoo my eyes," Valkyrie said. "He sees what I see. He wants to watch me shoot and kill Omen."

"That's impressively sick. So what can I do?"

Valkyrie didn't know. She was making this up as she went along. "Do you think I see you?" she asked. "Like, do you actually think I'm seeing you physically?"

"Yes," said Kes. "That's how seeing things works."

"But no one else can see you."

"Yeah, because no one else is tuned to my frequency. And you can only see me when I want you to see me."

"But am I seeing you through my eyes," Valkyrie said, "or am I seeing you with my mind?"

Kes hesitated. "Ah."

"If I'm seeing you with my mind, then Cadaverous won't be able to see you."

Kes moved behind her, like she was pacing. "I don't know, Valkyrie. I don't know how this works. It might be a mind thing, it might be an eye thing, or it might be both. Why? What's your plan?"

"If Cadaverous can't see you," said Valkyrie, "then you can stand in front of Omen when I shoot him."

"What good will that do? The bullet will just pass through me."

"Not if you catch it."

245

Kes went quiet for a moment. "Oh my God," she said. "You want to shoot me."

"You can heal yourself."

"You want to actually shoot me."

"But you'll survive. Omen wouldn't."

"I've just teleported here, and now you want me to use my weak reserves of power to become tangible, and then you want to shoot me."

"Yes."

"No."

"Kes—"

"No way in hell."

"He's going to kill Alice unless I do this."

"Then do it," said Kes. "Shoot Omen. Kill him. It's not like anyone's really going to miss him when he's gone."

Valkyrie clenched her fists. "I'm not going to murder an innocent boy."

"But you're fine with murdering me?"

"You can heal yourself."

"You *think*. We don't know that I'll be able to. I can't even remain tangible for more than a few seconds. Besides, so what? Say I do stand there like an idiot and you shoot me instead of Omen – what then? Have you had a chance to discuss this wonderful plan with him? Does he know that he'll have to fall down and play dead?"

"No," Valkyrie admitted. "You'll have to zap him."

Kes laughed. "Zap him?"

"Like you did with Lethe. When I fire, you zap Omen, make him fall, make him lose consciousness."

"That's more power for me to use, Valkyrie. I'd be stretched thin as it is, just becoming tangible. But healing myself and zapping him? How do you know I wouldn't just fade away afterwards? Your plan is something I might not recover from."

"We don't have a choice."

246

"Yes, we do," Kes said. "Kill Omen."

"I'm not going to do that."

"It's Omen or it's Alice. Pick one."

"It's Omen, it's Alice, or it's you."

Kes laughed without humour. "Wow."

"You can do this."

"You don't know that."

"I do. You're strong enough, and we don't have any more time to talk about it. Please."

"You won't kill Omen, but you will kill me, is that it?"

"I'm willing to risk your life, yes. Just like I'd be willing to risk mine."

"All of this means nothing if Cadaverous can see me."

"I know," Valkyrie said, and turned, looking Kes straight in the eye. "Well, he either sees you right now, or he doesn't."

Kes didn't say anything. Valkyrie held the phone, and waited for it to ring.

When it didn't, she put it back in her pocket. "Please," she said.

Kes folded her arms, and didn't answer.

Valkyrie walked out.

"What do we do now?" Omen asked.

Valkyrie picked up the fallen gun. She checked it was loaded, and turned.

"Uh... Valkyrie?"

"I'm sorry," she said, aiming. "Cadaverous needs me to do this."

"Do what?" Omen said, his face going pale. "You're... you're not going to shoot me, are you? I mean... that'd kill me. You'd be killing me."

"I'm sorry."

He held up his hands. "But, now, wait. I don't understand. Why does he want you to kill me? I can be useful. I can help. I can... I don't know what I can do, but I can do it and you won't have to kill me. Valkyrie, please. You can tie me up. You can tie me up and lock me in a room."

"He's going to kill Alice if I don't do it."

Omen's face crumpled, and tears started to fall. He stayed standing, even though his legs were shaking. "Please don't kill me."

Her hand, the hand that held the gun, was surprisingly steady. She thumbed back the hammer. "This is a test," she said. "If I fail, he'll kill Alice right now and I'll never see her again."

Omen wiped his tears with his sleeve, but more fell. He looked down, his lip trembling. Then he looked up, and nodded. "OK," he said. "Get your sister back."

"What?"

"I'd do it," Omen said, "for my brother. Or I'd want to, at least. Probably wouldn't be brave enough. Probably mess it up. It's my fault anyway. I should have put up more of a fight. She's seven years old and I let him take her."

"This isn't your fault."

"Do it. It's OK. You can do it."

"Thank you, Omen."

He nodded again, and closed his eyes. "I forgive you."

"Why does he have to be so insufferably nice?" Kes muttered, and stepped in front of him, her hands on either side of his head. "Three," she said, "two, one."

Power pulsed from her fingertips and Omen's entire body jerked back as Valkyrie fired, the bullet catching Kes in the back. Omen fell and Kes cried out, twisted, and vanished before she hit the ground.

Valkyrie looked away immediately. A few seconds later, the phone rang.

"I didn't think you had it in you," Cadaverous said.

"He won't be the last person I kill."

Cadaverous chuckled. "So many delightful promises. It really

248

is quite disconcerting, you know, looking at the world through your eyes."

"Where's Alice?"

"Ah-ah, not yet, I'm afraid. You still have miles to go before you sleep, and stops to make along the way."

"No," she said, anger rising. "I killed a boy for you. I murdered for you. Tell me where my sister is and let's finish this."

"It seems that someone is forgetting her manners."

Valkyrie bit her lip. Hard. Then she started again. "I would like to see my sister again as soon as possible," she said. "Please, sir."

"Soon, Valkyrie," Cadaverous said. She could hear the smile in his voice. "But, before that, I'm going to need you to drive to the home of some friends of mine. The address is in the box Palter opened. Turn round. Good girl. See it there? On the floor."

A white card. She picked it up, shoved it in her pocket.

"This is fun," said Cadaverous. "I imagine this is what it's like to play a video game – although this is infinitely more entertaining. And pick up Omen, there's a good girl, and let's get back on the road."

Valkyrie frowned. "Omen's dead."

"And I can't very well have his corpse found at this early stage, can I? The City Guard will discover this scene of carnage and be stumped for a few vital hours. But if we leave Omen here, the skeleton will hear about it and link it to you and me. No, no, it's better to clean up after us as we go. Take him with you, there's a good girl."

44

Temper Fray barged past the jerk in the robes and pushed the doors open. Creed's office, here at the very top of the Dark Cathedral, was just as he'd imagined: bare, functional and a little bit creepy.

There was a desk with a circular window behind it and there were chains on the walls. Actual chains. On the walls.

"Why are there chains on the walls?" he asked.

"You cannot come in here!" the jerk in the robes shrieked. "You are infringing upon—"

"Leave us," said Arch-Canon Damocles Creed, who hadn't even looked up from the papers he was reading.

The jerk whimpered, and backed out, closing the doors after him.

"The walls," said Temper. "Why are there chains on them?"

"They act as a reminder," Creed said.

"A reminder of what?"

"The shackles that bind us."

"It's weird. That's all I'm gonna say about it. It's weird and off-putting. It's weird and off-putting and kinda unsettling. Do you have many visitors up here? I doubt you do. I doubt there are many people who want to come for meetings in the office with all the chains on the walls."

Creed sighed, and finally raised his big bald head. "I had forgotten how much you talked."

"I am a talker."

"What can I do for you, Officer Fray? I am very busy."

"I'd say you are, what with all the hijinks you're getting up to. You got your fingers in some pies, don't you, Damocles?"

Creed's eyes were heavy-lidded, which gave him the air of someone permanently unimpressed. But Temper had been there during Creed's sermons, when those eyes widened so much they threatened to bulge out of his head.

"We're on a first-name basis, are we?" Creed asked. "I can't remember us ever being so informal."

"I'm trying something new," said Temper. "I figured I spent enough time deferring to you when I was one of your mindless little drones that I should give disrespect a shot. You know what? I'm kinda liking it."

"You were never a drone, Temper," Creed said. "You were always one of my favourites." He sat back in the chair, his simple shirt stretched tight across his chest. "But now look at you, standing there in a uniform. Obeying the same rules, enforcing the same laws, bound by the same restrictions... I think you've finally become the mindless drone you feared you'd become."

"Those restrictions you mentioned – they happen to be connected to the Religious Freedom Act?"

"Ah," said Creed, "that's why you're here."

"We were just told about it. Apparently, all religious practices and rituals are now protected."

"The Sanctuaries should never have been able to dictate how any religious order is allowed to worship. The Supreme Mage agrees with me, and we are all the better for it, not just the Church of the Faceless."

"But, as far as I know, the Church of the Faceless is the only religious order to advocate human sacrifice."

"That's a ridiculous accusation."

"I was next on the list to be sacrificed."

"We do not kill."

"The Kith are as good as dead and you know it."

Creed sighed and stood, coming out from behind the desk, reminding Temper of just how massive he was. "The Kith will be first in line to meet the Faceless Ones upon their return. You would deny them this honour?"

"I would."

"Then it is a good thing that you have strayed from the path, Temper. You are unworthy."

"If I hear that's what you're up to – if people start going missing? The Religious Freedom Act won't save you."

Creed lowered his head, his heavy brow throwing a shadow over his eyes. His mouth widened into a smile that creased his face. *There.* That glint of madness.

"Do you know what the Religious Freedom Act means, Temper? What it really means? It means I could kill you right here, with witnesses just outside the door. It means I could tear you apart and have everyone hear your screams – and your colleagues in the City Guard wouldn't be able to arrest me for it, even if they wanted to."

Time slowed, and the space between them turned jagged.

Temper drew his gun and Creed batted it from his hand with surprising speed. Temper hit him – an elbow to the solar plexus that Creed didn't seem to feel – and stepped back to pull his sword. Creed closed his hand round Temper's wrist and squeezed, and Temper's fingers sprang open. The sword dropped and Creed kicked him in the chest and Temper hit the wall, the chains rattling. He rebounded, winded, rage coursing through him, took one step and prepared to unleash – and froze.

Creed's thin smile had never left his face, and now it split, revealing his teeth. "You could kill me if you wanted," he said softly. "Tear me apart. Decorate this room with my innards. But what would it cost you, Officer Fray? Everything? Or more?"

Temper cut off his anger. Starved it of oxygen. He straightened. Adjusted his uniform.

Creed walked back round his desk and sat, resumed reading the papers. "Get out," he said. "And close the door after you."

Temper picked up his weapons and left. He didn't close the door.

He returned to the Vault, that concrete block of a building that housed the City Guard, and changed out of his uniform and into some civilian threads. Skulduggery was waiting for him outside.

"Sorry I'm late," Temper said. "I had a thing to do before my shift ended."

"Take a walk with me," Skulduggery said, and Temper shrugged and fell into step. "Has there been any breakthrough with the portal device?"

"Not yet," said Temper, "but the guy who's in charge of the reverse-engineering is confident he can figure out how it works. A little guy named Forby. Nice enough, if a little weird."

"I heard the portal itself was shut down this morning."

"Yeah. What you may not have heard is that there were another ten thousand mortals waiting on the other side when the button was pushed."

Skulduggery tilted his head. "I was under the impression that they'd all come through."

"I'm afraid you were misled. Mevolent's forces were getting too close, apparently. Rather than risk a confrontation, the device was deactivated and our people pulled out – which left those ten thousand mortals pretty much defenceless."

"China gave that order?"

"I can only assume so."

"Those people will have been slaughtered."

"As Commander Hoc personally reminded me when I brought up that exact point – they ain't our mortals, and it ain't our problem."

"That's the Commander Hoc I know and adore," Skulduggery responded. "So all our hopes lie with this Forby, do they?"

"They do," said Temper, "and I don't envy him having to deliver on everything that's expected of him. If he doesn't figure out how to stop portals like that from opening anywhere at any time, there'll be nothing to prevent Mevolent from attacking. Hell, we could be talking a full-scale global invasion. Skulduggery?"

"Yes?"

"I'm talking invasions and you're barely listening."

"I'll have you know that I was listening to every word you said. But I was also checking on the gentleman who's been following me for the last half-hour."

Without looking round, Temper said, "The guy in the baseball cap or the guy in the green jacket?"

"The gent in the jacket is merely lost. Our baseball-cap-wearing friend is the one we're interested in."

"Are we leading him somewhere?"

"We are," said Skulduggery.

They turned down a side street and waited for the guy in the baseball cap to hurry by. Skulduggery stepped out from behind cover and grabbed him, threw him against the wall. The cap came off. The guy beneath was scruffy and startled.

"Argosy Pelt," Skulduggery said.

Pelt tried to run off and Temper shoved him back. "You know him?"

"I've glanced at his file," Skulduggery said. "He had been incarcerated in Coldheart Prison when Abyssinia took it over."

"For a crime I didn't commit!" Pelt blurted.

"Shut up," said Temper, and frowned at Skulduggery. "Did you glance at the files of all the inmates?"

"Of course."

"How many was that?"

"Seven hundred and thirty-two."

"And you recognised his face from his mugshot?"

"It's a memorable face."

"Is it?"

254

"Look at it."

"I am, but I'm forgetting it even *as* I'm looking at it. Do you remember anything you read in his rap sheet?"

Skulduggery shrugged. "He's been arrested before, multiple times, spent a total of thirty-seven years in various gaols for assault, robbery and murder."

"I never assaulted, robbed or murdered no one!" Pelt screeched.

"He was sentenced to nineteen years in Coldheart for killing a mortal in a bar fight three years ago."

"I'm innocent!" Pelt roared. "I wasn't even in that bar! My reflection did it!"

"And he always says his reflection did it," Skulduggery continued.

"It did!"

"You've been examined by Sensitives, Mr Pelt. They all say you committed those crimes."

"My reflection's got them all fooled!" Pelt roared. "Listen to me, OK? My reflection sneaks out of my mirror at night while I'm sleeping. It goes out and commits crimes. Then it sneaks back into my house and transfers its memories back to me, and that is what the bloody psychics see when they go poking around my head! I'm an innocent man, I tell you!"

"Then why haven't you thrown out the mirror?" Temper asked.

"I can't. The reflection's blackmailing me, see. It's committed worse crimes, and it's got evidence, and if I get rid of the mirror then the evidence will be sent to the Sanctuary and I'll be locked away *forever*."

"That is one hell of a devious reflection you got there, Mr Pelt."

"I know," Pelt said, his eyes brimming with tears. "I used it too much, see, when I was younger. I broke it, and now it's evil. Or, you know, smarter than me."

"Why are you following me, Argosy?" Skulduggery asked. "I'm assuming you were sent because Abyssinia thought I wouldn't recognise you."

Pelt nodded. "I was told to stay at a distance, but keep you in sight. It wasn't easy. I thought I'd lost you, like, at least three times."

"You did," said Skulduggery. "And then you were following the wrong man for ten minutes."

"I was?"

"The tall man in the brown suit."

"That wasn't you?"

"Is my suit brown?"

Pelt looked at Skulduggery's suit. "Oh," he said, "it's blue. But – but I found you again, didn't I?"

"I let you find me, Argosy."

"Oh."

"Why were you following me?"

"It wasn't anything bad, I swear. I wasn't sent to kill you, or anything. Abyssinia just told me to keep you in sight, and she'd call when she was ready and I'd tell her where you were."

Pelt's phone rang.

He looked at Skulduggery. He looked at Temper.

He twisted, lunging for his phone, ripping it from his pocket as he lashed out, hitting no one, managing to trip over himself while Temper and Skulduggery just stood and watched.

"They caught me!" he yelled into it. "It's a trap! It's a trap!" He stopped rolling around on the ground and listened for a moment, then held the phone out to Skulduggery. "She'd like to talk to you," he said.

Skulduggery took the phone and held it to his skull. "Hello," he said.

Temper pulled Argosy Pelt to his feet. "Your reflection is framing you, is it?"

"I swear it is. I swear."

Temper nodded. "I'll look into it."

"Thank you. Thank you so much! I'm going to run away now, if that's OK."

"Yeah, sure, man, whatever."

Pelt smiled gratefully, and fled. Temper turned back as Skulduggery was telling Abyssinia what street they were on. Then he hung up, and dropped the phone.

Temper raised an eyebrow. "This is risky."

Skulduggery adjusted his tie. "She wants to talk."

Temper looked round, saw Nero and Abyssinia teleport in on the other side of the street. She was wearing a red bodysuit that practically sparkled in the afternoon sun. She spoke a few quiet words, and Nero stayed where he was while she walked over.

Temper and Skulduggery took out their guns.

Abyssinia held up her hands. "Don't shoot," she said. "As unlikely as it sounds, I come in peace."

Skulduggery thumbed back the hammer. "I think I might shoot you anyway."

"I'm here because I need your help. Cadaverous Gant has Caisson."

"Isn't Cadaverous on your side?" Temper asked.

"He was," said Abyssinia. "He's not any more. Call it what you will – a disagreement, a falling-out, a betrayal – the end result is the same. I need to find Caisson, retrieve him safely, and kill Cadaverous."

"And to do this," Skulduggery said, "you need my help. This is an interesting request, Abyssinia, seeing as how I can't see why on earth I would ever possibly help you."

"Because he's our son, Skulduggery."

"Wait," said Temper, "what?"

"Skulduggery is the father," Abyssinia said. "Well, it's either him or Lord Vile, I can't be too sure." She smiled. "But I know which one I'd prefer."

Temper stared at Skulduggery. "Is this true?"

"So she claims."

Temper took a moment to process the possibility. He had a

friend who'd used magic to have a kid. It wasn't exactly common, but not unheard of, either. He shrugged. "Congrats."

"She's undoubtedly lying," Skulduggery said, "and has yet to provide me with a good reason not to shackle her right here."

Abyssinia lowered her hands. "Because you're going to need my help, too. If Cadaverous has gone so far as to make an enemy out of me, then he knows his time is ticking away. Which means he will attempt to tie up any unfinished business he might have left."

"Meaning what?" Temper asked, but Skulduggery was already pulling out his phone.

Temper watched him dial and then put the phone against his skull. When no one answered, Skulduggery marched up to Abyssinia and pressed his gun to her forehead. "Where's Valkyrie?"

"I assure you, I don't know," Abyssinia answered calmly. "But wherever she is, our son will probably be there, too. So I'm coming with you."

"The only way you're coming with us is if you can help us," Skulduggery said. "If you don't know where he's taken Valkyrie, then who would?"

45

It took under an hour to get to the address on the white card. Valkyrie pulled up outside the small cottage just outside Ferbane in Offaly just as the clock on the dashboard turned 8.30, with Omen still unconscious in the back seat of the car.

Three and a half hours to get Alice back.

Valkyrie got out, jogged up to the door, and a white-haired old woman in a floral dress and a heavy cardigan opened it before she could knock.

"Come in, come in," said the old woman.

Valkyrie hesitated, then entered, walking into a warm kitchen where a fire burned in an ancient stove.

"I'm Rosemary," the old woman said, closing the door behind them. "That useless lump over there is Pádraig."

The old man in the armchair smiled and gave a nod, then went back to reading his newspaper.

Rosemary waved at a rickety chair by the table. "Sure, take off your jacket there and have a seat. Can I get you a cup of tea?"

"I'm OK, thank you, and I won't be staying long."

"Not even for a cup? Be God, but it's warm in here. Are you not roasting, altogether?"

"My, uh, my jacket's pretty light."

Rosemary peered closer. "That's some outfit, that is. What's it made of? Is it leather?" She reached out, caught a crease between her thumb and forefinger and rubbed gently. "No, not leather. Much softer. What is this?"

"I don't really know," Valkyrie said, resisting the urge to move away.

"Pádraig, come over here and feel this."

Pádraig rolled his eyes. "I'm sure the nice girl doesn't want us feeling her clothes, Rosemary. For God's sake, leave her alone."

"She doesn't mind," Rosemary said. "You don't mind, do you? Can I try it on?"

It took a moment for Valkyrie to answer. "My jacket?"

Pádraig laughed. "Sure, that's not going to fit you, woman! You're huge!"

"Shut up, you!" Rosemary snapped. "I'm only asking to try it on!"

"You're embarrassing her," Pádraig said.

"No, I'm not! How am I embarrassing her?" She smiled at Valkyrie. "I'm not embarrassing you, am I?"

Pádraig lowered his paper. "She's hardly going to say yes, now is she? She doesn't want to insult you."

"And how would she insult me?"

"By telling you you're way too big to be wearing a jacket that size. Look at her, would you, and then look at yourself. She's a grand girl, big and strong, but compared to you she's a stick. And you? You're the opposite of a stick."

"Oh, really?" Rosemary said. "And what exactly is the opposite of a stick?"

"Ah, I don't know," Pádraig responded. "The rest of the tree, I'd imagine."

"And I suppose you're some fine specimen of a man!" Rosemary said. "I suppose you're perfect in every way, are you? With your ears and your nose and your big hairy belly?"

Pádraig grinned and patted his stomach. "It's a sight to behold, all right."

"I'm sorry," Valkyrie said, "but I'm in a bit of a hurry, so if I could just get what was left here for me..."

Rosemary flapped her hands at the notion. "That's the problem with the world today, in my opinion. Everyone's in a hurry to get somewhere else. Sit down there now and I'll make you that cup of tea."

"Thanks, but I really have to get going."

"Just one cup!"

"Sorry, no."

"Ah, you'll have just one cup, won't you?"

"Go on, go on," muttered Pádraig, and laughed.

"Shut up, you big eejit," Rosemary scowled, then turned her smile back on. "You must think we're awful thicks. It's just... we've been very excited about this. We know who you are. *The* Valkyrie Cain. I've heard so much about you. Mr Gant never stops going on about how much he wants to kill you, how much he wants to bash your brains in." She laughed. "But I'm sure you're used to that sort of attention, a pretty girl like you. Probably have men lining up down the street to get a chance to bash *your* brains in."

"You're embarrassing the girl again," Pádraig said, not looking up.

"You have something for me?" Valkyrie asked. "Something from Cadaverous Gant?"

"Yes, we do," Rosemary said, "yes, we do. He has your sister, doesn't he? He told us about that. Isn't this exciting? He has your sister and he's going to kill her. Ooh!"

Valkyrie stopped herself from throttling this woman. "Could I have it? Whatever he left for me?"

"Yes, yes," said Rosemary, and started looking around. "Pádraig. Pádraig!"

Pádraig sighed. "I heard you the first time. What is it?"

"Where's the card?" Rosemary asked.

"What card?"

"The card, you daft eejit! The card! The card!"

"You can repeat yourself till the cows come home," Pádraig said, "but I still don't know what it is you're looking for."

Rosemary froze, like she'd just been reminded of something, then turned to Valkyrie with a worried look on her face. "You've got those sigils, don't you? Mr Gant told us about them. On your eyes? So he can see what you see?"

"Yeah."

Immediately, Rosemary straightened up and started tugging at her hair. "Pádraig!" she whispered loudly. "Mr Gant! He can see us!"

"Ah, Jaysis," Pádraig said, throwing the newspaper to one side and getting to his feet. He smoothed down his scruffy V-neck jumper.

"Mr Gant," Rosemary said loudly, looking Valkyrie straight in the eye, "I would just like to once again thank you for the honour of being included in these activities. I have led a humble life, as has my husband, but we are endeavouring to—"

"He can't hear you," Valkyrie said.

Rosemary faltered. "Beg pardon?"

"He cannot hear you."

"Well... maybe not, but I'm sure he can lip-read."

"Right," said Valkyrie, "I've been as polite as I can with you people, but I don't have time for this. Cadaverous Gant gave you something to give to me. So give it to me before I lose my goddamn temper."

Rosemary's hand fluttered to her chest. "Oh! Oh, well...!"

Pádraig hurried over, patting his wife on the back. "You're OK there, Rosemary."

"I'm in shock, Pádraig," Rosemary said, sagging against him. "Shock, I say!"

Pádraig glared at Valkyrie. "Look what you've done, and in our own home, no less!"

Rosemary clutched at him. "Oh, Pádraig! I think I might faint!"

White lightning tore a chunk out of the wall behind them, and

Rosemary and Pádraig cried out and whirled to Valkyrie as energy crackled between her fingertips.

They blinked.

"Pádraig," Rosemary said, her voice quiet, "go get that card, there's a good man."

Pádraig made sure Rosemary wasn't about to fall over, then went into another room. Rosemary took a moment to compose herself, and walked to the cutlery drawer.

"Mr Gant left something else, as well," she said. "Told us to make sure you put it on before you're given the card."

She took out a bracelet made of burnished gold metal and passed it over.

There were sigils carved into the metal – sigils Valkyrie recognised. She got the sense that Cadaverous was looking through her eyes right at that moment, so she put the bracelet on, made sure he could see it click shut round her left wrist. The sigils glowed once and she felt her magic dull.

"Can he still see?" she asked.

Rosemary folded her arms. "What?"

"The bracelet binds my magic," Valkyrie said. "Does it have any effect on the sigils on my eyes?"

"Do you know nothing?" Rosemary responded, a sneer on her lips. "Those are passive sigils. Passive sigils can't be bound quite so easily. So don't you be worrying, girly, Mr Gant can still see what you see, so you better keep behaving or he'll cut your little sister's throat."

Valkyrie shoved Rosemary back. "Say that again," she said. "Say one more thing about my sister. See what happens."

Rosemary's eyes narrowed. "You're a nasty girl. I knew it the moment you stepped in here. You're dirty, aren't you? Dirty girls are all the same. Harlots. You're probably oozing with diseases, aren't you? Dirty, filthy girl."

Pádraig walked back into the room, holding up an identical white card to the one in Palter's metal box. "Found it," he said.

Valkyrie strode over, snatched it out of his hand. "Is that it? The bracelet and the card: that's all he gave you to give me?"

"That's all he gave us," said Pádraig.

"And he didn't say anything else?"

"He did say one other thing," Pádraig replied, and frowned. "Rosemary, what was that last thing? After we give her the bracelet and the card, what did he say we had to do?"

"Whatever we wanted," Rosemary said.

"Ah, yeah," Pádraig said. "That's right."

Valkyrie stuffed the card into her jacket pocket and turned for the door. "Well, I'll leave you both to it, then. Have a nice life, you frickin' psychos."

"Where are you going?" Rosemary asked, and swung something hard against Valkyrie's head.

Valkyrie stumbled, tripped on the edge of the rug and fell, turned over as Rosemary advanced.

"Mr Gant told us we could do whatever we wanted with you," she said, and swung the poker again.

46

Temper didn't like being teleported – it made him feel queasy and off balance. He especially didn't like being teleported by a murderous little psychopath with bleached hair. That just upset him at a fundamental level.

But, most of all, he didn't like being teleported straight into Coldheart Prison, where hundreds of convicted killers, terrorists and general whackadoos walked freely and without shackles.

The convicts stared down at them from the higher tiers as Temper and Skulduggery followed Abyssinia to the dais that hovered over the deadly energy field.

"What has Cadaverous been doing lately?" Skulduggery asked. "Where has he been spending his time?"

"I'm afraid I don't know," Abyssinia replied. "He would get in that black car of his and disappear for days. As for what he's been doing, I've been assigning him his duties – duties that he deemed unworthy of his skills."

"He was unhappy here?"

"Apparently. I will admit, I did notice his growing discontent as my search for our son continued."

"Don't call him that."

"I can't wait for you to meet him."

"Let's get back to Cadaverous."

"Of course," said Abyssinia.

"Traitor," Nero muttered.

Temper looked over his shoulder. "You say something, buddy?"

Nero scowled. "You betrayed us."

"How'd you figure that?"

"You pretended to be one of us."

"I was undercover, jackass. Pretending to be one of you is what undercover means. I can't betray you if I was never one of you to begin with."

"You said you were my friend."

"If it makes you feel any better, you still hold a special place in my heart."

"Shut up."

"Need a hug?"

"Shut. Up."

Temper grinned.

"Cadaverous killed one of my most promising sorcerers," Abyssinia was saying, "I think to spite me. A wonderful young man called Avatar. I suspect that his body was thrown overboard or vaporised in the energy field. Speaking of which – watch your step."

She came to the end of the walkway and hopped over the gap on to the dais. Skulduggery did the same, and Temper followed, keeping his eyes off the crackling lake beneath.

When they were all on the dais, it started to rise. They passed tier upon tier of silent convicts, itching to tear them apart.

The dais stopped at the very top and Abyssinia led the way off. A huge convict stepped out of his cell once Abyssinia had walked by.

"The Skeleton Detective," the big guy sneered. "You got some nerve coming in here, coming into *our* house. You think we're gonna let you leave here in one piece, little skeleton? You think we're gonna let you—"

Skulduggery grabbed him, twisted, and threw him over the balcony, and the big guy screamed all the way down.

"Sorry," Skulduggery said to Abyssinia, "you were saying?"

They resumed walking, and Temper waved to the convicts he recognised.

"Nero, Razzia and Destrier were with Cadaverous when he took Caisson," Abyssinia said. "I've looked into their minds – they had no idea what he was planning."

"We'll need to speak to them," Skulduggery said.

"I assumed as much."

They came to a large cell filled with books and a comfortable-looking bed. Razzia and Destrier stood at the open door.

"These are Cadaverous's quarters," Abyssinia said. "We haven't yet conducted a search. I thought you would like to be the first one to do so."

"Very much appreciated," Skulduggery said. "Razzia, very good to see you again."

She smiled back. "G'day, Skulduggery."

"Cadaverous's home — do you know where it is?"

Razzia frowned. "You're looking at it."

Skulduggery shook his head. "Cadaverous's home is his castle. He transforms it into whatever his imagination can conjure. That's where he's gone. That's where he's taken Caisson, and that's where Valkyrie is. He's drawing us in to where he has all the advantages." Skulduggery glanced at Abyssinia. "Your power won't mean a whole lot in there. You realise that, yes?"

"It doesn't matter," she answered. "He has my son."

"I liked you better when you were evil," Razzia said. "You were more fun. You threatened to kill people more."

"I'm still fun, Razzia. You just have to give me a chance."

"He spoke about it once," Destrier said.

Skulduggery swivelled his head. "Cadaverous spoke about his home? What did he say?"

Destrier's eyes were on his shoes. His hands were intertwined. His fingers tapped nervously against each other. "Not much," he said. "He thought I wasn't listening but I was. I hear everything,

267

but most of it doesn't interest me. Not very much interests me, apart from the things that do. They interest me very much. He didn't say where it was, but he said he had a new home."

"When was this?" Temper asked.

"Five years and two months ago. And twelve days."

"Any idea which country it was in?"

Destrier shook his head.

"Cadaverous has been preparing for this for a long time," Skulduggery said.

"If that's true," Abyssinia responded, "then he managed to keep it from me when I was inside his head. A clever boy, that Cadaverous. Truly cunning."

Skulduggery stepped into the cell, and went straight to the bookcase. "Shakespeare's plays are all in chronological order apart from this one," he said, taking *The Tempest* from the shelf. He flicked through it, caught a white card as it fell out. "An address," he said.

Abyssinia clapped her hands delightedly. "We've found him!"

Temper raised an eyebrow. "A bit too easy, don't you think?"

"I'd agree with Temper," Skulduggery said. "But it's a lead."

"Then we'll follow it wherever it takes us," said Abyssinia, and smiled at Skulduggery. "Together again, eh, my love? The way it was always meant to be."

47

She lifted from the murk and the world sharpened, and she opened her eyes. She lay on the floor, her hands bound behind her with tape, her legs bound at the ankles. It hurt to move her head.

Valkyrie turned over, on to her side. Pádraig was working at the stove.

"Mr Gant isn't going to be happy," Valkyrie said.

Pádraig looked round, and smiled. "You're awake! You must have a hard head! And don't you worry about Mr Gant. He told us that once we'd passed over the card we could do whatever we wanted with you. And we're going to eat you."

He turned back to shove more wood into the stove.

"I'm sorry?" Valkyrie said.

"We're going to eat you," Pádraig repeated. "We've been eating people for years now, Rosemary and I."

"You're cannibals?"

Pádraig looked at her over his shoulder. "Ah, now, we don't like the word, so we don't. We don't like it. It has unpleasant connotations. But yes, essentially, cannibals are what we are. But we only eat magical folk. They taste the best."

"Are you going to eat me alive?"

Pádraig laughed. "Jaysis, no! Would you eat a chicken alive?

Or a cow or a pig? No, no, no. We're going to cook you and then eat you. Well, first we're going to boil you, and you'll be alive when you're being boiled, but I doubt you'll stay that way for very long. It's our way of marinating you before we start the cooking."

"Mr Gant wants to kill me himself."

"Yes and no," said Pádraig. "This is a test, you see. If we eat you – and we will – then you'll have failed the test, and so it wouldn't be worth his time killing you. If you escape us – and you won't – then you'll have proven yourself worthy. You understand?"

"Am I going to be given any kind of a fighting chance?"

Pádraig looked puzzled. "This is your fighting chance." Satisfied with the stove, he took a cookbook from the shelf and laid it on the table, and started flicking through the pages.

"What time is it?" Valkyrie asked.

He checked his watch. "Almost nine."

She groaned. "I've only got three hours left. OK. Could you hurry this along? I really don't have time to waste."

He chuckled. "You're really not getting this, are you? It's over. You're over. You're tied up and you've got no magic. D'you know where Rosemary is right now? She's on the toilet, emptying herself and making room for you. Because in three hours you're not going to be saving your sister. You're going to be a midnight feast."

Valkyrie turned over on to her knees. She got her toes under her and rocked back on to her heels, then stood.

Pádraig looked up, and sighed. "What are you doing?"

"You're not going to stop me."

"If I let you sit in the armchair, will you quit being silly?"

"Sure."

Pádraig came forward, arms out to guide her. "You're going to have to hop over there. I'm not as strong as I used to be."

Valkyrie waited until he was close enough, then slammed her forehead into the space right between his eyes. Bright light flashed behind her vision and she had to jump madly to stop from toppling over, but when she regained her balance Pádraig was sprawled out on the floor, hands tapping feebly at his face. Blood gushed from his broken nose.

"Guess you're right," she said as she hopped over. "I do have a hard head."

She jumped, came down on his belly with both knees. Pádraig whooped and she fell sideways as he curled up in silent agony. She ran her hands down the back of her legs, struggling a little to get them over her boot heels. When they were over, she sat up, drew in her feet, started to rake at the tape round her ankles. It was thick, but she managed to scratch a small hole in it, and she kept going, making the hole bigger.

She heard a toilet flush.

Valkyrie looked around. Under the table was a fork. She rolled over to it, grabbed it, sat up again and used it to tear into the tape.

"I feel ten pounds lighter, so I do," Rosemary said, walking in. "Pádraig? Pádraig, where are you?"

Rosemary's heavy footsteps came closer, heading for the stove. Any moment now and she'd see her husband. Valkyrie hacked.

"Pádraig!" Rosemary cried, and stumbled into view, about to fall to her knees at her husband's side. But at the last moment she saw Valkyrie and she straightened up.

"You!" she snarled. "How could you do this to him? He's an old man!"

Valkyrie didn't bother answering. She just kept hacking.

It took a moment for Rosemary's eyes to flicker downwards, to realise what Valkyrie was doing. "Oh, no," she said. "Oh, no you don't."

Rosemary clicked her fingers, summoning a ball of fire into

her hand. Valkyrie turned over as she hurled it, felt it strike her back, and then Valkyrie was on her feet, tearing her ankles apart while Rosemary grabbed a meat cleaver.

Valkyrie kicked Rosemary in the chest, hearing bones crack and sending the old woman flipping over the table. She landed on the floor on the other side and started yelling in pain. Valkyrie ignored her, exchanged the fork for the sharpest knife she could find and used it to cut away the tape round her wrists.

Her phone rang.

She freed herself and answered.

"They're always trying to eat people," Cadaverous said, chuckling. "I was introduced to them through a friend of a friend. They're not friends of mine, per se – I try not to associate with known cannibals – but they do have their charms, don't they?"

Valkyrie pulled the card from her pocket. There was an address printed on it. "Do I go here now?"

"Valkyrie, Valkyrie... you sound impatient."

"I'm just keenly aware of how little time I have."

"Oh, I guess you have a point. Yes, Valkyrie, that's where you go, and it's the last stop before you get to your sister. It's forty minutes away if you drive really fast. Tick-tock goes the clock, Valkyrie.'

Pádraig moaned as Valkyrie hurried past. She didn't even bother to kick him.

She got in the car, swung back out on to the dark road, the headlights splitting the night.

She heard another moan now, from behind her. She fixed her eyes straight ahead. "Omen," she said. "Omen. Omen."

"Uhhh..."

"Don't sit up."

The moaning stopped. "Valkyrie?"

"You're meant to be dead," Valkyrie responded. "So no sitting up, understand?"

"You... did you shoot me?"

"Do you have a bullet in you? No? Then I didn't shoot you. But Cadaverous thinks you're dead, and we're not going to do anything to break that illusion."

"My head feels—"

"I don't care."

"You didn't shoot me."

"Of course not."

"Is he... is he looking through your eyes right now?"

"I don't know. I doubt he's looking every single moment, but I have no way of knowing, so I'm assuming that he's constantly watching."

"Where are we going?"

"I've got one more stop before he tells me where Alice is. I expect there'll be someone there who's going to try to kill me."

"Valkyrie?"

"What?"

"Thank you for not killing me."

She softened. "No problem. Thank you for understanding."

"Should I sneak away and call Skulduggery?"

"No," she said. "We can't call anyone. If Cadaverous even gets a whiff that I'm not playing by his rules, he'll kill her."

"So... so you don't have any back-up? At all?"

"I have you, don't I?"

"I suppose. What should I do?"

"Lie back there and pretend to be dead."

"But I must be able to help," Omen said. "I mean, Cadaverous holds all the cards, right? This is his plan, he's a step ahead, but he doesn't know that I'm alive. So, like, this is where we turn the tables."

"I appreciate the optimism, Omen, but you're not my secret weapon. I don't want you doing anything, at any time. I want you to stay in the car and not move. That's all."

"I don't know, Valkyrie – that seems like a waste. We have the element of surprise now. Shouldn't we use it?"

"No, not really."

"I wouldn't let you down."

"I know you'd try your very best, and, a lot of the time, that'd be enough. But Alice's life is in danger. I can't take the risk."

"Yeah," Omen said sadly. "I get it."

48

Nero teleported them back to Roarhaven, to the Bentley parked by the side of the street.

"Why are we taking a car?" Nero asked, confusion riddling his pretty face. "I can get us anywhere in an eyeblink, remember?"

Temper watched as Skulduggery turned and put a hand on Nero's chest to stop him. "You're not coming with us."

"Oh, you think so, do you?"

Skulduggery seemed unimpressed with Nero's sudden posturing. "I only barely trust one Teleporter with silly hair, Nero, and that's not you. Abyssinia, send him away."

"We'll be much faster with Nero than with a car," Abyssinia said.

"Send him away or this partnership ends right here, right now."

Abyssinia sighed. "Yes, fine. Nero, shoo."

"You want me to go?" Nero said, frowning. "But... but you won't have any back-up."

"I'm the Princess of the Darklands. I don't need back-up. Go on now."

"Yeah," Temper said. "Shoo."

Nero glared, and vanished.

While Skulduggery got behind the wheel, Temper opened the passenger door, pulled the seat forward, and motioned for Abyssinia to climb in the back.

She peered in. "You want me to get in there? But it's so cramped."

"I've already called shotgun, I'm afraid," said Temper. "In you go."

Sighing, Abyssinia manoeuvred her way in with no small amount of grace. Temper returned the seat to its original position and got in.

49

The country house, every detail captured in the warm glow of floodlights, was as big as Grimwood and even grander. It had a fountain in the driveway that Valkyrie circled, before parking facing the exit – in case she needed to make a quick getaway.

She looked in the rear-view. Someone was walking over.

"Stay down," she said to Omen as she undid her seatbelt. She got out.

The man who approached wore fox-hunting gear – a green jacket with four brass buttons, riding hat, jodhpurs and polished boots. He looked to be in his forties. He was tall, and observed her disdainfully. "You are late."

Valkyrie ignored the voice in her head that told her to punch him. "What am I here for?"

He observed her for a bit longer, then sighed and turned. "This way."

She followed as he led her round the house, to where the countryside rolled to the starry horizon on dark waves, spotted here and there with the lights of isolated houses and passing cars. A line of thirteen horses stood directly behind the house, their riders in an assortment of black, green and tweed jackets. Standing in front of the horses were maybe twenty people. They looked nervous. Jittery.

At the bottom of the hill was woodland, and built into that woodland, twisting in and around the trees, was a massive hedge maze, like nothing Valkyrie had ever seen.

The man in the green jacket indicated that Valkyrie should stand beside the scared people. She did so, as he climbed into the saddle of the biggest horse. Now that she could see them properly, Valkyrie realised the riders were all wearing grotesque masks.

She sighed, and turned to the woman next to her. "We're going to be hunted, aren't we?"

The woman met her eyes, and laughed with an excitement that Valkyrie found disturbing.

"At the centre of that maze," the man in the green jacket said loudly, "is safety. Anyone who reaches it will live. Anyone who doesn't will die."

Valkyrie stepped forward. "Do I have to do this? You seem to have a thing going on here, but I'm just looking for my—"

"Back in line!" roared the man in green.

Valkyrie glared, and stepped back.

"For those who reach the middle," he continued, "you will join the Wild Hunt at our next meet. You will be one of us, with all the privileges that go with that. Every hunter you see before you has been where you are. We understand your fear." He glanced at Valkyrie again, and irritation washed over his face. "As for you, there is a card in the middle of the maze. Written on that card is an address. In the unlikely event that you survive, that will be your reward."

He took off his riding hat, pulled on a carved mask, and put his hat on over it. "I am the Master of the Hunt," he said, "and I tell you to run!"

The men and women around Valkyrie ran. She hesitated long enough to see the hunters draw curved swords, then bolted after them.

The grass was wet and slippery. Already some of her fellow

targets had lost their footing and were tumbling uncontrollably down the hill. Valkyrie passed the excitable woman, who reached out to grab her. Valkyrie shoved her away and kept going.

Behind them, a horn blew, and the night trembled with the thunder of approaching hooves.

Someone fell in Valkyrie's way and she leaped over him, reached the bottom of the hill and sprinted on, finding herself near the front of the charge. There were some seriously unfit people running for their lives. She passed a wheezing woman who was slowing with each step. She was about to reach out and pull her along when an arrow thudded into the woman's head and she dropped dead.

Valkyrie started zigzagging as she ran.

There were screams behind her as the horses caught up to the stragglers. Valkyrie glanced back, caught the flash of a curved blade, saw an arc of blood.

An arrow hit her shoulder and bounced off. Another one pierced the ground at her feet. A third landed ahead of her, but this one exploded in a burst of liquid.

A similar arrow hit a man to her left, made him stumble but didn't hurt him. He ran on, his back drenched, disappearing through the entrance to the maze.

Something hit her in the small of the back. She reached behind her, felt the wetness, and then she was through, into the maze.

Valkyrie slowed down to catch her breath. Outside the maze were the screams of the dying – inside was the hushed panting of the desperate. They plunged on without thought, without strategy, barging past Valkyrie in their eagerness to win a place in the Wild Hunt.

Psychos, she decided. Hunters and hunted, both as bad as each other.

There was a rule about mazes, she knew there was. Keep right, maybe? Keep trailing your hand along the wall to your right and it will lead you to the centre?

Or was it left?

She looked back as the hunters streamed into the maze on foot, swords glinting.

She turned right and ran.

The hedges ranged from knee-height to three metres tall. Sound worked differently here. All around her were the sounds of the pursuers – their footsteps, their calls, their laughter, their shouts – and the sounds of the pursued – their footsteps, their cries, their sobbing, their screams – but these sounds crept up from odd angles. Sometimes they were behind, sometimes in front. Sometimes above, and sometimes just over her shoulder.

The deeper Valkyrie went, the further from the lights she moved, the darker it got. She crouched, listening to someone begging nearby. There was a laugh, and a sudden, gurgled moan, and the begging stopped.

There was someone coming for her.

Valkyrie moved on, keeping low. She tugged at the bracelet round the wrist, but there was no way it was coming off.

She stopped. Her hand. It was luminous orange.

She twisted, looking down at herself, hissing a curse under her breath. Her jacket, her trousers, drenched with that liquid, now glowed in the dark, a beacon to the hunters who were closing in.

Footsteps. Rushing her. Valkyrie spun and the hunter stopped running. He laughed beneath his mask.

She sagged. "Come on then," she said, allowing her voice to tremble. "Get it over with. If you're going to kill me, kill me. Just... just make it quick."

She raised her chin and turned her head a little, giving him a clean swing at her neck. He marched forward, confident in her submission and his inevitable victory. He raised the sword as he walked, and when he was in range he swung. Valkyrie stepped into him, left arm wrapping round his right while her other hand cracked into his chin. He stumbled but she held on, hit him a few more times as he went down, then hit him a few more times after that.

She straightened, looked around for the sword. It had flown from his grip and was now lost in a hedge somewhere.

"Here!" another hunter shouted, and Valkyrie bolted.

She tore off her jacket as she ran, dropping it, thankful that the T-shirt beneath was black. She took a corner. There were two hunters ahead, hacking a man to death, and Valkyrie ducked behind the next corner before they saw her, then slipped backwards into the shadows. She crouched, doing her best to hide the parts of her that glowed, and held her breath. The hunter on her tail ran past.

"She come this way?" the hunter, a woman, barked.

"Who?" one of the other hunters asked.

The woman didn't bother answering. She hurried back to the corner, and Valkyrie squirmed further into the darkness.

The woman passed, sword in hand, and Valkyrie stepped out, wrapping an arm round her throat – but the hunter grabbed her arm and twisted and Valkyrie flew over her shoulder.

She managed to pull the hunter down with her and they both hit the ground. The woman did her best to scramble up, but Valkyrie dived on her, grabbing the wrist that still held the sword.

The hunter squirmed, scratching Valkyrie's face, trying to push her off. Valkyrie kept control of the woman's sword hand, worked her way into a dominant position, and started to ram her elbow into the hunter's jaw. The hunter was strong, roughly the same size as Valkyrie herself, but it didn't take much to put her out.

Valkyrie swapped her trousers for the hunter's jodhpurs and pulled her boots back on.

Someone screamed. Someone else laughed. Valkyrie carried on.

She got through the next few minutes without meeting any

more hunters. When she came to smaller hedges, she climbed over them, heading for the light she could see every now and then through the leaves. She quickened her pace, and her feet hit something and she tripped, went tumbling.

"Shush!" said the man she'd tripped over. "Shhhh!"

Valkyrie glared at whoever it was. "You saw me coming," she whispered. "You could have warned me you were there."

"You should look where you're going!"

"It's dark!"

"That's no excuse!" the man said, straightening up. "Now I have to find another hiding spot!" He turned, walked right into a sword thrust.

"Eryx?" he said, gasping.

The hunter peered closer. "Pyramus?" he said through his mask. "It *is* you. Hey. Uh... oh, man. Sorry." Pyramus gurgled, and fell down, and Eryx the hunter turned to Valkyrie. "He was a friend of mine," he said. "I encouraged him to take part. I feel really bad now."

Valkyrie nodded, and ran.

He ran after her.

She scrambled for the corner, sprinted down another path, turned the corner and immediately ducked and spun and crouched.

She heard Eryx running up. Getting closer. Closer.

She powered out of her crouch, catching him in the side as he turned the corner. He went flying and she slipped on the wet grass. The sword landed next to her.

She grabbed it as Eryx came up to his knees, holding his ribs, struggling to breathe. He looked around for his sword, saw it in Valkyrie's hands and froze.

She stood. He held up his hands.

"Please don't kill me," Eryx said.

"Take off the mask."

He did as he was told. His face was unexceptional, and shiny with sweat.

"Hands on your head," said Valkyrie. "Interlace the fingers."

"Oh, God," Eryx said as he complied. "You're going to kill me, aren't you? You are. Just say it. Just tell me. You're going to kill me."

"Shut up, Eryx."

"I'll beg if I have to."

"You're already begging."

"I'll beg more. I'll beg better. Please don't do it. I have a family. I have a wife and children."

"Is that so?" Valkyrie said, stepping closer, tapping the tip of the sword on one of the brass buttons on Eryx's jacket. "What's your wife's name?"

He blinked. "She... she's my ex-wife."

"What's your ex-wife's name, Eryx?"

"I... I can't remember."

"I think you're lying about the family, Eryx."

He shook his head. "I love them very much. Please don't deprive my children of their father. They need a strong male role model in their lives."

"You murder people, Eryx."

"You can't blame them for that. Please. Think of my kids. Think of little Timmy."

"I think little Timmy will be fine without you, Eryx."

"He won't," Eryx said, crying. "He's useless."

"Do you know this maze, Eryx? How do I get to the middle?"

Sobbing, he looked around. "We're quite close to it," he said. "Keep going that way. Look for the openings to get narrower. The narrower the better. They'll take you right to the middle."

"Thanks for that," Valkyrie said, and hit him behind the ear with the pommel of the sword. Eryx fell forward and she carried on.

She followed his advice, chose the narrower of the options available to her, and in under three minutes she stepped into a clearing. Before her was a fountain surrounded by a small hedge. No one else was here yet, but upon the ledge of the fountain lay a white card.

And then a blade pressed against her throat from behind.

50

Valkyrie dropped the sword and turned so, so slowly.

Two hunters stood there – a woman in a black jacket and a man in a green one. The Master of the Hunt. It was the woman's sword that scraped her windpipe.

"I reached the middle," Valkyrie said.

"No," said the Master. "That's the middle. Over there. You haven't reached it, which means you're going to die."

"Cadaverous won't be happy with you. He wants to kill me himself."

"You think I care what Cadaverous Gant wants?" the Master said. "I owed him. I agreed to include you in tonight's hunt in order to repay my debt. Now we're square. In fact, I rather enjoy the idea of killing someone he wants to kill himself. I really don't like him."

Valkyrie licked her lips. "I'll pay you."

"We don't do this for money."

"Well, hold on now," the woman in the black jacket said. "Tell me more."

"A relative left me a lot of money," Valkyrie said. "He was a writer. Gordon Edgley – you heard of him?"

The woman lowered her sword. "*The* Gordon Edgley?"

Valkyrie nodded. "He left me his fortune. I can pay you, both of you, to walk away."

The Master looked at the woman. "Hypatia, no."

"How much?" Hypatia asked.

"A lot."

"You're lying," the Master said. "She's lying."

He went to stab Valkyrie, but Hypatia held him back. "How much?"

"Most of it is tied up in investments and policies and things, but I'm pretty sure I can get you a million. Each."

"Not interested," said the Master.

"Maybe *you're* not interested," Hypatia said, "because you've got money. You've been around for two hundred years. But I'm young. A million each, you say?"

"In cash."

"You expect us to trust that you'll live up to your end?"

"This is a big reward," Valkyrie said. "You've got to take a big risk to get a big reward."

"Stop this," said the Master. "This very conversation is cheapening the name of the Wild Hunt. Hypatia, maybe I was wrong about you. Maybe you're not one of us, after all. I think I'll have to talk to the others."

Hypatia stuck her sword through the Master's chest. He gave a surprised sigh, and crumpled.

"Two million," Hypatia said. "For me."

Valkyrie nodded. "Agreed."

"If you try and cheat me..."

"I won't, but I'm going to need some way to contact you when I have the money."

Hypatia took out her phone and held it up. "I'm recording," she said. "Give me an email or a number or something."

Valkyrie recited her number and Hypatia put her phone away. "Three days," she said.

"Agreed," Valkyrie said, and ran to the fountain. Upon the card were printed five words:

Midnight at the Midnight Hotel

She spun. "What time is it? The time, quickly!"

Hypatia looked at her phone. "Ten to ten."

"Is there a shortcut out of here?" Valkyrie asked, hurrying back. "I need to get to my car."

"For two million," Hypatia said, "I think I can give you a lift."

She wrapped an arm round Valkyrie's waist and brought the air in, boosting them high over the maze. They leapfrogged like this all the way back up the hill, coming to a stop at the country house.

"You know," said Hypatia, "you did reach the middle of the maze, so technically you're invited to join the Wild Hunt."

"Is this what you do, then? Hunting down people and killing the ones you catch?"

Hypatia shrugged. "It's not *all* we do. We're an interesting group. I think you'd like us, if you gave us a chance."

"Thanks, but I've got enough friends."

Valkyrie started running for her car.

"You can never have enough friends!" Hypatia shouted after her. "I'll call you!"

Valkyrie jumped in the car.

"I heard horses," Omen said from the back seat.

"Alice is in the Midnight Hotel," Valkyrie said, starting the engine and putting her foot down. The car kicked up stones as it sped for the road.

"Huh," said Omen. "Suppose that fits."

"You know about it?"

"Yes," he answered. "Well, kind of. We just covered it in school."

"Then you know where it is?"

"It changes location every twelve hours."

"I know that – I mean do you know where it is when it's in Ireland? I've been there, but Skulduggery always drove and I didn't really pay attention. Do you know the address?"

"Um..."

"What? What's wrong?"

287

"I, uh... I'm not very good at remembering facts about things. I know that the hotel is planted at each new location. There are these green seeds that grow in the bushes around the hotel – you put one in the ground and you add water and a new hotel just... sprouts up, and the people inside are teleported straight in to it. The existing hotel, like, wilts, or whatever it is it does, withers away to nothing. I saw a video of it, taken back before people had proper phones. They had the camera looking out the window and everything outside is so big, because the hotel is only growing, you know, and everyone inside is tiny? It only takes a few minutes for it to reach full size, though, and then there's a brand-new hotel. It's pretty cool."

"Omen. I need the address."

"I... I don't know."

"I know roughly where we're going, but I really need you to think now, OK? I need the exact address?"

"It's... um... it's in... Wait." He frowned. "Oh my God," he said. "I know this. I actually know this! I've remembered something from school!"

"Student of the goddamn year," Valkyrie said, and gunned the engine.

51

The address on the card led them to a small apartment building that had popped up behind a newsagent's in somewhere called Mountmellick – which was in Laois, apparently. Temper had never been to Laois before. It seemed like a nice enough place.

Skulduggery activated his façade and went to pick the lock of the side door, but Abyssinia just kicked it open and strolled through. Temper watched Skulduggery lecture her on the way up the stairs. Abyssinia agreed with everything he said, but was obviously ignoring him. It was kind of amusing.

They reached the door to Cadaverous's apartment.

"If this is Cadaverous's home," Skulduggery said, "we might be walking into something we're not ready for."

"Let's go," said Abyssinia.

"Hold on," Skulduggery said. "He likes to say that in his home he is God. And, while that may be grandiose, it's not untrue."

"Let's go in and find out."

"Just wait a second, would you?"

She grabbed Skulduggery, slammed him against the wall. "Our son is in there!"

"We don't know that," Skulduggery responded coolly. "Also, hands off the suit."

"I could crush you," Abyssinia snarled.

"Hands. Off. The suit."

The door to the neighbouring apartment opened, and a man with a shaggy beard came out, a knapsack over one shoulder. He looked at the three of them.

"Howyeh," he said.

Temper waved. "Hi there."

The bearded man hesitated, then closed his door, walked between them and moved on to the stairs.

When he was gone, Abyssinia released Skulduggery and stepped back, a smile sweeping the anger from her face. "You're maddening," she said. "You never used to be like this. Razzia was right. You're more fun when you're evil."

"Aren't we all?" Skulduggery said, straightening his tie. He knelt by the door to pick the lock.

Abyssinia looked at Temper. "We were in love," she said.

Temper nodded. "Love is nice."

Skulduggery put his lock picks away, and stood. "When I open this door, anything might happen. Cadaverous has had five years to build the nightmare of his dreams – we could literally be walking into hell."

"I'm ready," said Abyssinia.

"I could wait in the car?" said Temper.

Skulduggery deactivated his façade and drew his gun. "Then let's go."

Temper drew his, too, and when Skulduggery pushed the door open they swarmed in –

– to an empty apartment.

"Huh," said Temper.

There was one item of furniture – a table with a white card placed upon it. Temper read what it said.

"Abyssinia – you didn't think it would be this easy, did you? We're going to play a little game, you and I. I call it Let's Save Caisson. The objective is simple. You've got forty-eight hours to find him, and you have to do this alone. No Teleporters. No back-up. Your first stop will be to—"

Abyssinia snatched the card out of Temper's hand and read the rest of it herself. "He thinks he can make me play his game? The insolence of the man! I will find him and crush him."

"Again with the crushing," Skulduggery muttered, coming out of the bedroom.

"If his plan was to draw Abyssinia in like this," Temper said, "then maybe he's done the same thing with Valkyrie."

"Call Omen," Skulduggery said, checking the empty cupboards. "He was babysitting Alice this afternoon."

Temper dialled Omen's number and waited.

"What are you doing?" Abyssinia asked Skulduggery.

"Looking for clues," he said.

"Are you finding any?"

"Not really."

"Then you're just wasting time while Caisson is in the hands of a lunatic. I heard that you had become this great detective in my absence, but, aside from finding a card in a book, I have yet to see you detecting anything."

Temper put his phone away. "Omen isn't answering. You think Cadaverous has Alice?"

"I do," Skulduggery said.

"You think he has Omen?"

"If Omen is lucky – yes. If he isn't lucky, he's already dead."

"Damn. Omen's a good kid."

"Who cares about the Darkly boy?" Abyssinia snapped. "He isn't even the important one! No one will mourn for him! We have to focus on what matters – finding Cadaverous before he kills Caisson. Everything else is an irrelevance."

Skulduggery opened the cupboard under the sink. "Nothing is irrelevant," he said, stepping back to let them see the body curled up against the pipes.

"A clue!" Abyssinia cried.

Skulduggery pulled the body out. Now little more than a skeleton, it crumpled to a pile of bones on the kitchen floor.

"This must be kinda weird for you," Temper said.

"Not really," Skulduggery replied, picking up the skull. He tilted his head. "I think I know him."

Temper frowned. "How can you tell?"

"I recognise him from somewhere."

"I don't mean to be... uh, whatever... but how can you recognise him when he's... like this?"

Skulduggery looked at Temper. "You don't think all skulls look alike, do you?"

"Kinda, yeah."

"You do?"

"Of course."

Skulduggery started searching its clothes. "Did I ever tell you that I lost my skull once?"

Temper sighed. "Yeah, you did. Goblins ran away with it."

"And for years afterwards I wore a replacement skull. For years, I walked around with a different head. The jaw was different, the cheekbones were different, the nasal aperture was hilariously off – I'm still surprised people recognised me at all."

"Maybe the fact that you were a skeleton..."

Unable to find any ID, Skulduggery tore off a large strip of the deceased's shirt. "The point is, a skull is as unique as the face that sits upon it."

Skulduggery laid the cloth over the head, and manipulated moisture out of the air to dampen it until it clung to the skull. Then he put both hands up under the jaw and ever so gently the air began to flow, filling out the cheeks and the eye sockets from beneath.

"No," Skulduggery murmured, "that isn't it..."

Temper watched as the cloth face billowed slightly, somehow giving the corpse lips, lending it the appearance of substance. Every so often, Skulduggery would give another murmur. He was like a sculptor: happy with one part of the face, he'd move on to the next, until it became something definite.

"Satrap Beholden," Skulduggery said, removing the cloth from the corpse's skull as he stood. "I haven't heard from him in years. Haven't seen him in a decade."

"You sure it's him?"

"There's no mistaking Satrap."

"Who was he?" Abyssinia asked. "And why is he dead in Cadaverous's apartment?"

"He would have told you himself that he was nobody of consequence. He stayed out of the war, he didn't bother anyone..."

"How did you know him?"

"I met him when he was going out with Anton Shudder," Skulduggery said. "The relationship lasted five or six years. He helped Anton run the Midnight Hotel before they broke up."

"When was this?" Temper asked. Skulduggery turned his head like he was listening to something, but didn't answer. "Hello?"

"The Midnight Hotel," Skulduggery said softly. "When Anton died, it would have been passed on to his next of kin. Anton didn't have any family. If he'd named Satrap in the will, he mightn't have had time to change it before his death."

"So Satrap here inherited the Midnight Hotel," Temper said. "And Cadaverous killed him for it?"

"What is this Midnight Hotel?" Abyssinia asked.

"It's a building that moves," Skulduggery said. "Every twelve hours, it grows in another location around the world, and everyone inside goes with it. For someone whose power is rooted in where they live—"

"A moving house is a dream come true," Abyssinia finished. She held up the white card. "He thought he would lead me on a treasure hunt that would take me forty-eight hours. Instead, we can go straight there."

"And catch him off guard," Skulduggery said.

"To the car!" Abyssinia announced, tearing the card in two. "I call – what's the phrase? – shotgun."

She walked out.

52

All the lights were on in the Midnight Hotel.

Valkyrie drove up slowly, the tyres crunching on gravel and twigs. A two-storey building. Faded white plaster. Dark wooden door and windowsills.

"Are we here?" Omen asked quietly.

"Keep your head down," Valkyrie said, gently pressing the brake.

Her eyes flickered to the clock on the dash. An hour and thirty-five minutes until midnight. Alice was still alive – providing Cadaverous Gant could be counted on to keep his word.

"What's wrong?" Omen asked.

"His last home looked completely normal on the outside, too, but the inside was all metal walkways over a lake of fire. The moment I go in there," she said, "he's got all the power."

"Well," Omen responded, "and I don't want to be mean, but doesn't he have all the power anyway? He's got Alice and he knows you're coming. This is a huge big trap that you have no choice but to step into. The only advantage you've actually got, and I know I've said this before and you're probably getting sick of it, but the only advantage you've got is that he thinks I'm dead."

"You're not coming with me, Omen. Now that I'm here, you've got to find your way to a phone and call Skulduggery."

"Cadaverous will kill you."

"Not immediately he won't."

"I'm not going."

"Yes, you—"

"You were going to shoot me!" he blurted. "I mean, I know now that you weren't *really* going to do it, but I didn't know that then, did I? So I stood there and thought you were going to kill me, and I was going to let you do it. I was willing to die, Valkyrie, because I thought it would get Alice back and also, kinda, because it was my fault she was taken. Valkyrie, please. You don't owe me anything, but you sort of owe me this. Let me help."

"Omen..."

She stopped. Cadaverous Gant stepped from the shadows at the side of the house. He waved to her, smiling, then turned and walked away.

"Stay down," she said, and eased off the brake.

She started to circle the hotel, giving it a wide berth.

At the rear of the building was a garage. Cadaverous stood in front of the roller door, waving to her. His smile was a rictus grin. The door started to open.

"Seatbelt," Valkyrie snarled, gunning the engine and spinning the wheel, the car fishtailing slightly, and now she was looking at the old man straight down the bonnet. The roller door behind him had risen to waist-height.

"Brace yourself!" she shouted, and stomped on the accelerator.

Cadaverous ducked under the door and Valkyrie followed right after, her eyes tightly shut as the car hit the door and crashed through, the windscreen cracking, the airbag exploding, knocking her back in her seat as she braked.

Her foot still on the brake, she reached out, put the car in neutral. She sat there for a moment, her eyes still closed, the engine's low growl the only sound.

When she was like this, the windscreen could have cracked because either the roller door had hit it, or because Cadaverous had. When she was like this, the old man could either have been injured and alive in front of the car, or dead beneath her wheels. Anything was possible, so long as she stayed like this. Like the cat in Schrödinger's box, the old man was both alive and dead. Until she opened her eyes, she was both a good person and a killer.

Alice. She had to find Alice. Alice was the only thing that mattered.

Omen groaned behind her.

She pushed the deflating airbag to one side, squinting against the harsh garage light as she kicked the door open. She was halfway out when her eyes adjusted.

The light wasn't coming from a bulb. It was coming from a blazing sun. It wasn't a garage floor she had stepped out on to. It was hard-packed dirt.

She stood, and looked back the way she'd come. The garage door was still open, and through it she could see the trees and the small road and the dark sky, could still make out the tracks her car had made in the mud – but the door was cut into a vast wall of rock. It was a cliff face, wide enough to vanish into distant horizons on either side, tall enough to reach the sky.

She stepped back, craning her neck. It did reach the sky, and then it folded back, *became* the sky. The sky, rather than an infinite expanse, was a ceiling as high as a cathedral's, with drifting clouds and its own sun – brilliant but not blinding – directly overhead.

And on the surface of the sun: clock hands, counting down to midnight.

The sheer impossibility of Valkyrie's surroundings – an environment much too big for its walls to contain – made her dizzy and she almost stumbled, had to lean against the car for support. A hot breeze stirred.

She was on a dirt road on a hill. The dirt road led down, becoming a real road a few miles further on. The road swerved through a forest of dark trees and then narrowed, became the main street of a small town on the edge of water. The water was black, the reflection of the sun on its waves sending splinters of a migraine deep into Valkyrie's brain.

Beyond the town was a bridge to a small island. It was too far for her to make anything out, but she knew that was where her sister was.

Her eyes widened and she jumped away from the car. The bonnet, though scraped, was clear of any dead man's body. She dropped to her belly. The underneath was clear also. No corpse. No Cadaverous.

She got up again, slowly, brushing the dust off automatically.

A phone rang. A payphone, right there on the side of the dirt road. She looked at it while it rang. Let it ring a good long time. Then she walked over. Slowly. She reached out to pick it up, and it stopped.

"Real mature," she murmured.

She kept her eyes on it. A minute went by. She turned to go back to the car and it rang again.

She answered.

"Welcome," Cadaverous said, "to my humble abode."

53

"I'm here," Valkyrie said. "I made it. Give me my sister."

"Ah-ah, you haven't made it quite yet," Cadaverous responded. "Just a little bit further, that's all. The woods are lovely, dark and deep. But you have promises to keep—"

"And miles to go before I sleep," Valkyrie finished. "Yeah, I know a few poems, too. Wanna hear one? There once was a man from Nantucket—"

Cadaverous cut her off with a laugh. "You are proving to be every bit the adversary I had been hoping for, Valkyrie. This wouldn't be nearly as satisfying if you weren't up to the task."

"I'm glad you're enjoying yourself. I'll be interested to see if you're still having a good time when I drag you out of here."

"Now, now, we both know that's not going to happen. This is my home, Valkyrie. Granted, it's a little different from my last one, but I needed a change. Do you like it? I knocked down a few walls to make more room."

"I can see that."

"I spent a long time on this place, Valkyrie. Five years, in fact. I poured my heart and soul into it. I constructed every pebble, every speck of dust. That breeze you're feeling? That took two weeks to get just right."

"Once again, you prove yourself the master of hot air."

"Master of my *domain*, Valkyrie. Remember that. In here, I am God."

"So why don't you strike me down? Huh? I'm standing right here. Come get me."

Cadaverous chuckled. "No, no, no, Valkyrie. That's not how this is going to work at all. Your journey isn't over yet, and time is still counting down."

"Bull," Valkyrie snarled. "You said get to your house by midnight. I'm here with an hour and a half to spare."

"But that's not the house I meant," Cadaverous said. "The house I meant is at the end of this road. You'd better hurry. Your sister is waiting."

He hung up.

Valkyrie slammed the phone back on to its cradle. Picked it up and slammed it back down again. A shout of frustration welled up inside and escaped, and she kicked at one of those pebbles that Cadaverous had designed and watched it skip across the road, raising little puffs of Cadaverous-designed dust as it went.

"Valkyrie?" Omen said from the car.

"Stay there!" she snapped, and stormed back to the car, pulling the deflated airbag from the steering wheel. She got in and slammed the door, put the car into gear. She glared into the rear-view mirror, hoping Cadaverous was watching, and gave him the finger.

The car shot forward.

54

The Bentley pulled up outside the Midnight Hotel and they got out.

Skulduggery stopped at the front door and drew his gun. "OK," he said. "When we go in—"

"Enough talk," Abyssinia said, marching past him and into the hotel.

Skulduggery muttered something and followed, and Temper came last.

They were suddenly in the mountains somewhere, and it was daytime. The air was crisp, the sky blue, the trees tall. Temper looked back. The doorway was the mouth of a cave. Through it, he could see the dark sky and the Bentley.

"This is like the TARDIS," he said.

"I don't know what that is," Abyssinia responded, still looking around. "We're in the Carpathian Mountains."

"You recognise this?" Skulduggery asked.

"I recognise it from the trips I took into Cadaverous's head. This is where he spent the first eight years of his life before moving to America. He's replicated it exactly. Even the..." She trailed off.

"Abyssinia?"

"My son is here," she said, and started walking, away from the path and into the woods.

Temper started after her, then turned to Skulduggery. "You coming?"

"The sun," Skulduggery said, looking up. "There's a clock in the sun."

55

The road was wide and smooth and there were signs everywhere, all with Alice's name on them, all pointing straight ahead.

"How fast are we going?" Omen asked from the back seat.

"Shut up," said Valkyrie.

"OK."

Her foot eased up on the accelerator, though. Just a little. She'd be no good to her little sister if she crashed before she got to her.

She passed a sign different from the others – small, sticking out of the ground by the side of the road. It had *Help* scrawled on it.

There was a similar sign ahead, beside a bigger one that had Alice's name in lights. Again, it said *Help*.

The road turned slightly, then straightened out again. More big signs, goading Valkyrie on. But more small signs, too, this time with arrows, all pointing left. A minute later, Valkyrie came to a left turn.

She slowed. The big signs told her to go straight on, told her that Alice was waiting ahead. But the small signs, the ones written by hand, told her to go left, down a narrower road.

"Is everything all right?" Omen asked, and Valkyrie ignored him.

She turned left.

They drove for five minutes, until a city rose up in the

windscreen. Cars passed and people walked. Valkyrie pulled into the kerb and waited. Her fingers tapped the wheel, gently but quickly.

"Can I sit up?" Omen asked.

"No."

"It's not very comfortable like this."

"I don't care."

"Are we there yet?"

"I don't know where we are, or who these people are."

A car turned towards her. She resisted the urge to duck down. It slowed as it approached. It was an old car. Boxy. It belonged in the eighties. It passed and she got a look at the driver.

"Cadaverous," she said.

"Where?" Omen asked.

"He just passed." She put the car in gear, prepared to make a U-turn, maybe smash into the back of him, drag him out and kick his head in, but right before she stomped on the accelerator she glimpsed a man in an overcoat out for a walk.

Cadaverous. Again.

Valkyrie turned in her seat, watched the boxy car drive away, then looked back at the other Cadaverous.

"What's wrong?" Omen asked. "Valkyrie?"

"There are two of them," she muttered, then turned off the engine and got out.

"Give me my sister," she said, striding up to Cadaverous.

He blinked at her. "I'm sorry?"

She slapped him, the heel of her hand slamming into the hinge of his jaw. Cadaverous fell backwards, unconscious before he hit the pavement. Valkyrie frowned. She hadn't expected it to be so easy.

"Hey!" someone yelled from across the street. A woman, in a flowing skirt and heels, ran over. "Get away from him! I saw what you did! That's assault!"

The woman got closer and Valkyrie jumped back. It was

Cadaverous, in lipstick and eyeshadow, with long hair, wagging his long, bony finger at her.

"I'll call the police! I saw everything!"

Valkyrie stared at him. "What are you doing?"

Cadaverous knelt down beside the other Cadaverous. "This poor man! What did you do to him?"

Three people hurried closer – a businessman and a couple in jeans and jackets. All three of them were Cadaverous Gant.

"She attacked him!" the Cadaverous in the dress said. "An unprovoked attack!"

Valkyrie backed off.

"Where do you think you're going?" said the Cadaverous dressed as the businessman.

"I'm calling the cops," said one of the Cadaverouses wearing jeans. "Where's the nearest payphone?"

Valkyrie ran.

She ducked into an alley, sprinted its length, splashing through a puddle and nearly falling over an old-fashioned dustbin, the galvanised steel kind she'd only seen in movies. A trash can, really. Crossing the next street she came to, she hurried down another alley. She got halfway through when she stopped. There was a puddle ahead of her. Beyond that, an old-fashioned, galvanised trash can. The kind she'd only seen in movies.

She ran a hand along the wall. It looked rough, uneven, but it was smooth to the touch. She walked back the way she'd come, back through an alley identical to the one she'd just left. How many of these identical alleys there were in this city, she couldn't begin to guess. Cadaverous had designed everything here – she supposed she shouldn't have been surprised to find that he'd used duplicates for some of it, and hadn't bothered with exact detail in the parts that didn't matter.

Maybe that applied to the people, too. He needed a population, after all, and she supposed that the easiest thing would be to populate it with versions of himself. It was weird, sure, but kind of understandable.

She turned left, feeling calmer now, heading for the cars and people. She reached the corner and stood there, watching.

People passed, all wearing Cadaverous's face. They ignored her, for the most part, but it didn't seem to be out of spite. Rather, they each appeared to be caught up in their own thoughts. Like regular people. Those who did happen to glance at her, to catch her eye, didn't fly into a rage or call on the others to attack. Instead, they gave a quick nod and carried on walking, chatting or driving. A city of Cadaverous Gants, and not one of them recognised her.

A Cadaverous shuffled by, using a walking stick. Valkyrie walked beside him.

"Excuse me?" she said.

He looked at her, irritated. "Yes?"

"I'm terribly sorry, but I think I'm lost."

"So why are you apologising to me?"

She smiled. He was a mean-tempered old grouch. "Could you tell me where we are? The name of this city?"

He grunted, eyes returning to the pavement on which he was walking. "Cities don't have names. Everyone knows that."

"Oh," said Valkyrie, "of course. What's your name? I'm Valkyrie."

"That's a stupid name."

"What's yours?"

"Why do you want to know?"

"I think we could be friends."

He grunted again. "Charlie," he said. "I'm Charlie."

"Hi, Charlie. Where are you off to?"

"Home."

"Is that close?"

"Round the corner."

"I'm looking for someone. Maybe you've seen her? Her name's Alice. She's my sister, and I think she's somewhere here."

"Don't know any Alice," Charlie said.

"She's only seven. Have you seen any kids? Charlie?"

He stopped, reluctantly giving her his full attention. "Why do you want to be friends with me? Eh? Everyone hates me and I hate everyone."

"I'm sure not everyone hates you."

"Of course they do," he said, barking out a laugh. A Cadaverous in a scarf walked by. "Hey, you, do you like me?"

The Cadaverous in the scarf glared. "I hate you," he said. "Everyone does." And he walked on.

"See?" Charlie said. "Nobody likes me. Not in college. Not in work. Not in life."

"What did you do? For a job?"

"I taught," he said, chest swelling a little. "I'm retired now, but I taught English literature to idiots and airheads. Gave them a little culture, not that it did them any good. Ungrateful lot. Do you know the problem with the younger generation? They're victims. They think they've got it worse than anyone who's ever come before them. They collect weaknesses like badges, wear them for all to see."

"I'm young," said Valkyrie. "I'm not a victim."

"You could be," Charlie said. "Just as easily. You could be." He looked at her for a long while, then grunted. "A sister, eh? I think I've seen a little girl somewhere around here."

Valkyrie's eyes widened. "Is she here? Is she close?"

He started walking again. "Come along. Come this way."

Valkyrie wanted to pick him up and run with him, but she forced herself to match his pace, agonisingly slow though it was. They turned the corner on to a residential street, lined with identical houses.

Perfectly identical houses. Two-storeyed. Wooden. Dark. The curtains were drawn at every window.

Charlie shuffled up to his front door. "In here, I think," he said. "I think she's in here."

He led the way in. Valkyrie followed. Inside it was dark. Musty. "What a nice house," she said.

"Yes. The house where I grew up. Come now. Your sister is in here."

He opened another door and stood there, walking stick in hand, waiting for her to rush past. His eyes were bright. He looked eager. Expectant.

"You had another house, didn't you?" Valkyrie asked. "Bigger than this, I'd say."

He shook his head. "Lived here my whole life," he said. "Come now. Hurry."

"You had another house," she said again. "It had a lot of different builders working on it. There were doors that led nowhere. Hidden stairs. Hidden rooms. Traps. You remember all that, Charlie?"

He frowned. "You must be... you must be getting me mixed up with someone else."

"You sure it doesn't ring a bell? It was when you were living in Missouri."

"I... I've never..."

"Yes, Charlie?"

"I've only ever lived here. I've never lived in..." He shook his head. "I've never lived in St Louis."

"I didn't say you lived in St Louis. I said you lived in Missouri."

He rubbed his forehead. "What are you doing to me?" he muttered. "What are you doing to my head?"

She walked up. "I don't think you are who you think you are, Charlie. Parts of you are missing. Why did you want me to come inside? Were you going to kill me?"

"No."

"I think you were going to try and kill me, just like you killed all those other people. Most of them were your students, weren't they? The idiots and airheads who didn't appreciate what they were being taught? You invited them in and then what did you do? Did you hunt them? Did you hunt them through your little house of horrors?"

A smile broke through Charlie's confusion. "Yes," he said.

"You hunted and killed them, didn't you, Charlie?"

"Yes," he said, eyes brightening.

"You're not whole. There's something missing. You can feel it, right?"

Charlie nodded. "I'm not me," he said. "I'm not who I am."

"There's a man out there, Charlie. His name is Cadaverous. He's got all your thoughts and memories, and he made you. He made this city, and all these people. But he didn't bother making you whole. He left bits out. Important bits. The bits that make you who you are."

"The bits that make me happy."

"Yes. Yes, those bits. He's a sloppy creator. He's waiting for me, Charlie. He took my sister and he wants me to go to him. He wants to hurt me. He wants to kill me."

"Kill you."

"But I think my sister got away from him. I think she left me signs to come here. Is she here? Where would she hide, if she were here?"

"Kill you," Charlie muttered, and swung his walking stick at Valkyrie's head.

She dodged back instinctively, and Charlie launched himself at her, teeth bared. She stumbled, wrestling with him, then got a hand to his throat, pushed him back and kneed him between the legs. He jerked, and stiffened, and then crumpled slowly, unable to even gasp. He sank to his knees and Valkyrie resisted the urge to break his walking stick over his head.

"You've got to help me."

Valkyrie turned.

A teenage boy stood in the doorway. He was dressed in frayed trousers and a threadbare shirt. His shoes were heavy. Looked uncomfortable. She recognised Cadaverous in his features, but not his eyes. He had sad eyes.

"You put up those signs?" she asked.

"I'm sorry," he said. His accent was American with a hint of something else – Russian, maybe. "I had to talk to you, but I cannot leave this city. He will find me if I do."

"Who will find you? Cadaverous?"

The boy nodded. "He does not know I'm here. He thought he'd destroyed me, long time ago. He almost did. I'm nothing to what I was once."

"Listen, I'm sorry to be the one to tell you this, but he's seeing you right now, through my eyes."

"Yes. And I feel his rage. But he cannot find me. This city, for him, it's too confusing."

"But he built it."

"He did, to store thoughts, to put them away and never think them again. This land he's made, it's him. His mind. To create something so big... is something he has never tried before. He controls most of it, but there are areas where he fears to tread."

"I need to find Alice."

"She's waiting for you, in his house. On the island, beyond your town."

"My town?"

"He spent five years building this land, but he kept a space for you. He built it specially. It's powered by a distorted Echo Stone that will draw from your memories and construct your town when you get close. He wants to hurt you. He wants to kill you for what you did to Jeremiah."

"I didn't do anything to Jeremiah," Valkyrie said. "He attacked me. He fell."

"You're responsible," the boy said.

"I'm not arguing about this, OK? You got me here, fine. How do I beat him?"

"In here, you can't. You have to get him outside."

"Can you help me do that?"

"I can't do anything."

"Then what do you need? How can I help you, if I can't beat Cadaverous?"

"You can't win," he said. "He has your sister and he will kill her. This is going to happen. When he does this, I fear, you'll attack him. Then he'll kill you, too. And this place will go on, and I'll stay here and hide here and nothing will ever change. Unless..."

"Unless what?"

"Unless you accept your sister's death."

"No."

"You must. Do it now, so that, when it happens, you are ready. Don't play his game. When she is dead, run. Lead him out of this place, and kill him. When he dies, destroy this land."

"I'm getting out of here, with my sister."

"No," the boy said sadly, "you're not." He frowned. "You'd better go. The city is starting to notice you."

He stood aside. Valkyrie hesitated, then went past him, emerging on to the street.

A car slowed, then stopped. The driver, Cadaverous, looked straight at Valkyrie.

Across the road, people stopped walking. They looked over.

"You'd better run," said the boy.

Valkyrie wanted to get back to her car, but there was a crowd coming round the corner so she darted across the road. A car pulled up, narrowly missing her. Cadaverous opened the door and tried to grab her.

She ran. There were people chasing her. There were people in front, running at her. Cadaverous lunged out of a doorway just ahead and she jumped, slammed a knee into his chest. He went down and she stumbled over him, managed to stay on her feet. Ran on.

There was a park on her left, but the fence was too high to

scale. She rolled across the bonnet of a parked car, avoiding the hands that reached for her. She landed on the other side, punched someone. Someone else grabbed her and she headbutted him, tore free, sprinted. The streets surged with people, everyone wearing Cadaverous's face, like antibodies flushing out a virus. They were right behind her. She couldn't turn back. The road ahead was blocked. Crowds flooded in from either side. She stopped running. Nowhere to run to. She turned. Turned again. They were all around her. They closed in, ready to tear her apart.

A phone rang.

The city stopped. It just... stopped. The people, all those snarling Cadaverouses, stopped moving, stopped snarling. Not a sound but for the ringing phone. No distant car engines. Not one singing bird. Nothing.

Just that ringing phone.

The telephone box stood next to a streetlamp. Like everything else in the city, it looked like it was from the eighties. Her breathing under control after all that running, Valkyrie walked towards it slowly. All those Cadaverous eyes watched her, but not one of those Cadaverous feet moved.

She pulled the door to one side. It opened like an accordion, folding in on itself. She plucked the receiver from the cradle and held it to her ear.

"You're not supposed to be there," said Cadaverous Gant.

"I took a detour," she told him. "Talked to a nice young gentleman."

"He shouldn't have done that. Now I know where he is."

"He seems to think you're afraid to come here. Is that true? What would happen if you did? Would you get lost? Would you be consumed by all these versions of yourself?"

"I should kill little Alice right this second."

"What do you call this place, anyway?" Valkyrie asked, her voice dripping with a confidence that sprang from somewhere desperate. "Cadaverousburg? Gantville? Yeah, it looks like a Gantville."

"Didn't you hear what I said?"

"You're not going to kill her," said Valkyrie. "You do that and the game's over. I've still got an hour to get to you. Those are the rules."

"You'd better hurry."

"I'll get to you when I get to you," she said, and hung up.

56

After five minutes of trampling through the Carpathian Mountains as remembered by Cadaverous Gant, they came to three wooden shacks in a clearing.

"Recognise these?" Skulduggery asked.

Abyssinia shook her head. "I was never able to get this far into Cadaverous's mind. Tread carefully."

There was a rustle of movement and Temper turned in time to see a hatchet swing for his head.

He jerked back and his attacker, a scrawny man in filthy clothes with hatchets in both hands, swung at him again and kept swinging, his bearded face contorted in fury. One of the hatchets swished by Temper's face and he stepped in, his knee buckling the guy's leg while his fist cracked against the guy's jaw.

His attacker hit the ground, one of his hatchets spinning out of his grip. He scrambled up and launched himself back into the fight and Temper sent him to the ground again, this time with an arm twisted and Temper's knee on his chest.

"Thank you," Temper said to Skulduggery and Abyssinia. "Thank you for just standing there."

"You had it covered," Skulduggery said.

Abyssinia walked over, looked down at the squirming wild man. "And who might you be, my unshaven friend?"

He snarled at her in a language Temper didn't know. It sounded vaguely Russian.

Abyssinia looked at Skulduggery. "You're the genius. What's he saying?"

Skulduggery tilted his head. "I'm expected to know all the languages?"

"You're four hundred and fifty years old. What else have you been doing with your time?"

"Punching people, mostly."

The wild man tried to break free, but Temper wrestled him down, then glanced at Abyssinia. "Can't you read his mind or something?"

"Oh, he isn't real," she said. "He is no more self-aware than that rock, and even that rock isn't real. Everything you see here has been conjured in some fashion by Cadaverous, and acts according to the rules of this world."

"I can understand roughly every third word that he's saying," Skulduggery said. "He is not pleased to see us, and he's calling us some very bad names."

Abyssinia raised an eyebrow. "How dare you. I am royalty."

"Now he's threatening us. He doesn't seem particularly perturbed to be in the presence of a talking skeleton, by the way, but I put that down to the limitations of his programming rather than a true reflection of whoever he's meant to be."

There was a screech behind them, and a kid of about six tore from the trees, a hatchet in his hand.

"I'm not hitting a child," Temper said immediately.

"Well, I'm not doing it," said Skulduggery.

"I'll do it," said Abyssinia, and stepped forward to kick the boy in the face.

He flipped over backwards, unconscious before he'd even landed.

"Jesus," Temper muttered, the wild man going nuts beneath him.

"I do so love kicking children," Abyssinia said. She looked up. "Oh, come on. He's not even real."

"He's real to this guy," Temper responded, twisting the wild man's wrist in an effort to control him.

"Ask him where our son is," Abyssinia said. "He's close. I can sense him."

"For the last time," Skulduggery said, "stop calling him our son."

Abyssinia smiled. "Admit it, darling. You're coming round to the idea of being a father again, aren't you?"

"Are you going to stop, or is this partnership over?"

"I'll stop," said Abyssinia. "For now."

Skulduggery spoke to the wild man, and the wild man responded with his usual snarls.

"He claims not to know," Skulduggery said, then asked the wild man something else, mentioning Valkyrie's name.

The wild man snarled and spat.

"You are most disagreeable," Skulduggery murmured.

He babbled further.

"What's he saying now?"

"I'm not sure." Skulduggery listened for another few seconds. "Something about an axe. A man with an – no, an Axe-Man."

"Is he the Axe-Man?" Abyssinia asked.

"No. He says the Axe-Man's coming."

"Well, that'll be nice," Abyssinia said. "The Axe-Man sounds friendly. Maybe he'll tell us where my son is."

A shape moved, out by the trees.

For a few seconds, there was nothing, and Temper was about to look away when a man appeared. He was made of muscle, close to eight feet tall and covered in blood with a sack tied over his face. He dragged a gigantic axe after him, the blade making furrows in the dirt.

"Um," said Temper.

Abyssinia looked round. "What?"

"I could be wrong," he said, "but I think the Axe-Man's here."

57

The town ahead of them wavered, like it was caught in a heat haze, but it solidified as they grew closer. Bushes, trees, hedges, low walls and lamp posts – landmarks that had evolved since Valkyrie's childhood, lining the road to Haggard. They passed the graveyard and the wide gates of the nursery, passed the service station on their left and the cottages on their right, the bus stop, and the Chinese restaurant that everyone still regarded as the new Chinese place even though it had been there for the last ten years. There were people, too, and cars on the road.

"They've stopped looking like him," said Omen.

"Down," she said, keeping her eyes away from the rear-view mirror.

"I'm just peeking," Omen said. "Look at the people. They're not like Cadaverous any more."

"No," said Valkyrie. "They're taken from my memories."

She had become aware of a pressure, somewhere in the back of her mind, like the tentative prodding of fingers. She eased her foot off the accelerator, let the car slow right down as she focused.

"Are you OK?" Omen asked.

"Quiet."

"Sorry."

She'd had a few lessons on how to shield her thoughts from a psychic assault, and she took what she'd learned and built a wall around her mind. The townspeople flickered in and out of existence. She built the wall taller, made it thicker, and the street emptied of both people and cars.

Omen looked around. "Where'd they go?"

The car drifted and the front wheel hit the kerb and Valkyrie veered off and braked. The people were suddenly back.

"This is so weird," Omen whispered.

They stayed where they were, pulled into the side of the road. Cars behind her slowed, waited for the opposite lane to clear, and overtook. All very normal.

Valkyrie focused, building the wall up again.

"Um," Omen said, sitting forward and pointing. "Is that real Alice or an Alice from your memories?"

Valkyrie looked up as Alice crossed the road in front of them, got to the pavement and ran off.

Tearing off her seatbelt, Valkyrie threw open the door, forcing a passing car to swerve. The driver honked his horn, but she ignored him as she jumped out.

"Valkyrie, wait," Omen said. "It might not really be her!"

"Stay there!" Valkyrie shouted back, and ran after her sister.

She passed a neighbour, out walking her dog. She passed her old friend, J. J. Pearl, who nodded a hello she didn't return. She got to the corner just as Alice darted through the door into Hogan's Flowers, and Valkyrie slowed.

The front window was filled with flowers of extraordinary colour. Every Valentine's Day as a kid, she'd accompany her dad as he went to buy her mum a bouquet. She'd help him pick out the perfect selection, and then they'd tell Mr Hogan and he'd chuckle and start picking and plucking and arranging. Every time, every single time, he'd take a lollipop from the jar beside the till and hold it out to her, and she'd walk up shyly and take it from him. Then he'd chuckle again and go back to work.

But there was something about Mr Hogan that had always unnerved her. The look in his eyes, maybe, or the fact that when he held out the lollipop he'd never step forward. She always had to go to him. Then there was that afternoon she'd been playing hide-and-seek with her friends up and down Main Street. She'd ducked into the flower shop to hide and Mr Hogan had flown into a rage, had grabbed her by the arm and yanked her into the corner. His fingers, like steel, round her arm, his face, contorted in anger, her only way out blocked by his bulk... She'd had a recurring nightmare about that moment. She'd forgotten that.

Valkyrie stepped into the flower shop.

"Alice?" she called. "Alice, come out."

The inside of the shop was dark. Flowers lined the walls and spilled from the shelves. Hanging baskets swayed slightly on thin chains. There was an opening to a cellar in the middle of the floor that she didn't remember being there in the real shop. Greasy yellow light bled out from the gloom.

Mr Hogan shuffled out of the darkness, a potted plant in his hands. He saw her and chuckled. "Look who it is," he said. "Little Stephanie Edgley. Haven't seen you around in ages."

Her mouth was dry. "I'm looking for my sister," she said. "She came in here."

"Did she now?" Mr Hogan said. "Well then, she must be somewhere, mustn't she? Feel free to take a look."

Valkyrie tried to build a wall again, tried to make him vanish, but the bricks were crumbling even before they could set.

She walked forward on stiff legs, quickly checking behind shelves and peering into alcoves. She turned and cried out as she jumped back – Mr Hogan was standing there, a yellow lollipop in his hand.

"Want a sweetie?" he asked.

That's what he used to say when she was a kid. Only, no, it wasn't quite right. There was something else, something he used to call her...

"Want a sweetie, sweetie?" he asked.

318

Valkyrie shook her head. "I just want my sister."

He chuckled. "She's probably downstairs, then." He stepped back, allowing her a clear path to the steps leading down to the cellar.

She was shaking. She was shaking and her knees were weakening. "Is she down there?"

"That's where they all go," said Mr Hogan, shuffling away.

This was all wrong. She'd never been this scared of Mr Hogan before. He was a creepy old man who turned nasty when there weren't any adults around, but this fear was coming from somewhere else. This was a kind of fear she'd only become familiar with recently, in the last few years. It had sidled up to her, lain at her feet like a dog, had started to accompany her wherever she went. It was the kind of fear that weakened her. That paralysed.

The steps down to the cellar were old and wooden. The smell of flowers was pungent in the humid air, like they were ripe, like they were starting to rot. Valkyrie stepped on to the dark floor, into the mulch of petals and leaves and stalks that covered it like a carpet. Crates and wooden boxes were stacked away from the single bulb that didn't try very hard to pierce the gloom. Some of those boxes looked like children's coffins.

"Alice?" Valkyrie called. Her voice was quiet. It sounded scared.

She walked further away from the light bulb. Further away from the stairs. The darkness beckoned her.

She stopped. Stepping into darkness was beyond stupid, so she allowed her voice to go on ahead. "Alice," she said again, louder this time. "Alice? Are you here?"

Nothing. It hadn't been her. Alice would have answered. Alice would have come running. Valkyrie was certain. She turned, headed back to the stairs.

And yet...

Maybe Alice was frightened. Maybe she was too frightened to emerge from hiding. Maybe she was crouched somewhere, tears in her eyes, waiting for her big sister to come and find her, counting on her big sister not to be scared of the dark.

Goddammit.

Valkyrie went to the stairs and looked up. "Mr Hogan," she called, "do you have a torch I could borrow?"

No sound from up there. No movement.

"Right," she said, still speaking loudly as she turned and strode into the gloom. "Alice, I'll be right there. Hold up your hand when you see me. Call out for me. Can you do that? Of course you can. You're a brave little thing, aren't you?"

Into the gloom, into the darkness, checking the corners, moving aside crates, the cloying smell of flowers making her feel sick with every moment she spent down here. Still she moved, still she marched, making lots of noise, talking all the time, pretending to be brave, pretending to be her old self.

The ground was getting softer. With every step, Valkyrie had to pull her foot out of the sickly sweet-smelling muck that sucked at her boots – and then the ground gave way and her lower leg plunged down into it. When she put her weight on her other leg to try and free herself, that foot began to sink. She immediately stopped what she was doing, but it was too late.

She looked around for something to grab. There was a table beside her. She reached for it, but it was too far away. She coiled, then sprang, but the ground had her and wasn't letting go. She splashed down, tried to push herself up and now she'd lost her left arm up to the shoulder.

Panic squirmed deep in her belly.

The mulch was like quicksand. She had no base under her, no solid ground from which to stabilise. She craned her neck, keeping her chin above the muck as her body sank like a lead weight.

"Help," she said. Then again, louder. "Help." She wasn't even able to scream. Screaming required movement and she couldn't afford to move.

Muck tipped off her chin. It was cold.

"Someone," she said. "Help me."

She tried to twist, tried to lunge, and that was a mistake.

With a last, desperate breath, she went under.

58

"I don't get it," Temper said, his back braced against the door of the shack as the Axe-Man's fists pounded on it from the outside. "Why doesn't he just use his ridiculously large axe to break through?"

The shack was small. Rustic would have been generous. There were two beds – one of them tiny – in the corners. A rocking chair, covered in pelts, stood next to the fireplace.

Abyssinia, sitting at the small table in the middle of the shack, crossed her legs. "Maybe he's stupid," she said. "Skulduggery, perhaps you'll be able to use his stupidity against him. It might be more effective than your bullets."

Skulduggery, who had already used the Axe-Man as target practice, reloaded his gun thoughtfully. "If you think that's a practical option, please, toss him a book of Sudoku and we'll sneak away while he puzzles over it."

"I don't know what Sudoku is," Abyssinia responded, looking up at the ceiling and sounding bored. "I've been a heart in a box for two hundred years."

"As you never tire of reminding us."

"Are you implying that I talk too much of the time you tried your very best to kill me?"

"I've tried to kill lots of people," Skulduggery replied. "You don't hear them complaining about it."

"Excuse me," Temper said, "could you two possibly stop bickering and come up with a way to get out of whatever the hell is going on here? Also, the kid's awake."

They looked over at the boy, lying on his bed in the corner, arms and legs bound.

"Try not to kick him in the face again," Skulduggery said.

"He's tied up," Abyssinia replied. "There's no sport in it. Ask him who he is."

"I already know who he is. This is Cadaverous Gant you're looking at."

Abyssinia raised her eyebrows with renewed interest. "It is? My, my. Running around with a hatchet, strange Axe-Men coming to kill him... No wonder he grew up to be a serial killer."

"So this is a memory?" Temper asked. "An eight-foot-tall lunatic who doesn't mind getting shot really did attack his house with an axe?"

Skulduggery peered out of the window as the Axe-Man continued to pound the door. "We don't know that," he said. "For all intents and purposes, we're inside Cadaverous's mind right now, so we shouldn't be too surprised if things get a little muddled. Temper, you should probably move away from the door."

Temper nodded and straightened up, just as the axe blade came through right where his head had been.

"He's using his axe now," Skulduggery explained helpfully.

59

Dark.

Wet.

Cold.

Valkyrie tried bringing her hands to her face, but the muck was too thick. She was still sinking. She could feel it. Tried to turn. Couldn't. The earth was in her nose and ears and mouth. Her lungs begged to inhale something. Anything. Even muck. They didn't care. She could feel her body start to respond. Against every command she was issuing, her body was going to breathe in the filth and then she was going to die.

She tried to kick herself to the surface, even though this wasn't water, even though she couldn't move her legs.

Apart from her foot. Her right foot. It was moving. She could move it.

And now her left. One moment it was just the foot. Then it was the ankle.

She kept sinking. The more she sank, the more she could move.

Her right knee. She could bend her right knee.

With her lungs burning, Valkyrie kicked out, felt herself sink faster. She was emerging from the other side, whatever it was, wherever it was, so she squirmed, and her hips were free now, and she squirmed more, and more –

– and she fell, dropping, gasping, and she splashed into mud,

mud that grabbed at her, pulled at her, and she wiped her eyes clear, saw that she was still in the cellar, and before the muck claimed her she looked up, saw the muck on the ceiling, and then she was submerged once again.

This time she didn't try to raise herself up. This time she focused on burrowing herself down, and after a moment her foot broke free of the mud, just like last time.

She was going to sink and fall and sink and fall, and it was going to go on until she drowned.

Her hips were free, and she could picture her legs dangling from the ceiling. She kicked them up behind her, plunging them into the mud even as her torso kept sinking.

There was a moment when she thought she'd messed up, a moment when she hung there, on the verge of dropping but not being able to, and then she was out and falling once again. This time she covered her face with her hands, twisted her body and sucked in a deep, deep breath.

She hit the mud with her elbows first, her head went in shoulders deep, her body splashing down behind. Squirming to go faster, she kept her feet out of the mud for as long as she could.

She sank head first. When she couldn't move her feet any more, she knew she was close to being through. Seconds passed. Long, long seconds, and a lot of them. Again, she became afraid that she'd miscalculated.

And then she emerged. She gasped, took her hands away from her face, cleared her eyes, blinking rapidly.

The cellar looked different from up here.

The table beside the muck. If she could grab it, she might be able to pull herself out of this crazy cycle. When her waist was free, she started swaying, and by the time her thighs were emerging she was swaying back and forth, trying to time it right.

Suddenly she was falling.

She reached out, stretched with both arms. Her hand slapped

325

against the table and then she was in the dirt again – with one hand closing round a table leg. She went to pull herself out, but only succeeded in yanking the table closer.

She started sinking again.

She pulled the table round, grasping the second leg with her free hand, and tugged them both into the muck. With her full weight pressing down, this end of the table sank quickly. Once she'd made a ramp, Valkyrie started dragging herself up.

She clambered on to the table, welcoming the painful knocks, and rolled across, landing on the floor. Despite her exhaustion, she didn't stay down in case the mulch here started pulling on her, too. She heaved herself to her feet and stumbled to the stairs. She almost cried when her foot found the first step. How firm it was. How solid. She started up, and a shadow fell across her.

"Want a sweetie, sweetie?" Mr Hogan asked.

His bulk blocked out the light, transforming him into a shape of pure darkness.

Then he grunted, and fell forward, and Valkyrie dodged back as he crashed down the steps.

Omen peered down. "What happened to you?"

60

The Axe-Man was shredding the door to splinters. Temper was not happy about this turn of events – not happy at all.

Even Abyssinia was on her feet, though still looking bored.

"Why don't you do something?" Temper asked her. He had to speak loudly to be heard over the racket. "You're all super powerful and stuff, right?"

"I am super powerful, this is true," she responded, "but we're in Cadaverous's world now, and here I'm probably just as completely weak and useless as you are."

"Right," said Temper. "Thanks."

Skulduggery walked over to the wild man and started untying him.

"What are you doing?" Temper asked.

"The enemy of my enemy is my friend," Skulduggery said.

"Not all the time," Abyssinia countered.

"Well, no, not all the time, but definitely some of the time."

Abyssinia made a face. "That's debatable. A lot of the time they take the opportunity to try to kill you, too."

"This is also true," Skulduggery said. He pulled away the last of the rope. "But hopefully not in this case. Temper, hand him his hatchets."

Temper stared. "The hatchets he tried to kill me with?"

"Unless there are others you can see."

"He tried to kill me with them, Skulduggery."

"But I doubt he'll try it again when there's a blood-drenched man with an axe trying to get in and he's got his son to protect."

Temper grabbed the hatchets, hesitated, and tossed them over. The wild man caught them, but didn't attack any of them. Yet.

Skulduggery untied the kid, who leaped up and backed into the corner.

The door, or what little there was left of it, broke apart and the Axe-Man came through, hefting his giant axe in his giant hands.

Skulduggery glanced at Abyssinia. "Do you want to try first?"

She seemed to consider it, then shook her head. "Not especially. I vote we all attack together. *Unus pro omnibus, omnes pro uno.*"

Temper frowned. "Say what?"

"One for all and all for one," Skulduggery translated.

"Ah," Temper said, "*The Three Musketeers.*"

"I don't know what that is," said Abyssinia.

The wild man gave a war cry and ran forward, hatchets at the ready, but the Axe-Man cut him in two with one mighty swing. As both halves of his body hit the floor, Abyssinia let out a sigh.

"Does no one speak Latin any more?"

Temper scooped up one of the fallen hatchets as the Axe-Man stepped further into the shack.

Little Cadaverous whimpered in the corner.

Skulduggery adjusted his cuffs, and took a single step towards the Axe-Man. He said something Temper didn't understand. He waved his hands. The tone of his voice indicated that he was making a joke. The Axe-Man, however, appeared immune to Skulduggery's charms, and Skulduggery had to dodge back to avoid the blade that cut deep into the floorboards.

"Get him!" Temper shouted, leaping forward. "While his axe is—"

The Axe-Man pulled his axe out easily.

"Never mind," Temper said, leaping away again.

The Axe-Man turned his sack-covered head in his direction. "That," Temper said to him, "is a really nice sack. Skulduggery?"

"Lovely sack."

"Abyssinia?"

"It's a sack," she said. "I'm not going to say it's anything special when it's just a sack."

The Axe-Man turned to her.

She folded her arms. "Don't act offended. You wear a bag on your head."

The Axe-Man swung, impossibly fast, and Abyssinia barely ducked in time. Skulduggery snapped his palm against the air and the air rippled and the Axe-Man stumbled backwards. But then he charged, knocking Skulduggery off his feet. Abyssinia crashed into him, tried to suck out his life force, but the Axe-Man's massive arm swept her into the wall like a tidal wave. She fell to her knees, gasping.

Temper turned, grabbed the little boy, and ran for the door.

The Axe-Man immediately lost interest in Skulduggery and Abyssinia, and started thundering after them.

Temper ran round the corner of the shack, plunging into the trees before the Axe-Man caught sight of him again. The kid clung to him, terrified.

Temper moved quickly, staying low and keeping to the treeline. He waited for the sounds of the Axe-Man crashing through branches before he crept back out of the trees and raced over to the second shack. The door was open and he ran through, put the boy down, put his finger to his lips.

The kid, Cadaverous Gant as a child, nodded. He had big eyes.

They were in a small barn. There was a table laden with rough farming tools and a few cloth sacks in the corner. There were more tools leaning up against the wall, but nowhere to hide if the Axe-Man came looking. Temper turned back to the door to peek out, saw the Axe-Man coming straight for them.

Cursing, he jumped back, reached for the kid and couldn't find him. The little creep was digging his way under a gap in the far wall.

The Axe-Man had to turn sideways to fit through the door.

Temper backed off, but the Axe-Man went straight for the boy. Grabbing a pitchfork, Temper ran up behind him and sank the prongs into his back. He got an elbow in the face for his trouble and that knocked him to the ground, too stunned to do anything but register the Axe-Man turning in his direction. At the last moment, he noticed the axe rising, and his brain kicked into gear and he rolled under the table. The axe came straight through, sent the farm tools clattering, but Temper had already got to his feet on the other side.

The Axe-Man pulled the pitchfork from his back and flipped it in his free hand. He kicked the remains of the table to one side and Temper backed off, his avenues of escape cut off. The Axe-Man thrust the pitchfork at him and Temper skipped sideways, almost fast enough to dodge it.

Almost.

Two prongs sliced into him and he gasped as the Axe-Man forced him backwards. He hit the wall and stayed there, eyes wide, the pain just beginning to blossom. The Axe-Man let go of the pitchfork and strode across the shack, grabbing the kid by the ankles and hauling him back. The little boy screamed and struggled. Temper went to help, but the pitchfork was pinning him to the wall.

The Axe-Man lifted the sack on his head, exposing a huge, misshapen mouth that seemed to grow as it widened –

– and he dropped the kid into it.

Temper stared. The Axe-Man let the sack cover his head again, and adjusted the rope that secured it. Then he paused, and looked at the wall. Cocked his head.

He strode out of the shack.

Temper pulled the pitchfork from his side, cursing in pain as he did so. With his hands over the wounds, he stumbled to the hole the kid had been trying to escape through and dropped down. He could see across the clearing to where Abyssinia was approaching the third shack. The Axe-Man's boots passed in front of the hole and Temper jerked back, stifling a moan. He got up as Skulduggery appeared at the door.

"You're hurt," Skulduggery said.

"He stuck a fork in me. I'm done." Temper laughed without humour. "He's going after Abyssinia."

"Where's the child?"

"He swallowed him."

"He ate him?"

Temper shrugged. Even that was painful. "I didn't see any chewing. I just saw swallowing."

From outside, the sound of a fight, but Skulduggery wasn't moving from the doorway.

"Are we going to help?" Temper asked. He had a packet of leaves somewhere on him. He knew he did.

"I've been thinking about that," Skulduggery said.

Blood was soaking through Temper's clothes as he searched his pockets. "You want the big guy to kill her."

"I doubt he'd be able to kill her," Skulduggery said, "but he might be able to injure her enough so that I can cut out her heart again."

Temper found the leaves, stuffed them in his mouth. The pain lessened. "Man," he said, "that is cold."

"You object?"

"Me? Naw. But that doesn't warm it up any."

"I suppose not."

There were crashes now. The sound of wood splintering.

"And what do we do if he does beat her?" Temper asked. The pain was nothing more than an irritation now. "How do we stop him?"

"We don't have to stop him," Skulduggery said. "We avoid

331

him. We walk away. He hasn't actually killed anyone – not anyone real anyway. If he doesn't pose a threat to innocent life, why would it be our problem?"

"I guess so. Course, now I feel stupid for risking my life to save a kid that doesn't exist."

"He existed once."

"Not like this, though. I mean, this can't be a memory if Cadaverous's younger self gets swallowed whole by the big guy. Unless he manages to tunnel out somehow. Which is just weird."

"This isn't pure memory," Skulduggery said. "I think it's a reinterpretation of the day his father was killed."

"So who's the Axe-Man?"

"Right now I'm thinking it might be the physical manifestation of his own violent urges."

"Man, I hate those," said Temper, and then Abyssinia came crashing through the wall in an explosion of wood and splinters.

61

Valkyrie used Omen's jacket to wipe the mud from her face and arms as she drove. She handed his jacket back to him and he thanked her unenthusiastically. Her T-shirt was soaking, and clung to her, and the jodhpurs were stained black. She turned on to the road that swept by the pier and up to her family's house – but slowed as she came to the turn. The pier wasn't a pier. In Cadaverous's world, it was a wooden bridge that crossed the water, linking up with the island in the distance.

She manoeuvred the car on to the bridge – it was narrow, with no railings – and drove slowly, the dark water lapping on either side. She glanced up through the windscreen. The sun hadn't moved its position, but, when the clock hand ticked over to 11.15, the sun immediately darkened to a burning amber that infected the sky, and a multitude of blazing reds and oranges washed over and banished the blue.

"Cool," Omen whispered.

Forty-five minutes left. Forty-five minutes to save her sister.

62

Abyssinia dusted herself off and, without looking at either of them, said, "One for all and all for one, huh?"

"We were just about to go and help," Skulduggery said.

She looked at Temper. "And you?"

He showed her all the blood. "I'm injured. I need medical attention."

"I'm disappointed in you both. I thought we were a team."

"We were making plans," said Temper. "Discussing theories. Skulduggery thinks the Axe-Man is a metaphor."

"So I was thrown through a wall by a metaphor?" Abyssinia asked. "Well, that's nice."

"Speaking of whom," Skulduggery murmured, and walked to the hole Abyssinia had made.

Temper joined him, and they peered out. The sky had become a painting of bleeding red and burning orange. The sun was darker, too, but still in the same position. They watched the Axe-Man walk back to the cabin. He started swinging the axe into the front door again.

"The door's been fixed," Temper said. "How did the door get fixed?"

"I doubt that's the only thing that's been reset," Skulduggery said.

"You think the gentleman with the hatchets and the child are in there, don't you?" Abyssinia asked.

"I think they're on a loop, yes," Skulduggery said.

"Good," said Abyssinia. "Now that he's distracted, I can take a look inside that revolting little shed."

She walked out. Skulduggery and Temper followed.

They crossed the clearing to the smallest shack. Abyssinia led the way in. Temper went last, and immediately gagged at the smell of rotting meat and congealing blood.

The shack was split into two rooms. In the first one, animal carcasses hung from chains and black clouds of flies rose from mounds of furs and pelts. A large table, stained with blood and scarred with notches, took up most of the space. Despite the history of death carved into it, the table was neat. Orderly.

Not so the smaller table, for the smaller hunter, that sat in the corner. This table was littered with the butchered remains of animals. There was no evidence of the practical, pragmatic skinning and preparing of prey. Here was evidence of a psychopath's delight.

Abyssinia ignored all this. She went straight to the other room like she was pulled there.

"Caisson!" she cried.

Temper and Skulduggery glanced at each other, and followed her in.

63

The bridge narrowed even further, and Valkyrie had visions of the tyres slipping off the side and the car plunging into the sea. She took a deep breath and continued on.

The island was a flat, grassy pebble. There were no trees, no other vegetation.

She stopped the car. The two-storey house at the island's exact centre was tall and dark and pointed. The porch was wide, supported by square columns. There was a rocking chair beside the door, which stood open.

"I suppose I should stay here," said Omen from the back seat.

"No," Valkyrie said. "I might need your help."

"Really?"

She turned to him. "Omen, if we find Alice and you get the chance, you grab her and get the hell out, OK? You forget about me and you run. Do you understand?"

Omen hesitated, then nodded.

They got out of the car. Valkyrie raked her fingers through her hair, coming out with fistfuls of drying mud that she flung at the ground as they entered the house.

Most of the doorways on the ground floor were arched, and lacking any actual doors. Valkyrie could see straight through to the corridors that stretched to the rear of the deceptively large building. Corridors lined with too many closed doors for all of them to actually lead anywhere.

A wide staircase rose lazily along the wall to her left, its bottom step beginning just beyond the doorway to the living room – a wood-panelled room with a large fireplace and a single armchair.

To their right, through a corridor, the kitchen.

"Alice?" she called. "Alice, where are you?"

For a moment, there was nothing, and then—

"Stephanie?"

"Alice!" Valkyrie shouted, striding for the stairs.

"Stephanie! I'm here!"

Valkyrie took the stairs two at a time, Omen right behind her. "Where are you? Describe where you are!"

"I'm in a room!" Alice shouted back from far away. "It has a bed and a chair and a bedside table with a lamp!"

Valkyrie got to the landing. "Is there a window?"

"No! But there's a door!"

"Bang on the door, Alice! Let me hear you!"

Somewhere in the house, she heard little fists beating upon a door.

"Keep doing that!" she shouted, moving again. "I'll find you!"

They followed the sound down a corridor, picking up speed, running now, feet on floorboards that creaked sharply with each step, now on to a thin rug, then back to floorboards, then back to a rug that gave way beneath her and Valkyrie dropped, her momentum slamming her into the side of the pit. She hung there, fingers digging in for purchase, legs dangling as the pit swallowed the rest of the rug. She glanced down, saw another hole beneath her, revealing a drop right into the basement.

Omen reached down, grabbed her, and pulled her up.

"Traps," he said.

She nodded. "This house will be full of them."

They moved on, more cautiously this time, and followed Alice's voice to a door.

Valkyrie tried the handle. It was locked. "Alice, I'm here."

"Stephanie! Let me out!!"

"Stand back from the door, OK? Stand against the wall."

Valkyrie stepped back.

"OK!" Alice called. "I'm against the wall!"

Valkyrie kicked and, although the door shuddered, it felt as sturdy as hell under her boot. She kicked again, and again, and then rammed her shoulder into it. That hurt.

"Hold on, Alice," she said, and turned to Omen. "Find something to—"

A door opened behind Omen, and Valkyrie grabbed him, pulled him behind her as Cadaverous Gant stepped out. The real Cadaverous Gant.

"You made it," Cadaverous said. "And it's not even midnight. But you seem to have broken the rules. Omen Darkly, aren't you supposed to be dead?"

"Let Alice go," said Valkyrie. "Whatever plans you have for me, let Alice go. She can't hurt you."

Cadaverous smiled. "Neither can you, Valkyrie. Not in here. In here, you are as ineffectual as a five-year-old."

"I'm seven," Alice said from behind the door.

The smile widened. "Kids, eh?"

64

"Caisson," Abyssinia whispered, kneeling by her son. "What have they done to you?"

Caisson was unconscious on the floor, next to the rear wall of the shack, and was in no condition to answer. His silver hair was long and matted. His face was drawn, his skin an unhealthy pallor. He wore an old hospital gown, and his wrists were shackled.

Temper and Skulduggery watched Abyssinia check her son for any obvious injuries.

"He doesn't look a whole lot like me," Skulduggery said.

"I wouldn't take it personally," Abyssinia responded. "My family's genes have always been dominant. I hope you get to meet him properly one day – assuming you survive your encounter with Cadaverous."

"You're leaving, I take it."

Abyssinia scooped Caisson into her arms, and stood. "As precious as this little team of ours is, yes, I am. I feel our special bond ended when you decided to let that monster with the axe try to kill me. I hope you find Valkyrie. I'd hate for her to miss that particular sensation of you betraying her the way you betrayed me."

"I thought you came here to rescue Caisson *and* kill Cadaverous."

"Oh, I did, but if you love someone you must prioritise, and our son is much more important to me than the chance to exact some childish revenge."

Skulduggery turned to Temper. "Go with her," he said.

Temper frowned. "What? Why?"

"You're hurt."

"I feel fine."

"You're hurt, and you're losing too much blood. I can find Valkyrie on my own."

"Seriously, man, I can do this, and you need the back-up. I've got plenty of leaves to keep me going."

"Your packet is empty."

"No, it's not," Temper said, taking it from his pocket. "See?"

Skulduggery plucked it from his hand and clicked his fingers and Temper watched the leaves flare and burn.

"I cannot believe you did that," he said softly.

"There's more leaves in the Bentley," Skulduggery said, handing him the keys before walking to the door. "Better hurry or you won't make it."

Temper watched Skulduggery leave the shack and rise off his feet, disappearing from sight.

Abyssinia carried Caisson to the door and, too late, Temper saw a string that ran from Caisson's shackles to the wall. It went taut, and he started to shout a warning when the string broke, and a tiny bell sounded.

That's all. No trap was sprung. No pit opened beneath them.

Abyssinia kept on walking, and Temper frowned and followed.

65

Cadaverous halted, his head turning slightly, like he was listening to something in the distance.

"Huh," he muttered, "she's early." He smiled at Valkyrie. "I'm afraid I'll have to divide my attention. But you will stay here, won't you? You won't find some way to escape? If you do, I promise I'll tear your little friend's arms off."

Moving impossibly fast, he grabbed Omen and shoved Valkyrie. She spun backwards, righting herself just in time to see him dragging Omen through a door that slammed shut after them.

66

Omen went stumbling forward, falling to his knees on the dirt as Cadaverous strode by him. He was outside, in a clearing with a few rickety old wooden shacks. He was in the mountains. He looked around. Definitely in the mountains.

Someone moved in the doorway of the nearest – and smallest – shack, and Abyssinia stepped out into the sunlight. She carried an unconscious man with hair as silver as her own. Caisson.

"You played my game better than I anticipated," Cadaverous said, smiling.

"Ah," said Abyssinia, "I was wondering when you'd appear. Thank you for keeping my son safe for me."

"It was entirely my pleasure," Cadaverous said. "Was it a joyful reunion? Were there tears?"

"I was practically overcome with emotion."

Temper Fray emerged from the shack behind her. His eyes narrowed when he saw Cadaverous, then widened when he saw Omen.

"You're alive," he said.

Omen didn't know how to respond to that, so he nodded and said, "Yes, I am."

Abyssinia turned, and passed Caisson to Temper. He grunted as he took the weight. "Take my son out of here," she said. "If you harm him, or leave him behind, I will crush you. Do you understand?"

Temper didn't appear to have anything much to say to that, so he just nodded and said, "Yup."

Cadaverous and Abyssinia met in the middle of the clearing. "Is this my punishment?" she asked. "For neglecting you?"

"You didn't neglect us," Cadaverous replied. "You abandoned us. You promised us glory, power, redemption... but the moment we helped you come back you forgot it all. You betrayed us."

Temper motioned quickly to Omen, and Omen got up and scurried over to him, giving a wide berth to the two evil nutballs.

"You keep saying us," Abyssinia said, "yet all I see is you."

Cadaverous smiled again. "I'm the only one who isn't scared."

"In here, you mean. Out there, you would never dare say these things."

"But we're not out there, are we? Out there, you would rip me apart without a thought. But I brought you here, straight to my home, where I hold the power. I gave you more credit, Abyssinia. I'm disappointed in you."

"I do so hate to disappoint my children."

Cadaverous laughed, and attacked her.

Omen reached Temper. "How did you get here?" he whispered.

"I came with Skulduggery. He flew off to find Val. Here, help me with this."

Omen did his best to take Caisson's weight while Temper repositioned himself. When he straightened up, Temper was carrying Caisson in a fireman's lift. "We're getting outta here," he said.

Omen took his eyes off Cadaverous, who was throwing Abyssinia around like she was a broken doll, and noticed Temper's bloody shirt. "You're injured. Oh, God, you're injured. Do you have your phone? We could call Never."

"My phone doesn't work in here, slick. We're gonna have to do this the old-fashioned way."

"You're... bleeding really badly."

Temper grimaced. "Then I guess we'd better hurry."

67

Valkyrie found a poker downstairs, and used it to try to force the door open. The wood splintered but didn't give.

"Alice," she said. "Hey, sweetie. What's the room like?"

"Um," Alice replied. "It's square. The walls and the floor are made of wood."

"Is there any furniture?"

"No. Can you get me out of here?"

"I will, Alice, I will. I promise. How you doing? Are you worried?"

"No, I'm OK."

Valkyrie smiled. "Good girl. That's what I like to hear. I'll have you out as soon as I..." She turned her head, frowning. Then she heard it again, closer this time.

Skulduggery, calling her name.

"Up here!" she shouted. "I'm up here!" She heard him running up the stairs and shouted, "Be careful of booby traps!"

Skulduggery came round the corner at speed, his feet centimetres above the ground, floating over the hole she'd fallen into.

She ran to him as he landed, hugging him. "So glad you're here."

"Of course you are," he said. "You're covered in mud, by the way, and this is an exquisite suit."

"Sorry," she said, releasing him. "How did you find us?"

"Your car is parked on an island just off what appears to be an exact replica of your hometown. Where else would you be?

"Alice," Valkyrie said, banging her fist against the door. "Stand back."

"I still am!" Alice responded.

Skulduggery swept his arm wide and the door flung open, and Valkyrie scooped Alice up in the biggest hug she could manage, noticing Skulduggery activating his façade just in time.

"The two of you have had adventures," he said.

"Omen's here, too," Valkyrie said. "Cadaverous took him, just a minute ago. Skulduggery, you need to fly Alice out of here."

"I'm sure I can manage that," he said, his hand on Alice's back as they turned for the stairs.

But a door opened before them and Cadaverous came through, dragging a broken and battered Abyssinia after him. "And where do you think you're going?" he asked.

Skulduggery tossed a fireball into Cadaverous's face, then pushed at the air. Cadaverous's clothes rippled wildly, but he didn't even sway, so Skulduggery strode up to him and lashed a kick into his knee.

Cadaverous laughed, swung a punch that Skulduggery ducked, laughed again as Skulduggery kicked at his other knee. It didn't so much as buckle.

Keeping Alice behind her, Valkyrie watched as Cadaverous grabbed Skulduggery and marched him backwards. With his free hand, he slapped the wall and the wall opened, and Cadaverous shoved Skulduggery into the darkness beyond. He slapped the wall again: it closed up, and he turned to Valkyrie as she picked up Alice and ran.

His laughter following her, Valkyrie leaped over the pit and kept going towards the stairs.

Halfway to the bottom they trembled beneath her. She grabbed the banister with her free hand and jumped, jamming her feet against the wall as the top of each step slid back into the riser, exposing the upturned rusty nails waiting beneath.

"Hold on," she said to Alice, and sprang over the banister, adjusting her grip as she did so. Her feet hit the wall below. She let herself hang, then dropped to the ground. She hefted her sister in her arms. "You OK?"

Alice nodded, and Valkyrie ran for the front door, but a hatch in the ceiling opened and Cadaverous dropped through.

Valkyrie hissed, turned, sprinting into the nearest corridor. They followed it round, and it narrowed as they reached the door at the far end, which opened towards them. Beyond was more corridor and another door.

Valkyrie glanced behind. No sign of Cadaverous.

She carried on, but had to put Alice down. The second door was smaller than the first. Through they went, and round the corner. The third door was smaller still, and Valkyrie had to duck her head to get through. The corridor was tight. Her shoulders brushed the walls on either side.

Alice hurried through the next door without an issue, but Valkyrie had to bend double. They had no choice but to move in single file now.

Another corner turned, and they came to a wall with a tiny door.

Valkyrie lay flat, pushed it open. The corridor returned to normal proportions on the other side. "Go on," she said to Alice. "Wriggle through."

Alice obeyed, crawling through quickly and easily. Valkyrie stuck her head in after her. There was a rope on the wall next to her, looped round a bracket. She couldn't look up far enough to see what it was connected to.

Her shoulders brushed the top of the small door as she passed through. She tried to heave herself in the rest of the way, but her rear end hit with more force than her shoulders and she heard a clack and suddenly the rope was unravelling.

"Grab the rope!" she shouted, and Alice lunged, got her hands to it and the rope went taut, jerked her off her heels for a moment. Valkyrie twisted, looked up, saw the guillotine blade hovering above.

"Your bum is too big," Alice said.

"Apparently so," Valkyrie whispered.

"This rope is heavy," said Alice.

Valkyrie held out her hands. "Give it to me," she said, smiling.

The normal-sized door at the other end of the room opened, and Cadaverous came through. "There you are," he said, smiling.

Valkyrie yanked on the rope, tried to wriggle through, but Cadaverous had already taken Alice's hand.

"Leave her alone," Valkyrie said. "Alice, come back!"

But then he was leading her away.

And then they were gone.

68

Temper stumbled over a tree root, falling to one knee. "Aw, hell," he murmured.

Omen tried to catch Caisson before he dropped off Temper's shoulder, but all he could do was slow his descent to the ground.

"I may need urgent medical attention," Temper said. His breath was laboured and he was sweating. His clothes were drenched in blood. "Also something for the pain. And possibly a stretcher."

"How far is the exit?" Omen asked.

"Not sure," said Temper. "Or if we're even on the right track."

"You think we might be lost?" Omen asked, panic rising in his chest. "But you just came this way!"

Temper wiped his forehead. "Slick, I can navigate my way through any urban jungle without an overabundance of hassle. But over a mountain? All these trees look the same. All these rocks look the same. See that bush? I don't know if it's my first time seeing that bush or the fourth. We might be totally screwed here, kid, and I have to admit I ain't thinking so straight."

"OK," Omen said, nodding fiercely, "I'll take care of it. I'll get us out."

"You're taking charge," said Temper. "That's what I like to see. That's good. I feel better now. Though I might need a lie-down."

"You can't," Omen said, pulling him up when he tried to sit.

"You're losing too much blood. Our only chance is to keep going, all right? We need to find the exit and get to the car."

"I can't carry this guy any more."

"Maybe, um, maybe I could."

"I don't see that happening."

"Then... then how about we drag him? We each take an ankle and just drag him behind us?"

Temper wiped the sweat from his brow. "Yeah, we could try that, I guess. Help me up."

Omen heard a loud tick, and looked up. Through the trees he watched the sun flip like a coin, revealing the moon on its other side, and the sky changed to a deep, dark and ugly purple.

It had just turned 11.30.

69

Both hands gripping the rope, Valkyrie pulled, raising the guillotine blade. She turned slightly, squirmed through, tucking her knees to her chest as she released her hold. The blade *thunked* into the ground behind her and she rolled to her feet and ran on, barging through the door.

"Alice!" she shouted. "Skulduggery!"

Lights were flickering on all over the house, throwing back the darkness as Valkyrie panicked. She shouted for her sister, shouted again – and finally heard Alice respond.

"Alice!" Valkyrie yelled, bursting into the living room.

Cadaverous was sitting in the armchair. There were suddenly roaring flames in the fireplace, but no sign of Alice or Skulduggery.

Valkyrie stalked over. "Where are they?"

Cadaverous smiled. "Close by."

"If you've hurt them—"

"Why would I have hurt them already?" Cadaverous interrupted. "You think I'd go to all this trouble and not even have you present for something like that? No, no, no. You have to watch. You have to see them in pain; you have to see them die. Then, and only then, will I allow your pain to end."

"And that's it, is it? Then it's all done?"

"Then it's all done." He stood. "Are you ready?"

"No."

"Well, fortunately, it's not up to you."

"That's not what I meant," Valkyrie said. "When I spoke to the boy, the younger version of you—"

"He's not real," Cadaverous said irritably. "He never existed."

"He's real somewhere. Somewhere in your head, that boy is real, and he is you, a version of you that didn't sink into all this evil. When I spoke to him, he told me something. He told me not to play your game."

Now Cadaverous laughed. "My dear girl, in here, my game is all there is."

"I know," said Valkyrie. "Which is why we shouldn't be playing."

She backed off, turned to a door, lunging through, Cadaverous's laugh following her into the hall. She ran to the kitchen, careful not to touch anything, wary of booby traps. She ignored the back door. In the old house, the real house, in St Louis, the back door had been rigged to deliver an electric shock. Instead, she clambered up beside the sink, kicked at the window, cracked it, kicked again, smashed it, the glass trying to get through the jodhpurs. She cleared the edge with her boot and crouched, then slid through, dropping into weeds and scrub that snatched at her ankles.

Round the corner of the house she ran, sprinting for her car.

The front door opened and yellow light spilled out and from that light Cadaverous came, jumping down the steps, snatching at her, but she ducked him and his foot hit her own and they both went down, sprawling away from each other. Valkyrie rolled, came up with her keys in her hand, leaped on to the bonnet and slid across.

Pulled the door open. Key in the ignition. Engine roaring. Knocked the car into reverse and the wheels spun, throwing dust, Cadaverous punching a hand through the passenger-side window, reaching for her.

She yanked the wheel, spinning the car, leaving Cadaverous to stagger, leaving him for the gloom to swallow, and she gunned the engine and was off. She flicked on the headlights, lit up the bridge a moment before she reached it, and then the wooden slats were thundering beneath, and on either side were the dark waters of Cadaverous Gant's mind.

The other side of the bridge approached quickly and then shot by. No more thunder. Just the engine now, and the familiar crunch of tyres on tarmac as Valkyrie followed the road up into the town that wasn't Haggard. Before she swerved on to Main Street, she raised her eyes to the rear-view mirror. Glimpsed headlights.

"Come on!" she shouted. "Come and get me!"

Main Street was empty now. She drove down the middle of the road, got to the bend opposite the service station, nearly jumped the kerb and hit the wall, but she forced the car back under control and kept going, biting down on her lower lip the whole time. From here on, it was a straight blast to the graveyard, and her foot got heavier on the pedal.

The darkness blurred by. The engine's roar filled her ears. Valkyrie gripped the wheel and kept her elbows locked. At this speed, one mistake, one tiny mistake, would flip the car, would bring this manufactured world crashing in on top of her. Her seatbelt. She wasn't wearing her seatbelt.

The graveyard approached. She didn't let her eyes flicker.

Once beyond the graveyard, Valkyrie eased off the accelerator. The roar decreased. She turned the wheel slightly and the car slid, and she tried turning into the skid, but then the car was spinning, and she cracked her head against the window and came to a sudden, rocking stop in the middle of the road.

A moment to sit there, just a moment, to make sure she hadn't crashed, she hadn't killed herself, then a glance around to establish where she was. The town that wasn't Haggard in front of her. The way out behind. And, speeding towards her, Cadaverous Gant's Cadillac.

Reverse. Foot down. One hand on the wheel, the other across the headrest of the passenger seat, looking behind as much as in

353

front. The Cadillac's headlights filled the car like water. Bumper to bumper, she fled and he chased. Reflected light gave her a glimpse of that grinning, manic face.

Her free hand, pulling the seatbelt across her body. Switched hands. Clicked it in. Braced herself. A foot on the brake and a sharp turn of the wheel. The Cadillac hit her and she spun and the Cadillac swept by and now she was following it, cursing at it, ramming into the back of it. They followed the curve of the road, up to the woods. Up to the narrow, narrow road into the woods.

She pulled alongside the Cadillac, going faster with every heartbeat. He bashed into her, shaking the car. She bashed into him, harder. Did it again, nudging him over, making him give up the middle of the road. She aimed the car at the gap between the trees and went faster, faster, way too fast – Jesus she was going to kill herself, going to hit one of those trees on either side and go up in a fireball, everything blurring. One tip from that Cadillac and it was all over –

– and then she was plunging between the trees, her rear-view flashing with the Cadillac's swooping headlights as Cadaverous swerved away to avoid an impact.

Valkyrie's foot eased off the accelerator and tapped the brake. Still going fast, but managing it. Controlling it. Slowing down more as she came to the bend in the road. She had time. She took one hand off the steering wheel and flexed the pain from her fingers. Did the same with the other one. She tasted blood in her mouth. Her bottom lip was bleeding.

She slowed further. The end of the woodland was just ahead and Valkyrie rolled towards it, and stopped.

She turned off the engine, and got out. She stood beside the car, eyes on the bend in the road behind. Listening. This wouldn't work if he'd given up. This wouldn't work if he'd already gone back to kill Alice and Skulduggery.

Please let him not have gone back.

Through a gap in the branches, high overhead, she could see the clock moon. It was twenty minutes to midnight.

"I'm here!" she shouted at the dark trees. "I'm right here! Come and get me, you coward! Come on!"

In the woods, there was no warm breeze. In the woods, there was only stillness.

And then headlights snapped on at the bend in the road, like a great beast opening its eyes, and the Cadillac came roaring for her.

70

Valkyrie jumped in the car, twisted the key and floored it. The car leaped forward, but the Cadillac still bashed into the back of her. She was thrown about in her seat as the car fishtailed, scraped a tree, ricocheting from one side to the other, the Cadillac behind her straight as an arrow.

Out of the trees her car screamed and now there was the hill, there was just the hill, and then she'd be out, and that's where she led him and that's where he followed, so determined to catch her, to kill her, that maybe he didn't notice, maybe he didn't care how close they were to the exit. The Cadillac came up on her right and crashed into her in a shriek of tortured metal.

Still they sped on, locked together. Up the hill. Towards the exit.

Cadaverous reached through her window, fingers closing round Valkyrie's sodden T-shirt. She cursed, tried to break the hold, but he was already pulling her out of the car. Her foot left the accelerator and her hand left the steering wheel and the car turned on its own, flipped, left the ground and rolled through the air as the Cadillac sped on, leaving Valkyrie's car to crash to the ground behind them.

Now, instead of trying to break free of his hold, Valkyrie held on, desperately keeping her feet off the speeding road.

They were at the top of the hill now, passing the payphone, and Cadaverous braked hard and the Cadillac swerved and skidded to a halt, a stone's throw from the exit. The engine was turned off.

Sudden silence. Valkyrie let her feet touch the ground. Cadaverous pulled her in close and smiled. His breath was hot, like the breeze.

She grabbed his wrist, tried to twist it. She dug her thumb into his eye. He didn't even flinch. He laughed at her struggles. He was God here, after all.

But out there, out through that garage-door-sized hole in the cliff face, he was just a man.

Valkyrie managed to pull her T-shirt loose but Cadaverous snarled, grabbed at her again, yanked out a clump of her hair that brought tears to her eyes, but she was free and she was running. She heard him jump out of the Cadillac, heard him run after her, but she was right there, she was so close, just another three steps and she'd be out.

He kicked at her ankles and she hit the ground, biting her tongue, the hard-packed dirt scraping at her skin as she skidded and bounced.

Her elbows, scratched and cut and bleeding, rested on the cement lip of the Midnight Hotel's garage. It was cold out here, out in the real world. The air was chilled.

Fingers closed round her ankles and dragged her back.

Valkyrie twisted, tried to break free, but he just laughed, swung her a little and let her go. This time, when she hit the ground, she did her best to roll, but she was so tired, so exhausted, that while she managed to come up on one knee, she immediately fell back.

"Are you quite done?" Cadaverous asked, standing between her and the exit.

She spat blood and didn't answer. She sucked in a deep breath, turned over and got up very, very slowly. She nodded at the battered Cadillac. "Last time someone damaged your car, you went spare."

"Spare?" Cadaverous said, raising an eyebrow. "Must be an Irishism I haven't sampled before. I did indeed 'go spare', but only because my car is a thing of beauty. The vehicle you see before you isn't my car. The real Cadillac is parked nearby and is quite safe, I assure you. This is merely the Cadillac I constructed for use in here. They're almost identical, aren't they? Almost but not quite. The interior and the grille are different, and the wheels are not—"

Valkyrie held up her hand. "I was just making small talk before you killed me. I really don't care about your stupid car."

"How many times do I have to tell you? You're not going to die before your sister and the skeleton. That would spoil the fun." He waved his hand, and the boot popped, and slowly opened. "In you go," he said.

"I'm not getting in there."

"I could throw you in, if you'd prefer, or you could climb in yourself and maintain some degree of dignity."

"Dignity's not going to do me any good stuck in a car boot."

"Very well," he said, and walked towards her.

She tried to dodge past him, but he grabbed her easily, his hand closing round the back of her neck. His fingers squeezed so tight she went light-headed, almost didn't notice him dragging her towards the Cadillac. She got her feet back under her, took her own weight. His grip loosened slightly. Not enough for her to break free, but enough so that she wasn't going to black out.

"...today's generation," Cadaverous was saying. "No dignity. No self-respect. You don't work for anything any more. You just expect it all to be handed to you. Dignity is earned. It comes from perseverance."

Valkyrie managed a laugh. "Your little friend Jeremiah didn't show much dignity when he died."

Cadaverous stopped walking for a moment. Before Valkyrie could start to prise his hand away, however, he lunged at the Cadillac, slamming her face into the side.

He held her there, pinned, unable to do anything about it, and then he leaned down.

"Don't you talk about him that way," Cadaverous said.

She didn't want to say anything else. She didn't want to utter one more word. All she wanted was to stay quiet and let him dump her in the boot. All she wanted was for him to stop hurting her.

Instead, she made herself smile. "He squealed."

Cadaverous leaned down. "What did you say?"

"When he fell," she said. "Or, when I let him fall, I mean. He squealed all the way down."

His eyes positively bulging from his gaunt face, Cadaverous hauled her back, and now all she could see was the Cadillac. The pretty, pretty Cadillac, all dented and bashed and scraped and covered in dust from the chase. The passenger's side window was rolled up. It was the one part of the car she could see that had yet to sustain any damage.

Then it was hurtling towards her and she closed her eyes and the world crashed and went dark.

71

The Cain girl had gone limp in his hands.

Cadaverous dropped her, disgusted, and she crumpled – less like a human body, more like a sack of human remains. Blood ran freely from the cuts on her face. At least she wasn't saying anything any more. At least she had shut up now, had stopped spewing all those lies about Jeremiah. Of course she had lied. It wasn't even her fault. She was a woman. It was in their nature. He had learned this a long, long time ago, had learned it as a child. His mother had been a liar. She had lied to his father so many times that it had reduced the man to nothing. Sharp words were like the blade of an axe – enough swings and they would chop down the tallest of trees.

He took hold of the girl's ankle, dragged her easily, enjoying the strength his home provided him. His back didn't spasm when he bent down to pick her up, and his muscles didn't strain when he lifted her into the trunk. His age didn't mean anything in here. In here, his energy was limitless.

He shut the trunk, went round to the driver's side, got in behind the wheel. He paused for a moment, wondering if he'd killed her. He didn't want her dead just yet. That would spoil his plans.

He focused on looking through her eyes, expecting nothing but darkness. Instead, he saw a red light. The interior of the trunk.

She was conscious again, and she was alive. He wasn't surprised. She had survived a lot worse than getting her head smashed through a car window. She was tough. It was one of the things he almost respected about her.

He left her to the red light, the steering wheel swimming back into view. Jeremiah hadn't been tough, not like that. In many ways, in fact, Jeremiah had been weak. Sometimes even petulant.

But he'd been talented, and that had meant a lot. The way he'd worked had been a wonder to behold. Watching Jeremiah, Cadaverous had often been reminded of himself as a young man.

He started the car, made a U-turn, was almost to the payphone when he glanced in the rear-view and saw that the trunk was open.

He braked. Leaped out. Sprinted after Valkyrie Cain as she stumbled for the exit.

She passed through. He felt her leave and it hit him like heartache.

He stopped, right at the doorway. She turned to him. Blood masked her face, ran in rivulets down her throat, mixing with the mud that caked her T-shirt. She stood just out of reach. To grab her, he'd have to step out of his home. He'd be vulnerable there. He'd be strong, and fast, but not this strong, not this fast. One more step and she'd have a chance to stop him.

"I'll kill them," he said. "I'll kill the skeleton first. I'll tear him apart and burn his bones. I'll scatter his ashes. Then I'll kill your sister, your helpless, terrified little sister."

"You're going to kill them anyway," Valkyrie responded, spraying small drops of blood every time her lips moved.

"I have to kill him," Cadaverous said. "For my own future survival. I can't have Skulduggery Pleasant running around after I've killed the great and terrible Valkyrie Cain. But I don't have to kill *her*. I can let her go, so long as you come back inside. I give you my word."

"You expect me to trust you?"

"I have never broken my word," Cadaverous told her. "I do not intend to start now."

"Everything you say is a lie."

Cadaverous shrugged. "You can believe that, if you wish. If it makes you feel better. If it lets you walk away. But, if you do walk away, then I will definitely kill her. If you leave, you will be cutting your own sister's throat."

"If you hurt her, I swear to you I'll kill you."

"Maybe you will. But that won't bring her back to life. And I can stay in here a mighty long time."

Valkyrie raised a hand to her head, as if she was just noticing her injuries. She looked at her hand, looked at the blood that covered it, and her legs gave out and she stumbled backwards, collapsed.

Cadaverous fought the urge to lunge at her during this moment of weakness. Even with her magic cut off, she was a formidable opponent, and he couldn't be sure that she wasn't faking this vulnerability in an attempt to draw him out. So he stayed where he was, watching her as she got to her hands and knees.

"We both know you're not going to run away," he told her. "It's not in your nature. You're going to exchange your life for your sister's, so let us forgo the pretence and get it over with. Midnight is almost upon us."

She stood. She looked genuinely unsteady, and her face – what little he could see of her skin beneath all that blood and dried muck – was startlingly pale. He began to think that maybe she wasn't faking it, after all.

He took a step over the border, into the real world.

Valkyrie used her dirty T-shirt to wipe some of the blood off her face. Her cuts were still bleeding, though, forging new rivers that dripped into her eyes, off her nose, off her chin. She was blinking rapidly, half blind, two steps away. Just two steps.

Cadaverous reached for her and saw a grin start to form and

he jumped back over the border, safe in the world in which he was all-powerful.

And Valkyrie laughed so hard she doubled over. "You're such a coward!" she cried. "You're such a typical little bully! Scurrying back to your safe place!"

Cadaverous felt that old anger rising up. She was starting to sound like the rest of them now.

"You're big and strong when you're on home turf, aren't you?" she said, taunting him in that way they did, where their words needled into his mind, prised away his control. "But the moment you step out into the real world you realise how small you are. How pathetic."

"Shut your mouth," Cadaverous snarled.

"How insignificant."

"I'll kill her," he said, walking back to his car. "Your sister is going to die and it's your fault. You could have saved her, but you were too busy showing off."

"Jeremiah died screaming!"

Cadaverous spun. "You shut your lying mouth!"

"He took after you," Valkyrie said, a snarl of her own on her face. "He talked tough and then it all fell apart. He begged me to help him. When he was about to fall. He begged me to help. He was crying. Know what else he said? He said, 'Please, Mr Gant, please save me.' How pathetic is that, huh? And then I let him go, and he fell, screaming, begging, with your name on his lips."

His fists were clenched. His muscles knotted. "I know what you're trying to do. You're trying to get me to lose control."

"No. I'm trying to get you to be a man."

A screech rose from somewhere within. "Who are *you* to question *me*?"

Valkyrie shrugged. An innocent, insouciant little shrug. "No one," she said. "I'm just a girl. Just a weak, helpless little girl. I don't even have my magic to defend myself with. But who are you? You're a big, full-grown man. And you're too scared to come and get me. You killed, what, a dozen women back when you were a serial killer? And how many people have you killed since you discovered magic? Do you even remember? I suppose it doesn't matter, because obviously none of them, not a one, ever challenged you. Not one of them was in a position to fight back. And then you meet someone like me, someone who is going to fight back, and you're too scared to come and get me."

He looked at her, and his fists unclenched, and he chuckled. She frowned.

"You've overplayed your hand, my dear," he said. "It was close. It was. You almost got me. Male pride is a surprisingly fragile thing, especially when a weak, helpless little girl like you is poking at it. But, of course, you're not a weak and helpless little girl, are you? You're dangerous, and you have a history of snatching victory from the jaws of defeat. So forgive me, Valkyrie, if I'm not prepared to play your little game tonight." The Cadillac's door opened as he walked over to it.

"Coward!" she shouted at him.

He glanced at the moon, then back at her. "You have ten minutes, and then the skeleton and your sister die. Who's the coward now, Valkyrie?"

72

He left her there, drenched in blood and impotent, and drove through the woodland, through the town and across the bridge. He stopped outside the house and walked up the steps to the front door. A calmness had settled over him. She'd either follow him and he'd kill her, or she wouldn't and he'd kill her sister. Either way he'd win. Either way he'd beaten her.

The house whispered to him when he entered, welcoming him back. He patted the table as he passed. The floorboards creaked and he smiled. The ceiling groaned.

He paused, swapping his sight for Valkyrie's. It was dark where she was. He watched her hands pulling apart weeds and branches. She was looking for something. Her movements desperate. Good.

The living room swam back into view and suddenly Abyssinia was in front of him, her hands clamped on to either side of his head.

But he just laughed.

"You think you can drain my life force?" he asked. "You think that's even possible in my own home?" He gripped her by the throat. "I am God here."

He hurled her through the wall, the wood splintering, and she crashed into the hidden room beyond. Skulduggery Pleasant, wearing a false face and holding Alice with his left arm, ignored her as she rolled to a stop at his feet, and raised his gun. Six bullets hit Cadaverous. Three to the chest and three to the head. None of them pierced the skin. None of them made Cadaverous so much as flinch.

There was an odd ripple around Alice's head.

"What a nice thought," Cadaverous said. "Using the air to protect her delicate ears from all that gunfire. Not that she's going to need her hearing. She won't exactly be getting any older after tonight."

Pleasant put the gun away. "At the risk of stating the obvious," he said, "she is only a child. You don't have to kill her."

"Valkyrie must learn that there is a cost to shirking one's responsibilities."

"She got away, then."

"I'm sure she'll be back," Cadaverous said. "She wouldn't just abandon the two of you, would she? I doubt she'd be able to live with herself afterwards."

"So what do you propose we do now?" Skulduggery asked. "Wait for her to arrive?"

"No. I want to inflict pain. Put the child down and come forward."

Pleasant hesitated, then looked at the little girl. "You're going to have to be brave now, OK? Can you do that? I'm going to put you down and I want you to stay as far back as you can."

The little girl nodded her delightful little head.

Cadaverous smiled. "Are all children so well-behaved? This whole time, she hasn't cried or complained once. A lot of grown-ups I know could learn a lesson from her."

Pleasant put the girl down and she wandered off to the back wall.

"So obedient," Cadaverous said, and the table crashed into him from behind.

He stumbled slightly, and laughed, and Pleasant waved his arms again and the armchair lifted off the floor and flew at him. It knocked him back a few steps, but only made him laugh louder.

"You can't do it," he explained, adjusting his tie. "You can't beat me in here. Don't you understand? You boast so much about how intelligent you are, but sometimes I truly do doubt it."

A fireball hit him, exploded across his face, and when he wiped it away Pleasant was on him, hands grasping either side of his head, thumbs digging into his eyes. Cadaverous ignored it all, and pressed his hand against Pleasant's shirt, felt the material, stiff yet soft, precisely what was required of a shirt that gave the illusion of a flesh-and-blood body beneath. But of course there was no flesh-and-blood body beneath, and Cadaverous sank his fingers in, gripping the ribcage. Pleasant gasped, tried to pull back, but Cadaverous raised him off his feet and threw him across the room. He hit the wall pleasingly, dropped and came back up.

"Ow," the skeleton said, brushing dust from his lapel. Cadaverous had to hand it to him – he had style.

Pleasant darted in. Cadaverous went to bat him away, but the skeleton did something, some fancy move that Cadaverous had never seen before, and suddenly he was behind him and Cadaverous's head was in his hands again and Pleasant wrenched it to the side.

But Cadaverous's neck didn't break, because Cadaverous was God here, and God's neck doesn't break.

He hit Pleasant with the back of his hand, little more than a lazy swipe, and Pleasant twisted and went stumbling.

"Isn't it disheartening," he asked as the skeleton straightened up again, "to be consistently denied the kill that you so richly deserve? Because I admit it – you deserved to kill me there. Both times. You came in, got past my defences, and went straight for the head. Straight for the kill. And yet, there you stand. Denied. I know how you feel. I know what that's like. Time and again I have been denied what I deserve."

Pleasant nodded, then suddenly pushed at the air, sending furniture crashing into the far wall. But not a single hair stirred on Cadaverous's head.

Cadaverous hit him. Hit him again. Hit him a few times and then hit him a few times more. He wished the skeleton wasn't a skeleton. He wished he was a flesh-and-blood man, so he could break the flesh and spill the blood. Another pleasure denied him.

Still, at least the skeleton felt pain. At least he felt each punch as it landed. At least he felt it when his bones cracked and fractured.

"I like your suits," Cadaverous said, as Pleasant tried to crawl away. "Where do you get them?"

He picked Pleasant up and launched him through a door that splintered open on impact.

Pleasant went rolling. Groaned. "A friend of mine," he muttered, "made them for me."

"Do you think he would consider making one for me?"

"Sure," Pleasant said, standing. "I'll introduce you."

He swung a punch that cracked against Cadaverous's jaw, but inflicted no damage, and Cadaverous responded with another backhand that sent Pleasant sliding across the floor. His face melted from his skull, retreating under his collar.

Cadaverous smiled, and dragged the skeleton back into the living room. The little girl was trying to wake Abyssinia, but she looked up when Cadaverous called.

"Look at this," he said, holding Pleasant up so that she could see him properly. "Look at Skulduggery. Look at what he really is, when he's not wearing a mask."

He expected her to scream, or to cry, or to do something. Instead, she just stared.

"That was anticlimactic," Pleasant muttered, and Cadaverous let him collapse.

And then the moon began to chime.

73

"Midnight," Cadaverous said, smiling again. "And Valkyrie Cain hasn't come to save you. Are you disappointed in her? I thought she was made of sterner stuff."

Pleasant waved a hand in his direction. "I have a retort," he said from the floor. "And it's a good one. Just wait there. It'll be worth it, I promise."

"I am dreadfully sorry," said Cadaverous, "but your time has run out. No more waiting for you. No more procrastinating."

The little girl ran up to stand between them. "Stop hurting him," she said. Her little hands were on her little hips. It was almost adorable.

Pleasant moaned. "You tell him, Alice."

"Hurting people is wrong, and you shouldn't do it." The little girl wagged her finger. "You are being naughty."

Cadaverous hunkered down, and peered at her. "You don't feel any fear, do you? Not an ounce. Not one jot."

"I'm brave," the little girl said. "Like my sister."

Cadaverous smiled and shook his head. "I'm sorry to be the one to tell you, but your sister is not brave. If she were brave, she'd be here right now, fighting for you."

Alice frowned, and looked back at Pleasant, who was on his feet and testing his jaw, probably to make sure it hadn't fallen off. "Is he right?" she asked.

"No," Pleasant said. "He's just a cranky old man who doesn't know what he's talking about. If your sister isn't here to fight for you, then I am. You'll always have someone, Alice."

Cadaverous straightened. "Oh, I apologise, are we not telling her that she's about to die? It's just, once she sees me kill you, the idea might occur to her anyway."

Pleasant moved Alice behind him, and took out his gun. "I've got my second wind," he said. "And I've been studying your moves. I know exactly how to beat you."

"You do?"

"Yes," said Pleasant, and threw his gun. It bounced off Cadaverous's head.

Cadaverous laughed. So did Pleasant.

"I'm going to kill you now," Cadaverous said.

Pleasant squared his shoulders. "I'd imagine so."

And then Valkyrie Cain called Cadaverous's name, from outside the house.

"Huh," said Cadaverous, and walked to the front door. Pleasant followed, holding the little girl's hand.

Valkyrie stood waiting in the moonlight, her clothes caked in dried mud. Most of the blood flow had stopped, which allowed Cadaverous to see the deep lacerations along her forehead. The skeleton's car was parked beside her, and she was chewing on something – probably those foul-tasting leaves – in an effort to dull her pain. She held no weapons, and the bracelet on her arm was still secure, so she obviously hadn't found whatever she'd been hunting for.

"You're late," Cadaverous said, "and, sadly, the offer I extended to you was time-sensitive. I'm afraid I can no longer allow your sister to live."

Valkyrie shrugged. "I wouldn't worry about that, if I were you. I'm about to give you an ass-kicking like you wouldn't believe."

"Is that so? I'll admit, such a proclamation would ordinarily have me positively quaking in my boots, but unless you found a God-Killer weapon hidden somewhere in the undergrowth, I sincerely doubt it."

Valkyrie wiped a trickle of blood away from her eye. In the moonlight, the blood looked black. "I don't need a God-Killer to stomp your head into the ground," she said, and started walking.

Cadaverous watched her, oh so casual, oh so cool, as she disappeared round the side of the house. He reached back, took Alice by the arm. "Come along," he said. "You, too, Detective. You wouldn't want to leave Alice alone with me, would you?"

He walked after Valkyrie, not even feeling Alice as she tried in vain to struggle from his grip. They got to the side of the house and kept walking. Cadaverous was enjoying this. No matter how weak her hand would turn out to be, Valkyrie was acting as if she was leading him into a trap from which he would not escape. He was looking forward to watching the confidence slip from her face. He was looking forward to catching sight of the first flickers of fear. That was one of his favourite moments.

They came round the corner, and Cadaverous stopped, and frowned.

"I wasn't looking for a weapon," Valkyrie said, standing on the roof of a building that shouldn't have been there, a building that was no taller than Valkyrie herself. "I was looking for a seed."

It took him a moment to recognise the building. It was the Midnight Hotel, and it was growing slowly before them.

But... but no. They were *in* the Midnight Hotel. This didn't make any sense. They were both in the Midnight Hotel and outside it at the same time.

Holding the chimney for balance, Valkyrie raised her foot and brought it down hard on the roof, and thunder shook the sky and made the moon tremble.

He should have leaped forward. Should have pulled her down

and snapped her neck. But in his confusion he could only say, "Stop." He could only say, "What are you doing?"

She brought her boot down again and, to the north, the sky over the mountains splintered –

– and a giant foot broke through.

74

Valkyrie gazed down through the hole in the roof, and saw the mountains below.

Then she looked up, saw them in the distance, across the water, and saw her boot dangling above them like God's own foot. She wiggled it, just to see it wiggle, then pulled her leg up and stamped down again. The crash, from both the roof below her and the world around her, was a thunderclap of monstrous collisions.

She reached down, grabbed a jagged collection of timbers. The roof, not even close to being fully formed, peeled away, leaving her with a gap just about big enough to drop through.

She caught Alice's eye, winked, then stepped into the hole and let herself fall. She landed, bending her knees, in the middle of the mountains. They were uneven and she almost twisted an ankle, but she reached out, steadied herself by grasping the tallest snow-capped peak. She took a moment to orientate herself. The mountains came up to her shoulders. The dark sea was now no more than a small pond, and, beyond it, the island with Cadaverous's house.

Valkyrie straightened, the top of her head brushing the sky, and stepped out into the sea. The water didn't go higher than her calf.

She hurried to the island, kicking up a tsunami with every step. If the thought occurred to Cadaverous to climb on to the hotel and follow her down, it was all over. The only thing stopping that from happening was the sheer shock he was hopefully feeling, and his own lack of imagination.

She passed under the moon, paused, and moved the big hand almost all the way round.

Her head hit the moon and she scowled and continued on.

Any hope she had of ending this by just squishing Cadaverous beneath her boot vanished when she saw him walking towards her. He was growing with each step. If she was the size of a mountain, he was the size of a house, and then a church, and then a tower and then a skyscraper, and when he stepped off the island and into the sea he was as big as she was.

"Not nearly clever enough," he said, and threw a punch.

Valkyrie saw it coming and stepped into it, absorbing it along her upper arm. It didn't send her flying. It was a good punch, a strong punch, but it wasn't strong enough to stagger her. She realised how tired Cadaverous now looked – as if the effort to grow to this size was taking all of his energy.

She snapped out a jab that rocked him, then grabbed his shoulder and lunged in with an elbow that sent him backwards. He fell, toppling, into the sea.

"This is embarrassing," said Valkyrie, backing away a little.

"How dare you!" he screeched, splashing about as he got up. "How dare you!" Wiping blood from his nose, he stalked after her as she led him away from the island. "I am God here! This is my world! This is my creation!"

He dived at her and she rammed her forearm into the side of his neck. He gasped and she dragged him over her hip and flipped him. He hit the water, managed to break free, rolled away and stood, cursing her. He seemed smaller now. He *was* smaller. Not by much, but he had definitely lost some height.

She skipped in, kicked at his leg. He howled, staggered back. The more she hit him, the smaller he got. She grinned, liking this game.

He ran at her. She tried to flip him again, but she mistimed it and they both went down, splashing into the sea. Cadaverous snarled, going for her eyes. She gripped his wrists, turning him, wrapping him with her legs. He got a hand free and pulled her hair and she hissed, tried to break the hold. He scratched at her, shoved her off and scrambled on top. His hands at her throat, on her face, forcing her head underwater. Lungs burning, eyes shut, she wrapped him up with her legs again, crossing her ankles and extending her body. Squeezing him. That wasn't working. His fingers were like iron.

She slammed a fist into the crook of his elbow and his arm bent and she surfaced, gasping for air. Yanking one of his arms across her body, she swung her right leg up on to his shoulder and then shifted her weight, hooking her left knee over her own right instep. Eyes bulging, he forced her back and she took a breath before submerging. She didn't mind it this time. After a moment, he stopped trying to drown her and devoted his attention instead to getting himself out of the triangle choke.

He brought his feet in under him, struggling to stand. Valkyrie did her best to keep him on his knees, but he was too strong. He straightened, taking her up out of the water with him. He turned, staggered a few steps, Valkyrie still stuck to him like a limpet. She glanced over her shoulder, saw where he was bringing her. The bridge.

He fell forward. Valkyrie hit the bridge and smashed through it, and felt something give in her side. All sensation left her fingers and toes and darkness clutched at her vision. She waited until it started to recede, then shook her head and flexed her fingers. She could feel them again.

Cadaverous was on his feet, drawing in lungfuls of air. Valkyrie went to get up, but he snarled, and lashed in a kick, his shoe striking that broken rib. Exquisite pain lanced through her.

He tried another kick, but she brought her knee up, her boot absorbing some of the blow. Gritting her teeth against the pain in her side, she grabbed his leg and scrambled up. Cadaverous hopped angrily, trying to maintain his balance. Valkyrie backed off, taking him with her, then spun him, and he hopped and cursed and it would have been funny but for the broken rib and the bruises and the cuts and the fact that he was trying to kill her.

It was getting harder to control him. The smaller he got, the stronger he got. But Valkyrie was shrinking, too. While the interior dimensions of this new Midnight Hotel were all messed up due to Cadaverous's magic, the fact was that the hotel was still growing, and every passing moment robbed her of any advantage she might still possess.

He tore his leg from her grip and they collided, stumbling out of the sea and on to dry land. They crushed houses, flattened trees, left footprints in roads. She headbutted him, was rewarded with a definite reduction in his size, but he punched her square in the chest and that blasted her backwards, into the city. Her hip scraped against an apartment building, her elbow smashed through a skyscraper, but she found something to grab on to to stop herself from falling.

She was still taller than the skyscraper she'd just damaged, but only just.

Breathing heavily, blood dripping from a gash across the bridge of his nose, Cadaverous followed her in, demolishing an overpass like he was kicking at weeds. The more she damaged him, the more he shrank, the more dangerous he became. This was not a winning strategy. Her only hope was that Skulduggery was at least taking advantage of the distraction to fly Alice back into the real world.

If that was actually possible. The moment she'd planted that seed, Cadaverous's world and everyone inside it were immediately transported to the new hotel that had begun to grow within the old one. Valkyrie tried to figure out what that meant for the exit, but before she got too far down that train of thought, Cadaverous was attacking her again.

She ducked under him, but felt her ribs slide against each other and gasped, faltered, and he shoved her and she fell. Clutching at herself, Valkyrie tried to cry out but couldn't. Out of the corner of her eye she saw Cadaverous breaking a spire off the top of a tower. Holding it like a dagger, he jumped on to her. She brought her knees up and they crashed against his chest, but there was nothing she could do about the spire that was coming for her face except raise her left hand, and the spire went clean through.

Valkyrie found her voice, and screamed.

Spittle flying from his clenched grin, Cadaverous tugged the spire one way and then the other and Valkyrie's screams reached new heights. She grabbed his wrist with her free hand, fought to get her feet between them, and then she pushed him back with her legs. He hit a building and went straight through, collapsing floors on top of himself, and Valkyrie got up, stumbled and ran, holding her left hand close to her body.

She kept low and darted right, followed a long street, turning slightly to stop her shoulders from hitting the buildings on either side. She went left, right again, glanced back to make sure Cadaverous couldn't see her, and sank down with her back against something that looked like a bank. She watched tiny cars brake and tiny people, all with Cadaverous's face, shout at her. She pulled her feet out of the park opposite, pulled them close. Only then did she dare look at her hand.

The sight of it made her want to be sick. The spire, to her, was maybe the length of a pencil, but she was shrinking, which meant it was growing, which meant she couldn't afford to let it stay where it was. She tried to take hold of it, but even touching it like that was too much and tears sprang to her eyes. She was dimly aware of all those little Cadaverous-people laughing at her.

She scooted forward, tore a tree from the park, then scooted back again, pressed her spine against the bank building. She put the tree between her teeth and clamped down. There was a crowd of the Cadaverous-people beside her, pointing up and jeering.

She slammed her hand on top of them. The crowd squelched beneath her and the spire shot up and she did her very best to muffle her scream. She tasted bark and blood in her mouth, and whipped the spire from her hand and let it fall.

Blood poured from the puncture wounds. She spat out the tree and sat there, gasping, crying, trying not to make a sound. She wiped away the tears with her forearm, the park once again coming into blurry focus. Only then did she remember the tattoos on her eyes.

75

Cadaverous reached over the bank with both hands, grabbed her by the hair and hauled her up and dragged her back, spine arched across the roof of the bank. He landed a fist in her belly and she curled up, fell sideways off the bank roof, knees flattening cars and snapping lamp posts. Cadaverous took hold of her head in both his hands and picked her up, walked her backwards, grunting out curses and obscenities the entire time. He cracked the back of her skull off a building and stood over her as she collapsed.

When she was lying on the ground, he stepped on her head, grinding it into the street.

"How many times," he asked, "do I have to beat you before it registers?"

Valkyrie wanted to throw him off, to jump to her feet, to knock that triumphant gleam out of his eyes, but she was way too tired and far too hurt. His shoe scraped against her cheek. His heel crushed her ear.

From down here, she was seeing the city from a new angle, and realised that this was the street she'd visited earlier. It looked quite different now, like a playset. Rubble and glass covered the road, and all the little Cadaverous-people had scampered away. It was quiet and still, so that when Valkyrie glimpsed movement it stood out like it was caught in a spotlight. She watched Skulduggery – tiny, tiny Skulduggery – creeping up, using the debris for cover.

Cadaverous, all the way up there, hadn't noticed him yet.

"You're not worthy of this," Cadaverous said. "You know that, don't you? You're not worth the time and the effort that has gone into killing you. You should have been just another name added to the list of the people I've killed. That's all you deserved. And yet somehow, somehow, you've survived up until now. Why is that, do you think?"

Skulduggery crouched, waiting for something, waiting for Cadaverous to look away. Valkyrie didn't know what he was planning to do, or what he even could do. He was about the size of her thumbnail.

"Do you think you're special?" Cadaverous asked. "Do you think you're unique? Do you think I view you as a mortal enemy?"

Skulduggery launched himself forward, flying low to the ground, and disappeared under her bracelet.

The sound of Cadaverous's voice changed slightly, and Valkyrie knew he was looking down at her. "I do not view you as any such thing," he said. "You are an annoyance. That's all you ever were. And you're lucky. I will give you that. But luck, like blood, runs out eventually."

Cadaverous gave Valkyrie's head a push, then stepped away. Clutching her left wrist to keep her injured hand steady, she hid Skulduggery from view as she sat up slowly. Cadaverous hunkered down next to her.

"This was a good attempt," he said. "Growing a new hotel, smashing your way into it... That shows ingenuity. It shows initiative. I respect that, much as it pains me to admit it. Jeremiah... Jeremiah wouldn't have thought of something like this. It would, sadly, have been beyond him. It's even got me confused, and I'm a very smart man. Let me see if I've got everything in the correct order. The hotel you dropped into — that's what we're in right now, yes? We were all teleported into it the moment it took root. But then you left the hotel we were in, and dropped into here, which is still the hotel we were in, but... not. Am I right? Am I making any sense? I don't think I am. Let me try again."

He laughed, closed his eyes, focusing, and Valkyrie did her best not to gasp as the bracelet sprang open and magic flooded her body. She immediately twisted her arm so that Cadaverous wouldn't see what had happened. Skulduggery vanished behind a building.

"Let's think about exits," Cadaverous said. "If we were to walk out of here the way we came in, we'd emerge into the first hotel, wouldn't we? And when we walked out of that the way we came in, we would actually be outside, wouldn't we? I think we would." He laughed again, and clapped. "This is wonderful! Are we caught in a paradox? I've never been caught in a paradox before. It's quite fun. And why haven't the old versions of the hotel withered away yet? Are we damaging it beyond repair by forcing previous versions to maintain their structures? Will I need to find a new home when all this is over? Oh, I do hope not, not after all the work I've put into the place."

"I should never have come in here," Valkyrie muttered.

"What was that?" Cadaverous asked. "What did you say?"

She cleared her throat, and spoke more clearly. "I should never have come in here."

Cadaverous nodded. "Obviously."

"Will you let her go? My sister? She hasn't done anything. She's a child."

"She is a child, yes," said Cadaverous, "and a relentlessly upbeat child, at that. It would actually please me no end to allow her to leave after I've killed you and the skeleton."

"Thank you," said Valkyrie.

"But I'm afraid I can't do that," he continued. "In ten years, she'll be formidable – especially if she follows your example. And she'll remember me, and she'll come after me. I'm dreadfully sorry, I just can't have someone out there who harbours any kind of grudge, let alone a vendetta. I'll have to kill her."

"Cadaverous, she's a kid. Please."

He waved a hand. "I don't see why you're getting upset. You're going to die now. Why should you care what happens to anyone after you've died? It seems to me to be a waste of energy." He stood, towering over her. "You really shouldn't have come in here. Look at you. You're growing smaller every moment."

He was right. The hotel must have hit a growth spurt in its final stages, because cars that Valkyrie could have crushed between two fingers a moment ago were now bigger than her hand.

"I suppose your failure isn't entirely your own fault," he said. "It's not every day you fight a god."

Gritting her teeth against the pain from her broken ribs, Valkyrie started getting up. "Actually, I've fought gods before." She straightened, and flicked her wet, filthy hair out of her eyes. "They're not so tough."

Cadaverous looked displeased, opened his mouth to say something and she raised her right hand and sent an arc of lightning straight into his face.

He stepped back, cursed, turned away, the damage already fading, but Valkyrie hopped on to a nearby building and sprang at him, crying out in pain as she wrapped an arm round his throat.

First rule of fighting gods is to keep them off balance. If they can't form a coherent thought, they can't assert their power.

Valkyrie kicked at the back of Cadaverous's leg and his knee buckled and they toppled backwards. She tried to steel herself before they landed, Cadaverous on top, but her ribs sent daggers shooting through her side. Tears streaming from her eyes, she wrapped her legs round his waist while she locked in the sleeper choke. He thrashed wildly, pulling at her arms, almost breaking the hold by pure strength alone. If he'd kept at it, he could have snapped her bones, but both air and blood were being cut off from his brain, and Cadaverous was doing what everyone did in that situation – he was panicking.

Valkyrie clung on as he rolled to his hands and knees. He tried standing but she pulled at him, toppling him again. He was shrinking now and she had to adjust her position, had to tighten her arms. There were a few moments when they were of equal size, but he was shrinking faster than she was.

She squeezed. She squeezed with everything she had left. Her exhausted arms were little more than useless bands of rubber, and still she squeezed. She didn't stop. She couldn't. Her sister was in here. She had to save her sister.

Valkyrie squeezed and squeezed and shut her eyes and gritted her teeth, and when she let go it wasn't because she wanted to, it was because she had no other choice. Her arms failed her and sprang apart as she collapsed back, Cadaverous rolling off to one side.

But he didn't get up. He just continued to shrink.

She took a few deep breaths, then heaved herself on to her knees and, moving slowly and awkwardly, with her left hand held away from her body, she stood. Skulduggery ran up, Alice in his arms. Valkyrie was twice as big as him.

Skulduggery put Alice down and turned Cadaverous on to his belly. He tried snapping the cuffs on, but Cadaverous's wrists were still too thick.

Another few seconds. That's all they needed. Another few seconds and this would all be over.

Cadaverous opened his eyes.

He threw Skulduggery back and ignored Valkyrie's lightning as he got to his feet.

"That was close," he said. "That was astonishingly close. Congratulations might well be in order – but failure is failure, and the game is at an end."

"Not yet it isn't," Valkyrie said.

"What else do you have?" Cadaverous asked. "What else is there? You have nothing. Do you still think your little bolts of lightning are going to hurt me in here?"

"I've got more than lightning."

"Do you now? And what might that be?"

Valkyrie showed him.

76

Omen and Temper dragged Caisson out through the front door of the Midnight Hotel, and Temper collapsed and Omen dropped to his knees beside him.

"Car," Temper said. "Leaves. For the pain."

Omen looked around. "There is no car. Temper, there is no car. Listen to me, I need your phone. Temper, please, your phone. I can call Never. I can call for help."

Temper dug into his pocket, came out with the phone and unlocked it, then handed it over and lay back and blacked out. Omen jumped up, dialled a number –

– and Razzia snatched the phone from his hand and tossed it behind her.

"Oh, hell," said Omen.

Nero walked by, stood over Caisson and nudged him with his foot. "He's still alive," he announced.

"She'll be happy about that," Razzia said, then looked down at Omen. "Where is she, mate? Where's Abyssinia? I haven't heard her voice in my head since she told me to come here."

"She, um, she's in there," Omen said, jerking a thumb at the hotel.

There was another woman with them, a dark-haired lady with an angry scowl on her face. "Go get her, or we'll kill your friend."

Omen's eyes widened. "No, no, don't do that! I can't get her

384

– I don't know where she is. Inside there, it isn't like the inside of the hotel, it's a whole other—"

"We know what Cadaverous can do," Razzia said.

"All I know is that Cadaverous has Abyssinia," said Omen. "They fought, kind of, and he... well, he beat her. And he took her away."

Razzia frowned, and looked at Nero. "We'd better go in."

Nero made a face. "In there? The old man will murder us."

The scowling woman stepped forward. "Valkyrie Cain," she said, "is she in there?"

Omen nodded, and the scowling woman turned that scowl on Nero. "We're going in."

77

Valkyrie reached for Cadaverous's thoughts with her mind. She could hear them, faint though they were, like a muffled conversation held behind a closed door. She had to get closer. She had to open the door.

Valkyrie lunged at him and he laughed, let her come, let her clamp her right hand on to his head, and suddenly the door burst wide open and his thoughts became loud and clear and overwhelming.

But she expected this and so narrowed her search, cutting through to his memories, just like Abyssinia had done. Valkyrie copied her technique precisely, following those memories down a flickering tunnel of sights and sounds and emotions, burrowing past his adult life, past the people he'd killed and the people he'd met and the people he'd known, back and back, deeper and deeper, to a childhood that was sharp at the edges and cold in the centre.

Time stopped. Cadaverous's childhood didn't so much lie before her as unspool around her. Suddenly Valkyrie knew. She knew his earliest memory as surely as she knew her own. She knew the smells of the cabin he lived in. She knew the hunger. She remembered his mother. She remembered his father.

His mother was her mother. His father was her father. Valkyrie was Cadaverous. His hatred and frustrations crowded her mind.

She knew now why he killed. She understood now the compulsions that drove him, the urges that twisted his potential, that set his life on the course it took. She had killed the same people he had killed. She had killed for the same reason.

Her mother and her father. She had watched her mother die at her father's hands. He had beaten her, and strangled her while Valkyrie screamed, while she tried and tried to pull him away. But Valkyrie was small, and her father was big and strong and even as Valkyrie struggled harder, her mother's struggles weakened.

Her heart broke. The only love she'd ever known in the world drifted from her mother's dull eyes. Now it was just the two of them, her father and her, alone in those mountains. Without anyone to protect her, Valkyrie was beaten by hand, by belt, by branch. She knew pain, and fear, and helplessness. Her life progressed in cuts and bruises and broken bones. They were how she measured the passing of time.

He was going to kill her. He was going to use her up and discard her, a rattling thing of jangled bones with dull eyes. So she picked up that hatchet, and she cleaved his skull in two while he slept, and she felt relief and a peculiar kind of joy. It would be a long time before she felt that joy again. Killing small animals would only offer a taste. She would have to wait until she had been taken to America, until she had killed that homeless man, until she had bashed his head in with a broken brick and watched his blood drip on to her shoe, watched the gentle way it splashed—

No. That wasn't her. That was Cadaverous. That had happened to Cadaverous and Valkyrie could see it, his memories playing all around her like projections on the walls of an attic, projections she could walk into. Touch.

Change.

She went back to Cadaverous's father strangling his mother, and she thought about his hands lifting away from her neck, then watched it happen.

This was hard. This was worse than hard, this was painful. She couldn't feel her body any more, but she could feel the pain this was causing her. Nevertheless, she persisted.

She thought about her own life, the love her own parents had shown her, had demonstrated for her again and again, and she took that love and released it here. She fed Cadaverous the love she had known, the smiles and the laughter. She fed him the support and the understanding. She fed him the light, a light that beat the darkness back.

She knew Cadaverous, knew what drove him, but now she also saw this clumsy veil she had pulled over his pain. It was stretched tight, and wouldn't last, and was already beginning to tear as she backed out of his thoughts. But it was love, and it was something Cadaverous had never truly known.

Valkyrie blinked. She was standing, her hand pressed against his head. Cadaverous's eyes were glazed. She let go, almost stumbled.

His voice cracked when he spoke. "What did you... what did you do to me?"

She stepped back, ignoring the headache. She felt blood run from her nose and wiped it away.

"Are you all right?" she asked.

He focused on her, and frowned. "I don't... What did you do to me?"

"I don't know," she answered honestly.

She heard footsteps behind her. The teenage boy walked forward. Cadaverous stared at him.

"Help me," Cadaverous said.

Slowly, the boy put his hand on the old man's face. "I don't think I can."

Tears rolled down Cadaverous's cheeks. "Please," he said.

"We're too damaged," the boy said, and smiled sadly. "You didn't have a chance."

"It hurts."

"I know it does." The boy turned to Valkyrie. "Go," he said. "Thank you, and go."

Valkyrie turned, tried to pick up Alice, but her ribs wouldn't let her. Skulduggery put his hand on her arm. She looked up.

Abyssinia stood there, with Nero and Razzia and Skeiri.

"You've been in my head," Abyssinia said. Her face was bruised and bloody, and she was standing like her bones were broken. "Don't look so surprised: you left footprints all over the place."

Skeiri's face was pure hatred. Her teeth were bared, her eyes narrowed to slits. Violence radiated from her whole body.

"You're powerful," Abyssinia continued. "You don't know how powerful you are. But you're... inelegant. I could trace you from one memory to another. You crossed the bridge between us, Valkyrie, and then walked through my memories."

"I didn't build that bridge," Valkyrie said. "That was you."

Skeiri suddenly launched herself at Valkyrie, but Abyssinia caught her and in an instant had drained her, healing her bones and her bruises.

Abyssinia sighed, much happier. "Ooh, that's better," she said. "And it doesn't matter who built the bridge, Valkyrie. What matters is you crossed it. This cannot go unpunished." Her eyes flickered briefly to Cadaverous. "You went trampling through his memories as well, didn't you? I can see the alterations you made. A clumsy... what did you call it? A clumsy veil. Clumsy but effective. You've actually cured him. Temporarily, of course, and with significant flaws... Cadaverous, how does it feel to have love in your life?"

The boy stood in front of Cadaverous. "You could have done this for him," he said. "You could have helped him."

"Perhaps," said Abyssinia. "I would assuredly have done a better job. Maybe I'd have cured him completely, taken away this urge to kill that has haunted him since he was a boy."

"Leave," Cadaverous said, his hand on the boy's shoulder. "All of you."

Abyssinia smiled. "You can feel it beginning to slip away, can't you? Do you want to spend your last few minutes alone with your memories? They're not yours, you know. She's merged her memories with your own. The people you're thinking of have never been your real parents."

"I don't care," Cadaverous said. "Leave me."

"Of course. There's just one thing I need to do."

Valkyrie felt Abyssinia's thoughts dart into Cadaverous's mind, piercing the clumsy veil and slashing it open. Cadaverous cried out, hands at his head as he fell to his knees, the teenage boy doing his best to catch him.

Abyssinia looked at Valkyrie. "Stay out of my head," she said, and Nero teleported them away.

Skulduggery picked up Alice, practically threw her into Valkyrie's arms. "Get her out of here. I'll hold him off."

"Won't do any good," Cadaverous said, and let the boy fall, his neck broken. "You should have killed me when you had the chance. Now no one gets out of here alive."

Valkyrie crouched wearily. "Don't worry, Cadaverous. I'm not done with you yet." She took a seed out of her pocket, showed it to him before dropping it on the ground and covering it with dirt.

His eyes widened.

"What," she said, "you thought I only grabbed one of these things? If the last few years have taught me anything, it's to always have a back-up plan. Skulduggery, some water?"

Skulduggery waved, and a light rain fell just over her hand.

"No!" Cadaverous snarled, scrambling up even as the new hotel began to sprout.

Skulduggery shot off his feet, straight into Cadaverous, who staggered under the impact. Skulduggery punched him, sent him reeling, but Cadaverous was regaining strength with every moment that passed. He got hold of Skulduggery and they wrestled, kicking up dust.

Valkyrie hunkered protectively over the hotel. It was the size of an apple now, but soft. If they trampled it, they'd all be killed. They came close and she cursed, charged into them, managed to push them away.

They fell, all three of them, a tangle of arms and legs.

Cadaverous closed his hand round Valkyrie's throat. It was like she was caught in a vice. Skulduggery fell back, swinging a kick that would have smashed bone into splinters – but all his foot did was bounce off Cadaverous's jaw.

Cadaverous smiled.

Then the world was nothing but deafening thunder and apocalyptic earthquakes and Cadaverous released Valkyrie and she fell, hands over her ears, glimpsing the horizon shatter and the hand of a god pulverising mountains, levelling cities and filling the sky as it reached in and reared above them. And then the hand was falling, those impossible fingers curling, and Cadaverous shrieked as he was plucked from the ground, vanishing into their folds.

Valkyrie glimpsed beyond the hand, to the shattered horizon, where she saw a giant's eye blinking at her.

She looked around at the growing hotel, still no bigger than a child's lunchbox, and at her sister, who was reaching through its broken wall.

Alice took back her hand and the god's appendage withdrew from above them, taking Cadaverous with it. Alice came over. She held out her hand, showed Valkyrie the tiny Cadaverous Gant, lying helplessly in one of the creases of her palm.

Then Alice looked at Valkyrie, smiled, and clapped.

78

Dawn split the darkness, and a new day broke across Roarhaven. Shadows stretched as the sun rose, and then shrank as it rose higher, feeding some warmth into the chill air. Sebastian arrived at Lily's house before eight, but Tantalus was already there. Sebastian watched him through the window. Sebastian had already told Bennet and Forby about the fight in the tunnel when he'd handed over the scythe the previous night, but now Tantalus was telling his version. The other members of the Darquesse Society listened. Not one of them was arguing.

It occurred to Sebastian that he needed them much more than he'd realised. Yes, Forby and the device were essential to his plan, but he was alone in this city. He had no friends. He had no one he could talk to. This group of oddballs was the closest thing he had to a family any more. He couldn't lose them.

Steeling himself, he knocked. Lily answered, let him in. He joined the others in the living room. Forby gave a little wave.

Tantalus glared at him. The others looked uneasy. It was all very awkward.

"Plague Doctor," Tantalus said, "so good of you to join us. We've been talking amongst ourselves regarding your future with us. While we have appreciated your input and suggestions over the last few months, we feel that you may not be the right fit for our little group."

"Right," said Sebastian. "I don't suppose I get a chance to argue my case, do I?"

"Let's not make this any more uncomfortable than it has to be," Tantalus said. "I think we should take a vote. Hands up, all those who think the Plague Doctor should be excluded from the Darquesse Society."

He put his hand up.

Nobody else did.

"What?" Tantalus said, looking around. "What's wrong? Didn't you understand the options?"

"Hands up," said Bennet, "all those who think Tantalus should be excluded."

All hands – except Tantalus's – went up. It was so utterly overwhelming that Sebastian didn't even have to raise his own hand. But he did it anyway.

"You can't be serious," Tantalus said, his eyes wide.

"We're sorry," said Kimora.

"You can't kick me out of my own group!"

"Wait," Ulysses said, "since when is it your group? It's *our* group."

"It was started in my living room."

"That doesn't make it yours."

Tantalus went quiet for a moment, then pointed at Sebastian. "He assaulted me."

"You attacked him with a knife," said Bennet.

"I didn't! He's lying about that! I didn't even *have* a knife! *He* assaulted *me*!"

"Why? Why did he assault you?"

"He tried to kill me, because then he could blame it on the Cathedral Guards and he'd be free to take over as leader."

"You're not the leader, Tantalus," Lily said.

"Then why does everyone do what I say?"

"Because you never stop moaning whenever we don't," Tarry responded. "It's an easier life if we go along with your stupid rules. But you can't just attack people."

Tantalus folded his arms. "You can't stop me from coming to the meetings."

"We're not going to tell you when the meetings are."

"This... this isn't fair. Why are you all taking his side? We don't even know who he is! He could be the enemy!"

Demure frowned. "What enemy?"

"We have loads of enemies, you just don't see them! Everyone is against us; everyone hates us! For all we know, he's one of them! I mean, why won't he show us his face?"

"He can't take his mask off for health reasons," said Bennet.

"He's keeping his identity secret for a reason, you idiots!" Tantalus screeched.

"We all have our secrets," Bennet said. "I don't mind that he doesn't take off his mask. It's kinda cool."

"I think it's cool, too," said Kimora.

"I wish I had a mask," said Forby.

"Sorry, Tantalus," Bennet said. "You're going to have to go."

A vein popped out on Tantalus's forehead. "You... you are all making a big mistake."

"Say hi to Wendy for me."

"Die, Bennet. OK? Just die."

Demure gasped. "Tantalus!"

"Oh, shut up! For once in your life, Demure, just shut up, will you? Allow the rest of us the luxury of you shutting up!"

"That's no way to speak to Demure," said Tarry.

"Oh, here he comes!" Tantalus cried. "Rushing to Demure's defence yet again! She's never going to leave her husband for you, Tarry! She barely notices you're alive!"

Tarry gaped, and went bright red, and now everyone was arguing with Tantalus and Tantalus kicked over the coffee table.

"That's it!" he roared. "I'm out! I'm leaving all you losers behind! I hope you all die!"

And he stormed out of the house.

Bennet helped Lily right the coffee table as Tarry tried smiling at Demure.

"I don't... uh... I don't want you to leave your husband," he said.

"Of course not," said Demure, avoiding his eyes.

Sebastian cleared his throat. "I just want to say... thanks for sticking up for me. I don't have any friends in Roarhaven right now, so that means a lot."

"You're one of us," said Bennet, shrugging.

Sebastian smiled. "Thank you." He turned to Forby. "So was it worth it? Could you get any Faceless Ones' DNA from the blood?"

"I did," said Forby. "Or what passes for their DNA anyway. It'll take a few days to align the device, but we should be able to begin the search by the end of the week."

"That's amazing news," said Sebastian. "Any idea how long it'll take?"

"None. Not a clue. By my calculations, it should be able to scan up to six thousand dimensions an hour. That sounds like a lot, until you factor in the possibility of an infinite number of dimensions. I can adjust the search parameters as we go, but we need to be prepared for three possibilities. One, the search takes a day. Two, the search takes fifty years. Three, the search takes forever, and still doesn't find what we're looking for."

"That's sort of depressing," said Kimora.

"Nonsense," Sebastian responded. "It'll just mean that when we do find Darquesse it'll be even more astonishing, that's all. I've got a good feeling about this. I think it's going to work."

The others glanced at each other, and nodded to Bennet.

"Will you be our leader?" Bennet asked.

Sebastian paused. "Me?"

"You seem to know what to do," Demure said.

"I thought we didn't really *have* leaders, though."

"We don't," said Lily. "But we could start. So... will you?"

He hesitated. He'd never been asked to lead before. This was a whole new experience for him.

"Yes," he said eventually. "Yes, I will be your leader."

They cheered, and Sebastian beamed.

79

Omen's arm was bruised where Cadaverous Gant had grabbed him. Four distinct bruises, and a fifth where Gant's bony thumb had pressed into his flesh. A mark of violence. A badge.

Omen pulled his sleeve down, covering it, and went back to eating lunch.

"Hey," Never said, smoothing down her skirt before she sat in front of him.

"Hi," said Omen, his mouth full.

Never applied a bit of gloss and smacked her lips before speaking again. "Listen... I was thinking about the babysitting thing, you know? I don't think you should do it again if Valkyrie asks. I mean, she's using you, isn't she? She's going off, having adventures, and she asks you to come in and take care of her little sister because she knows you'll say yes. That's not right. She's taking advantage of your eagerness."

"I don't think she is."

"Of course you don't. She's kind of your idol. When she was your age, she was going off with Skulduggery and saving the world and that's what you want."

"I'm, uh, I'm not sure it is, actually."

Never raised an eyebrow. "Since when?"

"I've been thinking about it, thinking about what she goes through every time she has one of these adventures. It's not just a... a fun rollercoaster. People's lives are in danger. Innocent people, sometimes. There's blood and broken bones and you get hot and sweaty and you ache and..."

"And it's real," Never said quietly.

"Yeah," said Omen. "It's real. So, like, maybe I'm OK being who I am. Maybe I will leave the dangerous stuff to the professionals."

Never chewed her lip, and for the first time she looked up and met Omen's eyes. "I have something to confess," she said. "Um..."

"You have a new boyfriend?" said Omen.

"No."

Omen leaned forward. "A new girlfriend?"

"No, not that, either. I don't really know how to say this, so I'll just say it. I've been... helping Auger."

Omen sat back. "Oh."

"They needed a Teleporter," Never said quickly. "He told you about what was going on, didn't he? With Mahala being possessed, and then Kase...? He asked for my help and, you know, what was I supposed to say? No? I couldn't do that, so I... I helped out."

"Right."

"You're mad at me, aren't you? Oh, God, you hate me."

"I don't hate you, Never."

"Yes, you do. You hate your gorgeous, glamorous friend Never."

Omen had to smile. "I don't hate you."

"Are you mad at me?"

"To be honest, I don't know what I am. But I don't blame you for saying yes. Of course you said yes. Who wouldn't?"

"I just feel bad about it. I feel like I've betrayed you or something. You wanted the adventure, and I went off on one and left you behind to, like, babysit Valkyrie Cain's little sister. That's hardly fair, is it?"

"Don't worry about it."

"You're taking this really well."

"Is it over?" Omen asked. "Is Kase all right?"

"He's back to normal," said Never. "The evil has been vanquished. Good guys rule. Status quo maintained. Auger's waiting to talk to you, actually, but I wanted to be the one to tell you."

"Is it going to be a thing now? Are you, like, part of my brother's gang?"

Never hesitated. "I don't really know. What would you think about it if I was?"

Omen tried his best, but there was no way to disguise the sadness in his voice. "I'd be fine with it."

"We'd still be friends."

"I know that. Never, seriously, you don't have to feel bad."

"Thanks, Omen." Never watched Auger approach, and stood up. "I'm gonna head. Talk to you later?"

"Sure," said Omen, and Never walked off while Auger took her place at the table. "It's like a tag team here."

Auger smiled. "How are you feeling?"

"About Never helping you out? I'm fine with it. I'm not made of glass, you know. I'm not going to break."

"I know," said Auger. "Hey, remember what we were talking about before, when you asked me who I wanted to be once the prophecy is fulfilled?"

"Vaguely."

"I think I want to be normal," said Auger. "I think I want to be like everyone else. I still want to be able to do the things I do, but... I don't want the pressure to have to do them. You know? Is that selfish?"

"I don't think so."

"It sounds selfish. If you have gifts, don't you have an obligation to use them to help others?"

"By that stage, you'll have done that," said Omen. "You'll have beaten the King of the Darklands. You'll deserve a quiet life."

Auger thought for a moment, then shrugged. "Anyway, that's who I want to be."

"You seem almost cheerful."

Auger laughed. "I am, actually. Life after the prophecy was always just a haze for me – but now I can actually see it. I can see myself being happy."

Omen smiled. "That's cool. That's so cool."

"And it's all thanks to you," Auger said, "for bothering to ask a question that nobody else asked. Thanks, dude."

"Um... sure. No problem."

Auger stood. "Gotta go. I've got a test to study for. What've you got next?"

"We're actually going over to the City of Tents now with Miss Gnosis, so I'll be missing double maths."

"Result," said Auger. "Say hi to Aurnia for me, won't you?"

Omen smiled. "I will."

After lunch, Omen got into a small bus with Axelia and the other volunteers. The back seat was loaded with heavy cardboard boxes.

"OK," Miss Gnosis said, turning to them, "today we're going to be handing out pamphlets containing phone numbers and websites that our friends are going to need when they move into their new homes."

"They have homes?" Axelia asked.

Miss Gnosis smiled. "They're moving into Roarhaven. The Supreme Mage has organised accommodation – she's got people arranging training schemes and all kinds of wonderful things. They've got a home again, and I got a letter from the High Sanctuary thanking every one of you for your efforts in making the refugees feel comfortable and welcome. So well done, the lot of you."

"Do they even know what a website is?" someone asked.

"Well, no, they don't – not yet anyway. But that's what the training schemes are for, to get them up to speed with our world. I'll be splitting you into groups of three. The usual rules apply, got me? No one wanders off alone and everyone stays within visual range. Questions? No? OK then."

They got to the City of Tents, and Omen and the only other boy who'd volunteered, an American student named Navada Machete, unloaded the boxes. Omen was put into a group with Navada and Axelia, and they each took an armful of pamphlets and off they went. The mortals were busy packing up their meagre belongings, but they took the pamphlets because they dared not say no to a sorcerer. Omen tried offering a reassuring smile with each pamphlet he gave out, but he wasn't sure it was working.

A slender hand plucked a pamphlet from his grip and he turned.

"What's a website?" Aurnia asked, reading from it.

"It's a page on a computer," said Omen.

"We were told about those," Aurnia said, "but we don't have any."

Omen smiled. "Every house in Roarhaven has one. Do you know where you'll be living yet?"

Aurnia folded the pamphlet and put it into her jeans pocket. It was weird, seeing her in regular clothes. "Not yet," she said. "But Supreme Mage Sorrows told us we'll all be living in the same area. Thank you, by the way."

"Me?" said Omen. "I didn't do anything."

"You made me an ambassador," said Aurnia. "If I wasn't an ambassador, I'd never have met Grand Mage Sorrows. She is... unearthly."

"I suppose she is. So, like... you're moving into Roarhaven. We'll be neighbours! Kinda."

"Yes," Aurnia said, smiling broadly. "We have a new life here. I... I can't tell you what that means to us. Our lives back home were... difficult. Bandits would attack, or sorcerers would arrive and destroy half our village just for fun. I thought that was existence. I thought my life was always going to be this way.

"And then we came here, and we were terrified; we were

somewhere new and scary, somewhere we didn't understand. And then you arrived, handing out blankets, telling us that it was going to be OK. Thank you, Omen."

"I'm, uh, I'm glad I could help. Maybe we could spend some time together, y'know, once you're in your new house and everything? I could give you that tour I promised you."

"That'd be nice," Aurnia said, smiling.

A moment passed, and Omen wanted to lean in and kiss her. He wanted to kiss her so badly. This was the perfect moment. He knew it was. He took a deep breath.

"Please don't kiss me," Aurnia said.

"Yep," Omen responded, nodding, "OK, fair enough."

"I'm... I'm sorry," she said. "You just looked like you were going to try to kiss me."

"Did I? I wasn't. Well, no, I was. I mean, I was going to ask if I could. But, obviously... I can't."

"I'm sorry," said Aurnia, and she looked genuinely sad. "There's a boy that I've liked for a very long time, and I didn't think he liked me back. But then he heard about you and that made him come up and tell me that he did like me, and he asked if we could... I don't really know what the word for it is here."

"Go out?" Omen ventured.

"Is that it? He asked if we could go out? So... I said yes. I'm sorry. I didn't mean to do this. I didn't know it would happen. But I've liked him my whole life and he's... I suppose he's one of us..."

"And not a sorcerer," said Omen.

"No. He's not. It's easier. My parents, especially, they didn't understand... you."

"I get it," Omen said.

"You'd like him, I think. He's just like you. He's funny and smart and so nice. You'd really get along."

"That's cool."

"I didn't mean to hurt your feelings. Can we still be friends?"

Omen looked away for a moment, then back. "I would love that," he said.

Aurnia smiled. "Good. It was nice seeing you again, Omen."

"You, too."

He watched her walk off. After a while, he became aware of someone standing beside him.

"Rough," said Axelia.

Omen laughed. "Don't worry about me."

She frowned at him. "You keep saying that. You keep telling people not to worry about you. Why is that?"

"Uh..."

"Do you want to know what I think?"

"Not if it's going to be mean."

"I think you don't view yourself as someone who is worth worrying about. I was talking about you with my friends."

"Oh, God."

"Shush. We've come to the conclusion that Auger got all the attention and all the affection growing up, and maybe you were starved of it as a child and now you walk around, not believing that you deserve any for yourself. That's what we think." She shrugged. "We might be wrong."

"I... I thought your friends hated me."

Axelia frowned. "Why would they hate you? You're lovely. You're nice to absolutely everyone. The whole school likes you."

Tears, actual tears, came to his eyes. "What?"

"You're so silly," she said, and walked on, giving out pamphlets to the mortals who passed.

80

After Reverie had given both of the Edgley sisters the all-clear, Valkyrie got changed into a clean set of clothes and drove back to Haggard in a car she'd borrowed from the High Sanctuary. Alice chatted the whole way like she hadn't just been through the absolute worst kind of hell. Valkyrie didn't know how she did it.

They got to the house, and Valkyrie followed her little sister into the living room where Kes was waiting with her arms folded. She responded to Valkyrie's look of delighted surprise with a glare.

Alice got halfway across the room when she froze.

Valkyrie frowned. "Alice? You OK?"

Alice turned slowly.

"What's wrong?" Valkyrie asked. "Alice, talk to me."

"I think," Alice said at last, "that I need to pee." She scrunched up her face, and nodded. "Yep." Then she ran off to the bathroom.

Valkyrie breathed out. "For a second, I thought she could see you."

"How awful that would be," Kes said. "I'm alive, by the way. No thanks to you."

"I knew you'd survive."

"Yeah? Because I didn't. It took everything I had to heal myself, and for the rest of the night I had to just lie there on the pub floor. The City Guard came and they kept stepping on me and through me and I wasn't even strong enough to crawl into the corner."

"Thank you," said Valkyrie.

"Whatever."

"No, seriously – thank you. I needed you to do something incredibly risky and you did it. That means a lot."

Kes grunted. "You got the munchkin back, then."

"Yeah," Valkyrie responded, smiling. "You should've seen her – she was so brave."

"What are you going to tell the folks?"

Valkyrie hesitated, and Kes laughed.

"You're going to lie to them, aren't you?"

"I think it's the wisest thing to do," said Valkyrie.

"And do you think Alice will be able to maintain that lie?"

"I don't know, to be honest – but what choice do I have? If they find out what happened... I don't know what they'd do."

Kes shrugged. "Maybe they'd figure it's safer for Alice to grow up without her big sister around that much."

"Yeah," said Valkyrie. "Maybe."

"They're probably right."

"No," Valkyrie replied. "This was a one-off. No one has gone after my family like this before this, and no one will after this."

"Tell that to Carol."

"That was different. That was... That won't happen again."

"You know what?" Kes asked as Alice came back in. "You sound like you're trying to justify what you're doing."

"Do you want to see my dancing?" Alice asked.

"You sound like you know you're wrong and that you're being selfish and that the best thing for the people you love is to stay as far away from you as possible—"

"Stephanie? Do you want to see my dancing?"

"– but you can't bring yourself to do it, can you?"

Valkyrie forced herself to smile at Alice. "Yes," she said. "I would love to see your dancing." A happy smile on her face, Alice ran off.

"I just got back," Valkyrie said quietly. "I spent five years without them. Without her. I can't do it again."

"You could quit," said Kes. "Wouldn't that be the best compromise? Living your life as a normal person would make sure that no one comes after your family ever again. So retire. Leave magic behind. Leave Skulduggery behind."

A car pulled up outside. The Bentley.

"But you can't do that, either, can you?" Kes asked. "Because you're addicted. You're addicted to magic and you're addicted to him."

"I can handle it," said Valkyrie. "I can make sure my family is safe from now on."

"I like you, Valkyrie," said Kes. "You're my only friend in the whole entire world, so I'm kinda forced to like you. But you're not being honest with yourself."

The doorbell rang, and Kes disappeared.

"It's Skulduggery!" Alice yelled out from the hallway. "Stephanie, it's Skulduggery!"

The sound of a door being opened, and Alice's excited chatter mixing with Skulduggery's velvet tones, and Valkyrie stood there, burying her anxiety and her doubts and her fears in a big hole in her mind and filling it in, shovelful after shovelful, faster and faster, until she could turn and smile as they both came into the room.

"Skulduggery's here!" Alice exclaimed, leading Skulduggery by his gloved hand. "He has a face!"

"I called at your house," Skulduggery said. "I thought you might be here. Am I interrupting?"

"No," said Valkyrie, "not at all. We're waiting for Mum and Dad to get back. Alice was about to show me her dancing."

"Oh, yeah!" Alice said, and ran out of the room again.

Skulduggery was wearing a navy three-piece. His façade flowed away. "How are you feeling?" he asked.

"Sore," she said, holding up her bandaged hand. "And I look like a bus hit me. Apart from that, I'm fine. How's Temper?"

"Patched up and walking around. I paid a visit to that country house, by the way. I found the maze and plenty of blood, but no sign of the Wild Hunt or their victims."

"What about my clothes?"

"No sign of them, either, unfortunately."

She sagged. "But Ghastly made them for me."

Alice came in, tapping the screen of a tablet. "Found it," she said.

Skulduggery hunkered down next to her. "And how are you feeling, Alice?"

She looked at him. "I'm fine, thank you. How are you?"

"I'm fine, too. How did you sleep last night? Did you have any nightmares?"

Alice shook her head.

"Were you scared, at all?"

"No," Alice said. "The bad man is gone, isn't that right, Stephanie?"

"That's right, sweetie," Valkyrie said.

"Can I dance now?"

"Of course."

Alice put the tablet down and a song played. She started dancing.

Skulduggery stood beside Valkyrie and they watched the performance. "She seems to be in good spirits," he said softly.

"She is," said Valkyrie. "She's going to tell Mum and Dad that we played games and danced and watched movies yesterday. She says she's not going to mention anything that happened."

"Do you think she'll be able to do that?"

"She's coping really well so far. I don't see why not."

"And do you think this is the wisest course of action to take?"

Valkyrie sighed. "Not you, too."

He tilted his head. "Who else has been talking to you about this?"

"No one," she said quickly. "I didn't mean it like that. I meant it, like..."

"Hey!" Alice called. "You're not watching!"

"We are," Valkyrie assured her. "Sorry. Continue."

Alice went back to dancing.

"Anyway," Valkyrie continued, "I think she'll be able to keep the secret."

The song ended, and another began, and Alice hesitated. "I don't know the dance for this one."

"Make it up," said Valkyrie. "Like this." She took Alice's hand and started dancing, and Alice laughed and did her best to copy her big sister's moves.

"When did you learn to salsa?" Skulduggery asked, clearly amused.

"I learned all sorts of things when I was away," Valkyrie replied, and held out her hand to him. "Come on. I'm not doing this on my own."

Alice laughed again when Skulduggery took Valkyrie's hand. She danced with them for a verse or two, then broke free and started doing gymnastics across the floor. Skulduggery spun Valkyrie out, pulled her back in, and they danced like that, Valkyrie enjoying every single step despite her aches and pains.

"Mommy!" Alice yelled, suddenly sprinting from the room.

Valkyrie turned off the music, glanced at Skulduggery for moral support, and followed her sister out into the hall just as the front door opened. Her mother swept Alice into her arms.

"Hello there!" she said.

"Mom! Did you miss me?"

"I did, I did, so much."

"Did anyone miss me?" Desmond asked, closing the door behind him.

"I did, Daddy!"

"Well, that's nice to hear. Did you have a good time with Stephanie?"

Valkyrie tried to fix a smile on to her face, but it wouldn't attach properly.

Alice nodded vigorously. "I slept in my own room at Stephanie's house," she said. "And we played games and I played with Xena. Can we get a dog?"

Desmond groaned. "Should've known this would happen."

"I'd really like a dog like Xena. Stephanie, does Xena have a sister or a brother?"

"I don't think so, sweetie," Valkyrie said.

Her mum's eyes widened when she took a proper look at Valkyrie. "Oh God. What happened?"

Valkyrie smiled. "Nothing. Don't worry about it."

"Your face is–"

"I'm fine, Mum. Really."

There were suddenly tears in Melissa's eyes that she quickly blinked away. "Well, OK, you know what you're doing," she said with a smile as fake as Valkyrie's. "Is Skulduggery here? We saw his car outside."

"I'm just leaving," Skulduggery said, stepping out of the living room, wearing a new façade.

"Oh, you don't have to leave," said Valkyrie's mum.

"I have business to attend to," Skulduggery said. "It was very nice seeing you again. Alice, an absolute pleasure as always."

Alice grinned at him. "Bye, Skulduggery."

Valkyrie followed Skulduggery out, closing the front door behind her. If she'd spent another moment with her mother she would have burst out crying.

"Alice handled that well," she said, thankful to focus on something else as she walked him to the Bentley. "She even added that bit about Xena. She's a born fibber, that girl – I should probably be worried."

"You probably should," Skulduggery said quietly.

Valkyrie frowned at him. "Everything OK?"

The façade melted from his skull. "You're right," he said. "Alice handled that well. She handled it very well. Impossibly well."

Valkyrie shrugged. "She's an Edgley. Impossible is our thing."

"Any other child of that age – any other person of any age – would probably be traumatised by what happened. Alice is not traumatised. She's happy."

"What's wrong with that? She's always happy."

"You've mentioned that before, actually. The fact that she's always happy. Can you think of an instance when she wasn't happy?"

"Why?"

"Indulge me."

"Kind of a weird thing to indulge you with."

"Please."

Valkyrie sighed. "Sure, OK. Um..."

"Have you ever seen her cry? I don't mean from a grazed knee or a stubbed toe. Have you ever seen her cry because she's sad, or upset, or angry?"

"Of course I have."

"When?"

"Well, I mean... I can't remember exact— OK, I don't think I have, but so what? I've been gone for most of her life. What are you getting at, Skulduggery? You're starting to freak me out a little."

"Have you ever used your aura-vision on her?"

Valkyrie stared at him. "Why would I do that?"

"Maybe you should."

"Why?"

"I don't know," he said. "I just know that Alice should not be as happy as she is – not after everything that's happened to her."

"You think there's something wrong with her?"

"Yes."

Anger boiled, mixed with the dread that was suddenly coursing through Valkyrie's veins. "What do you...? What do you expect me to see?"

"I'd prefer not to say."

"Tell me."

"No," he said. "Not until you look."

She was shaking. Her knees were trembling. She clenched her jaw to stop her teeth from chattering.

Somehow she turned; somehow she walked back towards the house. She peered through the living-room window. She could see them in the kitchen, her parents and her sister, talking and laughing. She tried to turn the aura-vision on. Tried again. It wouldn't work. No, it would work – she just didn't want to do it.

She forced herself to switch it on, and she peered in again. Her parents shone with a strong yellow light – warm and healthy.

But Alice... Alice didn't have a light.

Valkyrie staggered back from the window. "No," she said. "No. No." Skulduggery caught her and she pulled away from him. "What is it? What's wrong with her?"

"What did you see?" he asked.

"She doesn't have a c-colour," Valkyrie stammered. "She doesn't h-h-have one. What's wrong with her? What did he d-do to her?"

"This wasn't Cadaverous," Skulduggery said. "This isn't a recent thing."

"Wh-what are you talking ab—?"

She stopped. She couldn't feel her body. She couldn't feel the tears that she knew were running down her cheeks.

"I did it," she said. "When I killed her and brought her back... I damaged her. She doesn't have a soul because of me."

"Valkyrie—"

He reached for her and she took a step back. Energy crackled between her fingers. She could feel it behind her eyes. Building.

"Valkyrie," Skulduggery said, "listen to my voice. It's going to be OK. You just... you just have to calm down."

She shook her head. The energy was all around her now, building like a scream, and then it tore loose and she shot off the ground, into the air, lightning trailing behind her. She clutched her head and twisted, shrieking her pain and her rage and her guilt, spinning through the sky, into the clouds, roaring her grief at the planet that curved beneath her.

81

He found her hours later, huddling on one of the tiny islands off the Haggard coast. Her clothes were scorched, and hanging off her. Her trainers had burst apart. She didn't remember them doing that.

He dropped from the sky gently, quietly, and took off his jacket. He draped it over her shoulders, and sat beside her. They watched the water lap at the small, stony beach.

"What have I done?" she whispered.

He put his arm round her, and pulled her tight. "We'll fix her," he said. "We'll make her better."

82

Flanery didn't like to be in the Oval Office past five at the very latest, but it was nearing midnight and he was still here, still sitting behind his desk, still being president. Sometimes he took a few moments out of his day to think about how far he'd come in his sixty-seven years, from the son of a humble millionaire to a self-made billionaire to the leader of the free world, and he couldn't help but wonder how his life would have turned out if he'd made different choices.

But he didn't think about it for too long. Introspection was for losers.

Wilkes knocked on the door and Flanery called him in.

"I was just checking to see if there's anything you need before I punch out?" Wilkes said, smiling like an idiot.

Flanery smiled back. "I don't think so," he said. "I think I've got everything under control. Don't you?"

"Oh, yes, sir," Wilkes said, and laughed. "If anyone does, you do. Goodnight, sir."

Flanery nodded, and waited for Wilkes to almost reach the door before he asked, "Did you call Abyssinia, by the way?"

Wilkes hesitated, then turned. "She's proving elusive, sir."

"Elusive, huh?"

"I'll try again in the morning."

Flanery leaned back in his chair, clasping his hands over his stomach. "What do you think of my idea, to move up the operation? Be honest now."

Wilkes chewed his lip for a second, then stepped further into the room. "I thought it was good, sir. You're absolutely correct: you need the country to get behind you. My only concern is that this operation needs to be pulled off perfectly the first time. We're really not going to get a second chance."

"I agree," said Flanery.

Wilkes blinked. "You do?"

"Of course. I listen to you, Wilkes, even when you don't think I do. You've been with me from the start. You helped get me elected."

"Thank you, sir, but I reckon that was all you."

"I just told the people what they'd been waiting to hear," Flanery said. "All they needed was someone who understood them. And I do understand them. I know what they want. I know what they love and what they fear. They're my people, Wilkes. All of them."

"Yes, sir, Mr President," Wilkes said, and gave a nod and a smile before turning to leave.

"Are you going to call her?" Flanery asked.

"Sir?"

"Abyssinia. Are you going to call Abyssinia?"

"Oh," said Wilkes. "You, uh, you still want me to tell her to move up the operation?"

"No, no," Flanery said, waving his hand. "We've just decided that we can't afford to rush that, haven't we? No, I was wondering if you're going to call her to brief her on what I've been up to."

"I'm not sure I understand..."

"You don't?" Flanery said, raising his eyebrows. "Correct me if I'm wrong, but... you *are* her spy, aren't you?"

Wilkes laughed. "Uh, I'm no spy, Mr President."

"No? I was misinformed?"

"You must have been, sir," Wilkes said, having a good chuckle. "Goodnight now."

"That's so weird," said Flanery. "So your sorcerer name isn't Vox Askance?"

Wilkes froze.

"I know all about you," Flanery continued. "I've known for weeks. I didn't believe it at first. I said Wilkes is too spineless to be a spy. Weak-Willed Wilkes, I called you. But then I was shown proof."

Wilkes turned slowly.

"You betrayed me," Flanery said. "You lied to me and betrayed me. You're one of them. You're a filthy, degenerate weirdo."

Wilkes was standing differently. His back was straighter, his shoulders no longer stooped. "Who told you?"

"You betrayed me!" Flanery screamed, jumping to his feet.

"You know what?" Wilkes said. "I'm glad you know. I'm delighted. Do you have any idea how hard it has been, these last few years, to even be around you? You are detestable. You are ignorance personified. I've been around some nasty people, I've been around *murderers*, but you? You are by far the worst. And that's saying something."

Flanery sneered. "You think you're—"

"Shut up," said Wilkes, and snapped out his hand. A gust of wind hit Flanery so hard it toppled him backwards over his chair, and he went sprawling on to the carpet.

"You were shown proof, were you?" Wilkes said, walking up to the desk. "Was it with pictures? Because it sure as hell wasn't a written document. God forbid you ever have to *read* something."

Flanery scrambled up. "Get – get away from me."

"You're an insufferable little man, you know that? I deserve a medal for what I've had to put up with. Abyssinia should make me a general for not snapping your neck every time you blatantly lied about something you knew I knew. Abyssinia's plan? It wasn't your idea, you moron. It was hers. I was there when Parthenios

Lilt explained it to you. And then you try to take credit for it? What is wrong with you?"

Flanery lunged for the button on his desk, but Wilkes grabbed his wrist and twisted. Flanery cried out. He tried to hit Wilkes, but he'd never thrown a punch before and it bounced off Wilkes's shoulder.

Wilkes laughed. "Everything about you is soft," he said, forcing Flanery backwards until he was pressed against the wall. "Your arms are soft, your belly's soft, your hands... dear God, your hands have never done a moment's hard work, have they? Not a single moment."

"Help," Flanery whispered. "Help me."

"Oh, don't worry, Mr President. I'm not going to kill you. Abyssinia wouldn't want that. She needs you for the plan to work. *Her* plan. We can still work together, can't we? Sure, there'll have to be some changes. You'll be treating me a lot better, for one thing. Hell, you'll be treating everyone a lot better. In fact, I reckon you're going to turn over a whole new leaf, Mr President. What do you think about that?"

Flanery licked his lips. "Help me."

Wilkes leaned in. "Has that fragile mind of yours finally snapped? I'm not going to help you. I'm the one threatening you."

"I think he was talking to me," said the tall man in the checked suit behind him.

Wilkes turned and Crepuscular Vies hit him in the throat.

Gasping, gagging, Wilkes stumbled to the desk and slid along it. Crepuscular followed, walking slowly. Flanery had never seen him in the light before. He didn't have any lips. His gums simply merged with the skin that was stretched too tight round his head. His cheekbones and eye sockets were pronounced, and the eyes themselves bulged like they were going to pop out at any second.

Flanery stared, his fascination mixing with revulsion, and

watched as Crepuscular reached out, pulled Wilkes towards him, and broke his neck.

Wilkes fell.

"You... you killed him," Flanery whispered.

"Did I?" said Crepuscular, and glanced down. "Oh, so I did." He moved round to Flanery's chair, laid his pork-pie hat on the desk, and sat. "Look at me," he said. "I'm the President."

His black hair was parted in the middle, like they used to do in the 1920s. He leaned back, put his feet up. His socks were brightly coloured, and matched his bow tie.

Flanery's trembling legs took him to the middle of the room, and he turned in a circle, panic rising within him. "What are we going to do? What are we going to do?"

Crepuscular raised an eyebrow. "About what?"

"About Wilkes!"

"Don't worry about Wilkes," said Crepuscular. "We'll tell Abyssinia he disappeared, and we'll keep going along with her little plan for as long as it's in our best interests."

"I meant the body! I meant the dead body!"

"Oooooh. Well, leave that with me, Martin. I'm your go-to guy now. If I can't get rid of a corpse from the Oval Office, what use am I?"

"You didn't..."

"What's that? Sorry?"

"You didn't tell me you were going to kill him."

Crepuscular fixed him with a stare from those hideous eyes. "You're not my president, Martin. I didn't vote for you. I'm not even American. So I don't have to tell you *anything*. I didn't have to tell you that Wilkes here was a spy for Abyssinia, but I chose to, because we're in this together. I didn't have to tell you that the secret magical government of the world has been subtly influencing you and your people... but I chose to. Why?"

"Because we're... we're in this together?"

Crepuscular tapped a finger against an invisible gong. "Exactly.

And, now that it's official, I'm going to be introducing you to a lot of interesting people who can do a lot of interesting things for you."

"More people like you?"

"Heh. There's no one else quite like me, buddy boy. But I'll be introducing you to friends of mine. Sorcerers and the like. In particular, there's a doctor I want you to meet, a thing called Nye. It has a proposal for us that just makes me giddy with joy."

Crepuscular was sitting behind that Oval Office desk like he was born to it. Now that the shock was wearing off, that little fact was starting to worm its way down the back of Flanery's spine.

"What's in it for you?" he asked, feeling the old bravado returning.

"Me?" said Crepuscular.

He put one hand on the desk and vaulted over it, plucking up his hat with the same hand and placing it on his head as he loomed over Flanery. "I've got scores to settle, buddy boy. I've waited hundreds of years for this, and my time is finally here. I've got a list of things I want to destroy and a list of people I want to kill, and you're going to help me do it."

Flanery swallowed. "OK."

Crepuscular put an arm round Flanery's shoulders. "This is the start of something special, Martin. Can you feel it? I can feel it. Together, we're going to smash everything good in his life and kill every last thing he loves, and I'll stand over him, right at the end, and I'll say, 'See? I beat you. I won.'"

"St-stand over who?"

"Hmm? Oh, sorry, buddy boy," Crepuscular said, and laughed. "His name's Skulduggery Pleasant. I'm going to kill Skulduggery Pleasant."

Skulduggery Pleasant

NUMBER ONE BESTSELLING AUTHOR
DEREK LANDY
Skulduggery Pleasant
MORTAL COIL

NUMBER ONE BESTSELLING AUTHOR
DEREK LANDY
Skulduggery Pleasant
DEATH BRINGER

NUMBER ONE BESTSELLING AUTHOR
DEREK LANDY
Skulduggery Pleasant
KINGDOM OF THE WICKED

NUMBER ONE BESTSELLING AUTHOR
DEREK LANDY
Skulduggery Pleasant
LAST STAND OF DEAD MEN

NUMBER ONE BESTSELLING AUTHOR
DEREK LANDY
Skulduggery Pleasant
THE DYING OF THE LIGHT

NUMBER ONE BESTSELLING AUTHOR
DEREK LANDY
Skulduggery Pleasant
RESURRECTION
YOU CAN'T KEEP A DEAD MAN DOWN.